When the Phoenix rose from the temple, She spoke to the priests in a voice made of ash.

"Why are they fighting for this land?"

As She spoke, armies waged war at the foot of the mountains. If one walked to the front steps of the temple, one could hear the faint sorrows of battle: the clash of metal and the short-lived screams of men. The Phoenix looked from priest to priest, but none could meet Her eyes—not only because of their shame, but also because they could not see past the clarity of Her flames.

All except one.

A priestess met the golden eyes of the Phoenix and spoke in a small yet steady voice.

"It is because they do not realize their mortality," she said.

The Phoenix stared down at the priestess, but she did not waver.

"Then it is you," the Phoenix said, and so it was done. Her Eternal Fire rose in answer to its new master and wrapped around the arms and limbs of the priestess. It enveloped her, covered her, welcomed her. The Phoenix raised Her wings, and a beam of light erupted from the heart of the fire to the sky above. The armies below saw it. The whole world saw it.

The Prophet was chosen.

THE PHOENIX KING

THE RAVENCE TRILOGY:
BOOK ONE

APARNA VERMA

orbitbooks.net

Copyright © 2021 by Aparna Verma
Bonus chapter copyright © 2023 by Aparna Verma
Excerpt from *The Jasad Heir* copyright © 2023 by Sara Hashem

Cover design by Lisa Marie Pompilio
Cover illustrations by Shutterstock
Cover copyright © 2023 by Hachette Book Group, Inc.
Map by Tim Paul
Author photograph by Aparna Verma

Orbit
Hachette Book Group
1290 Avenue of the Americas
New York, NY 10104
orbitbooks.net

First Orbit Edition: August 2023
Originally published as *The Boy with Fire* in paperback and ebook by New Degree Press in August 2021

Orbit is an imprint of Hachette Book Group.
The Orbit name and logo are trademarks of Little, Brown Book Group Limited.

The Hachette Speakers Bureau provides a wide range of authors for speaking events. To find out more, go to hachettespeakersbureau.com or email HachetteSpeakers@hbgusa.com.

Orbit books may be purchased in bulk for business, educational, or promotional use. For information, please contact your local bookseller or the Hachette Book Group Special Markets Department at special.markets@hbgusa.com.

Library of Congress Cataloging-in-Publication Data
Names: Verma, Aparna, author
Title: The Phoenix king / Aparna Verma.
Other titles: Boy with fire
Description: First Orbit edition. | New York, NY : Orbit, 2023. | Series: The Ravence trilogy ; book one | "Originally published as The boy with fire"
Identifiers: LCCN 2023012400 | ISBN 9780316522779 (trade paperback) | ISBN 9780316522892 (ebook)
Subjects: LCGFT: Fantasy fiction. | Novels.
Classification: LCC PS3622.E7456 B69 2023 | DDC 813/.6—dc23/eng/20230331
LC record available at https://lccn.loc.gov/2023012400

ISBNs: 9780316522779 (trade paperback), 9780316522892 (ebook)

Printed in the United States of America

LSC-C

Printing 1, 2023

*To those who believe that their stories
don't matter, keep a fire burning.*

You never know whose beacon you will become.

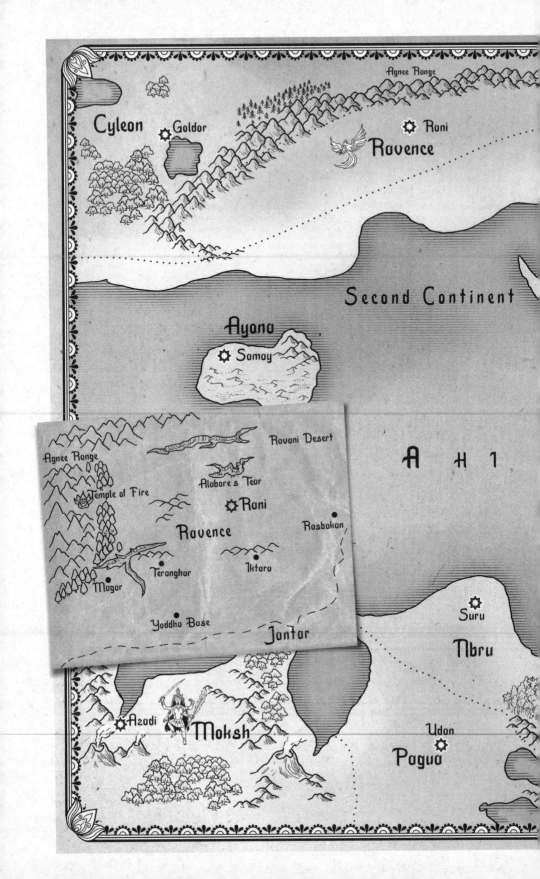

Harven

Sard

Veran

Eravon

Amirin Mtns.

Jantar

Rhea

Sona Range

Tsuana

Janoon

Rysanti

S E A

Ajgar

Seshar

First Continent

The Claw

Mandur

Narasir

Map by Tim Paul

PROLOGUE

BURNING DAY

One dead king, and Yassen Knight would be free.

He slid close to the wall, tucking himself in the darkened corner where the guards above could not see him unless they were brave enough to weather the storm and lean over the stone edge. The rain lashed down, drenching him. It wasn't like the thunderous, refreshing monsoons that swept across the deserts of Ravence leaving a riot of color in their wake. This storm bit down, clenching the coast in its grey jaws, unwilling to relent until it blended the world into hues of slate and brown.

Yassen shivered. He was lucky; he had been able to climb up the craggy cliff before the storm had hit. It had taken him nearly half an hour, from the hidden cove to the hidden blind spot of the wall, clawing for footholds and hollow pockets as the wind lashed at him. There was no surveillance here; clearly, the king believed no man foolish or brave enough to attempt the climb. He was right, Yassen thought bitterly as he felt another raindrop trickle beneath the collar of his jacket and down his spine. He wasn't foolish or brave.

He was desperate.

Lightning splintered across the darkening sky, followed by a great boom of thunder that rattled the coast with such force that Yassen felt its echoes in his bones.

He stood on a thin ledge, the cliff dropping steeply behind him, the black stone wall looming before him. His pulse gun was holstered beneath his jacket, the silencer tucked above his heart. He was carefully putting the metal stakes he had used during the climb into his small knapsack when his holopod pinged.

Yassen pulled out the pod, a smooth silver circle no bigger than his palm. Two holos blinked awake: The first showed the time, a quarter to the hour, which meant the guard change would happen in ten minutes; the second showed live cam feeds of the inner compound.

King Bormani of Veran had insisted on building his summer home on the easternmost point of his coast so that he could be the first to see the sun rise over his kingdom. The vanity of it. The sun rose everywhere, Yassen thought, so why did it matter if you saw it first? But that was the way of kings: excessive, unnecessary. Yassen had known many such nobles. Most had been too blinded by their own pride to see that the danger lurked on their own doorsteps.

Above him, two guards huddled along the inner wall, their heads tucked inside their thick jackets, their hands thrust into their pockets. They looked miserable.

His pod pinged, this time with a message.

Guard change stalled. Climb.

Yassen checked the cam feed, and sure enough, the two guards above him glanced at their own pods. One guard, the bigger one, sprang up at once.

"Damn time," Yassen heard one say.

"Don't you think we should wait for the others?" his companion said.

The big guard whirled around. "In this weather? I can't feel my crackin' toes. Stay if you like but I'm *out*."

The smaller guard grumbled but stood up. He stepped forward, toward the outer wall, and Yassen stilled. If he leaned over...

But the rain was thick, and the guard, probably thinking it was better to warm up with a bowl of soup than risk his neck peering over slippery stone, turned and hurried after his companion.

Lightning struck again, angrier this time. Despite himself, Yassen thanked the heavens. He had long ago lost his belief in the gods, but habit made him kiss his three fingers and press them to his chest for good luck. He did not invoke the Phoenix. Instead, he slipped off his gloves and rubbed chalk from his knapsack over his palms.

Yassen placed his hands against the wall and closed his eyes. The rough, slick stone brushed against his bare skin like a familiar friend. He had grown up climbing canyons and dunes, the warm sun on his back, sand and grit in his nails. For a moment, Yassen cradled that memory, but then the pod chimed again, and he felt the memory curdle. He would never feel the rough grit of sand again. That was his past. Yassen gripped the stone and looked up. The wall loomed over him, black and bleak. Just one more climb, he reminded himself. One more dead king, and he would be free.

He tapped his toes together, and two blades made of Jantari steel flicked out. They cut through the stone like a knife through flesh. Handhold here, insert foot here. Shift right. Shorn rock, move slow. Yassen fell into his familiar rhythm, sweat and rain beading down his forehead. The lip of the wall loomed closer. Fifteen feet, then ten, then five.

Yassen peered over the edge. The wall was empty. Yassen pulled himself over and, in one smooth motion, slipped out his pulse gun and silencer. His boot knives slid back. The rain drummed down, hard and mean like tiny pebbles. Yassen crept toward the staircase, gun balanced in his left hand, the other cradling a thin throwing knife that had been hidden in his boot.

When he reached the main floor, Yassen cautiously peered out across the grounds. He could see the two guards in the distance, hurrying down a garden path toward a grey, low building. The servants' quarters. Beyond the building, he could see the faint silhouette of the king's compound. He would be asleep right now. All Yassen had to do was climb onto the roof and slip into the topmost right hallway...

A sudden sound to Yassen's right made him freeze, finger curled around the trigger. The rain muffled most noise, but Yassen was sure...

There! It sounded like a squeal, raw and painful; the sound a marjarah squirming on the butcher's table would make. The Verani considered the meat of the catlike animal a delicacy. But the noise came from the direction of the king's compound, not the kitchens.

3

Yassen crept forward as a far gate swung open and three guards ran out. They were shouting orders.

"Got out!" Their voices, dampened by the rain, came in little snatches. "Southside...Garden path!...Inform the king."

Damn it! Yassen looked at the right topmost window of the king's compound. It was still unlit. He had a few precious minutes to scale onto the roof. Perhaps he could make it through, shoot the king and the guards. But then how would he get out unnoticed?

For a moment, Yassen debated abandoning the assignment. *The mission was compromised*, he imagined himself telling Akaros, his handler. But then how many more assignments would they send him on before they finally granted him peace? How much longer until he could be free?

No, he had come too far. This would be his last job. He would fade away, slip past the Arohassin using the methods they had taught him. He had already made the rearrangements. An alias, Cassian Newman, with a passport from Nbru, a country that the Arohassin had no foothold in. Instead of sailing back to the rendezvous point, he would head out into the Ahi Sea.

Yassen waited until the guards were out of sight and then sprinted forward. Speed and confusion were his only advantage right now. He stuck to the perimeter of the circular garden, slipping between the dark, hunkering ferns.

A gutter ran up the backside of the grand, sprawling building of the king's chambers.

He had just gripped it when a figure flickered from around the front of the house. A guard, head bent against the rain, his back to Yassen. He sounded annoyed, bickering into his pod.

"I told you I don't know where it went! The old man shouldn't even have it as a pet. It got scared by the storm and got out. There's no need to wake up the king for his stupid—"

As the guard turned, Yassen's knife sliced cleanly into his eye. The man's body stiffened, his mouth frozen in shock, and then he fell onto his knees. Yassen quickly closed the distance, and in one deft motion, he slipped out the knife and sliced the guard's throat, covering his mouth. The guard gasped against his palm, then lay still.

A voice continued arguing through the guard's holopod. Yassen picked it up.

"—going to be angry! The damned thing only listens to him—"

Yassen cut the line and slipped the holopod into his pocket. He heaved the guard's body back and laid it against the far wall, blanketed by shadows. Guilt snaked around his chest. His task was to eliminate a king, not his subjects. It was not their fault that they had gotten embroiled in politics beyond their control.

Yassen kissed his three fingers and pressed them against the guard's forehead.

"Go in peace, wherever that is," he murmured.

He took off his jacket and draped it over the guard's body. The others would find him, eventually. *But please, heavens above, let it be after.*

The side entrance lay open. Yassen stepped inside, knife in hand, pulse gun primed. He closed the door softly. He could hear loud, stress-filled voices down the corridor. To his left, a staircase curved upward into darkness. At the top, Yassen pressed his ear against the door on the landing. Nothing. Carefully, he propped it open an inch. The hallway was dark and muted, shadows flickering and dancing across the walls from the large window above. All else was silent.

Yassen slipped into the hall, his footsteps light. Little raindrops dripped down his clothing, a spattered trail that couldn't be helped. Ahead of him was another staircase, this one grander and more ornate, swathed in soft carpet. He took the stairs two at a time, the fabric swallowing any sounds, and paused at the second level. The hall forked left and right, sconces glowing gently at intervals. Murmurs drifted from the right, where the king's bedchamber lay.

Activating his silencer, Yassen crept toward it.

A guard appeared at the far end of the hall. Yassen stopped, heart thundering, pressing back into the shadows. The guard walked slowly, hands outstretched.

"Here, Adria." The guard made kissing sounds. "Here, girl. It's all right."

He thinks I'm the cat. Yassen wanted to laugh, but then he thought of the other guard, lying cold and dead in the rain. He holstered his gun, slipping his knife back into his sleeve. The guard inched closer, searching the shadows of the opposite wall.

"Adriaaa, I have treats," he sang.

When the guard's back was to him, Yassen leapt out. The man whirled, but Yassen was faster. He turned on his heel, sidestepping the guard's confused punch, and wrapped him in a choke hold. The guard kicked his feet, the thud of his heels muffled against the carpet.

Yassen squeezed harder. Slowly, and then all at once, the guard's body fell limp. Yassen checked his pulse. He was alive, but he would be unconscious for at least a few minutes. Yassen quickly emptied the guard's pockets, donning the man's hat and jacket.

Thunder boomed around him as he jogged down the hallway. Another guard paced in front of the king's door but stopped when Yassen approached.

"Did you find her?" he hissed.

"No," Yassen said in a Verani accent, his hat tilted down, "but I did find this."

He threw the unconscious guard's holopod across the floor. It slid across the carpet, hitting the other guard's feet. He bent to pick it up, eyebrows knitting in confusion, and when he looked up, Yassen kicked him solidly in the face. The guard crumpled to the floor with a loud thump. Yassen winced at the sound, but no one else appeared in the corridor.

Unholstering his pulse gun, he opened the king's door and slipped inside.

The room was wide and swathed in silks and velvets of rich purple. A fire crackled softly in a hearth beside the window. King Bormani was sitting up in his bed, rubbing his eyes. He blinked sleepily as Yassen entered.

"Briske," he said, "what is all that noise? And would you close that crackin' window?"

The windowpanes creaked in the wind. *It must have blown open during the storm*, Yassen thought. He peered at the king. He had no gun, no knife. The man had only his robe, which was quickly on the verge of unspooling as he yawned. Yassen hesitated. He had made an oath, long ago, to never kill a man without a weapon. And he had followed it, as best as he could. But now...

The window panels banged against the building.

"Ah, Briske, get the damn window!" Bormani snapped.

Just one more dead king. One more dead king and he would fucking finally be free.

Yassen swallowed his pride and glanced quickly between the king and the window. Suddenly, it fell into place. *Yes, it can work.* Yassen strode to the window, escape route in mind, finger curled around the trigger.

A log snapped and sparks fluttered in the air.

Three things happened at once then.

First, the king paused, as if finally noticing Yassen's pulse gun. "Heavens above, Briske, what do you have that for?" he said as Yassen raised the weapon.

Second, an alarm blared. Loud and piercing through the house.

Third—and this Yassen would remember in the days to come—the fire. That damned, forsaken fire.

A single log snapped and rolled from the hearth, flames lashing out and catching Yassen's leg. He yelled as he pulled the trigger. The pulse zipped through the air, missing Bormani's head and ripping through the headboard.

The king shouted as Yassen tottered back, beating at the flames with his hands. His pants were wet, so the fire was sluggish, turning to steam. Relief filled his heart—just as his heel met the log and he tumbled. Flames leapt onto his dry jacket, laughing. They spread quickly, viciously.

Yassen screamed.

Guards barreled through the door. Bormani sprang from his bed and ran. The confused guards rushed to protect their king as Yassen pulled himself over the window ledge and rolled over.

He slammed onto the tiles of the roof below, the impact knocking the breath out of him. He tried to stop himself, but he was moving too fast. He fell off the slanted roof, crashing into the garden bushes. Thorns and branches whipped his face. The flames hissed angrily as they died. Yassen was aware of a searing sensation in his right arm, but adrenaline and the sheer desperation of survival kept it at bay as he staggered to his feet.

Sirens blared through the compound. Guards streamed out of the servants' quarters in the distance.

Yassen ran.

He sprinted to the stone staircase as pulse fire shredded the air. He made it to the wall when he felt a pulse zip above him, barely missing his shoulder. Yassen stumbled back. A guard, hiding behind one of the supply huts on the top of the wall, shot again. Yassen backed down the staircase as the pulse blasted the spot where he'd just been.

One last job. After this, you're done.

Oh, what Yassen Knight wouldn't do to be free.

Voices behind him, getting closer. He darted forward, knife in hand, and spun on his toes, flinging his arm as the guard popped up from behind the hut again. The knife cut through the man's throat. The guard made a wet, gurgling sound.

Yassen ran to him, grabbing his knife and the guard's pulse gun. Inside the supply hut, he found more guns, along with blankets, a half-eaten bowl of soup, holopods, and—*yes*—a rope.

He grabbed the rope and began to knot it, but his hands were trembling, his fingers too slick as they slipped over the knots.

The searing sensation in his arm grew worse. Yassen winced, teetering. White spots danced in his vision. He grabbed the rampart to steady himself as footsteps thundered up the staircase.

Come on, he said to himself. *Almost done.*

Finally, he knotted the rope to the rampart of the wall. It made a slithering sound as it fell over the edge, the line stopping ten feet short of the ground.

Yassen put the handle of the knife in his mouth to stop himself from screaming. With his left hand, he grabbed the rope and hauled himself over. He kicked off the wall, bouncing down, down, down, the rope sliding through his hand, burning his palm. He moaned into the knife handle. When he reached the rope's end, Yassen stopped.

The drop below him was not too far, but the ledge was narrow. Beneath, the grey waves beat against the cliff.

"He's over here!"

Yassen looked up. The guards were leaning over the wall edge. One guard trained his gun and shot. The pulse burned the stones just above Yassen.

Yassen stared down at the churning sea, despair filling his heart.

One last job. And then you'll be free.

He kicked off the wall and plunged into the sea.

CHAPTER 1

YASSEN

The king said to his people, "We are the chosen."
And the people responded, "Chosen by whom?"
　　　　　　—from chapter 37 of *The Great History of Sayon*

To be forgiven, one must be burned. That's what the Ravani said. They were fanatics and fire worshippers, but they were his people. And he would finally be returning home.

Yassen held on to the railing of the hoverboat as it skimmed over the waves. He held on with his left arm, his right limp by his side. Around him, the world was dark, but the horizon began to purple with the faint glimmers of dawn. Soon, the sun would rise, and the twin moons of Sayon would lie down to rest. Soon, he would arrive at Rysanti, the Brass City. And soon, he would find his way back to the desert that had forsaken him.

Yassen withdrew a holopod from his jacket and pressed it open with his thumb. A small holo materialized with a message:

Look for the bull.

He closed the holo, the smell of salt and brine filling his lungs.

The bull. It was nothing close to the Phoenix of Ravence, but then again, Samson liked to be subtle. Yassen wondered if he would be at the port to greet him.

A large wave tossed the boat, but Yassen did not lose his balance. Weeks at sea and suns of combat had taught him how to keep his ground. A cool wind licked his sleeve, and he felt a whisper of pain skitter down his right wrist. He grimaced. His skin was already beginning to redden.

After the Arohassin had pulled him half-conscious from the sea, Yassen had thought, in the delirium of pain, that he would be free. If not in this life, then in death. But the Arohassin had yanked him back from the brink. Treated his burns and saved his arm. Said that he was lucky to be alive while whispering among themselves when they thought he could not hear: "Yassen Knight is no longer of use."

Yassen pulled down his sleeve. It was no matter. He was used to running.

As the hoverboat neared the harbor, the fog along the coastline began to evaporate. Slowly, Yassen saw the tall spires of the Brass City cut through the grey heavens. Skyscrapers of slate and steel from the mines of Sona glimmered in the early dawn as hovertrains weaved through the air, carrying the day laborers. Neon lights flickered within the metal jungle, and a silver bridge snaked through the entire city, connecting the outer rings to the wealthy, affluent center. Yassen squinted as the sun crested the horizon. Suddenly, its light hit the harbor, and the Brass City shone with a blinding intensity.

Yassen quickly clipped on his visor, a fiber sheath that covered his entire face. He closed his eyes for a moment, allowing them to readjust before opening them again. The city stared back at him in subdued colors.

Queen Rydia, one of the first queens of Jantar, had wanted to ward off Enuu, the evil eye, so she had fashioned her port city out of unforgiving metal. If Yassen wasn't careful, the brass could blind him.

The other passengers came up on deck, pulling on half visors that covered their eyes. Yassen tightened his visor and wrapped a scarf around his neck. Most people could not recognize him—none of the passengers even knew of his name—but he could not take any chances. Samson had made it clear that he wanted no one to know of this meeting.

The hoverboat came to rest beside the platform, and Yassen disembarked with the rest of the passengers. Even in the early hours, the port was busy. On the other dock, soldiers barked out orders as fresh immigrants stumbled off a colony boat. Judging from the coiled silver bracelets on their wrists, Yassen guessed they were Sesharian refugees. They shuffled forward on the adjoining dock toward military buses. Some carried luggage; others had nothing save the clothes they wore. They all donned half visors and walked with the resigned grace of people weary of their fate.

Native Jantari, in their lightning suits and golden bracelets, kept a healthy distance from the immigrants. They stayed on the brass homeland and receiving docks where merchants stationed their carts. Unlike most of the city, the carts were made of pale driftwood, but the vendors still wore half visors as they handled their wares. Yassen could already hear a merchant hawking satchels of vermilion tea while another shouted about a new delivery of mirrors from Cyleon that had a 90 percent accuracy of predicting one's romantic future. Yassen shook his head. Only in Jantar.

Floating lanterns guided Yassen and the passengers to the glass-encased immigration office. Yassen slid his holopod into the port while a grim-faced attendant flicked something from his purple nails.

"Name?" he intoned.

"Cassian Newman," Yassen said.

"Country of residence?"

"Nbru."

The attendant waved his hand. "Take off your visor, please."

Yassen unclipped his visor and saw shock register across the attendant's face as he took in Yassen's white, colorless eyes.

"Are you Jantari?" the attendant asked, surprised.

"No," Yassen responded gruffly and clipped his visor back on. "My father was."

"Hmph." The attendant looked at his holopod and then back at him. "Purpose of your visit?"

Yassen paused. The attendant peered at him, and for one wild moment, Yassen wondered if he should turn away, jump back on the boat, and go wherever the sea pushed him. But then a coldness slithered down his right elbow, and he gripped his arm.

"To visit some old friends," Yassen said.

The attendant snorted, but when the holopod slid back out, Yassen saw the burning insignia of a mohanti, a winged ox, on its surface.

"Welcome to the Kingdom of Jantar," the attendant said and waved him through.

Yassen stepped through the glass immigration office and into Rysanti. He breathed in the sharp salt air, intermingled with spices both foreign and familiar. A storm had passed through recently, leaving puddles in its wake. A woman ahead of Yassen slipped on a wet plank and a merchant reached out to steady her. Yassen pushed past them, keeping his head down. Out of the corner of his eye, he saw the merchant swipe the woman's holopod and hide it in his jacket. Yassen smothered a laugh.

As he wandered toward the homeland dock, he scanned the faces in the crowd. The time was nearly two past the sun's breath. Samson and his men should have been here by now.

He came to the bridge connecting the receiving and homeland docks. At the other end of the bridge was a lonely tea stall, held together by worn planks—but the large holosign snagged his attention.

WARM YOUR TIRED BONES FROM YOUR PASSAGE AT SEA! FRESH HOT LEMON CAKES AND RAVANI TEA SERVED DAILY! it read.

It was the word *Ravani* that sent a jolt through Yassen. Home—the one he longed for but knew he was no longer welcome in.

Yassen drew up to the tea stall. Three large hourglasses hissed and steamed. Tea leaves floated along their bottoms, slowly steeping, as a heavyset Sesharian woman flipped them in timed intervals. On her hand, Yassen spotted a tattoo of a bull.

The same mark Samson had asked him to look for.

When the woman met Yassen's eyes, she twirled the hourglass once more before drying her hands on the towel around her wide waist.

"Whatcha want?" she asked in a river-hoarse voice.

"One tea and cake, please," Yassen said.

"You're lucky. I just got a fresh batch of leaves from my connect. Straight from the canyons of Ravence."

"Exactly why I want one," he said and placed his holopod in the counter insert. Yassen tapped it twice.

"Keep the change," he added.

She nodded and turned back to the giant hourglasses.

The brass beneath Yassen's feet grew warmer in the yawning day. Across the docks, more boats pulled in, carrying immigrant laborers and tourists. Yassen adjusted his visor, making sure it was fully in place, as the woman simultaneously flipped the hourglass and slid off its cap. In one fluid motion, the hot tea arced through the air and fell into the cup in her hand. She slid it across the counter.

"Mind the sleeve, the tea's hot," she said. "And here's your cake."

Yassen grabbed the cake box and lifted his cup in thanks. As he moved away from the stall, he scratched the plastic sleeve around the cup.

Slowly, a message burned through:

Look underneath the dock of fortunes.

He almost smiled. Clearly, Samson had not forgotten Yassen's love of tea.

Yassen looked within the box and saw that there was no cake but something sharp, metallic. He reached inside and held it up. Made of silver, the insignia was smaller than his palm and etched in what seemed to be the shape of a teardrop. Yassen held it closer. No, it was more feather than teardrop.

He threw the sleeve and box into a bin, slid the silver into his pocket, and continued down the dock. The commerce section stretched on, a mile of storefronts welcoming him into the great nation of Jantar. Yassen sipped his tea, watching. A few paces down was a stall marketing tales of ruin and fortune. Like the tea stall, it too was old and decrepit, with a painting of a woman reading palms painted across its front. He was beginning to recognize a pattern—and patterns were dangerous. Samson was getting lazy in his mansion.

Three guards stood along the edge of the platform beside the stall. One was dressed in a captain's royal blue, the other two in the plain black of officers. All three wore helmet visors, their pulse guns strapped to their sides. They were laughing at some joke when the captain looked up and frowned at Yassen.

"You there," he said imperiously.

Yassen slowly lowered his cup. The dock was full of carts and merchants. If he ran now, the guards could catch him.

"Yes, you, with the full face," the captain called out, tapping his visor. "Come here!"

"Is there a problem?" Yassen asked as he approached.

"No full visors allowed on the dock, except for the guard," the captain said.

"I didn't know it was a crime to wear a full visor," Yassen said. His voice was cool, perhaps a bit too nonchalant because the captain slapped the cup out of Yassen's hand. The spilled tea hissed against the metal planks.

"New rules," the captain said. "Only guards can wear full visors. Everybody else has to go half."

His subordinates snickered. "Looks like he's fresh off the boat, Cap. You got to cut it up for him," one said.

Behind his visor, Yassen frowned. He glanced at the merchant leaning against the fortunes stall. The man wore a bored expression, as if the interaction before him was nothing new. But then the merchant bent forward, pressing his hands to the counter, and Yassen saw the sign of the bull tattooed there.

Samson's men were watching.

"All right," Yassen said. He would give them a show. Prove that he wasn't as useless as the whispers told.

He unclipped his visor as the guards watched. "But you owe me another cup of tea."

And then Yassen flung his arm out and rammed the visor against the captain's face. The man stumbled back with a groan. The other two leapt forward, but Yassen was quicker; he swung around and gave four quick jabs, two each on the back, and the officers seized and sank to their knees in temporary paralysis.

"Blast him!" the captain cried, reaching for his gun. Yassen pivoted behind him, his hand flashing out to unclip the captain's helmet visor.

The captain whipped around, raising his gun...but then sunlight hit the planks before him, and the brass threw off its unforgiving light. Blinded, the captain fired.

The air screeched.

The pulse whizzed past Yassen's right ear, tearing through the upper beams of a storefront. Immediately, merchants took cover. Someone screamed as the crowd on both docks began to run. Yassen swiftly vanished into the chaotic fray, letting the crowd push him toward the dock's edge, and then he dove into the sea.

The cold water shocked him, and for a moment, Yassen floundered. His muscles clenched. And then he was coughing, swimming, and he surfaced beneath the dock. He willed himself to be still as footsteps thundered overhead and soldiers and guards barked out orders. Yassen caught glimpses of the captain in the spaces between the planks.

"All hells! Where did he go?" the captain yelled at the merchant manning the stall of wild tales.

The merchant shrugged. "He's long gone."

Yassen sank deeper into the water as the captain walked overhead, his subordinates wobbling behind. Something buzzed beneath him, and he could see the faint outlines of a dark shape in the depths. Slowly, Yassen began to swim away—but the dark shape remained stationary. He waited for the guards to pass and then sank beneath the surface.

A submersible, the size of one passenger.

Look underneath the dock of fortunes, indeed.

Samson, that bastard.

Yassen swam toward the sub. He placed his hand on the imprint panel of the hull, and then the sub buzzed again and rose to the surface.

The cockpit was small, with barely enough room for him to stretch his legs, but he sighed and sank back just the same. The glass slid smoothly closed and rudders whined to life. The panel board lit up before him and bathed him in a pale blue light.

A note was there. Handwritten. How rare, and so like Samson.

See you at the palace, it said, and before Yassen could question *which* palace, the sub was off.

CHAPTER 2

ELENA

*When the future king arrived at the unforgiving desert, he called to his
followers, "There, we will build our city." He led them under the cloak
of night when the sand had finally cooled. They built bricks of clay
until their hands were coarse and peeling. The twin moons watched,
compelled. They stayed in the sky longer that night to give the followers
relief from the burning day.*

—from chapter 41 of *The Great History of Sayon*

Elena ducked underneath an arch brimming with loyarian sparks. The
little flecks of light appeared in clusters in dark awnings during monsoon season, like tiny fairy flames. The priests insisted it was an act of
the divine, though Elena vaguely recalled a tutor offering a more prosaic
explanation to do with moisture and sand.

The Phoenix blesses us, the priests insisted. *She sends us a sign of good luck.*

As the sparks wafted down, Elena gently brushed them from her hair
and skin. Luck was not what she needed right now.

Her hand drifted underneath her shawl to rest above her hip where her

16

holopod was hidden. Though lighter than a sack of tea leaves, it weighed heavily, cold against her sweaty skin. What she needed, what she wanted, was Varun to be as foolish and greedy as he had been the day she had learned about his true desire.

"Phoenix Above, it's hotter than Her cursed fires," Ferma said. She pulled at her collar as sweat trickled down her brow. "Are you sure they're meeting *now*?"

"Yes," Elena said, hopping over a stray shobu sprawled out on the sand. It merely yawned, shaking its lionlike mane before curling back to sleep. On the balcony above, an artisan flapped out a newly dyed scarf, sending droplets of carmine and amber raining down.

"Of course, the fire fanatics picked the hottest time of day to meet," Ferma muttered.

The Yumi guard pulled her scarf tighter, hiding the trademark hair of her race: thick, long, silky strands that could harden into sharp shards and cut a man's throat.

Ferma had been trained from infancy to be a soldier. There weren't many of her people left on the second continent after the Burning of the Sixth Prophet, who ended nearly the entire Yumi race, but the ones who had lived served as army captains and warriors. Only the very best graced the royal halls. Ferma had been her mother's Spear, as well as Elena's mentor. She was the one who had taught Elena the art of holding a slingsword between her shoulder blades, how to keep it undetected before brandishing it with a quick flourish of her hips.

When Elena's mother had died, Ferma had presided over Elena's studies of history and politics, tended to her wounds after sparring sessions, pressed cool compresses to her forehead when she caught fever. Without a word, Ferma could command a room. Without a sound, she could murder a man.

Elena admired her elegance and her power. But it amused Elena that the one thing Ferma just couldn't handle was Rani's heat.

Elena's lips twitched. She was about to make a joke of it when someone shouted behind them. They both turned to see two black-and-blue-haired Sesharian teens whiz by on floating bladers, laughing as a merchant gave chase. On the bazaar corner, a group of drunk fans let out groans. The floating bank of holos played back the Cyleon goalie blocking Ravence's shot and winning the Western Windsnatch Title. One fan threw down his drink, spraying the running merchant with beer.

"At least they didn't pick a boring neighborhood." Elena grinned. Ferma frowned in return.

Despite the cloying heat and dust, she enjoyed the bazaar's winding streets and congested alleys. The capital was a jumble of incongruous sounds and architecture, of the stubborn past and marching modernity; tall pillars of blasted sandstone housed storefronts of holo-infused gauntlets and decked-out gamesuits. Merchants wheeled their carts, crying out the prices of the day for saffron, sage, and cloves, parrots from Cyleon, and spangled glass bracelets from the first continent. It was an uproar of hovercars beeping, drivers shouting, and pedestrians calling out as they crossed the road without the faintest fear of traffic; a rush of orphans crying, fathers begging, and businesswomen cursing as they rushed to the hovertrains in their pincer heels; a whirlwind of people rubbing elbows, knees, palms, and dreams. She could feel their collective breath, their sweat, their liveliness that was so unlike the long, cool halls of the palace.

She craved it.

"Dealer!" a merchant called.

Elena turned to see Eshaant pushing his cart toward them. Fresh makhana, sprinkled with ghee and spices, sat steaming in paper cones.

"Merchant." Elena smiled, face hidden beneath her scarf. "What's this? I thought you sold jalebi."

"Ach, the rent for my spot was too high. Fucking Lohan raised the price and kicked me out. I'm telling you, these Sesharians are greedy little—"

Ferma stepped forward, and Eshaant stopped.

"Oh right, right. Sorry. I forgot that you and your friend support the refugee efforts."

"They just want a home, same as us." Elena nodded toward his cart. "Those look delicious."

"Want one? I can throw you three for the price of two. Special deal just for you." Eshaant winked.

"I'm tempted, but no." Elena glanced at Ferma. "We have a rally to attend."

At this, Eshaant's smile fell. "Don't tell me you have business with the gold caps, dealer."

"Business is business," Elena said lightly, though the words felt cheap.

"Mm-hmm." Eshaant sniffed. "Be careful. I'd rather deal with a cheap Sesharian than an ass-kisser of the king like Jangir. Ego the size of Palace Hill, balls as big as makhanas."

Ferma chuckled, and even Elena smiled.

"Bring a chilled pitcher of chaas. Add more spice to the makhana, and give two for one," she said. "And when it's too spicy for them, charge them for a glass."

Eshaant whistled. "Clever. But alas, I won't be here for long."

"Why not?" Elena asked.

"I'm leaving for Cyleon the week of the coronation," he said. "I can't take it anymore. City is too crowded, and the gold caps are growing too rough. Last week, they seized my friend's shop and forced him to pay double the rent. Or else they'd burn down his shop and blame rebels."

Elena stilled. "They can't do that."

Eshaant rubbed a hand across his face, wiping sweat. "By the law, they can't. But the law doesn't care. The king doesn't give a shit."

"I hear the new queen does," Elena said, and she saw Ferma shoot her a glance.

"Ah, the heir." Eshaant laughed, a thick, derisive sound that made her stomach twist. "She's a puppet just like the rest. If she cared, why hasn't she said anything yet?"

"Maybe it's not as simple as that," Elena said, her voice quiet.

"Maybe, maybe not." Eshaant shrugged. "Either way, I'll be gone. I hear summer in Cyleon is beautiful."

"Not as beautiful as in the desert," Elena interjected.

"No," Eshaant said. "But the desert isn't kind either. Don't worry, dealer, I'll send my regards."

He dipped his head in farewell and continued on. As Elena watched him go, she felt that same weight slowly sink down her shoulders, like a body buried in sand. *I won't be the same*, she thought.

"Don't mind him," Ferma said, her voice gentle. "Come."

They swept through the bazaar, weaving between the shoppers.

"They should be gathering in front of Jasmine's Tea Garden," Elena said, increasing her pace.

"They're already there. Jangir has begun his speech." Ferma tapped her earpiece when Elena looked at her in surprise. "I sent a few men ahead of us to keep watch."

Elena smiled. Of course, Ferma had thought ahead. But then, a smaller voice chided her.

You should have too.

Elena pushed back that needling voice of self-criticism and self-doubt. She would need all her wits about her today.

Music filled the square ahead of them. Elena spotted a street dancer, resplendent in her colorful lehenga and choli, twirling in rhythm to a musician playing the ravanahatha. A small crowd watched. Ferma pushed past them, but Elena paused to watch the dancer as she leapt, her face raised to the sun, her limbs long and brown. For a moment, Elena wondered what it would be like. To dance with wild abandon. To fill her heart with song and let it take away her worries, her fears. To be like the desert wind, letting the sounds of the city guide her feet as the ravanahatha guided the woman. Often, when she danced, following the rhythm set by her guru, Elena had to make sure each movement was precise, sharp, full of intention. But this woman spun without pretense. Elena craned her neck, trying to get a better look at the dancer, but then Ferma called for her, and with one last glance, Elena hurried after.

They turned down an alley so narrow she had to walk sideways to get through, underneath arches adorned with crimson flowers, around a corner and then a side street, before she arrived at the dark awning of her favorite spot in the city—Jasmine's Tea Garden.

Normally, she would have loved to duck inside and savor a cup of tulsi tea, but instead, she turned to the square where a crowd had gathered. It was larger than the last rally, men and women of all ages, Ravani and Sesharian alike. They all listened earnestly to a thin wheat stalk of a man who stood on a raised platform. Despite his size, the man spoke with a deep, booming voice that carried throughout the square, its timbre and richness reverberating through Elena. If she did not know better, she would have listened to Jangir for hours. Beguiled by his promises, captivated by his stories. But then she saw the golden cap on his head, on the heads of those in the crowd, and she remembered whose men they were.

"War is coming, my friends," Jangir declared. "The Jantari ready their guns and oil their zeemirs as we speak. They defile our walls and call our king a heretic and a fraud. They spit upon the name of our god and wish to quench Her fire."

Angry shouts broke out around her, the stamping of feet. Elena edged back and felt Ferma squeeze her shoulder, her hand firm and steady.

"Stay close," she whispered.

"They call his daughter, our shining soon-to-be queen, a whore. They mock our traditions, destroy our outer posts. Just months ago in Rasbakan, five of our soldiers, our *sons* were..." Jangir shook his head, his expression etched with sorrow. "Sorry, my friends, I cannot tell you the truth. It is too terrible."

"Tell us!" someone shouted.

"Tell us what they did!"

Jangir looked up, his eyes sweeping the crowd. For a moment, his gaze met hers. Elena's heart stuttered. Did he recognize her, despite the disguise? But then he looked away, and she breathed a sigh of relief.

"They," Jangir said slowly, his voice shaking with fury, "they were captured and sentenced to die in a Jantari prison."

Elena bit her lip as the crowd erupted in anger. It was not true, this she knew. She had been in the war room with her father and the generals when the news of the attack had come months before. A minor squabble. No injuries on either side, no prisoners, nothing to merit a war they could not afford. But her father must have pocketed that report. Spun it, embellished it, and fed it to his blind, foolish followers.

He *thought ahead*, that needling voice said. *He's always thinking ahead.*

She began to weave through the gathering, keeping her eyes on Jangir. He studied the crowd, felt their anger build, and did nothing to calm it. Elena thought she saw a ghost of a smile on his face, but she was too far to tell for certain.

"There he is," Ferma hissed, pointing. A large man, shorter than Elena, stood at the fringe of the crowd. *Varun.* Jangir's right-hand man watched his boss with a dark, clouded expression. His gold cap perched precariously on his head, as if on the verge of falling off.

"This way." Ferma tugged her free from the throng of bodies.

"The other kingdoms ignore our pleas, and the Jantari are cunning," Jangir continued. "They will lie and hide their sins while our sons and daughters suffer. War is coming, my friends, and we must be ready. Enlist.

Quell your fears and strengthen your hearts. We have the fire of the Phoenix on our side. And She will never leave us so long as the king is here."

So long as the king is here. And what of your shining, soon-to-be queen? Elena thought bitterly as they approached Varun. *Will you listen to her just as well as you listen to your king?*

"Brother," Ferma called out in a customary Ravani greeting.

Varun turned. He had thinning hair and beady eyes that were always roaming, always watching. His gaze landed on Elena and a weary smile broke on his face. "Have you brought me worthy news, dealer?"

"News that should be shared in private," Elena said.

Varun hesitated, looking toward the stage, but Jangir was still spinning his tale, holding the crowd rapt.

"Let's go inside the tea shop," he said.

When they entered the store, the rich, earthy scent of tea leaves greeted them, and Jasmine, the owner, bustled over at once. Her eyes widened when she saw Elena's clothed face. She was the only one who knew about Elena's disguise; Ferma, ever quick to react, kept steering Varun toward a table at the back, and Elena pulled Jasmine aside.

"Your Highness," Jasmine began, but Elena held up her hand.

"As far as he knows, my name is Aahnah," Elena said in a low voice. She nodded toward Varun. "Do you understand?"

Jasmine stiffened, her face turning pale. But before Elena could ask what was wrong, Ferma beckoned her.

"Just bring us a pot of tea," Elena said and hurried over.

She sat down across from Varun, Ferma by her side. Elena touched her scarf, ensuring that only her eyes showed.

"I have something you might like to see," she said, switching her accent to the rolling drawl of someone from south Rani.

"Ach, people always say they have something to show me." Varun waved his hand. "And they show their faces to me. If you can't even do that now that we've become acquainted for a few moons, then I'm not interested." His eyes met Elena's. "Show me your face, dealer."

"It's of someone powerful. That's all you need to know," Elena said coldly.

"I know many powerful people. And many who claim to know things about them." Varun picked up a biscuit from the plate before Jasmine even set it down. He crunched it noisily as she poured their tea. "Your business is in trading secrets. So, this better be one I haven't heard."

"This is about Jangir."

Varun paused chewing for only a moment, but Elena caught it. She smiled beneath her scarf.

"What about Jangir?" Varun asked, too casually.

"We heard you wish to replace him," Ferma said, her voice muffled from behind her scarf.

Varun laughed. Crumbs fell from his lips as he took another biscuit. "Nonsense."

"And we found a way that you can, without raising questions."

Varun sipped his tea, hissing when he burned his tongue. He seemed to be on the verge of shouting for Jasmine when Elena pulled out the holo-pod and set it carefully on the table. Varun stopped.

"What is that?" The laughter was gone from his voice.

Elena shared a sidelong glance with Ferma, as they had rehearsed. He took the bait.

"What?" he asked, leaning forward. His eyes darted between them. "What news do you bring?"

"Apparently your leader was scouted by the Jantari, over a sun ago," Elena said slowly. "He's been spreading lies and misinformation while sharing the recruitment numbers with his superiors. Why else do you think he campaigns so heavily for the war effort? In areas full of low-wage Ravani and Sesharian refugees, men and women who know nothing about war? He's not serving *our* king. He's serving the Jantari."

Elena patted the pod. "When you are alone, view its contents. And you'll see that *you* were serving a traitor."

It was a lie, of course. Jangir was a loyal royalist, but like her father, Elena had had no trouble concocting the reports, though she did have some difficulty replicating Muftasa's seal. But Varun would not know the difference.

Most people will believe what you put in front of them, her father had told her once. *Especially if you show them what they want to see.*

"How...how did you get this?" Varun asked finally.

"My sources are credible." Elena reached forward and turned over the pod, revealing the official insignia of the king etched into the metal. Varun gasped. His eyes widened in understanding, and when he looked at Elena, there was a new consideration in them. Respect. And cold calculation.

"Who are you, really?" he asked.

"My people believe you are the right man to lead the gold caps. And we wish for a quiet changing of power. Do you understand what I'm asking you?"

After a moment, Varun closed the pod and pocketed it. "I underestimated you, dealer. If that is what you really are."

"Consider me someone who cares deeply for the future of our kingdom."

She stood, Ferma rising with her. Varun gave her a quick nod.

"I will find a way," he said.

Jangir was still speaking in heavy, impassioned tones when Elena and Ferma left the square. His voice haunted Elena through the winding bazaar streets.

We have the fire of the Phoenix on our side. And She will never leave us so long as the king is here.

So long as the king is here.

Elena was to ascend the throne in just over a month, on her twenty-fifth birthday. She would become regent, the queen of the Fire Throne. This would become her kingdom, her domain. It would be her responsibility to protect and guard the Eternal Fire.

So why didn't anyone else seem to welcome her rule?

Once they were a safe distance away, Ferma touched her arm.

"Did you give Varun the right pod?"

Elena slipped out the other pod in her pocket, the twin to Varun's. She turned it over. Like the other, it bore the official insignia of the Phoenix, but below it was her family's personal coat of arms: the crossed sling-swords. Only she and her father could use such pods.

"You told Varun you wanted a quiet secession of power, but I thought—"

"I want them to tear each other apart." Elena stopped at a corner. In the distance, the Agnee Palace sat on its gleaming perch over the desert. "And I want my father to see it."

When Ferma made no response, Elena turned. Ferma dropped her hand from her ear, her eyes raised heavenward.

"Well, I don't think you'll have to wait for long."

Elena followed Ferma's gaze to the west. There, she saw the black oval shape of a hoverpod, like a smooth stone in a desert oasis. It descended in the direction of the dunes.

"Your father wants to see *you*."

CHAPTER 3

YASSEN

When the dragons began to leave, no Sayonai noticed. Not at first. It wasn't until the droughts came and fires raged throughout the country-sides that the people raised their eyes to the heavens and realized—no one was there.

—from chapter 17 of The Great History of Sayon

Yassen watched the sea glide past him as he sank into its murky depths, past driftwood and other detritus and into darker waters. The sub shuddered as it neared the mouth of a cave along the rocky grade.

Yassen barely got to study the cave before the sub shot forward at a breakneck speed, throwing Yassen back into his seat. He realized then that the cave was a tunnel, and that it glinted with blue light. Up and up they went until Yassen saw a small opening, a shining patch of water shaped like a silver coin. The vessel bolted out and the sky opened above him with mountains jutting on the horizon.

Yassen let out a shaky breath, his stomach queasy. The sub bobbed gently as the glass covering slid back. He was in the middle of a quiet lake surrounded by the soaring white peaks of the Sona Range. On the shore, a figure stood, waving.

Yassen recognized the set of his broad shoulders and chest, the wide-legged stance and bowed knees that befit a warrior, or a man who rode his horses hard. As the vessel glided closer, the man lowered his hand, and Yassen saw something flash on his smallest finger.

After all this time, he still wore his family crest.

"Welcome, Yassen," the man said. His voice was deeper now, a steady rumble like that of a waterfall. It expanded and lingered in the air long after he had spoken. The voice of a Sesharian who had never forgotten his island home.

The sub docked, and Yassen hopped on shore. "Hey, Sam."

Samson Kytuu was taller than Yassen, straight-backed with a high forehead and an aquiline nose. When he smiled at Yassen, it was a wide grin that reached the corners of his eyes—the same one he had given when they had been scrawny boys crouched outside a Ravani bakery many suns ago. Back then, the smile had promised a distracted baker's daughter and three loaves of honeyed bread. Now—Yassen wasn't sure what it promised.

Yassen held up the metal feather, and it glinted in the sun.

"Why this?"

"Don't tell me you didn't see it," Samson said, and Yassen squinted, studying the seal. Here, under the dancing gleams of the sun, he saw that it was not a feather after all, but a single, flickering flame.

"Of course," he murmured.

He had met Samson in Rani. They had been orphans, hungry and stranded. While Yassen scoured the desert for castaway trinkets to sell, Samson pickpocketed. They would pool their money to buy food, and when they had too little, they stole. Together, they had survived.

Yassen could feel Samson watching him, studying him, possibly experiencing the same shocks that came when meeting a childhood friend after a very long time.

The physical distance between them wasn't far, but the awkward silence seemed to stretch endlessly.

Suddenly, the sub gave a loud hiss, releasing a burst of steam; as one, Yassen and Samson jumped and drew their guns, gazes locked on the innocent vessel.

For a long moment, neither of them moved. Then Samson's lips twitched. They looked at each other and then the vessel, and the next thing Yassen knew they were both laughing so hard their bodies shook—a laugh that warmed the arid silence and melted guarded fronts, a laugh that they had shared as boys.

Samson holstered his pulse gun with a grin. He kissed his three fingers and pressed them against Yassen's forehead, the customary Ravani greeting given to friends and family.

"It's been too long, Cassian."

Yassen blinked. *Cassian.* It had been his code name when he and Samson were in the Arohassin, before Samson had escaped. It hadn't felt right to continue using that name when the person he had loved most was no longer there to whisper it.

"You remembered," he said.

"I still remember many things about you."

They took a stone path that curved along the mountainside. Retherin pines, their velvet trunks and tawny orange leaves shining in the sunlight, covered the grade. A mountain lark flitted above them, giving its three-note call of peace. The Jantari were known to mine these mountains, yet Yassen did not see the telltale ugly metal hulls of the rigs.

"I've bought the entire land from here to the next summit," Samson said, as if to answer his thoughts.

Yassen stared at him. "And they just...let you?"

"Of course not, Cass, you know better. In exchange, my soldiers protect the mines on the northern range," Samson said. "Easy work, though. I even made a small base in the middle—a training ground of sorts. Perhaps I'll show you sometime."

"There has to be more to it," Yassen said, eyeing him. "I've never heard of King Farin being the generous type."

Samson smiled slowly, though he stared straight ahead. "Always the observant one."

The path grew steeper. Yassen felt his calves begin to burn when they finally crested the hill, and the house suddenly rose above him as if to stun him with all its glory.

It was a behemoth, more a palace than the mansion of a successful militant. Melded of black Sesharian marble and Jantari steel, the building curved around the mountainside like two great wings of some mythic beast.

"You put a *mountain* in the middle of your house?" Yassen asked, turning to Samson.

"Welcome to Chand Mahal, Cass," his friend replied.

The moon palace. Austere, cold, beautiful—Yassen could see it.

Twin towers, modest in height yet resplendent with their embellished ridges of lapis lazuli flowers, stood on the edges of the sprawling gardens. Soldiers stationed there lowered their pulse guns and saluted as they passed.

Pale-kissed roses and glowing, dancing tiger lilies swayed in the breeze, spreading their aroma across the grounds. Yassen spotted gardeners snipping away vines. Though they wore gloves, Yassen could tell by their raven-black hair that they were Sesharians. They each bowed as Samson approached, but he paid them no mind.

Eventually, they reached the black, yawning entrance of the palace, with its arched marble columns and rippling sculptures of dragons. The guards beside the entrance bowed, and Yassen watched Samson raise his hand, murmuring some command to put them at ease.

"They treat you like a king," Yassen said mildly as they entered the foyer.

To say the outside of the palace was magnificent was an affront to its interior. Two spiraling staircases swept up and diverged in opposite directions toward two wings. A gem-encrusted dragon coiled across the marble floor. Above, a million tiny glass tiles reflected the sunshine, so it seemed that the very stars were within this room, within his reach. Yassen tried to stop himself from staring, but he couldn't.

"Some say so, but it's more out of respect than divine right," Samson replied.

Yassen tried to compose himself, looking back out the doorway where the gardeners, relieved of their master's presence, resumed their task of pruning.

"Do they know who I am?"

"A half-Ravani and half-Jantari mutt," Samson teased, but then he slung his arm around Yassen's neck, his voice lowering. "We're more than orphans now, Cass." He gazed up at the ceiling that captured the heavens. "That's all they need to know."

Yassen gazed around him. How different this was from the derelict ruins they had once slept in. Here, they could host and feed an entire army and still not know the pang of hunger. Perhaps this was what Samson had intended—to create a palace so grand that no one would ever think to mention his wayward upbringing.

Their wayward upbringings.

Yassen felt a numbness in his right arm, and he flexed his fingers with some difficulty. Samson had chosen a different path, and this was what he had to show for it.

"Let's eat. I know you must be starving," Samson said.

As if on cue, a servant with lips stained blue from indigo snuff appeared from the adjoining wing.

"Sires," he said, bowing. Yassen spotted the same bull tattoo on his hand.

"Yassen, this is Maru, my most trusted man. Maru, this is Yassen, my childhood friend," Samson said. He gripped his shoulder, hands harder than Yassen remembered. "A brother, actually."

Yassen warmed at the distinction, but he smiled warily. Though Samson appeared easy, he suspected his old friend still harbored doubts about Yassen's loyalties. He would have to convince Samson that he was done with the Arohassin. That what he truly desired, above all else, was a quiet morning on this mountainside.

"A pleasure," Maru said, his eyes lingering on Yassen's rumpled clothes. "The refreshments are ready for you."

"Splendid," Samson said. He pulled Yassen closer, grinning. "A little bird told me that you still like Ravani tea."

Maru led them down a long hall full of light and crystal. Yet another dragon coiled across the ceiling here, its scales fashioned with mirrors that reflected their steps.

They came to two great doors. A river curved along the edges of the gate and swirled inward toward the doorknobs. Samson stepped forward. A pale light scanned his hand. Another thin beam swept across his face. Samson blinked, and then the beam closed, the river hissed, and the door unlocked to reveal the mountain.

A pathway of metal and stone cut its way through a courtyard of carefully pruned palehearts. Above, a mountain peak glimmered in the glare of the sun, but Yassen did not squint. He could not appear weak before Samson.

The path led to a terrace furnished with ivory chaises. Samson motioned for them to sit as two Sesharian servants placed pots of tea and platters of sandwiches and sweets before them. As they poured tea into their cups, lazy wafts of steam uncurled in the air. Yassen drank in the rich smell of Vermi leaves and lemongrass. Arranged on a three-tier platter were an assortment of sandwiches filled with apricot jam, gingerberry beads, and smoked meat. Another servant brought out a selection of powdered dew nuts, syrup-coated figs, and cloud cookies that, when bitten, dissolved into honeyed air.

"They still your favorite, yes?" Samson smiled when he caught Yassen staring at the cloud cookies.

Yassen couldn't help smiling in return. He nodded and sank back in his seat.

A flutter of color drew their attention, and Yassen caught the fleeting image of a clawed falcon diving into the canopy for unseen prey. Its descent set off a flurry of calls. Among them, Yassen recognized the flutelike voice of a mountain lark.

"They can be a nuisance sometimes, but I swear, come dawn, they make the most beautiful chorus you've ever heard," Samson said. He bit into a cloud cookie, vapors of red escaping from between his lips.

At the edge of the courtyard, a gardener ripped out a cropping of silver-headed mushrooms that gave off such a strong, sulfurous scent that Yassen could smell it from the terrace.

"Are we having mushrooms for dinner?" he asked and turned to Samson, who was carefully applying a layer of gingerberry beads to a piece of toast.

"No, because I assume they still turn your stomach," Samson said. "Remember the time when you threw up all over Akaros's shoes? Skies above, he was livid. He must have made you scrub those filthy leather loafers a hundred and fifty times before he put them back on."

"I spat in them for good measure," Yassen said, and Samson laughed.

"How is that old man? Keeping the boys miserable as always?"

Yassen didn't answer; instead, he motioned to the signet ring on Samson's pinkie. "I thought you had given up on the family name. Or at least that's what the reporters say."

"What do you think?" Samson asked, and Yassen recognized the subtle edge in his voice. It was the same voice Samson would use when they had to interrogate their sources for information. He was testing him.

Yassen hesitated, eyeing his friend. Though he had the same smile, this man was a stranger, not the boy Yassen had once known. The boy who had clutched his arm so hard that Yassen found marks in the morning; the boy who had promised that he was done with his name, done with the Arohassin, and that he was leaving and would one day come back for Yassen.

Yassen felt the ghost of Samson's hand pressing into his flesh.

"I think that—as much as you decry your family name and the horrors it's brought upon you—you still miss Seshar. Maybe not all the people, but at least the horses." Samson chuckled at that. Yassen pushed on, picking his words with care. "But what I still don't understand is, with all the wealth and power you've built, why haven't you gone back? Why haven't you punished the people who killed your family?"

"I see you haven't changed a bit." Samson lowered his leg, sitting straighter. He reached for his tea, pouring carefully, but Yassen heard the coldness in his voice. "You're still obsessed with punishment. They drilled that one deep."

"You were supposed to come back," Yassen said, hating the faint crack in his voice. "You made a vow to get me out."

Samson stopped pouring. There was a slight tremor in his hand as he set the pot down.

"We both know the Arohassin would have cut off our heads if I had returned," he said softly. But there was pain in his eyes. Samson had abandoned him to a miserable fate. And now here Yassen was, a thin, scarred, burnt reminder of Samson's shortcomings. Perhaps the militant knew of guilt too.

"I see you've employed your people," Yassen said after a while, nodding to the gardeners and the servants. "Are they all Sesharians?"

"Every single one."

"And Farin gave them to you?"

"You don't give men. They're not slaves," Samson said, a hint of reproach in his voice. "I simply convinced Farin that not all colonized people make good miners."

"They make better soldiers," Yassen said pointedly, looking at Samson.

Samson paused and then gave a slow nod. "Some better than others."

A servant came to refill their cups. When she left, Samson cleared his throat.

"Look, Cass. I'm glad you called me. And, I-I'm sorry for leaving you behind. You'll never know how sorry I am. After you helped me escape during our squad mission, I wanted to come back. To find you. But it wasn't safe, for me or you." He paused, biting his lip.

"But when you told me that you had defected, I had to take safety precautions. You see"—he placed his hand in the space between them, the dragon insignia of his ring flashing in the light—"I already have an assignment for you. But I won't force you to take it. It's your choice. Heavens know you deserve rest."

His words were kind. But Yassen knew he really had no choice as Samson tapped the table and holos shot up. News clippings and images opened before them, but Yassen already knew what they contained.

"Ravence," he said simply before Samson could speak.

Samson shook his head. "I knew you'd figure it out. Yes. Ravence is about to crown its new queen, and they've asked me to provide security. You know why?" His eyes bored into Yassen.

Yassen met his gaze without flinching.

"Because the Arohassin plan to attack and assassinate the Ravani family on the coronation day."

"Did they tell you anything else before you ran?"

"Everything I know, I give to you," Yassen said and withdrew a holopod from his pocket. It contained names, meeting points, and—the mother trove of all—a map of the Arohassin sleeper agents in Ravence. "This is proof that I've truly defected. It's all there, Sam."

"Then you already know what I'm going to ask you," Samson said. He hesitated for a moment. "Come with me to Ravence. I've already spoken to King Leo. He's agreed to give you a royal pardon if you help dismantle the Arohassin. Freedom, Yassen. You'll finally have it."

Yassen looked down at his hands. *Freedom*, what a funny word. Here, in the heady mountain air, in the quiet, he felt so close to it. But Ravence...

He pinched the nerve between his finger and thumb, flexing his fingers. Ravence was his home. And despite the peace of this garden, he knew what he really longed for was the desert. The endless, rolling dunes.

He watched Samson sit back and look at him, not with the pretense of childhood familiarity, but with the cold, calculated air of a militant.

"Take out that flame I gave you," Samson said.

Yassen pulled the metal insignia from his pocket and placed it on the holopod. A confidential file opened—his own.

"That flame contains everything I have on you. Names, dates, even the serial numbers of your guns. It could lock you away for life. But I give it to you as a measure of good will," Samson said.

Yassen laughed. "So, you've been watching me."

"Watching and waiting for the right moment," Samson agreed. "I want no secrets between us. I said long ago that I would help you get home, and this—this is it. I mean to fulfill that promise. People are going to question my decision, but I know you. You haven't changed."

Yassen studied Samson, searching his face for a trace of dishonesty, but either he was true to his word, or too well trained in hiding his thoughts. The look on his face was one of belief. Actual belief. The same burning belief that opened a floodgate when Samson, gripping Yassen's arm after being whipped for failing his mission, had babbled about revenge and defection. The same belief that shone in his eyes when he told Yassen, in a rare instance of drug-induced clarity, that he, Yassen Knight, would survive. Survive out of all of them. Survive to live out old age and perhaps even forgiveness from the gods.

What Samson hadn't known was that Yassen did not find himself to be in the ranks of the forgiven. He was well beyond that point. The burns up his arms told him so. His long flight across the sea told him so. The faces he saw in the night told him so. Guilt, that snakelike poison, wormed its way down his throat as Yassen smiled—a smile he knew would break the cold, calculated air Samson held up as a shield because he, too, hadn't changed.

Yassen reached for the flame and slipped it back into his pocket.

"I'll go to Ravence with you if you get me amnesty," he said. "And then I'll be free."

Samson kissed his three fingers and held them in the air. Yassen did the same, and they touched their fingers together, sealing the promise.

CHAPTER 4

ELENA

The Prophet is justice in the corporeal form. Blessed by the Phoenix, the Prophet never dies but is reincarnated—life to ashes; ashes to life. The last Prophet, the Sixth Prophet, was known to live in this world five hundred suns ago. There are no records of her death, but after her disappearance, Alabore Ravence led his followers into the desert and created what we know now as the Kingdom of Ravence.

—from chapter 3 of *The Great History of Sayon*

They flew across the sea of dunes toward the mountains along the western border. Despite the arid desert, the Agnee mountains were filled with lush, towering pines. Legends said that when the Sixth Prophet rose, she created the desert to deter armies, but kept the mountain forests to protect the temple.

If it had been up to her, Elena would have burned it all down. It was easy for enemies to hide in the forest. The desert left no room for secrets.

Low clouds hung over the Agnee Range and turned the trees into silver spears. The hoverpod rose, climbing through the grey expanse before the mist gave way to the looming temple.

The Temple of Fire was older than the Kingdom of Ravence, older than the desert itself. It sat on the edge of a steep cliff, overlooking the forests. Shaped in the form of a lotus, it had eight ivory wings, or petals, that each represented a tenet of the Phoenix: Truth, Perseverance, Courage, Faith, Discipline, Duty, Honor, and Rebirth. Large multitiered lanterns were fixed at the top of every petal. The priests took rotating shifts to refill the diyas with mustard oil and keep the flames alive.

At the heart of the lotus was a pristine white marble dome. The Seat. A thick plume of smoke curled from its center.

The hoverpod docked and Elena walked out, breathing in the smell of ash and pine. Two royal guards, dressed in black uniforms with a red feather above their hearts, stood at the base of the steps. They bowed as she and Ferma approached. Elena craned her neck to take in the white granite staircase chiseled into the face of the mountain.

Her heart sank.

They could have docked behind the temple. But this was her father's subtle way of reminding her who was in power. The king, of course, could land right on the holy grounds. The heir would need to climb.

Elena sighed and began the long process of ascending, Ferma close behind, moving with the grace of a dancer. The stairs were steep, the climb winding, but Elena was determined not to show discomfort.

"Do you think he knows? About our visit to the gold caps?" she whispered to Ferma when they came to a landing midway up the stairs. They were alone here. A large fountain rose before them, its waters splashing loudly below the statue of the Phoenix soaring above the basin. When Elena glanced up at the statue, she shivered. The statue's red eyes glowed despite the lack of sunlight. It was unnerving.

"If he does, he'd be thrilled," Ferma responded. "The princess at a gold cap rally? Maybe she's starting to see some sense."

"Of course," Elena murmured. Her father had encouraged her to visit the rallies, to see the people who so ardently supported their throne and their rule. *Maybe he thinks we're finally on the same page*, she thought ruefully.

"Let me do the talking," she said.

"Trust me, I have no desire to face the king." Ferma grinned.

When they finally reached the top, two men awaited them. Elena recognized Majnu, her father's Spear. He was a large brute of a man with wary eyes, and he dwarfed the short, white-haired man beside him.

"Arish." She smiled, a true smile. She was fond of Arish, who served as her father's Astra—his highest-ranking advisor.

The man bowed deeply, his silver hair shining.

"Your Highness," he said in his soft, whispery voice. "His Majesty is already inside for the Ashanta ceremony."

How many times will he consult the heavens? Elena squeezed Arish's arm and then brushed past him.

"Wait out here," she called back to Ferma.

The temple's entrance was carved from firestone and pink marble, laden with jewels burnished from the heat of the desert, but when Elena stepped inside the dark stone hall, shadows awaited her. She could hear the hypnotic drone of the priests coming down the main hall. Carefully, she removed her shoes and set them aside. The stone was cool underneath her feet but grew warmer as she neared the center of the temple. The chanting of the priests grew louder. The scent of sandalwood incense and smoke wrapped around her. Shadows danced along the wall, a mirage of the fire that awaited.

When she reached the curve, Elena paused. Her throat was already beginning to tighten from the smoke, her heart fluttering in her chest like a moth. *It's just fire*, she told herself.

She closed her eyes and concentrated on her breath. Felt the warmth of the stone. Emptied out her thoughts and then walked forward.

It was like stepping into a furnace. The heat slammed against her face, chasing the air from her lips. Despite her resolve, Elena stumbled back. The Eternal Fire roared and shot up toward the domed ceiling and the golden statue of the Phoenix that soared above. A semicircle of priests stood around the pit of the fire, chanting.

Within the flames, on the raised dais, Elena saw a man, seated cross-legged, his head bowed but his back arrow straight. Saayna, the high priestess, dressed in a golden shawl, stood before the steps of the dais. She threw lotus petals into the Eternal Fire, and the flames grew. The heat intensified. But the figure did not even stir or tremble.

No wonder people feared her father.

Elena sank to her knees behind the circle of priests. She felt her chest begin to constrict like the windpipe of a desert bird in the hand of a butcher. Her palms grew sweaty. She rubbed them against her knees and blinked the sting out of her eyes. She forced herself to *be still*, to stop fidgeting, to look into the Eternal Fire and not be blinded by its light.

The priests gave their final chant, and then the high priestess poured an urn of clear mountain water into the pit.

She opened a leather-bound book, a rarity in Sayon, and smoothed the pages.

"Here sits the servant of Alabore Ravence, the one true king. The one chosen to lead his people to their promised land," she sang. "May the Phoenix bless Her followers from the ash of Her fire. May we take this ash and see the world with eyes unclouded by hatred. May She bless the son who carries Her legacy."

King Leo stood. Ash sprinkled down his shoulders as he stepped off the raised dais and walked down the stairs. The high priestess pinched vermilion powder between her fingers and drew three diagonal lines across the king's forehead.

"And so we the blessed few," she intoned.

"So we the blessed few," both Elena and her father returned.

Elena rose slowly as her father accepted offerings from the priests. He raised them to his lips, kissing lotus flowers, sweets of diamond rock, and petals of desert rose. Saayna saw her and smiled. Elena bowed as she gently pressed her hand to Elena's forehead.

"When you are queen, you too will sit in the flames," she said, and the wrinkles around her eyes deepened.

"Thank you, Saayna," Elena said, but she could feel her father's eyes on her. He probably sensed the insecurity in her voice. Because try as she might, she could not hold a flame, let alone sit in the Eternal Fire. She could not withstand the burn.

"Elena," her father said, and she turned to the king.

Her father was a tall man, straight-backed like the great pines, broad-shouldered like the mountains, and with the same high forehead as hers. He was over fifty suns but gave no signs of his age save a faint greying of the hair at the edges of his temples. Perhaps his rigid constitution and ability to withstand the Eternal Fire made him so, or perhaps it was the fact that he managed a kingdom constantly threatened by wars and coups, fanatical anarchists and greedy neighbors. Yet when Elena bowed and King Leo placed a heavy hand on her head, she knew the reason her father held the throne was not because of his cunning and tenacity. It was because he had lost his wife to madness—and his sense of fear had died with her.

Her father feared nothing. And that made the Phoenix King a dangerous and capable man.

The ground rumbled as the stone seal before the entrance slid away, revealing steps. The priests all retreated into their underground chambers, save the high priestess.

She pressed a small leaf-bound package into Elena's hands.

"The Immortal one's gifts."

Elena nodded. The high priestess was nearly as old as her father, if not older. Wrinkles crept around her eyes, but her skin was otherwise smooth and unblemished, her brown eyes clear and full of serenity. There was something surreal about her, superficial even—at times it made Elena uneasy. She accepted the gift, and the high priestess bowed and descended into the chamber below.

Once they were alone, King Leo sank down to his knees before the dais steps. Elena followed suit, and together they gazed into the Eternal Fire. Heat scraped against her face, and though Elena felt ash tickle her throat, she could not deny the fire's beauty. It was mesmerizing, how the flames danced. How they soared and touched the feet of the Phoenix like loving, devoted servants. Fire knew when to destroy. It also knew how to love.

"I was surprised to hear that you went to the rally," Leo said. "I thought you hated the gold caps."

"I don't hate them," she lied. "I just don't agree with their...methods. But I thought it was time to finally try to understand why you find them so *necessary* for our rule."

"Every ruler needs a group of stalwart supporters, even if most are fools." He dusted ash from his sleeve. "They keep your enemies in check. After all, the voice of a dissenter will always be drowned out by a mob—"

"—so you learn to control the mob," Elena said in time with Leo. He smiled. Her father had said this to her for as long as she could remember.

Control the people, Elena. Tell them how they should think. Learn when to grant or withhold their wishes.

The problem was, she did not, could not, view people like Ferma or even Jangir as spineless puppets, mouthpieces to disseminate the stories she saw fit when she saw fit. Perhaps that was why she could not withstand the inferno. She could not find the same cruelty of its heat inside of her.

"Well, what did you think about the meeting?" her father asked, looking at her expectantly.

"Illuminating," she said. Hope glimmered in his eyes, and for a moment, Elena's chest clenched.

If Varun ousted Jangir and fought for control of the gold caps, the group could collapse on itself. Elena would make sure of it. Others would sense power and jump at the opportunity. And her father would watch his beloved supporters destroy themselves, like snakes in a pit.

She should feel nervous, anxious, elated, and yet... and yet guilt nagged at her, souring her hopes. Leo smiled, and Elena could not meet his eyes. She turned back to the fire as it hissed below her feet.

I am only helping us, she thought. The Phoenix King, the title of the throne, was her birthright just as much as it had been his. But how could she assume the throne if he and his people were still controlling it? If her own people thought she was another spineless puppet?

Leo had allowed the gold caps to grow too powerful, too proud. And she had watched, silent and powerless against her father.

She's a puppet just like the rest, Eshaant had said.

He saw her as a complacent bystander, and Elena knew others did too.

"There's some news I want to share with you," Leo said. A fine layer of soot lined his saffron-colored kurta and white shawl. Her mother's necklace, a golden chain with a bird pendant crafted from jade and purple desert-stone, hung around his neck. It alone was without a single speck of ash. "The Arohassin attacked a sand port in Rasbakan."

She breathed in sharply. The Arohassin were an ideological criminal organization bent on destroying kingdoms in the name of a new world order, an order of governments created by the people and not kings. But Elena had seen the work of the Arohassin. They claimed freedom and brought anarchy. They quoted martyrs and spawned more in their wake. What good was their liberation if it only led to ash and ruin?

"Do you think that's somehow connected to the skirmishes with the Jantari on our southern border?" she asked.

"Perhaps, but Farin is too proud to hire someone to do his dirty work," Leo mused. "I believe the Arohassin acted on their own."

"Splendid. So now we have storms in our east *and* south." She shook her head, her voice fierce and low. "But the Jantari are our bigger concern, Father. We're not ready for war. At the rally, the people were telling each other to enlist but—"

"As they should. We need new recruits to bolster our forces—"

"But these people know nothing about fighting. Do you want me to start my reign with a war that could debilitate our country? We're better off negotiating for peace with Farin—"

"We can handle the Jantari," Leo said, and there was an edge in his voice, one Elena knew better than to challenge. She sat back, hands clenching her knees.

"It's the Arohassin I worry about," Leo continued. "I ought to cut off their heads, but I found something better." He paused, watching a shower of sparks fall from the fire. "I made a deal with Samson Kytuu. He'll strengthen our forces against the Jantari in the south and use his intelligence to root out the Arohassin."

"Samson Kytuu?" She had heard about the Sesharian militant; they all had. Born under Jantari colonial rule in Seshar, he had escaped indentured servitude and joined the Arohassin, only to escape and sell their secrets to the Jantari army. He had risen quickly through the ranks and found favor with the king, so much so that Farin had allowed Samson to lead a small mercenary band of Sesharians known as the Black Scales. Why that horrid name, Elena did not know, but she did know that when the Black Scales entered the fight, they never lost.

"Samson Kytuu is under Farin's thumb. His allegiance is to the Jantari. Why would he want to help us? What does he want?"

Her father looked at her knowingly with his stark grey eyes, the ones she had not inherited. She understood the answer before he spoke, and it was as if all the air was sucked out of the room and into the roaring flames.

Shadows of light and smoke passed across Leo's face.

"The marriage would help solidify our position," he said. "Despite his past, people love Samson. They adore him—"

"They're stupid," Elena said, fighting to keep the tremble from her voice.

"I know," her father said, "but we can't deny that Samson is a powerful man. Yes, he's a snake-oil type, but his track record is flawless. Annoyingly so. We've seen him turn the tide of battles with his Black Scales. He's smart, fast, crude. With a man like him at your side, Ravence will never lose."

Elena said nothing. She stared down at her hands, which suddenly looked so small and far away. In the crackles and hiss of the flames, she heard the voices of history, those past kings and queens who had suffered and sacrificed for this altar before her, this mounting fire that ate everything in its path. She felt its heat, its claim on her destiny. The smoke closed around her, narrowing her field of vision until she was only looking at the haunting, dancing fire. How did her father do it?

Without thinking, Elena reached her fingers toward the pit. The inferno roared and singed her skin. She yelped and yanked her hand back.

"Don't worry, Elena," her father said after a moment. "You'll learn."

Elena fought back a grimace. She curled her hand in her lap to hide the burn.

Leo leaned forward and scooped up a single flame. It seemed to leap into his hand, ready to claim new flesh.

"I would burn them all, just like your great-grandmother did in the Red Rebellion," he said. Elena felt her skin prickle as he brought the flame closer and held it up between them. "But there are smarter ways to change the course of this land. Sometimes, all you need is to present the threat and then watch people cower like shobus with their tails between their legs."

Gently, her father returned the flame back to its waiting hearth. He laid out his unscathed palm.

"I also chose Samson because of the recent influx of Sesharian refugees to our kingdom," he said.

Elena looked to him in surprise. "What does that have to do with him?"

"For one, Farin is furious that we've even offered the Sesharians refuge. He views them as laborers, not refugees. He wants them for his mines. You've seen his warnings. The blocked asylums. But the other kingdoms are growing wary of his antics. Even Tsuana has asked Farin to not prohibit their passage."

Elena nodded. Tsuana was a neutral kingdom. It had never participated in any of the past great wars or regional conflicts. Yet if the Tsuana queen had spoken out against Farin, then it meant Farin truly was unsettling the other kingdoms.

When Jantar had invaded and taken Seshar nearly seven decades ago, the kingdoms of the second continent had been too shocked to retaliate, and the ones on the first continent were too far away to give a damn. Many feared that if they spoke up, they would be next. But her great-grandmother had not kept quiet. She had been the first to offer refuge to the conquered Sesharians who had fled, and several other rulers had followed suit. Ravence's aid to Sesharians had always been a sore spot for Farin.

But since then, Jantar had found new, rich ore deposits deep in the Sona Range. They had forced the remaining Sesharian families to work their mines, leading to a fresh wave of refugees wanting to avoid the cruel rigs. Elena had heard stories of men starving in the dark. Mines caving with people still in them.

"Jantar has grown too powerful," King Bormani had once told her and her father during a royal visit. Veran was a small kingdom, known for its spoiled wine and fat nobles. "We can't afford risking a war with them."

Her father had only smiled. "And who would ever in their right mind go to war with *you*, Bormani?"

Elena stared into the fire. Why would Samson want to marry her, when he was nothing but a glorified servant of Farin? When he was a turncoat himself? The man had served in the Jantari army. Raised his ugly zeemir against his brethren. The very thought of using weapons against *her* own people made Elena's skin crawl.

"Farin needs to appease the other kingdoms before they see the sense in Tsuana's argument and make requests of their own. And you know how persuasive Queen Risha can be." Leo continued. "Farin knows of Samson's marriage offer. I believe that he *encouraged* Samson to ask for your hand. If he allows his pet Sesharian to marry a Ravani, he thinks it will show that he isn't as bigoted as *we* know he is. And, he thinks—"

"He thinks that Samson will be a puppet king," Elena finished.

Leo paused. "Indeed," he murmured.

"Do you think Samson is more than what he seems?"

"Perhaps," Leo said slowly. "He's a proud man. Ambitious. I have a feeling that he has grown tired of being under Farin's thumb. That he wishes for more than just an army and a mansion in the Sona Range."

"How do you know that?"

But her father did not answer. Slowly, he wrapped his shawl around his arm. The flames whispered as if enjoying some great secret.

"Yassen Knight is coming back to Ravence with Samson. He'll join your Spear and be a part of your guard until the coronation."

"Yassen Knight." Elena was sure she had heard incorrectly.

"Don't sit there with your mouth hanging open," her father said, not unkindly. "He defected from the Arohassin, and Samson picked him up. Apparently, they're childhood friends."

She scoffed. "The Arohassin burned his name in the sand."

To burn someone's name in the sand was to call for their death. She had seen the Arohassin do it before to defectors. They never lived for long.

"Having Yassen Knight in Ravence will attract their attention," she said.

"Yassen and Samson both know more about the Arohassin than we do," Leo replied.

"But, Father, it's *him*. He's the man who assassinated the Cyleon ambassador and General Mandar."

"I know," Leo said. "But Samson is offering Yassen and his intel as proof that he is committed to joining Ravence. They both are."

The king stood and bowed to the Eternal Fire. In the wavering shadows, he looked more than a man, close to a god.

His eyes met Elena's, and something dark shone in their depths. "And if they are lying, we'll watch them burn."

CHAPTER 5

LEO

The Prophet raised her eyes to the heavens and said today justice would burn the land and cleanse it of its sins. But she does not know what it means to burn. The pain of it. The sorrow of it.
—from the diaries of Priestess Nomu of the Fire Order

Leo watched the Eternal Fire roll back into itself, satiated. The Ashanta ceremony had calmed it for now.

Elena had left with a clouded expression, leaving him alone in the Seat. He had known, of course, that she wouldn't like Yassen Knight being a part of her guard, but Leo wanted that bastard close. The assassin wouldn't dare make a false move with so many eyes on him. And Leo would enjoy watching him sweat.

He looked up at the great statue of the Phoenix. The golden bird stretched over the Eternal Fire, Her wings curving around the room. Rubies, bigger than Leo's hands, adorned her eyes and reflected the dancing fire beneath. The first followers of the Fire Order had carved the ancient language of Herra into the temple wall. Though Leo could not read the writing, he knew it told the story about a vengeful god and an all-powerful Prophet who could make the world bend. One who could raise fire from nothing.

Leo had once believed he would be the Prophet. Any young Ravani brought up on tales of the beast of fire thought he was the one to ride it. But then he had learned how to sit in the flames. Learned how to respect fire and withstand its heat long enough to give the country a show. He had come to know the truth.

There was nothing special about fire. It burned and raged. Demanded sacrifice, worship. It had no need for a Prophet.

His dream had crumbled to ash, hardening him into a cold, steady king who knew how to inspire both fear and respect. Fire had taught him one thing—the power of myth. Give the people something to believe in. Make it strong enough, fearsome enough, and they would all bow.

The king turned at the sound of stone scraping. The high priestess emerged from the chamber below. She had taken off her golden ceremonial garb and was dressed in a plain red robe with an orange shawl to cover her hair.

"Your Majesty."

"Saayna," he said and then, taking in the look on her face, "What is it?"

"There is something you need to see."

They descended into the chamber, the heat gradually seeping away as the cool damp of the mountain wrapped around them. A vast network of tunnels spidered beneath the temple. Here, the priests slept and worked, emerging only to tend to the Eternal Fire and the temple diyas. The irony of the priests of the Fire Order living in constant shadow had always amused Leo.

He pushed his hair back, careful not to touch the tilak, the Phoenix's blessing. It was nothing more than lines of vermilion, but he had to keep up appearances. The Fire Order was necessary to his reign. A Ravani king and queen could only rule after receiving blessings from the high priestess and the Eternal Fire. Throughout the suns, he had made a point of increasing the temple's budget and encouraged citizens to give hearty contributions. Jangir and the gold caps always rallied sizable crowds for holy events. Leo gave the order their worshippers, and they in turn gave him access to the heavens.

Small floating lanterns shaped like orbs lit the underground chamber. Leo and Saayna followed it to the end, took a turn, and then emerged into a larger room. The roof was not made of stone like the rest of the tunnels;

instead, banyan roots and moss intertwined to create a living ceiling through which pale sunlight filtered in. Herbs hung around the wall, filling the room with the smell of turmeric and dry pine. A young priest lay in a cot on his stomach, covered by a thin blanket. A small priestess stood immediately as they entered.

"Your Majesty," she muttered. A star-shaped birthmark on her cheek collapsed and expanded with the movement of her lips.

"Leave us," Saayna commanded.

When the priestess scurried away, Leo approached the young man. His face was grey and slack. A slick sheen of sweat covered his body.

"What's wrong with the boy?" he asked.

"Yesterday, the Eternal Fire burned him across the back. It will take him weeks to recover," the high priestess said.

The Eternal Fire often lashed out. The day Aahnah died, it had leapt from the pit, burning his foot. He still had a scar that roped around his heel like a serpent. But Leo had learned how to control the flames. The Phoenix and Her fire commanded respect, like any god. Give that, and it would stay at bay.

"He should have been more careful." He began to turn away.

"It burned a message."

Leo froze. "What do you mean?"

The high priestess removed the blanket covering the young priest. A burn spread across his back. It was as if a hand had taken a dagger and carved into his flesh, shaping it into two runes. Leo peered closer. The one symbol he recognized was the feather of the Phoenix.

"Do you know what this says?"

"Daughter of Fire," the high priestess answered, her voice hushed. Reverent.

Leo glanced up and saw the fervent look in her eyes.

"*Daughter* of Fire?" he repeated. The meaning slowly dawned on him. He looked at Saayna and then the poor boy. The runes seemed to smolder in the low light.

"The Prophet comes," the high priestess whispered.

Leo felt something unspool within him. Disbelief perhaps, denial even, but deeper within, disappointment. *Daughter of Fire.* The next Prophet would be a woman. It would never be him.

After learning the nature of the flames, he had believed in the Phoenix and Her prophecy with a grain of sand. He went through the rituals and ceremonies because that was what he needed to do as king. Ravence was built on the back of an old religion. He had to cater to it. But this—this was something his predecessors had never prepared him for.

Leo looked to the high priestess.

"When?" he asked.

"I know only that the time draws near," she said. "She will come for Ravence."

His father had told him this as he slipped into old age and madness—a prophecy that warned of the Phoenix rising again.

"She will call forth a Prophet who will turn all of Sayon into a dry, brutal desert," the old king had gasped, his eyes red and swollen. "She will burn everything in her path, including this kingdom. All gone in a single swipe of a vengeful god."

"We struck a deal," Leo said to the high priestess. "Alabore Ravence struck a deal with the Phoenix, and he was blessed with Ravence. Why would the Prophet take the blessing back?"

"The Phoenix is mysterious in Her ways."

"Heavens be damned, Saayna!" He gripped her shoulders. She flinched, but her gaze was steady. "I've made my mistakes, but don't let Elena suffer for them. Tell me, do you know what the Prophet intends? Where is she now? Has she already been marked?"

Saayna's lips hardened, and she removed his hands with soft fingers. Slowly, she covered the young priest, moved to the wall, and with a wave of her hand, summoned a holo. A map of Ravence floated before them, along with pictures of the two runes. She plotted the symbols over Ravence, and Leo watched as the black lines cut through the desert, leading to Rani.

A map within a map.

"The girl has been marked," the high priestess said. "She is here, in the capital, but she has not come into her full powers yet. That day will come. I can feel it. Soon, we will all have to answer for our sins."

She turned to him, her eyes dark. "Especially you, Your Majesty."

Leo disliked the undercurrent in her voice, but he forced himself to stay calm. He knew he could not trust Saayna. He sensed a lie dripping from her lips like rattlesnake venom, but he couldn't place it. The Eternal Fire had spoken—that much he couldn't deny. But was Saayna's translation accurate? He glanced at her as she dabbed the boy's forehead with a soft cloth. She would defend the Prophet; it was her duty. But it was also his duty to defend his kingdom.

For a split second, he wondered if Elena was the Prophet…but no. She could not hold flames. She could not withstand their heat. Rage welled inside of him.

Damn this Prophet! Damn the skies above!

He needed to hunt down the fanatic. He and his ancestors had brought peace to this wild desert. He would not let it burn now.

"Saayna," he said, his voice measured, calm. "I'm placing you under arrest for treason. The guards will escort you out of this temple, and you will only return on coronation day. Until then, you will help me find this Prophet. You *will* defend Ravence." He looked at her and then the young priest. "Or else I will make sure he is the first to burn."

Saayna nodded, her face composed. She seemed to accept her fate willingly. These religious fanatics were always like that. They gave in to the gods without so much as a squeak of protest.

"As you wish, Your Majesty," she said.

Saayna moved toward the young priest, but Leo stopped her.

"We are leaving. Now."

She threw a look at the boy but walked to the door. Leo followed her up and out of the chamber. The stone slab slid back, and they reemerged into the Seat. The Eternal Fire cackled in welcome. It elongated, the flames curling and dancing as if they could sense Leo's distress. As if they were laughing at his fate to come.

When they walked out of the temple, the mist had evaporated. Golden light dusted the great pines, and beyond, the dunes spilled out, still and majestic. The desert knew of fire. It could withstand its heat, just like him.

Leo motioned to Majnu, who stood waiting by the entrance.

"Arrest the high priestess," he said. "Take her to the prison in the desert, and do not let her get close to fire."

If his Spear was surprised, he gave no indication. Leo watched as he led the high priestess away, her hair shining like spun bronze. She was a proud one. He would give her that. But he would make her bend like everyone else.

CHAPTER 6

YASSEN

The Sky People were said to build their kingdoms in the clouds. They flew on ancient lily pads guided by a Sky Scout to the upper mountains of Seshar. We have discovered some vestiges of their civilization, but most were destroyed during the Jantari invasion.
    —from chapter 13 of The Great History of Sayon

Yassen splashed cold water on his face with one hand, his body trembling. He had dreamed of fire, again, crackling up his leg and arm, forcing its way down his throat. Even now, his throat felt raw.

It's only a dream, he reminded himself.

But he could not forget the sensation: the slow suffocation from smoke. The ash pricking his nostrils like sharp, grey needles.

It's only a dream.

He turned from the basin and looked out the window. It was a moonless night. Tiny stars pinpricked the dark, heavy fabric of the sky. This was the time he had often slipped out to do his work. He would move like a shadow—smooth and supple. Become a part of the night.

50

He preferred a pulse gun over all other weapons. It was simple, neat. The barrel warmed with energy, and when released, a singular pulse zipped out, hot like a bolt of lightning. It could burn a hole through a man.

He almost missed it. The swift adrenaline. The quiet of the night when most men were asleep and he could walk through the world, pretending that it was his.

But the fire...

A dull pain spiraled up his right arm to his shoulder. He began the slow work of awakening whatever life was left in his arm. He massaged his numb fingers, pinching the nerve between his thumb and forefinger, counting until ten, until twenty, thirty.

As he did, he felt a cold, slow panic. *I'm still useful,* he thought. *I can still manage.* But his injury told otherwise. It spoke of his mistake, his replaceability.

His fingers twitched back to life, and he sighed in relief.

He was already dressed when Maru knocked on his door. Dawn had yet to color the sky as the servant guided Yassen to the main foyer. A week had passed since his arrival at Chand Mahal; he had grown familiar with its long hallways and grand rooms, but even now, Yassen paused. Despite the moonless night, the mirrored ceiling sparkled with stars, as if the heavens were already awake and within his reach.

A hoverpod was docked outside the entrance. Samson stood on its ramp, wrapped in a milky fur coat that looked like the skin of a fyrra, the long, three-tailed wolves that roamed in Jantari mountains. But the fyrra had grown rare in the past decade, driven to starvation as miners cut down forests to set up more rigs. Only Jantari elite wore such coats. Perhaps Samson had found one stalking his grounds.

And of course, he would wear it to the hot deserts of Ravence, Yassen thought, shaking his head.

A servant took Yassen's bag. Others carried Samson's luggage up the ramp, like ants marching up a hill.

"Mother's Gold, how much are you bringing?" he asked.

"You need help with your wardrobe," Samson said. "We can't go to the holy kingdom dressed as soldiers."

"I dress just fine."

Samson surveyed Yassen's loose, asymmetric white shirt and slacks. He stopped a servant guiding a rack up the ramp and grabbed a garment bag.

"Here," he said, throwing it at Yassen.

Yassen caught it single-handed. Inside was a beautifully soft kurta with a subtle black-and-blue jacquard finish and ivory buttons fashioned into lotuses. The jacket, embroidered in a similar pattern, had two lotuses pinned on the collar.

"I had it made and delivered late last night along with a few other things," Samson said. "We don't want you looking like you just washed up from the sea."

Yassen scowled. "They know who I am."

"Still, deception..." Samson began.

"...is not a felony," Yassen finished. The words came on reflex. It was a saying the Arohassin had beaten into them. That and: *Murder is not a sin, but an awakening of one's own mortality.*

It felt odd to hear Samson say it, for him to remember. He had denounced the Arohassin, calling their tactics egregious, animallike, but here he stood reciting their mantras.

Yassen followed Samson into the hoverpod as Maru barked out final orders to the servants. The two friends sat across from each other, sinking into the plush seats. A bottle of white wine chilled in a pitcher while an assortment of fruits and a pot of steaming tea sat on the table.

Samson removed his furs, and Yassen was relieved to see that he was wearing a kurta beneath. The Ravani king would laugh them out of the court if Samson strolled in with that monstrous coat.

As Samson poured their tea, the door slammed closed, and the hoverpod lurched. Maru stumbled and dropped a package, which rolled to a stop at Yassen's foot. Before he could grab it, Yassen picked it up, the suede cover falling back to reveal a corner of a map.

He whistled. "Paper?" It was a rarity in Sayon.

"It was a gift from Farin," Samson said, his tone a bit too casual.

Yassen noticed Maru studying him, saw the expectant look in Samson's eyes. He realized then that Maru's stumble had been on purpose. *They want me to look.* For a moment, Yassen hesitated, his fingers brushing the cover. But curiosity got the better of him. Carefully, he unrolled the map and smoothed out the corners.

He wished he hadn't.

In faded ink, the map showed a network of tunnels beneath the Sona mountains. The tunnels spanned the entire mountain range, running north to south. A jumble of lines crisscrossed at the center and southern point of the range, notating the chambers that ran east to west.

Yassen glanced at Samson, his heart hammering. Did he know about the cabin?

"It's a relic. Half of those tunnels are caved in or inaccessible anyway," Samson said. "Still, best not let it get too much air." He took the scroll from Yassen, gently returned the map to its cover, and handed it back to Maru.

Yassen stared at him, his mouth suddenly dry. He wanted to believe that the map was just a faded memory, the tunnels nonexistent, but he knew they weren't. After all, his father had died after discovering them.

"Everything is ready, sir," Maru said. "The troops will be arriving after sundown."

"Thank you, Maru," Samson replied.

The hoverpod rose as the sun began to peek over the horizon. The sky slowly blossomed, shaking off its dark slumber. Blue leached to purple to pink. The sun warmed the underbellies of the clouds, and Yassen watched Chand Mahal grow smaller and smaller until it disappeared. He tried to sit back and relax, but he couldn't. Samson, on the other hand, curled into his coat and fell fast asleep, his untouched tea growing cold on the table.

Behind them, the famous Sona Range unfolded, a series of lush mountains whose depths were peppered with silver-hulled mines. It was here that the Jantari collected their precious, blinding metal. Unlike other types of minerals, Jantari metal could weather any storm or rust for a hundred suns. And the Jantari were master smiths. From fashioning entire cities to carving delicate music boxes, the Jantari could bend and shape their special ore in ways the other kingdoms could not.

We create magic with our hands, Yassen, his father had said. *Magic.*

Before they had conquered Seshar and used indentured Sesharians to work their mines, the Jantari government had targeted poor, desperate Jantari youth. *Strike ore and claim a handsome amount! All it takes it just one lucky venture!* Thousands of men had signed up. Thousands had delved deep within Sayon until they could no longer see their hands before their eyes. Yet only hundreds survived. And of those, only a few were not driven to madness by the dark. Yassen did not know how his father had done it: mined in the black; rubbed his hands raw so that the cracks of his skin were filled with dirt.

The hoverpod banked, and then Yassen could no longer see the mountains. He sighed, trying to sleep, but the memory of the dream, of the cruel fire and its harsh smoke, made him break into a fresh sweat. So he stood. Walked around the hoverpod, found Maru reading on the lower level amid the luggage. The servant asked if he wanted anything, but Yassen waved him away. He climbed to the top level, to the pilot's cockpit.

"How long is the journey?" he asked.

"A couple of hours, sir. Do you need anything?"

But Yassen was already walking away. He paced up and down, the knot in his stomach growing tighter with each step. He knew the reason he couldn't sleep was not because of his dreams, but that with every second that passed, he grew closer and closer to his home.

Ravence.

The very name sent an ache through Yassen. Since joining the Arohassin, he had only returned to Ravence twice. Once, to smuggle the leader of the Arohassin to safety; the other time, to take out a target, a rich general with jade piercings down his neck. And after the second time, it had become too dangerous for him to return, unless he wanted to be burned.

The Ravani held no warmth toward him, and Yassen couldn't blame them. He had killed a prominent military strategist. Worked for an organization that sought the kingdom's destruction. But the real reason for their dislike was far more bitter.

Yassen caught his reflection in the glass and stilled. His pale, colorless eyes stared back. He had inherited them from his father, his hair as well, but his curved nose and high cheekbones were from his mother, his smile, his deep love for the dunes. He looked more Jantari than Ravani, yet he spoke with the rolling accent of the desert. His countrymen did not know what to make of him. Sometimes, he did not know what to make of himself.

"Yassen."

He whipped around to see Samson climbing up the stairs to the upper level.

"There's something I need to know." Samson leaned against the wall. "Your arm."

Yassen froze. "What about it?"

Samson narrowed his eyes. "Word is that it was burned. That you can't use it anymore. Is that true?"

"It still works, and I shoot with my left," Yassen said, flexing his right hand.

But the intensity in Samson's eyes did not change. "Some of them know about the accident. The Ravani Intelligence, the king, hells—even the generals. They may not know about your *injury*, but they know that you failed to kill King Bormani. The Arohassin burned your name in the sand, Cass. They're looking for you." He leaned closer. "I need to know, are you taloned?"

"I am. Your men must have told you about the guards in the port," Yassen said, squaring his shoulders. "Did that look like a man who can't fight?"

At this, Samson drew back. He regarded Yassen for a long moment and then turned to the window.

"There it is."

Yassen looked out and saw, unfurling beneath the clouds, the dunes of his childhood. The Ravani Desert spread out before him, sloping in easy, natural curves. To the west, far off in the distance, the Agnee mountaintops kissed the blooming sky. Somewhere within those mountains was the Eternal Fire, the bewitching power that had beguiled men for centuries. Sons had slain fathers, mothers had killed daughters, in hopes of one day controlling the flames. To conquer the Eternal Fire was to conquer the gods.

The horizon rippled with waves of heat. Toward the southwest, Yassen glimpsed the red, dusty canyons that connected the southern cities of Magar and Teranghar. The hoverpod flew forward, its shadow flitting over thorny brush and narrow valleys. The dunes unfolded and then, in sudden glory, the sandscrapers of the city of Rani rose as if to defy the heavens themselves. Hovertrains zoomed from the city center to the outskirts, carrying tired laborers. Crammed between the pristine buildings and extravagant chhatris were booming bazaars and poorly plotted side streets. As a boy, Yassen had spent hours wandering the city. At every turn, he found himself in a different village—no, a different country—listening to the sounds of the various languages, from the lilting accent of the northern Ravani to the rumbling growl of the Karvenese.

When he didn't have the money, which was quite often, Yassen had watched the street urchins and learned their ways. He learned how to pickpocket softhearted tourists while he handed them satchels of spiced lotus puffs; how to evade the silver feather guards during their routine rounds; how to use the alleys to his advantage when an officer gave chase.

As they approached the city, Yassen craned his neck to see flashes of familiar buildings and new, developed squares. He could feel the desert heat pressing against the hoverpod's glass. Yassen rested his head against it. He could almost hear the cacophony: the blare of hovertrains and ring of sky bells interspersed with bellows of merchants and curses of drivers; a city breathing the lives and dreams of three million people, twelve nations, seven districts, and one wayward boy.

And there, rising amid all the chaos, was the grand behemoth—the Agnee Palace.

Sitting high up on a hill, the palace overlooked the city. Its ivory chhatris and sandblasted towers glowed in the morning sun. Marble latticework and fiery red gems adorned its windows. Three twisting spires—one each to look south, east, and west (but never to the sacred north)—stood like stoic guardians. There were no walls around the palace; the hill and the towers were enough.

"She's a beauty, no?" Samson said.

Yassen caught glimpses of luscious courtyards and fountains. Then they were landing, lowering onto a sunken strip behind the palace.

Samson stood. "Do you remember the Desert Oath?"

"I could never forget it," Yassen said.

"Good." Samson grinned. "Ready?"

Yassen stared out the window, rubbing his arm.

"Yes," he lied.

CHAPTER 7

ELENA

When Ravence was still a young kingdom, sandstorms raged along the borders. Queen Ashara had claimed that her god brought the storms to ward off invaders. This is a lie. When examining the weather patterns of that era, one must note the freak occurrence called Barru. A passing of a comet amplified the northern winds, and thus, the storms. This all goes to show that the Phoenix is a myth and the kingdom a sham.

—excerpt from an opinion piece in *The Jantari Times*

Elena sat beside her father in the large golden throne room. Over twenty thousand intricate mirrors shimmered within the walls, reflecting the golden light of the sun. She watched marigold flowers on the ceiling blossom as the sunlight touched them. They emitted a sweet, hazy smell, a tactic Leo used to lull heads of state into a false sense of security. Elena found the smell sickening. She had already decided that once she sat on the throne, she would rip out the flowers. Grind them between her palms and throw them into the Eternal Fire.

Arish entered the room, bowing to Leo before kneeling on a cushion beside the throne.

"They have just docked, Your Majesty," the Astra reported.

"They're late," the king said.

Her father was dressed in a white silk kurta with an embellished golden scarf draped elegantly down his shoulder. Kohl rimmed his eyes and a singular jade earring glittered in his right ear. Thick ropes of gold chain and a brooch of the Phoenix hung across his chest. Though Elena did not see it, she knew that beneath it all, he wore her mother's necklace. He was never without it.

The king sat upright on the throne with the crown of Ravence resting on his temples. The circlet was neither large nor glamorous. The object that nations had slain for, warred for, was merely a band of gold cut into the shape of dunes. In its center, Alabore Ravence had fitted the jewel that contained the only feather the Phoenix had granted men. It glinted softly as her father and his thousand reflections turned to her. It was a humble token—and a symbol worthy of the Phoenix.

"Did you bring the sands?"

Elena unwrapped the bundle her guards had brought in, revealing a gold basin filled with pure white sand.

"Do they even know the Desert Oath?"

Leo settled back into the throne, his eyes watching the great bronze doors. "They do if they're not stupid."

Elena nodded. She had taken the oath on the eve of her seventeenth sun. It was the day she had returned from her registaan, the rite of passage for every heir. Half a sun spent in the grueling depths of the desert, alone. She had been sent with no guards, no food, no water. She had only her wits, her training, and her Ravani blood.

Elena had learned how the desert moved and slept. She had learned how to coax water out of hardy plants; how to find the shady groves of a sandtrapper; how to, when the heat became too unbearable and the nights too cold, sit still and meditate: to slow down the life in her body so that every second became a day, a week, a month. So slow was her heartbeat that rattlesnakes mistook her for a stone and slithered past her. When she finally opened her eyes, Elena had felt balanced and light, as if she could dance out the rest of her days.

And she had. She'd danced to the songs of the desert as sand skittered in the wind. She'd practiced the Kymathra and Unsung, the ancient fighting styles created by the first queens of Ravence. She'd steeled herself into the warrior poses of the famed Desert Spiders, the lithe and legendary female soldiers who had once guarded the kingdom. Legends said that the Desert Spiders had once been a special faction of Yumi, ones who could control fire with their hair. The Yumi called them the Yamuna. The higher ones. But after the Sixth Prophet had nearly wiped out their people, the Desert Spiders had lost their power to wield fire, becoming mere Yumi. It was only Alabore who had rediscovered and revived their martial art form by teaching it to his daughters.

When Elena had finally returned to the palace, her skin had warmed from olive to burnished gold. Even her father had barely recognized her. Maybe that was why, when she was alone with him for the first time since her return, he had taken off his crown and rested it on her head.

"Only a desert wind can withstand the desert heat," he had said.

Elena had nodded, pretending to understand. Despite its delicate form, the crown felt heavy. It pinched her temples.

Gently, she had removed the crown and placed it back in her father's hands.

"Until then, it's yours," she had said.

She had not felt its pinch or its weight since then.

The doors of the throne room swung open, and two men entered. Arish stood.

"Samson Kytuu and his party, Your Majesty," the Astra announced.

The newcomers bowed. Elena instantly recognized Samson. He was handsome, strikingly so, with a gait that reminded her of a lion in the desert, slowly circling his prey. He wore a sand-colored kurta that complemented his broad shoulders and frame. But her attention did not rest on him. Rather, Elena found herself drawn to his companion.

He was shorter than Samson, with dark golden, curling hair that fell in soft wisps across his forehead. He had a long, pointed face and high cheekbones, like most Ravani. Yet he walked with such ease and grace, and when he knelt, she noticed how he bent his body like a dancer ready to leap.

Only a skilled fighter could move like that. In fact, he called to mind one woman, and that woman served as her Spear. Suddenly, Elena felt curious. *Who is this man?* The sun dusted his head, but he seemed to shrink back from it. And then immediately, she felt disgusted by her curiosity. Yassen Knight was an assassin and a traitor.

"Your Majesty, Your Highness," Samson said as they knelt. "It is our honor to be graced by your company."

"You honor us by being late?" The king gave a cold, hard smile. "Rise."

They stood. Samson stepped forward while Yassen Knight kept his eyes on the red marble floor.

Coward.

"Your Majesty, my apologies," Samson said. If the king's rebuke unsettled him, he gave no sign of it. His smile was easy, and it warmed the corners of his eyes. "We were finalizing placement of my troops. A selected few will remain in the capital, as we discussed, while the others will be sent to the southern border. I will even send some of my men to guard the temple—"

"The temple will be guarded by Ravani forces alone," Leo said. "It is our sacred duty as wardens of the holy land."

"Of course." Samson motioned at the servants who had followed him in, arms laden with trays. "We come bearing tribute."

The servants laid down the trays and pulled back the cloths, revealing a wide array of gifts: Sesharian swords with silver hilts, jade elephants with diamond trunks, dresses woven with crystals, silk scarves of every color imaginable, and pile upon pile of glittering necklaces, bracelets, and gauntlets.

Elena sighed. She glanced at her father; he hated when guests brought him such gifts. It was an act of complacency, he had told her, a way visitors tried to woo them like the marigold flowers showering their scent from the ceiling.

Leo waved his hand and the servants wrapped up the gifts and took them away. Then he stood. Elena shot up to her feet. Even the pale assassin looked up.

"You come with a proposition," Leo said. "State it."

Again, if her father's candor derailed him, Samson made no sign. He turned to Elena, his eyes bright and clear, his voice steady.

"Your Highness, I come with a humble offer. Ravence has many enemies along her borders, but Jantar is her deadliest. And yet, your kingdom has decided to take on Jantar's ire by accepting Sesharian refugees. As a

Sesharian, I am thankful for your service to my people. And I would like to repay you. I am willing to give you my strength, my armies, if—"

"If I take you as my king," Elena interjected. She looked long and hard at Samson, long enough to make him sweat, before continuing. "I've gotten many proposals. What makes yours different?"

Samson glanced at Yassen and then to her father.

"Do you have the list?" Leo asked.

Samson withdrew a pod from his pocket and called up the holos.

Lists of names and coded maps spilled out. Elena recognized the city grid of Rani, but there were plotted points that she did not recognize.

"These are the active Arohassin agents in the capital right now," Samson said. "Their entire operating network is in here. We have names, locations—everything. I've had my men cross-check the information and it all holds."

"But have you tracked any of them down?" Arish asked.

"With the king's permission, we will." Samson placed the holopod in Arish's outstretched hand and took a step back. "This is my offering—redemption. A final blow to the Arohassin, the locusts that have plagued Ravence." He looked at Elena, his eyes bright, calculating. "And it will all be under your name, Queen Elena."

Elena met his calculating gaze with one of her own. It was wrong to call an heir queen before she took the throne, but he had done so to please her, and to stroke her ego. Samson was a crafty one.

But Ravence needed his men, the Black Scales, infamous for their efficiency, their coldhearted accuracy. Her father had failed to rid the country of the Arohassin. But she could.

Samson watched, waiting. A small part of her had hoped that one day—one day she might understand the love her father had given her mother. The meaningful silences they had shared. The look in her mother's eyes when Leo would find them in the library, surrounded by books, and would draw Elena in his lap so they could hear Aahnah read together.

Her parents had chosen each other out of love, not necessity. It was an intimacy Elena had only seen and wondered about.

But Samson was nothing like that. She knew only about his military feats and the promises he offered. The promises that would make her kingdom stronger.

Elena squared her shoulders and ignored the numbness in her bones. Marriage, if not for love, was made for compromise. The welding of kingdoms. The safety of generations to come. Intimacy was not something Ravence demanded from her. It demanded peace, safety, and those she would give it.

"I accept," she said. "Let us come together in union to rid Ravence of her troubles." Her eyes rested on Yassen. "All of them."

Yassen Knight did not falter under her gaze. She had heard of his failed mission; they all had. She had imagined him to be ruined, embarrassed by his mistakes, but he stood as still and impassive as the dunes on a winter night. She shifted, uneasy. There was something familiar about him . . . yet also something alarming.

"It's decided then," Leo said, not with warmth exactly, but with more cordiality in his tone than before.

Elena lifted the golden basin and set it between her father and their guests. She then produced two long matches from the depths of her lehenga and handed them to the king.

"We shall seal the alliance with the Desert Oath."

Elena watched as Leo struck the matches and threw them into the basin. A fire roared to life.

Together, Samson and Yassen knelt and held their hands over the flames, their voices unwavering.

"The king is the protector of the flame, and I its servant.
Together, we shall give our blood to this land.
I swear it, or burn my name in the sand."

Together, they brought their hands down into the basin. Pressing their palms into the flames, they left the imprint of their fingers, and their oath, in the ivory sand.

"So it is thus sealed," Leo said, and with a clap of his hands, the flames died with a whisper.

Arish brought forward a silver bowl of water. Samson and Yassen dipped their hands in it to ease their burns. Neither flinched as Arish wrapped cool, aloe-covered cloths around their palms. Elena caught Yassen's eyes, and she breathed in sharply. In the light of the room, they looked white as the tips of the far-off, snowcapped mountains. As white as the blinding glare of the sun.

He truly is one of the unforgiven.

"You have come a long way," Leo said. "Retire to your rooms and rest. We will reconvene later with my generals, and I expect your troops to be in position by then."

"You have my word," Samson promised.

Leo turned to Yassen and gave him a hard look. Then he leaned forward and whispered something in his ear that she could not hear. The traitor bowed deeper in response.

He then looked at Arish, signaling that this audience was over.

"The guards will escort you to your chambers," Arish announced.

The three men dipped their heads as she and her father exited. They entered the adjoining chamber, where Ferma stood waiting.

"Well, did he propose?" Ferma asked, a slow smile spreading on her face.

"I accepted," Elena said sourly.

"Then a celebration must be in order." Ferma grinned wider. "What say you, Arish?"

"Yes, we must announce the union soon," he said, closing the door behind them. "A ball, perhaps."

Elena turned to Leo, who took off his crown and set it on a cushion. He had been silent through all this.

"What do you think, Father?" she said.

"Whatever you wish," he said as he sank into the chair behind his red marble desk. Elena waited, but he said nothing more. Not even an utterance of congratulations. It stung her, his silence. He had chosen this marriage, and she had accepted (mostly) without complaint so that *their* kingdom could be safe. She did not expect praise, not even a smile. But surely, her father could spare his blessings.

Elena moved to speak, to remind him, but her father was looking away, his eyes far off. Her plea died in her chest.

"I hear Yassen Knight will join us. My team, specifically," Ferma said.

"Yes, he'll be a part of Elena's guard," Leo said, finally turning to them.

"But he's half-Jantari," Elena said, "and former Arohassin. Is it wise to keep him so close?"

"Yes. You can keep eyes on him," Leo said.

"Eyes I can't spare while preparing for a coronation. Let him stay with Samson."

"He will stay with you. Trust me, Elena," he sighed. "I know how to keep this kingdom safe, and shall do so until you are crowned its queen."

She wanted to tell him that she could help him, if he would only trust her. If he would only teach her to sit in the flames. But Elena, once more, held her tongue. The desert picked its battles.

In her chambers, the sheer curtains danced in the late summer breeze. Elena sank onto a bench before the large window. Below was her private garden filled with lotus flowers and the sweet jasmine her mother loved, or at least that's what Diya, her handmaid, had told her. A sand-colored yuani bird washed itself in the golden fountain. Elena watched it as Ferma sat down beside her.

"Your father is right," she said gently. "We can watch Yassen Knight closely."

"I don't believe him," Elena said. To her horror, the burn of tears threatened as she recalled the distracted look in her father's eyes. "Yassen Knight has no honor. He will escape when he gets the chance."

"Elena, there's no place to escape to. Only the desert," Ferma said.

"You don't know that," she said, almost to herself. The desert was full of hidden places. She had seen them, curled up in them. The desert opened itself up for those who knew how to use it, and something told her Yassen Knight was smart enough to realize that.

"In any case, I need to prepare your new guard," Ferma said, beginning to rise.

"Aren't you bothered?" Elena asked as she looked at the little bird in the fountain. "If my father really believed in you, he wouldn't have added a newcomer to my guard."

Elena did not need to turn to know that she had hit her mark. Ferma had trained her, raised her. There was no one in Ravence who knew her better than her beloved Ferma, and no one who Elena trusted more. But the Yumi was growing close to her retirement at fifty suns. Now, Elena wondered if Leo truly planned to replace her guards with his men.

Another string for him to pull, she thought ruefully.

"He made Yassen Knight your guard to keep him close," Ferma said. There was an edge in her voice that made Elena flinch. "If he is planning anything with the Arohassin, or the Jantari, we will know. This is to keep you safe."

"You and I can keep me safe." She turned and squeezed the Yumi's hand in apology. "We're more than capable."

Ferma said nothing, only squeezed her hand in response, then broke away. "You have training soon. Don't be late."

Elena nodded, and as she turned, she spotted that her diya was wavering. She rose quickly, walking to the small shrine in the corner of the room. Cupped the little flame as a breeze blew. Gently, she poured mustard oil into the bowl of the diya, then set it back beneath the feet of the Phoenix.

"May the Phoenix bless us with Her light," she murmured.

A knock sounded at the door behind them. Elena turned to see Yassen Knight standing in her doorway. He had changed into the black-and-red uniform of a royal guard, one that brought out his impressive set of shoulders and chest, she noted. But the sleeves were slightly short, and she caught a glimpse of a dark band on his wrist before he tugged the fabric down.

Ferma stepped in front of him. "You can't be here."

"The king instructed me to come," Yassen said.

"Not before your orientation."

"The king sent me here," he said simply.

"It's all right." Elena joined them, waving Ferma aside.

"Your Highness." Yassen bowed his head. "The king said I am to start immediately."

She did not answer, deliberately drawing out the silence, but Yassen did not shift nervously like the other guards. He met her gaze. From the way he stood, feet slightly apart, elbows out, Elena could tell that her first observation had been correct: He was a fighter.

And from the way he looked at her, Elena could tell he was sizing her up just as well.

But for what end, assassin?

"What kind of training do you have?" she asked.

"All kinds," he responded.

Ferma bristled at the nonchalance in his voice, but Elena touched her arm. "My father may have picked you, but I decide whether you stay." She nodded at Ferma. "You'll spar with my Spear in training this afternoon."

He glanced up at her guard, and for the first time, Elena noticed a tremor of doubt in his voice. "Against a Yumi?"

"If you have 'all kinds of training,' you should know how to fight a Yumi." Elena let the ghost of a smile grace her lips.

"As you wish."

Ferma stepped in between them and called down the hallway to the guard positioned there. "Please escort Yassen to the gamefield."

"And, Yassen," Elena said as he turned. "Mind your arm."

He flinched, just slightly. But she knew her guess had been right.

Yassen bowed and walked away.

She had noticed it first when he had knelt before her. He had knelt on his left knee, keeping his right side angled away. And when he had bowed before her just now, she had noticed how his right shoulder crept back as if he was protecting a sore spot.

Yassen Knight may have the gait of an experienced warrior, and perhaps he was even trained in the ancient arts of the Unsung, but Elena had made it a point to sense her opponent's weaknesses. It was a habit, drilled by her father. One of the few things she thanked him for.

"What are you playing at?" Ferma asked as Elena made her way to the window.

The bird was gone, the fountain still. She leaned forward, her elbows brushing the warm pink stone. Waves of heat shimmered above the distant dunes. Elena could feel the desert call to her.

"Inform the gamemaster," she said to Ferma. "Let's see how skilled our assassin really is."

CHAPTER 8

LEO

During the Golden Reign of the Third Prophet, storms washed the world until it was bright and new. Crops burst into valleys and along mountainsides. Children knew not of hunger. The world knew not of war. Will a time like this ever return?
　　　　—from the diaries of Priestess Nomu of the Fire Order

Leo sat at the head of the war room table listening to his generals bicker about Yassen Knight. He had told them as soon as he entered that the assassin was in the palace, and the room had broken into an uproar.

"As soon as his list checks out, I say we hang him," General Rohtak snarled. He was a big man with a hatchet nose and eyes of weathered steel. "Or better yet, flay him."

"It's true, there's nothing better to bring the people together than a scapegoat," General Mahira replied thoughtfully.

"In this case, it would only cause further insurrection. The Arohassin have burned his name in the sand. If we take his life, we cheat them of it," said a thin voice. Leo turned to Muftasa, the head of his intelligence network. She was a small bird of a woman, dressed in all black, with a sharp nose and mouth that puckered as if she were perpetually dehydrated or scrutinizing those around her. After more than thirty suns, Leo knew it was both.

"He can be of use to us," she said and looked pointedly at Samson.

Samson sat beside Leo, his leg propped up on his knee. Like Leo, he had been silent through the whole exchange, watching the generals with an amused expression. Leo had to give it to the young man. He knew when to wait and when to strike. But heavens, the boy had to rein in his pride.

"Yassen can be trusted," Samson said. "You forget that he was born here. Sand runs through his veins."

Leo was no fool; he knew Yassen Knight could not be trusted. He could feel it deep in his bones—an intuition that had never failed him.

But Yassen Knight was also a man tired of running, and that made him weak. He would do anything for his freedom, and that's where Leo's advantage lay. He had seen the look in the assassin's colorless eyes. It was a look of desperation, perhaps even exhaustion. Either way, Leo would rip out every secret until nothing was left to give. Desperate men always made mistakes.

"My men are already taking their positions in the capital and the desert outposts as we speak," Samson continued. "We've got holotracking sensors, desert suits, missiles, pulse guns, and slab grenades." He smiled as Mahira let out a low whistle.

"Sounds like you're building up your own army," she quipped.

"I already have one," he replied. His gaze never wavered, and eventually Mahira leaned back in her seat. "Every man of mine is ready to defend Ravence."

"Show me," Leo said suddenly. His eyes met Samson's. "Let's have a military exhibition on our southern border. Your Black Scales marching under the Ravani flag."

"But, Your Majesty—" Mahira began.

Leo held up his hand. "Farin's too smart to strike without a proper cause. He knows that going to war with us simply because we're accepting more Sesharian refugees won't stand among the other kingdoms. Cyleon, our friends in the north, would step in. Tsuana would call for a truce. But Farin's growing impatient. He wants to move—and he won't wait much longer to find his reason."

Ravence's borders met Jantar's to the south and to the east. Sandstorms, especially around this time of year, made an eastern invasion nearly impossible, so Farin had increased his military presence along the south. He'd done it slowly and stealthily, but Leo had the reports. Of course, Farin was biding his time, waiting for the passing of the crown, for a moment of instability. But Leo would not give him that.

If the metal king saw Samson's Black Scales with the Ravani army, saw the brute force of their numbers, perhaps he would falter. Perhaps that could buy Ravence more time.

"But, Your Majesty, should we not pursue peace talks as our first course of action?" Samson asked.

"Seshar tried that, before the Jantari invasion. How did it turn out for them?" Leo asked.

Samson fell silent, his eyes darkening. Even the generals shifted in their seats. General Mahira threw a look at Samson and then patted his hand.

"It's all right," she said quietly. "We all know the work of the Jantari."

And that is why, Farin, Leo thought, *your boy is not a puppet king.*

Blood ran deep. Deeper than allegiances to kings. If Samson truly did not care about his Sesharian brethren and their treatment within the mines, he wouldn't have flinched. But there—there was that darkness in his eyes. Leo knew the boy employed mostly Sesharians on his staff, promoted mostly Sesharians in his army. He had seen Samson's ring.

Leo glanced at Arish, who gave him a subtle nod. So, his Astra had noticed too. Leo made a note to speak with Samson further, once they were alone. Candidly.

"Peace and Jantar do not mix," Leo said. "We must be prepared. We will have the demonstration at the end of the week. Arrange it. And give it a name."

"A name?" mused Saku, the minister of defense. "What about...Black Sands Day?"

Black sands. It was an omen in the desert, a sign for storm winds and catastrophe. Pools of sand would curdle, as if boiling in hot liquid, and turn black as soot. Leo himself had never witnessed it. But his father had told him stories of the phenomena appearing before invasions like the shadow of an arrow before it pierces the unwary target.

"A tad dramatic, but it will do," he said.

Samson clapped his hands, an easy grin curving across his face. Whatever hesitations he had felt, whatever demons the mention of Seshar had unearthed, were gone. "I'm sure Farin will love it."

There was a chuckle around the table, one that Leo did not share.

"Now, valiant protectors of Ravence, may I turn your attention to this." Samson summoned a map of the kingdom, marked with several scattered dots. He zoomed into Rani as a carousel of faces floated along the wall. He stopped on a dark-skinned woman with hair so black it looked like liquid tar.

"The Arohassin have operated within Rani for decades, always evading your grasp. But I, gentleman, and ladies," he said, dipping his head toward Muftasa and Mahira, "bring you the trap that will ensnare them all." Leo watched his generals and ministers take it in, their faces carefully composed and their eyes alert. Like him, they were judging this young cub who had strutted into the lion's den with a fresh kill. "This is Maya. She's a lead Arohassin strategist, and the one responsible for the attack in the Rasbakan port and the theft of Ravani weapons. But she rarely emerges. Our luck is that Yassen has provided a list of informants she utilizes. If we can snare a couple, they'll lead us to her."

"Who is on this list?" Muftasa asked.

"Giorna Vistik," Samson said. An image of a young woman with fiery red hair and an upturned nose emerged. "Let's not waste time. Vistik operates right in the heart of old Rani, by Radhia's Bazaar," he said. "My men are ready to bring her in. I just need your word, Your Majesty."

In his long reign, the Arohassin were a constant reminder of Leo's failure. The only flaw in his legacy. Whenever he caught one, another emerged, like gophers in the desert. But here, finally, was his chance to crush them.

"Will capturing Vistik alert Maya?" Leo asked. One wrong move could warn the entire Arohassin network. One wrong move could endanger Elena and his kingdom.

"It's unlikely. She's a low-level informant; they all are," Samson said. "But when they have information to give, they are sent a location. We can track her that way."

Leo drummed his fingers against the table, thinking. "All right," he said finally. "Bring her in. And find the other informants. If any of these agents recognize Yassen Knight as a defector, we will not burn him. At least not yet." He looked at his generals and Samson. "Understood?"

"But we will burn him. Won't we?" General Rohtak asked.

"Yes," Leo said, his eyes on Samson. "That was our deal."

Samson merely dipped his head in acquiescence.

"Then let us turn to the matters of the coronation," Saku said.

Leo nodded, his mind elsewhere as his advisors discussed the coronation parade route and the blessing ceremony at the temple. He kept his gaze on Samson, who sank back into his seat with an inscrutable expression on his face.

Eventually, Arish tapped his shoulder. Leo turned to see Muftasa looking at him expectantly.

"Yes?" he asked.

"Your Majesty, I asked whether the high priestess will come by hoverpod or desert carriage? To the blessing ceremony."

Leo thought of Saayna locked within a prison in the middle of the desert. He remembered the runes on the priest's back, and his stomach twisted.

"Desert carriage," he answered, trying to keep his voice as level as possible.

Muftasa blinked. After suns of service, she likely detected his unease, but to her credit, she merely turned back to the generals and offered her suggested security plan for the high priestess.

"All right," Muftasa said once the meeting adjourned and all had departed save herself, Samson, and Arish. "What is it? Tell me."

Leo smiled. Only Muftasa could speak to him with such candor.

He motioned to Arish, who called up the image of the burnt priest and the runes on his skin.

Samson inhaled sharply. "Skies above," he whispered.

"Well, I suppose you could say the heavens have spoken to us," Leo said. "The Prophet will come."

Silence filled the room, sudden and heavy.

"It will be a woman," Leo said finally. "A young girl who has already been marked. If what the high priestess says is true, if the Prophet is to come, then we are dead men walking."

He walked to the northern wall and pulled up a map of Ravence.

"According to Saayna, the girl is in the city. Muftasa, I would like you to work with Samson to locate those who fit the description. Quietly. They will be marked. Maybe with a rune or a flame...I'm not sure. But I know they will not burn. You will find them, and you will bring them to me." He turned; the red light of the Phoenix rendered on the wall spilled down his shoulders. "We will not allow a religious heretic to dismantle our kingdom."

"But, Your Majesty. If the legends are true...we won't stand a chance before the Prophet," Muftasa said.

"We will if we execute her before the Phoenix rises," Leo said. And the silence that followed was even more damning. He could feel the weight of the heavens and seven hells bearing down on him, judging him.

"Find her," Leo said and looked pointedly at Samson. "If you want Ravence, you will bring me the Prophet."

Muftasa nodded, but Leo could tell by her shoulders that she was wringing her hands underneath the table. She did not meet his eyes.

"Say it," Leo commanded.

"I—I've recently seen a report," Muftasa began. Still, she did not meet his eyes. "My men have been tracking a family of anarchist sympathizers. The mother gives speeches that amount to little more than rants in parks. Nothing of importance, but...We think the father may work for Jantar."

"What does this have to do with the Prophet?" Samson asked.

Again, Muftasa hesitated. It was not like her. She was always outright with him; it was one of the things Leo respected most about her. But if even Muftasa was hesitating...

Worry, cold and sharp, stabbed through Leo.

"Muftasa," he began.

She sighed and opened a holo. It showed a girl with hair the color of starlight.

"Their daughter was recently taken to the hospital for burns. At first, we thought she had gotten caught in a fire, but then we learned that *she* started it. Claiming that she saw a vision of the Phoenix."

"Burn marks?" Samson asked. "But you said the Prophet doesn't burn."

"The Prophet does burn—but only once," Leo said. "It is said that the Phoenix burns the Prophet to mark her. After that, she will not burn again."

"But what if this so-called Prophet doesn't know of her powers? Maybe she doesn't understand the significance of not burning."

"She could be an ignorant fool," Leo agreed. "But that doesn't lessen the fact that she is the Prophet. With a burn test, we can root her out."

As he said this, Leo felt a cold fist clamp around his stomach. This girl perfectly fit the description. He should feel relieved, but he could only feel an impending sense of dread. If this girl was the Prophet, he would have to commit the highest sin in all the heavens. He would be hated, cursed. No amount of Ashanta ceremonies would save him.

But if the Prophet started her rampage, his sins would pale in comparison.

He knew the stories. When the last Prophet rose, she had gone mad. Burned down armies of men, turned forests into harsh, arid deserts. No one had been able to stop her. No one could.

"Wait, wait, wait," Samson interrupted. "This is madness. The Prophet? I know nothing about your religion, but do you honestly believe there's a vengeful god with a murderous prophet, set to rise again?" He laughed. "Do you truly believe in such stories?"

Arish bristled and Muftasa frowned as Leo turned to Samson. He meant to school the boy on Ravani religious beliefs, then hesitated.

Because the boy was right.

Who could honestly believe in such stories?

He hadn't. Not at first. A part of Leo was still in disbelief, still hoping that the old tales were simply parables engineered by priestesses like Saayna to force submission and fear into those around them.

But he had seen the runes on the priest's back. Smelled his burnt flesh. Saayna would never commit such an atrocity on her own order. And the Eternal Fire was a powerful force he could not deny. He had sat in its flames, felt its heat, its hunger.

The messages it sent could not easily be ignored.

"Wouldn't you," Leo said softly, "if fire burned runes like that into your flesh?" When Samson did not answer, Leo nodded to the floating image before them. "Stories can be shaped. Altered. But fire can never be denied. Do you understand this, boy? *It does not lie.* Prophet or not, someone or something is coming. And I am not going to take any chances. Not when we also have the Arohassin and the Jantari to deal with."

"But, Your Majesty," Arish said, "how are you so sure that this Prophet, the Seventh, will burn the world like her predecessor? The other Prophets before the Sixth were saints. Gods, in a way. Their yuga was one of peace and fortune."

Leo smiled sadly. Arish was a religious man, and so he clamped on to his beliefs like a lost traveler hugs his lantern in a sandstorm. "If only, Arish. But the yuga of saintly Prophets ended with the Sixth. The Seventh will be no different."

He turned to Muftasa. "Where is the girl?" he asked.

"In the western slums," Muftasa said. "Her name—"

"Don't tell me," Leo cut her off. The fist in his stomach tightened and turned. "I don't need to know."

It was better that the girl remained unknown to him. Names held power. They could corrupt, sway a man. Knowing her name would only make the job more difficult. Seeing her face made it hard enough.

"Shall we bring her in?" Muftasa asked.

Leo looked at the young girl with hair of spun starlight. She had unusually clear eyes that seemed to bore into him. He felt a pang in his chest—guilt perhaps, remorse even—but he pushed it down.

"Yes," he said, "and begin a search in the capital. Look for others and bring them to me. We must find her."

And then, to himself, *Before she kills us all.*

CHAPTER 9

YASSEN

The Yumi are proud, powerful warriors. Only the women are gifted with weapon-like hair. For centuries, they led the most fearsome armies, some even going on to lead as queens. Fewer still were granted the power of the gods and became the Yamuna. Fire wielders. However, the Sixth Prophet ended the Yamuna and killed many Yumi. Only a few hundred remain, and most have now closed themselves off in Moksh, their kingdom across the Ahi Sea.

—from chapter 30 of *The Great History of Sayon*

The gamemaster rapped on the changing room door.

"Ready?" she asked.

Yassen bit his lip as he slowly pulled the bulky gamesuit over his right shoulder. His arm had grown stiff since the morning flight. He felt old, clumsy. How could he expect to fight? When he had told Samson about the princess's challenge, the militant had begun to pace the room.

"It's a test," Samson had said finally. "You can't win."

"But if I lose, I won't be a part of her guard," Yassen had responded. It wasn't a test. It was a balancing act. If he lost, Elena would cast him out. If he won, he would dishonor her Spear *and* the princess herself.

And nothing was worse than an heir with wounded pride.

With a hiss of pain, Yassen yanked the zipper up and walked out. The gamemaster tapped Yassen's chest twice. The suit sucked in, morphing to fit the grooves and ridges of his body. Yassen flexed his hands, and the suit rippled in response, smooth like silk.

The gamemaster eyed the cut of his muscles and sniffed. "Not bad."

Yassen allowed himself a small smile. He hadn't been in a gamesuit since his training days with the Arohassin.

Kavach, they called their specialized suits. Armor.

Armor that had tracked every vital of the body—from heart rate to temperature fluctuation to reaction timing. The operators used the data to create personalized weapons for each recruit, given upon graduation. Yassen had been the first in his class to receive his pulse gun. He was better than most, which he had learned early on. When the other recruits balked, he had stood calm and steady. Firm, like the roots of a banyan. Even Samson, with all his wit and charm, could not hit a target as well as he could.

Yassen followed the gamemaster into a glass-encased chamber that overlooked a training field covered with black sand. When the gamemaster activated the field, the sand would rise and twist, adding a further challenge to the fighters.

Lotuses carved from onyx and granite lit up the ceiling, casting the field in a pale blue light. On the far wall, the insignia of the Phoenix smoldered.

Samson was seated before a circular array of panels but straightened as Yassen entered.

"I thought you went to see the king," Yassen said.

Samson pulled him close.

"Be smart," he whispered. "One false move, and we're both done for."

There was no time to say more. Ferma strode into the room, a shimmer of steam clinging to her gamesuit.

"Your turn," she said.

The gamemaster closed the door of the chamber behind Yassen. Sensors locked into their dockets on his suit, and he felt a familiar twinge of electricity zip through his veins.

A laser scanned Yassen's body as the suit cooled and expanded, testing his pressure points and reading back his vital signs. There was a soft beep as the suit squeezed his right arm. The gamemaster narrowed her eyes. She cast a glance at Yassen but said nothing. She tapped something into the screen, and the suit tightened there, adding more armor.

Within a minute, it was done. Yassen walked out and looked down. The suit felt even sleeker, akin to his own skin. Except it was unblemished and unbroken.

"You look like you've seen a ghost," said a lilting voice.

Elena stood beside Ferma. Her eyes traveled over him, sizing him up and, he noted, lingering on his shoulders and chest.

"I haven't been in a gamesuit in a while," he responded.

"Why is that?"

"Too many memories." He remembered how light the pulse gun had felt when his handler, Akaros, had presented it to him upon his graduation. How natural it felt to load the chamber. How cruel it all seemed now.

"All right, fighters, down into the field," the gamemaster called out. Two doors at the far end of the room opened. Yassen gripped Samson's elbow and squeezed.

"I think if I make one false move, *I'm* done for," he whispered and descended into the training field.

The blue lights flashed. The lotuses on the ceiling began to spin as the magnetic field thrummed to life. Ferma faced him. The suit revealed her lithe body and coiled muscles, the result of a lifetime of training, fighting, protecting. He wondered what scars the suit hid for her.

She unbound her hair, and it fell around her shoulders in long, silky strands.

Yassen knew of the power of the Yumi. Their hair was their shield, their strength. It could harden into a million sharp shards that could cut through a man. He had seen it once when pickpocketing in Rani; an off-duty Yumi soldier had caught a man trying to force himself onto a young girl. She had pierced his hands with her hair and then dragged him into Coin Square for all to see. Only then did she take him to the hospital, handcuffed.

"Fighters, ready," the gamemaster's voice rang out.

Ferma knelt, and Yassen did the same. The sand felt warm underneath his fingertips. He glanced up and saw Elena watching. An unspoken

challenge shone in her eyes but also a curiosity. He let his gaze linger...
and then the bell rang, and Ferma shot forward.

She was fast—surprisingly so. Yassen barely had enough time to move
as she whipped her hair forward. The shards scraped across the sand as
Yassen twisted and spun, kicking her shin. Her hair whipped around, and
he fought back a yelp as it struck his foot.

He hopped back as his suit recalibrated, soothing the bruised skin and
reconstructing his torn muscle. Ferma turned slowly, her hair coiling. Her
tawny eyes were bright. Yassen sucked in a deep breath as she stalked forward, wishing he had a weapon as lethal as Ferma's locks.

But then the sand hummed and shifted below his feet. Yassen lunged
backward as the ground caved in, forming a pit. Ferma tried to scramble
to safety, but her foot slipped; the sand began to swallow her. She growled
and twisted, her hair finding purchase over the lip of the pit. As she
climbed, Yassen took his opening.

When she crawled from the pit and leapt to her feet, he landed his first
real blow, square on her torso. She stumbled but did not lose her balance.
Her hair lanced up, black and sharp. One blade sliced Yassen on his cheek,
and he felt warm blood trickle down.

Clever.

Yassen wheeled around, sweeping his leg out, but Ferma was quicker.
She jumped lightly out of his reach and then rushed him. Yassen weaved
in and out of her blows as sand sprayed against his face. He began to feel
the rhythm of her moves, the pattern of her advances.

And so began their dance. Every time she advanced, he retreated. Every
time she twisted, he shot forward. Above them, Elena, the gamemaster,
and Samson watched.

Sweat beaded on his brow, but despite himself, Yassen enjoyed this.
This waltz. It all came back to him now. The flush of battle. The exhilara-
tion of landing a blow. The adrenaline pumping through his veins.

Yes, he might regret the things he'd done for the Arohassin. *But nothing*, he thought as Ferma spun low, *nothing can beat the rush of a game.*

The sand hummed again, forming columns. Ferma disappeared like a
shadow behind one, her hair hissing. Yassen crept forward, edging around
the column when Ferma pounced from behind. Her hair jabbed his right
shoulder, quick and savage.

Pain exploded down his burned arm. Yassen bit back a shout as he slipped behind the pillar of sand to escape her next blow. Ferma turned, and he noted the subtle catch of her breath, the very slight slowness of her movements.

Yassen waited until she was close and then, at the last second, grabbed her arm. She gasped in surprise, trying to stop her momentum, but it was too late. He ducked underneath her writhing hair and launched forward, delivering an uppercut squarely on the jaw, sending her sprawling. Ferma hit the floor, and the bell rang out.

"End of round," the gamemaster announced.

Yassen panted as the Yumi sat up. She looked stunned, angry even, as she collected herself and rose to her feet.

"We're the same, you and I," Yassen said quietly so that only she could hear.

"We're nothing alike," she spat.

"We're both warriors," he said. "And we both want the same thing— the best for Ravence."

"You want what's best for you," Ferma said, taming her hair.

The door behind her opened, and Elena stepped out.

"That'll be all, Ferma," Elena said. She was dressed in a gamesuit that revealed her supple curves and carved muscles. "I will test him myself."

Ferma glared at him, and he saw the unspoken threat. He would not dare hurt Elena; he would be a fool to even land a scratch. Elena knew this. He saw the cold, calculated hunger in her dark eyes as she watched him. She meant to hurt him, and he could do nothing but accept the blows.

The Yumi slowly stalked out of the training field. And then he was alone with the heir of Ravence.

Yassen bowed as the bell rang out again, and Elena immediately sprang. Not with the grace and agility of Ferma but with a sureness that made every movement purposeful.

Mother's Gold, she's trained in the Unsung.

He recognized the footwork, how she rested her weight not on her heels, but on the balls of her feet. Yet as they began to circle each other, he noticed how she danced. Like sand in the wind. Feet quick and light, arms raised and poised. As if she could spin off at a moment's notice, out of his reach, or leap right at him, her knee connecting with his jaw.

Yassen shook out his hands. His injured arm still rang, and a numbness began to creep up his elbow. He knew she was waiting for an opening, just as he had with Ferma.

Her eyes met his, and for a moment, time held its breath. There was a cold fury in hers, like a sleeping fire, ready to burst. But Yassen also saw something else: fear.

Every fighter felt nervous before a game, and if they didn't, they were lying. But fear. Fear was what soldiers and thieves and assassins felt. Fear was what he had felt when he dangled on the stone wall, the sea churning beneath him. Fear was for those who had something to lose.

What could the princess of Ravence possibly fear to lose?

The columns of sand hummed and bent. He faked left, a move so obvious that when she came up on his right, he tensed for the blow.

She hit him in the chest, a deep jab that made his breath catch as he stumbled back. The sand hissed and crashed down. He rolled out of the way as Elena advanced. She was light on her feet, determined. Yassen rushed her, grabbing her arm, but she recognized the move and brought her knee up to block his punch.

He dove out of her reach, breathing hard. She smiled. This time, when she shot forward, he stepped into it and let her foot hit him in the stomach. Pain whiplashed through his body, and Yassen gasped, the air knocked from his lungs. She made quick work thereafter. Blow after blow rained down on him.

He could feel the calculated precision in every strike. He raised his hands up to protect his face when she whirled, delivering a kick square into his chest. He smacked into the sand.

"Enough," Samson's voice rang out.

Through bleary eyes, Yassen looked up to see Samson at the glass above. His mouth was a hard line.

"I think you've proven your point, Your Highness," he added.

Elena shook out her arms. She looked down at Yassen sprawled on the black sand, fighting for breath.

"Next time, assassin," she said, her voice low so that only he could hear, "use the Unsung instead of allowing yourself to be a punching bag."

"I like to be of service, Your Highness." Yassen grimaced, touching his arm to his chest in salute.

Elena paused. For a moment, he thought he saw a smile play across her lips, but just as quickly, her lips hardened.

"Clean him up," she called out as she turned. "I don't want a bloodied guard following me around."

Yassen watched her exit, watched her say something to Samson behind the glass, watched Ferma follow her out. Only then, slowly, did he get to his feet. Pain lanced through his ribs. He hadn't taken a beating like that in a long time—and the man who had done it to him then was dead.

Samson waited while he cleaned up and donned fresh clothes. The gamemaster took his suit and handed him a block of ice with a sympathetic smile. Yassen pressed it to his cheek.

"Your arm," she said in a low voice. "You need to see a doctor."

"I will, thank you," he said.

She drew back, shaking her head. "That's what they all say."

She swept out without another word, leaving him alone with Samson.

"I'm sorry," Samson said finally.

"It's all right, Sam."

"No, Cass, it's not." He shook his head. His eyes held the same brazen look they had on the night he had promised Yassen an escape. "I gave you my word that I would help you, but these people..."

"I'm taloned, Sam. Quit pitying me," Yassen said. He dropped the ice in a waste bin and gripped his friend's shoulder. "If we stick through this, you'll be king, and I'll be absolved of my crimes."

Samson looked as if he was going to retort, but then he sighed.

"You're right," he said. "Go, you deserve rest. I'll call for you later."

Yassen clapped him on his back and left Samson standing alone under the blue lights.

He hurried toward his room, avoiding the stares of servants as they took in the bruises staining his face. Yassen glanced down at his arm, turning back the edge of his sleeve. He saw that the marks had changed; they were beginning to warm, to grow an angrier red. He could feel the creeping heat, the tingle in his nerves.

Spots swam in front of his eyes. He turned into the hallway to his room when the world began to tilt. He stumbled, his knees going weak. A salty, iron taste filled his mouth.

He grabbed the wall with his good arm and slunk forward. Darkness ringed his vision. Hot, blistering pain cracked up his arm. His fingers brushed something cold, sleek. *The panel.* He pressed his hand into the scanner. The door swung open, and Yassen fell inside.

A desert breeze licked his face, warm and delicate. He was faintly aware that the window was open. Strange, he had not left it like that. Yassen tried to crawl forward, but he couldn't move. The breeze whispered, and he smelled the sweetness of a summer storm mixed with the promise of wet sand as he slowly lost consciousness.

CHAPTER 10

LEO

There are three types of fire. There is that of the Phoenix—a wild, vengeful power. There is that of the dragon—a cold, haughty power. And then there is the third—a fire that provides, nourishes, and heals. I do not know from where it draws its powers. I have yet to find it.
—from the diaries of Priestess Nomu of the Fire Order

Leo and Arish came to his private office—the real one fitted beside his chamber, not the facade behind his throne room. As he entered, Leo breathed in the smell of wet sand. There would be a storm soon. Good. The city needed a little rain.

The study was a large circular room, hung with lavish red curtains. An intricately patterned rug his grandfather had loved covered the floor, and a black granite table with golden veins sat before the large, floor-to-ceiling window. Overhead, a glass dome filtered light onto a seating area with sandalwood chairs and a chaise large enough to fit three men.

But what Leo loved the most about his study was the fire.

A ring of flames writhed around the room, their hiss a comfort to Leo.

In the beginning, he disliked their heat, their unpredictability, the way a single flame blinded his eyes and made him see shadows afterward. But he had grown to appreciate the power of an inferno. Its chaotic beauty. His forefather had founded Ravence with a respect for fire, and it was a discipline Leo's father had instilled in him.

Leo went to his desk and placed his hand down on the inlaid panel.

The floor rumbled, and the emblem of the Phoenix separated to reveal stone steps that disappeared into darkness. Arish took a floating lamp that hovered beside the chaise and sent the orb down the stairs to light their way.

"Wait," Leo said. He waved at the fire, and the flames surrounding the room shot to the ceiling—a barrier should anyone enter his study unannounced.

He followed Arish down the stairs and into the underground tunnels.

Two hundred suns ago, King Farzand had built them as an escape route when Jantar's army had trekked its way through the dunes to lay siege on the capital. But he never had to use them. As the army approached, a storm had come at night. It started as a whisper, a slight touch against the skin, but in a matter of minutes, it snarled and wreaked havoc on Jantar's soldiers, making them easy pickings for Farzand's skilled desert raiders. When morning came, Jantar's army lay scattered and dead.

Farzand's successor, Queen Jumi, had taken a liking to the mystery of the tunnels and ordered their expansion. Soon, a vast network of tunnels and chambers snaked underneath Palace Hill, slithering into the desert and the city. Here she built the Royal Library, a tall, cool chamber that housed ancient scrolls and precious books.

Leo breathed in the musty scent of timeworn paper as they entered the vast room.

With a push, Arish sent the orb up into the darkness to reveal bookcases that rose farther than Leo could see. Scrolls upon scrolls, spines among spines, packed together into the dusty shelves. As the light rose higher, more lamps floating quietly along the wall awakened until the library basked in a warm, gentle light.

Leo scanned the multiple shelves, dread crawling up his throat. How in heavens could he decipher the runes when he did not even know where to start?

He had never had much use for books. He visited the library rarely and never for very long. The first time, he had been hardly more than a child, accompanying his father as part of his tutelage about his heritage. The second, he had brought his new bride to show her the wealth and richness of information she had just gained access to. And the last was when, a few months after his queen's death, Leo had returned to the place that had brought her so much joy.

Aahnah had loved books. She studied and read the scrolls. She knew how to navigate these shelves. At some point, she had learned the truth about Ravence—and then she had taken its secret to the grave.

And this library kept the ghost of her. He could feel her in here, his rani, his queen, his lovely Aahnah. She had touched these shelves. She had run her deft fingers across these scrolls. The thought of her, the mere breath of her memory, sent a vicious, wicked pain through Leo.

How many times had she asked him to work beside her in the library? How many times had he been neglectful, too distracted by the demands of the throne?

Leo traced the lip of a shelf with a trembling hand. What he wouldn't do to see her now, reading in this tall chamber. He would push aside his engagements if only to hear her talk about the conspiracies of Alabore Ravence one last time in that low, lulling voice of hers that made any tale, no matter how ridiculous or unbelievable, possible.

"I suggest we begin by searching for information on the Immortals," Arish said softly, pulling Leo from the past.

It was a wise suggestion. The Phoenix was an Immortal, and it was the symbol of Her feather that had been burned into the priest's back.

"All right," Leo said. Grief twisted his heart like a cold, miserable rag as they followed the curve of the shelves to the westernmost point. Golden script inscribed into the wood told them that shelves 1 to 322 housed texts and histories of the Immortals.

Staring up at the looming wall, Leo swallowed his sorrow. He did not wish to stay in this library longer than he needed.

He had been a young king, with only a few suns under his crown, when Aahnah told him that she had found a peculiar scroll.

"It tells a story about the creation of the world," she said. "That the world began not with the Phoenix, but with three types of fire."

He had been listening halfheartedly, his eyes fixed on updates about the recent flare of anarchists who called for the end of kings. They had become bolder in the last few months. Arish had suggested ignoring the anarchists, but Leo could not run the risk of insurgency, not when he had a baby on the way.

"Does it really?" he asked, gesturing a holo closer. It was information about a young royalist by the name of Jangir.

You need your own men, loyal to you, *not the throne, to be your eyes and ears in the kingdom,* his father had told him.

He often didn't take the advice of a man whose health and mind were deteriorating, but Leo had to admit that at least in this, his father was right. Or, to put it another way, he thought Jangir could be bribed to infiltrate the insurgent groups. Maybe he should talk to Muftasa...

"Are you listening to me?"

"What?" He glanced at his wife, his eyes falling to the bump blossoming beneath her kurta.

"Mother's Gold, Leo." Aahnah sighed and reached for a chair. He sprang up to help her, but she waved him away.

"Aahnah, the baby."

"Yes, yes, the precious heir of Ravence. You only care to listen when I bring it up." And though her tone was unfriendly, a tender smile played across her face. "I can feel her kicking."

"What, now?"

"No, when I read. When I found the scroll, she began to kick harder."

"Well, what did it have to say?" he asked.

Her eyes, so clear back then, brightened. She laced her fingers together and leaned forward, and as she began to talk, her voice rising with excitement, Leo felt a rush of love, warm and fierce.

She told stories in such a beautiful way.

"Well, according to this passage from Priestess Nomu's diary, the world began with three types of fire. The golden flame, fierce and bright, the hottest and the most dangerous. The blue flame, slow and wormlike, always burning, always waiting. And the red flame. The one that's said to burn even in the darkest of places. You'd think that they would devour one another, but the fires lived in harmony. Until one day." She paused for dramatic effect, but then her eyes widened, and she placed her hand on her belly. "Phoenix Above, she's kicking, Malhari."

Leo took her hands in his and kissed her knuckles. "She wants you to finish the story."

"Well," and at this, Aahnah's shoulders slumped. "There's no ending. Not quite. Priestess Nomu just said that something broke the harmony of the fires. But she doesn't know why."

"Hmm."

"What do you mean, hmm?"

He laughed, and he did not know what made him say it, what made him damn his wife with an idea, a curiosity that would drive her to madness. "Maybe you should finish the story. Find what Priestess Nomu couldn't find."

Aahnah rubbed her belly thoughtfully. "I'm no priestess but...I suppose I could ask Saayna..."

"She would call it blasphemous," they said together.

Leo kissed her knuckles again, and then up her arm, her neck, until he was leaning over the desk and kissing her, cupping her face as she smiled against his lips.

"Malhari."

"Hush."

In one of her moments of lucidity, before the madness had claimed her, Aahnah had told him about her system. The shadows of the fire in the hearth curved around her face, and he remembered how, in that moment, he found her both lovely and terrifying.

"My initials." She had laughed, and the music of it was like raindrops dripping from a ledge after a storm. "A. M. My maiden name."

"And why would you use that name?" he had asked.

"Because Ravence is cursed, my love," she had said calmly, as if she was stating a well-known fact. "Why should I use it if it's cursed? Surely you know that better than most."

Still, it was slow work, searching for order in his wife's chaos.

He went to the shelves that housed Priestess Nomu's writings, as that was where Aahnah had spent most of her time. Though Aahnah had marked the shelves, she had not told him her system of categorizing the scrolls. He thumbed through them, one after the other. Diary entries, prayer ceremony rituals, runes he did not recognize. The floating orbs bobbed and darted overhead as the hours passed. When he could no longer reach the higher scrolls, Leo stepped onto a circular stone platform. He hit his heel against it twice, and it lifted, carrying him up.

They stopped only when Arish realized the time. "Mother's Gold, you're supposed to have dinner with Her Highness now."

With a sigh, Leo tapped his foot twice. It was as the stone platform descended that Leo noticed it. There, right beneath the golden number demarcating shelf 52. *A. M.*, neatly inscribed.

Except this one was slashed through.

Heart racing, Leo scanned the scrolls. One of the parchments was neatly contained by a metal band, unlike the other scrolls he had seen so far. Stamped onto the metal was the feather of the Phoenix; it glinted red in the light.

Leo opened the scroll gingerly. The paper was delicate, as if it would dissolve in the slightest breeze. But there, clear in the lines of text, he saw the feather and the unknown rune. The same ones burned onto the priest.

Saayna had told him that the runes meant Daughter of Fire, but he wanted to decipher them himself. To find the nature of Saayna's lie.

He glanced back at the shelf. Two more scrolls had metal bands. Sweeping them all together, he carefully tucked them into his coat.

"Reschedule my dinner with Elena," Leo said when they had returned to his office, the flames crackling in welcome. Leo waved a hand to calm them, and they slowly subsided to glowing embers. "I don't want to be bothered for the next two hours."

But then the panel on his desk glowed. Arish bent forward, reading.

"It's Jangir, Your Majesty."

Leo slipped the scrolls in his desk drawer. Jangir Meena was the leader of the gold caps, and quite possibly his most valued informant. Leo had first met him during one of his early public appearances. Jangir had roared the loudest, sung the highest praises. But his flattery was not what had compelled Leo to take him in; it was the way Jangir had moved others in the crowd to cheer with him. How, when he raised his voice, it seemed to sweep through everyone else. It was Jangir who had swayed the public in favor of Leo during the anarchist rebellions, when Leo had still been a young king. Jangir was a politician, through and through. And Leo had learned to use him.

At first, he had given Jangir little tasks in exchange for small favors. A hovercar for tracking a corrupt official. A home overlooking the dunes for finding a rebel. An invitation to a ball for rallying support around the city's costly infrastructure. But as Jangir's influence and his band of gold caps grew, Leo found another use for them: as his eyes and ears throughout the country.

Muftasa and her agents kept a close eye on anarchist sentiments in Ravence, but Jangir and his men could do what Muftasa's agents could not. They were civilians, not spies. And being so, they had intimate access to the people and their homes that Muftasa's spies did not.

The gold caps quelled rebellions before they arose. Exposed rebels before they could utter so much as a word of protest. Used a forceful hand, when needed. If Leo hoped to thwart potential rebellions, or find the agents on Yassen's list, he needed both Muftasa's and Jangir's help.

"Patch him through," Leo said.

Jangir appeared in a holo before him. He bowed, sweeping his hat.

"Your Majesty."

"Jangir," Leo said. "What do I owe the pleasure?"

"I don't mean to disturb Your Majesty, but—" Jangir hesitated. "One of my top men, Leelat, was taken into police custody last night. He got drunk in a bar, and his attacker was rushed to the hospital. An overzealous officer believed that Leelat caused the fight, but I assure you, Your Majesty, that the other gentleman began it. I can call witnesses."

Leo had no doubt that Jangir had witnesses who would support his story.

"The gentleman, is he alive?"

"Yes, sir. He'll pull through."

Leo sighed. He felt slightly annoyed to be called for so trivial a request, but he nodded.

"I'll arrange for him to be released and all charges to be dropped." He fixed Jangir with a cold stare. "But you need to control your men. I can't have any of them misbehaving, not with Elena's coronation so close."

"Yes, Your Majesty. And we will bring men in full force for the queen's celebration."

"What about rebel activity?" Leo asked.

"There have been whisperings about a gathering," Jangir said.

"Credible?"

"Somewhat, but my men will investigate further." Jangir paused. "But if we find them to be true?"

"Then do what you must," Leo said without wavering. He had neither love nor patience for protestors or Prophets who threatened his kingdom.

Jangir bowed. "So we the blessed few."

When his holo disappeared, Leo turned to Arish.

"Anything else?"

The Astra hesitated. "Your Majesty, does Jangir know that Yassen Knight is now working with us?"

"No," Leo said flatly, "and I do not plan on telling him."

Jangir had called, quite loudly, for Yassen's death when he assassinated his brother, General Mandar. The grizzled war hero had been a particular favorite among the gold caps, often hosting private dinners with top officials. If Jangir knew that the throne now employed his brother's killer, he would march up Palace Hill himself. Create a public nuisance. And then Ravence and the world would know that the Ravani throne worked with a traitor. And that was something Leo could not afford. Not right now.

"Justly so," Arish said. "There's then the matter of your daughter's engagement. I believe we should announce it. Tomorrow. Having Samson appear next to Her Highness on Palace Hill will send a message to the Arohassin."

"Arrange for it," he said. "And set a meeting for me with Samson. It's time I talk to the boy."

Arish bowed and departed.

Only once the door clicked shut did Leo sit, unrolling all the parchments. They looked even more fragile aboveground.

Gently, he flattened each, and studied the rolling script. It was written in Herra, the ancient language spoken in the early days of Ravence, now all but obsolete.

Leo was careful not to smudge the handwritten ink as he tried to make sense of the symbols. On the first scroll, he recognized the feather and the rune shaped like the eye of a hurricane, an inward storm. He searched for some clue that would unlock their meaning, but the scroll held no such key.

The second scroll was longer, and Leo spotted the feather and the rune several times throughout. Like the first, it also had the feather in the upper right-hand corner, followed by a rune. Just as it had been on the priest's back.

Leo looked to the flames as they wavered and hissed. The feather represented the Phoenix, he knew that. Was the second rune an adjective? A description of the Phoenix's power? The high priestess had said that the runes meant Daughter of Fire, so did the second rune prescribe gender? Or was Saayna leading him on a wild shobu chase?

Leo racked his brain. Something nagged at him; he felt as if he had seen this rune before.

He looked at the third scroll. This one was the shortest, with no symbol other than the feather.

Leo peered closer. At the bottom of the page, written in tiny scrawl, was a familiar phrase.

So we the blessed few.

It was the phrase he always recited at the end of Ashanta ceremonies, the same one he whispered to himself before meetings with war ministers and generals. But here, at the end of the phrase, looping out of the last letter, was the second rune. A casual glance would catalog it as a mistake—a stray dash of a quill.

Before Leo could scrutinize it further, the room rumbled, indicating the hall to his study had opened. He slipped the scrolls into his desk drawer as Elena entered.

"I thought I told Arish not to let anyone in," he said.

"Not even me, Father?"

"Don't be coy." The chamber remained open, but no one else came through. "Where are your guards? Where's Yassen?"

"He went to dress his wounds." She sat down and reached forward, picking up the metal band he had tossed aside.

Leo cursed inwardly as she held it up to the light.

"Reading something?"

He pressed his hand against the desk drawer to ensure it was fully closed before grabbing the band. "Old texts that don't concern you," he said and deposited the band in the drawer.

She eyed him.

"Arish is organizing a public viewing on Palace Hill to announce the engagement," he said, wanting to forestall any other questions she might have about the library. "You should prepare a statement with Samson."

"I will." There was an intensity in her dark eyes, her mother's eyes, as she leaned forward, her voice earnest. "But I need you to teach me about the fire," she said. "Teach me how to hold the flame."

The surrounding embers crackled as if responding to her request. But Leo knew she wasn't ready. The last time she had tried to hold a flame, she had burned herself, and sent thick waves of choking smoke so high that it could be seen all the way from the capital. Newscasts speculated as to the cause before Leo had announced there had been no blaze; that the high priestess had come to perform a cleansing ritual in the palace.

No one could know that the heir of Ravence was not capable of withstanding fire.

Elena drummed her fingers against the desk to call back his attention.

"Not yet," he said.

"Every heir needs to hold fire," she said. "How can I be queen if I can't even get through the Ashanta ceremony?"

He could not tell her the truth, not now.

Fire demanded sacrifice. A sacrifice she was not ready to give. A sacrifice she could *not* give.

"The viewing will be tomorrow morning," he said.

Elena sat back, her mouth a hard line and her eyes, Aahnah's eyes, judging him.

"You're making a mistake," she said finally.

He said nothing.

Elena gripped the edge of his desk, a muscle working in her jaw. But after a few wordless moments, she swept out of the room.

The flames hissed. Leo sat back in his seat and wearily pulled out Aahnah's necklace from underneath his kurta, studying the finely carved pendant.

No one had told him he would have to sacrifice the one he loved when he came before the Eternal Fire for his crowning. His father had hidden the truth, only revealing it to Leo the day of his coronation.

Leo had been furious. He had refused to sacrifice Aahnah. The flames had tried to rip him apart in response.

Miraculously, he had survived. And he had lived under the delusion that the test was over, that the Eternal Fire was satisfied.

Aahnah was the one to discover it was not. She had found the truth in the scrolls.

Elena was but seven suns when they went to the temple for an Ashanta ceremony. The Eternal Fire had been hot, angry. It had snapped at him, and Leo had stumbled down the steps of the dais to escape, but the fire was faster. It had grabbed his ankle and would have tugged him into the pit when Aahnah, face resolute, had jumped. Within seconds, the Eternal Fire devoured her.

One moment, she had been there, holding Elena, and then she was gone, leaving Elena alone by the dais.

After her sacrifice, the fire had fallen back, quiet, satiated.

Only then did Leo realize why his father had hidden the truth. He wanted to protect him—just as Leo wished to protect Elena now.

To become the ruler of the Fire Throne, to claim the title of the Phoenix King, the heir needed to make a sacrifice. Either one of blood, or one of love.

It was a closely guarded secret, spoken only on coronation day, and never again. If the people had ever remarked why a member of the royal household had suddenly gone missing, stories were woven.

He got drunk and lost his way in the desert.

She traveled to the first continent and died of illness.

At least it was no secret that madness ran through the Ravani royal blood. His enemies liked to harp on it. *Why should Ravence be ruled by a mad king?*

Royalists pitied it. *They lose themselves in service to the Phoenix. What better worship than this?*

At first, the stories of madness had been part of the ruse to cover the far deadlier truth, but somehow, the stories themselves had become reality. The Ravence family had become mad. His father, *his* great-uncle before him, and on, and on. But had they become mad because they hid the truth, Leo wondered, or because that's what happened when one lost their anchor in the world?

Leo knew the sorrow of fire. And Phoenix Above, he did not wish for Elena to know of it too.

But there is another reason, isn't there? the flames seemed to whisper, and in their crackle, he heard Aahnah's voice. *Oh selfish, selfish Malhari.*

Slowly, Leo unrolled the scrolls again. Though he could not translate the message of the runes, he thought he understood them. The Eternal Fire had given him a warning—a reminder of his transgression.

But he would protect Ravence until his dying breath. Without him, the nation would fall into chaos. Elena would be alone to fend off the hyenas.

Leo called for Muftasa.

"The girl," he said. "The one with the hair of starlight. Bring her to me. Let's see if she burns."

THE LAST PROPHET

–from the historical records of the Fire Order

*W*hen *the Phoenix rose from the temple, She spoke to the priests in a voice made of ash.*

"Why are they fighting for this land?"

As She spoke, armies waged war at the foot of the mountains. If one walked to the front steps of the temple, one could hear the faint sorrows of battle: the clash of metal and the short-lived screams of men. The Phoenix looked from priest to priest, but none could meet Her eyes—not only because of their shame, but also because they could not see past the clarity of Her flames.

All except one.

A priestess met the golden eyes of the Phoenix and spoke in a small yet steady voice.

"It is because they do not realize their mortality," she said.

The Phoenix stared down at the priestess, but she did not waver.

"Then it is you," the Phoenix said, and so it was done. Her Eternal Fire rose in answer to its new master and wrapped around the arms and limbs of the priestess. It enveloped her, covered her, welcomed her. The Phoenix raised Her wings, and a beam of light erupted from the heart of the fire to the sky above. The armies below saw it. The whole world saw it.

The Prophet was chosen.

With a wave of her hand, the Prophet unleashed the rage of the Phoenix. A fierce inferno tore down the mountainside. Those who resisted perished. Those who begged for mercy perished. Those who simply sank to their knees in defeat perished.

There is no forgiveness in the eyes of the Phoenix.

When the last king had burned to ash, the Prophet turned to the priests.

"There will be no more wars for this land," the Prophet declared.

And so it was done. The flames pushed past the mountain to the land beyond, burning rivers, streams, trees, birds, and men alike. The priests watched as the land transformed from a fertile, green forest into an arid desert that shielded none from the unforgiving gaze of the sun. Only the deep forest that clung to the edge of the mountains continued to exist.

The Phoenix saw this and more.

She spread Her marvelous wings again, and in each glistening feather, the Prophet recognized the colors of the world—from the dark depths of the sea to the warm shades of a sunrise. And as she saw these colors, the Prophet felt her body morph. Her limbs grew and her eyes changed.

The priests say her eyes melted into the eternal gold of the Phoenix; her veins pulsed with the heat of a fire; her hair unfurled into curls of smoke; and her lips, which once sang hymns, became small and hard.

When she spoke, she spoke with the multitude of her former reincarnations.

"This fire will protect the land. Do not let it die."

And so the Eternal Fire came to live in the heart of the temple. The priests watched as the Prophet and the Phoenix rose as one, growing brighter and brighter until the priests were forced to look away. When they finally reopened their stinging eyes, both were gone.

Only the flame, bright and unmerciful, remained to see all that would come.

CHAPTER 11

YASSEN

Jantar's shining city of brass, Rysanti, was created five hundred suns ago by Rydia the Tyrant. When workers complained about the bright reflection of the sun on the brass fixtures, she ordered them to wear visors. Hence, the Jantari began to lose the color of their eyes.

—from chapter 33 of *The Great History of Sayon*

Yassen awoke to someone banging on his door.

He groaned, licking his dry lips. Needles of pain pricked his arm. He rolled onto his knees and winced, trying to move toward the door when it burst open, and Samson marched in.

"Dragon's tit! What are you doing on the floor?" he demanded.

Yassen leaned his head against the wall. "It's comfy."

Samson took in his unkempt clothes and tousled hair. He squatted down and gripped Yassen's chin.

"Did you pass out?" he asked, a genuine hint of worry in his voice.

"She kicked my ass," Yassen replied.

97

Samson turned his face side to side, squinting. "Actually, I think she improved your looks."

Yassen snorted and turned to the window. The sky was already growing dim, the twin moons beginning their nightly watch. He vaguely remembered a storm, but only a few stray clouds remained now, looming on the horizon.

Samson straightened. He surveyed the room, taking note of the untouched clothes laid out on the bed.

"Is it your arm? The gamemaster informed me. I said I would tell Elena myself."

Yassen recalled Elena's comment about his arm, how she had watched him like a desert hawk tracking its prey before smashing it against the rocks. She must have sensed his weakness. But then he remembered her eyes: brown and dark, filled with cold calculation as if she could hide the fear underneath.

"Do you think Elena is afraid?" he asked.

Samson laughed. "How would you feel if you had to become queen in less than a month? I'd be more scared than facing the seven fucking hells."

He had a point.

Yassen rubbed his arm as he sat down on the edge of the bed. Silk shirts from Nbru, linen jackets from Monte Gumi, and cotton pants spun on the quaint foothills of Beuron lay crisply across the soft sheets, untouched.

"Try one on. See if it fits," Samson said as he closed the window.

Yassen hesitated. He looked down at the clothes and gingerly picked up a blue linen shirt with golden buttons. "Give me a minute," he said and began to move toward the washroom when Samson stopped him short.

"Try it on here," he said.

They stared at each other for a long moment. Finally, Yassen sighed and dropped his gaze.

"I knew it," Samson said. "Show me?"

Yassen slowly peeled off his sweaty shirt to reveal his right arm. Deep burns sliced across his shoulder and bicep, his skin brown and reddish and wrinkled like a date left out in the sun. Touching his elbow, Yassen felt a familiar ache echo through his bones.

"What did the Arohassin do to you?" Samson whispered.

"They did nothing. I made a mistake." The memory and the pain it brought were still too raw. He remembered how the fire had grabbed his arm. The smell of seared flesh. The deep, blistering heat. "They were barely able to save it."

Samson slowly sank onto an ottoman and folded his hands beneath his chin.

It was an old mannerism. He had done the same when they had received their first assignment to kill.

Their targets had been fleeing prisoners. The Arohassin called it the Hunt. They were usually Ravani soldiers or officials that the Arohassin had kidnapped or captured for information, questioning them with varying degrees of *encouragement*, as they liked to call it. If they had survived, they served as target practice for their newest recruits.

"All right, boys and girls," Akaros had said as he handed them their weapons. "Pair up."

Yassen, of course, had found Samson. They had been inseparable back then. They listened, shoulders trembling against the other, as Akaros told them the details of their assignment.

"Now, there are going to be six of them. And they're going to be *fast*. Like a shobu running for his dear life from a snake. So you'll have to be quicker. Remember your training. Find your target, calm your breath, and shoot. Any questions?"

They had not been brave enough to ask, save for Samson.

"What's the twist?" It was the question they had all been thinking. Because Akaros, unlike the other handlers, always loved a twist.

He had smiled, the burn on his face crinkling like sand patterns on a dune. "Glad you asked, Ruru," mentioning Samson's code name. He spread his arms. "You all will have one shot. One *bullet*. Oh, don't shake your heads. Bullets have more character than a fucking pulse. Now, see your friend there. Yes, look at the man or woman beside you. Go on. Look them hard in the eye. Because they'll get rewarded if you make your kill. And if you don't, well." Akaros did not smile. Yassen preferred when he did; at least then he could predict the man's eccentricities. "You all know what happens when a target doesn't cooperate."

The twin moons had hidden behind the clouds that night. It was hard to see from their perch on the hill, but the escape door of the underground prison stood directly across from them while they lay in pairs beneath the shadows of boulders.

"Samson," Yassen had whispered. "Sam."

He noticed Samson's hand trembling around the gun.

"All right," Akaros had said in their comms, "they're coming out."

The first prisoner had peeked out from the gate and scanned his surroundings. He looked hesitant, his lips pale and eyes haggard as Yassen watched him through his scope. Five more peered out behind him. They debated among themselves. Yassen was trying to read their lips when the first prisoner took off running.

One of the boys fired. The shot echoed through the valley. The man stumbled and fell.

"Quick now," Akaros had said.

"Sam!"

"I—I can't do it. I'm sorry, Yassen."

Fear swept through Yassen, cold and savage. "What do you mean you can't? Samson, you must."

Another prisoner screamed and dashed out, swerving right. Swearing, Yassen tracked him. He could see the man's head perfectly centered in his viewfinder. This man was somebody's son, likely a brother and father. He could have been a decent man. But Yassen knew how Akaros took his time, how he would stretch the pain until a single needle prick became excruciating. He couldn't allow Samson to suffer like that.

His shot had been clean. The body had crumpled, legs folding beneath it as if made of string, not bone. When Yassen exhaled, his heartbeat thundered in his ears. His whole body trembled. For he understood in that moment, in the split second when the bullet ripped the man's consciousness out of his body, that it also tore a part of him—a part he could never mend.

The other recruits found their targets. Only one prisoner remained, and she ran for the hills. Yassen shook Samson, who lay frozen. Even his grip was slack.

"Samson, please," Yassen begged, but Samson did not move.

And so Yassen had wrenched his gun away from him and shot the prisoner. Two kills, his very first. Later, he had tried to convince Akaros that Samson had taken the shot, when their handler had checked the empty chamber. But Akaros knew.

"Don't," Samson had said when the handler had moved to grab Yassen. "Let me take his punishment as well. It was my fault."

"How *courageous* of you," Akaros said, the word curdling in his mouth.

Samson was whipped twenty times. Ten for him, ten for Yassen; all the recruits had to watch. Yassen did not remember if Samson had cried. He only remembered how, when they had returned to the barracks, Samson, addled by drugs for the pain, had whispered something in the dark.

"She reminded me of my sister."

In all the time he had known him then, Yassen had never guessed that Samson had siblings.

"It's all right," he had whispered back as Samson held his hand. "They're all dead. They don't suffer anymore, Sam."

It had been a terrible thing to say. He was not one who knew how to comfort, but Samson had fallen asleep then, mostly due to the painkillers. But that night, Yassen had made an oath to himself. To never kill, unless needed. And never to kill a man who had no weapon.

But he had broken that oath the day he went to Veran.

Raindrops hit the windowpane, and Yassen jumped. Samson went to the window and opened it again. A gust of fresh air—that raw, grainy scent of wet sand—filled the room. Yassen felt the cold touch of raindrops on his burnt skin.

"There isn't anything like a desert storm," Samson said.

Yassen flexed his fingers. "I can still fight," he said.

"I know you can. But I wonder if this kind of fighting will kill you."

"I've been through worse," Yassen replied. He tried to sound nonchalant, but his hand trembled, and he curled it into a fist to stop the shaking.

"There's an Arohassin agent on your list that we want to bring in," Samson said. "She operates in Rani, out in the southern district."

"I'll do it," Yassen said. "I can bring her in."

In the fading light of the sunset, Yassen saw Samson's shoulders slump. His head bowed. After a moment, Samson turned and met his gaze.

"If she doesn't check out, they'll kill you on the spot."

Yassen nodded, but he knew Samson had more to say. He could see the words in his eyes, could read them in the way he clutched the windowsill. "Is there anything else?"

"Just..." Samson smiled, soft and small, the same smile he had had when they were boys. "I'm glad you're here. Alive. You're tougher than a fucking mountain, Yassen, and I should know. I'm trying to drill into one." He laughed.

"Well, trying to survive while Akaros breathes down your neck has that effect," he said.

Samson's smile wavered. Guilt, dark and silent like a cat, stalked across his face. But Yassen knew he would not apologize. Samson never did. He was horribly obtuse when it came to apologies, either too ashamed or too prideful, and when Samson had escaped and not come back, Yassen had been furious. So furious. But when Akaros had offered for Yassen to hunt down his former partner, that fury had dissipated. Because there was one thing he had admired in Samson above all else.

His loyalty.

He was an idiot when it came to apologies, but he was fiercely devoted and protective of his men.

"I promise you," Samson said, his voice fierce. "The day you're free, we'll hunt down Akaros himself. I'll cut off his head."

Yassen said nothing. Nursing a grudge took effort, pain, and when he wanted to be free of his past, he wanted to be free of that too. Revenge. Bloodshed. The works.

A clean slate. A new name.

He did not have the heart for retribution.

"Fine. But do it after you see me off. I won't come with you," he said.

Samson began to retort and thought better of it. He chucked a white shirt at Yassen.

"This will suit you," he said. His eyes lingered on the burnt flesh of Yassen's arm. "Does it hurt?"

"Sometimes, like a ghost is traveling through my body," Yassen said. He straightened and grabbed a pair of cotton trousers. "Now, if you could leave."

Samson paused before the door. The rain was falling harder, thick wet drops that sounded as if a million tiny soldiers were waging battle on the roof.

"We leave right after dawn," he said. The door closed softly behind him.

Yassen dropped the shirt to the floor. He crossed the room and leaned out the window. The rain splashed his face, soaked his hair, trailed down his naked torso. He wanted to feel its chill in his bones.

Through the mist, Yassen could make out the silhouettes of the sand-scrapers and chhatris. Beyond them lay the desert suburbs and, somewhere in the outskirts, his home.

Home. What a strange word. It was meant to be a haven, a place where he could finally die in peace, but it felt more like a curse. A dream that perhaps he would never achieve.

He had never belonged in Ravence, with his colorless eyes. The Jantari spurned him as soon as they heard the desert on his tongue. He had always been an orphan, even before he became one.

His parents had tried to shield him, but they too bore the same ostracization. *Traitors*, they had called his family before they died. *Abomination*, they had called him.

And when his parents had died, his neighbors had stared at him with pity, as if he were a wounded shobu. *No one will adopt an orphan like him,* they had whispered. He had wanted to pluck the pity from their eyes and bury it deep in the desert.

Yet here he was on Palace Hill, in the palace, looking down upon the city that had spawned him. He, who had never even dreamed of setting foot within the royal courtyards, slept in its chambers.

Yassen closed his eyes and tasted the salty rain.

He, the orphan from the desert outskirts, would show them. He had to.

CHAPTER 12

ELENA

There is a rage that comes with fire. An all-consuming fury that boils away any sliver of fear. This is why the Prophet is so powerful. She serves the heavy hand of justice without the fear of death. Her lifetime contains a multitude of generations, and our life is only a blink in hers.
—from the diaries of Priestess Nomu of the Fire Order

Y ou lost control," Ferma said once she left her father's office.

"What?" Elena said, startled. She had been lost in thought, wondering why her father had visited the library. She peered at Ferma. "Lost control of what?"

"In the gamefield," Ferma said. "You beat the everlasting shit out of the assassin when he gave you the game."

"Oh, that." Elena sighed. "He's trained in the Unsung, Ferma. I could tell by his stance. But he wouldn't use it. I tried to goad him, but…"

"But he was smart enough to take the hit." Ferma shook her head. "You know better than to attack a fallen enemy."

Elena said nothing. She may not be queen yet, but she knew the way of kings: their swift cruelty; their harsh justice. King Farzand had ruthlessly killed the stranded Jantari army after they had gotten lost in the northern sandstorms. Those men and women had been helpless, but he had not wavered, not even to return their bodies to their families. He had burned them all in a great pyre, several miles north of Palace Hill.

She did not have the stomach to do what King Farzand had done. But at least she knew this: Never underestimate a fallen enemy.

She continued walking, heading for her rooms and her private entrance to the library. Every member of the royal family had a separate corridor to the library. It was something Queen Jumi had insisted upon. But Leo rarely ventured down there; it reminded him too much of her mother. If he had pushed away his hesitance to consult the scrolls, she needed to find out why.

"Are you listening?"

"Contrary to what it seems, I am," Elena said, her eyes sliding to the Yumi. "And you're right. I was a little too hard on the assassin. But you're wrong about one thing, Ferma." She stopped, and her Spear broke her stride. "I never lost control. Not once."

She held out her hand. It was steady. When she had first learned the Unsung, her body would tremble for hours after. Use of the form demanded concentration, energy. She had seen how Yassen Knight spun on his toes, how he slipped in between Ferma's advances. He had been using the Unsung, but only to a point.

Perhaps because of his injury, she thought. Despite his arm, he had guarded himself well, positioning his right side away from attack, using her momentum to spin her back to his left side.

He had been smart, and incredibly infuriating. But now Elena felt a wary curiosity toward her new guard. As well as a tremor of warning.

If Yassen Knight had been holding back, what was he like in his full capacity? What else was he hiding from her?

The library still smelled like old stone and stale sand. Elena spun in a slow circle, the ends of her skirts fluttering as the orbs lit up one by one, illuminating the tower of books and scrolls spiraling above her.

She turned to the sound of footsteps. Ferma descended into the chamber, brushing dust from her long, silky hair.

"I've moved the guards outside your door to the end of the corridor. They didn't hear the passage opening."

Elena approached a bookshelf along the eastern wall, running her hand along the stone. In the last few suns, her visits here had become less frequent. Preparations as heir and tracking gold caps tended to have that effect.

As a child, she had come to escape nagging tutors. As she got older, she would come to breathe. Something about the cold, quiet stone and the musty scent of timeworn pages calmed her still.

But more so, it was the closest that she ever felt to her mother. Aahnah had been the keeper of this library, organizing the scrolls into a secret order that she had taught her daughter. Often, Elena would find her here, reading runes and ancient prophecies about the world that came before.

"Tell me what you've read, Mama," she would ask, and her mother would smile and smooth her sari, indicating Elena to sit on her lap.

"Once, before the world began, there were three flames."

It had been Aahnah's favorite story, the one she obsessed over to the point that it had driven her to fever dreams of destruction and death.

As Elena walked around the library, her throat tight, she remembered how on one occasion, she had come into the library and found her mother flying haphazardly on the circular platform, throwing scrolls left and right.

"It must be here, Phoenix Above, I *know* you're here," she called out.

Reams of paper, bouncing on the floor. Elena had cried out. She tried to grab the scrolls, to return them back to their spots, but no matter how fast she moved, her mother had been faster.

"His Majesty has definitely been here," Ferma called out as she rose. Her voice rang through the tall chamber.

Elena stepped onto a stone circle, forcing the memories away. She joined her Spear before the western shelves.

Ferma pointed at a section. "The dust is unsettled there."

"Why would my father study the Immortal scrolls?" Elena muttered.

She knew these ledges like the back of her hand. The Immortals were an...odd section, to put it lightly. The knowledge about them was limited, spanning fewer shelves than any other subject contained in the library. It was also the place her mother had visited during the last days of her sickness.

Hands, so thin and fragile, gripping her with a force that made Elena freeze.

"I know the sorrow of it," her mother had gasped, eyes wide and distant. "I know her pain."

"Elena." Ferma's voice was soft. "We can come back later."

Elena twisted the end of her dupatta. To her horror, both her hands were shaking.

Enough, she thought. *No more ghosts.* She sucked in a mouthful of dusty air, and coughed.

"No, no, there's no time." Elena used her dupatta to wipe her face. "I need to meet Samson. And then I need you to track Varun in the city—"

Ferma touched her shoulder. "Come, there's something I want you to see."

Elena paused, hesitant. She knew this library as well as she knew the Desert Oath. What could Ferma possibly show her that she didn't already know? But the Yumi was already descending, and after taking one last glance at the Immortals section, Elena followed her.

They walked along the eastern wall and then slipped down a corridor. Elena knew this entrance and the familiar ivory tiles interspersed along the walls. It had been her mother's. But Ferma did not lead her to the room that had been Aahnah's study. Instead, she stopped in front of one of the tiles.

When Elena peered closer, she realized it was cracked, the lotus leaves peeling back as if to reveal something within.

"What is this?"

Ferma beckoned to an orb floating along the wall as she sharpened one strand of her hair. "You'll see."

And then Ferma inserted her hair into the broken tile, like a key to a lock, and the wall opened.

Elena gasped, stumbling back as a door emerged. It led to a chamber, one about the size of her balcony. In the middle sat a heavy chest.

"Ferma," Elena began.

"Your mother kept her favorite and most precious scrolls hidden within this chest. She swore me to secrecy. I had planned to show it to you as a coronation gift; then you decided to come to the library after so long. So. Surprise."

Elena turned to Ferma. She felt a grin—her first true smile in months, it felt like—spread across her face.

"Oh, Ferma." She grabbed the Yumi in a fierce hug, and Ferma wrapped her arms around Elena gently.

"I reason to myself that Aahnah would have wanted you to see this eventually," she said, her chin resting on Elena's head.

"Thank you."

Elena knelt before the chest as Ferma opened it, again with a lock of her hair. A thick stack of scrolls sat within, along with notebooks and bound leaflets. Elena picked them up gingerly. As she opened one, she saw that her mother had marked it, too, with her initials scratched in the corner.

Aahnah liked to leave behind signs of herself. She used to scribble her name everywhere, from the inside lapels of her coats to the margins of historic texts. When Elena had asked her why, her mother had become silent, a distant look in her eye, as if to tether herself to some far-off point.

"Your name is important, Elena. It tells you who you are. It tells the world who you are," she had finally said.

It had taken her mother's death for Elena to understand why she had marked everything. It was not so much a claim of ownership but rather a quiet, desperate act to be remembered. To keep herself from disappearing by scattering parts of herself for others to find.

Elena rubbed her mother's initials, wondering if Aahnah were here now, what she would say about the daughter who could not hold fire.

"What exactly are we looking for anyway?" Ferma asked. "Was His Majesty searching for something?"

Elena thought back to the metal ring on her father's desk; the look on his face when he refused to teach her about the Eternal Fire, about her own kingdom. "He's searching for answers. Which means he has even less time for me."

She waved the floating orb down as she pulled out a scroll and unrolled it carefully. The paper crinkled at her touch. It was written in Herra. Carefully, Elena set it back and grabbed another. She flipped through the notebooks for some sort of guide or key, but she could make no sense of her mother's atrocious handwriting.

Not all the scrolls were marked. *Strange,* Elena thought. And then the realization cut through her.

They were not all marked, because her mother had never returned to finish her reading.

I know the sorrow of it. I know her pain.

Or perhaps her mother *had* finished her reading and found the answer that had finally broken her. Suddenly, fear, cold and small, licked the underside of Elena's belly. What kind of answer did her mother find that had driven her to jump into the flames?

"We should go," Elena said.

"Are you all right?" Ferma said in surprise.

"I'm fine, I just need fresh air," Elena said and began to rise. She didn't notice the floating orb near her head, banging into it and sending it spinning.

"Ow," she cried, rubbing her head. The light within the chamber wavered. And then Elena saw it. Movement.

She froze and peered closer. The writing on a scroll was *moving.*

Elena motioned for the orb and it floated downward. She watched, fascinated, as the runes unlocked in the light, unspooling and lengthening, forming new figures and characters until she realized they weren't words at all, but drawings of women surrounding a single flame.

She studied the scroll further. It wasn't many women, it was the same woman. And she was dancing around the fire.

"What is that?" Ferma asked, peering over Elena's shoulder.

Elena stared at the scroll, her mind racing. It showed seven different stances. Elena recognized none from her training in the Unsung and Kymathra, but she recognized one thing, felt it deep in her bones: Here lay a path to power.

"This is the way to hold fire," she whispered.

There were translations beneath the runes, and Elena recognized her mother's handwriting. The seventh form was unclear, however, the text and woman torn off. Elena smoothed the lower corner of the scroll. Someone had drawn a small flower. A jasmine. Below it were her mother's initials, like the mark of an artist: *A. M.*

She rolled the scroll and slipped it into her skirts, already making for the exit.

"Elena, wait," Ferma called. "Maybe we should inform your father about this."

"Our gracious king doesn't want to teach me about fire," she said. "This will be our secret."

"Did you ever consider *why* he's hesitating?" Ferma asked. Her tawny eyes seemed to glow in the darkness of the library. "Do you even remember that day?"

No.

"Yes," Elena said, her throat tight. In truth, she only remembered moments: her mother's reverent eyes, her father's agonized scream. It was the only time in her life that she had seen him fall to his knees.

"He doesn't want you to have the same fate as your mother," Ferma said.

"She was delusional," Elena said softly.

Madness ran in Ravani blood, and although her mother was not of the royal family, madness had found her too, through the scrolls. Like all the fire fanatics, Aahnah had come to believe redemption could only be achieved through burning. She had leapt into the pit of the Eternal Fire, leaving Elena not even her ashes to scatter in the wind.

"Maybe if she had known how to hold fire, she wouldn't have burned," Elena murmured.

"Fire is dangerous. It's pure chaos," Ferma insisted, gripping her arm. "You can't learn to wield it with only a scroll. You almost burned down the palace the last time you—"

"Mother's Gold, Ferma, you sound just like the king—"

"I don't want to lose two queens, Elena," Ferma said.

At this, Elena felt her anger dissipate. She turned away to hide her flush of guilt.

"Leave me," she whispered, but her voice echoed through the tall chamber.

Ferma hesitated, but then she bowed deeply.

"Your Highness," she murmured.

Elena returned to her room to find a message from Samson.

Congratulations on our engagement. Attached was a statement he had prepared. As she read it, Elena felt a coldness slither in the pit of her stomach. Marriage was an inevitable fact of life; she had a responsibility to bear an heir. But Elena had always believed she could rule without a partner, just like her father had without his. It would be harder, yes, but at least she could focus solely on protecting her kingdom.

There came a knock on the door.

Elena quickly closed the message and stowed the scroll in her desk drawer. Then she nodded to the guards to let the visitor in.

"Your Highness," Samson said and bowed deeply.

"Skip the formalities." She beckoned toward the covered terrace. "Let us speak out here."

"Have you had time to read over what I sent?" he asked as her handmaid brought out tea and a platter of cloud cookies. Rain drummed against the balustrades and down in her garden as the banyan trees rustled in the wind.

"It's a bit rough, but I can fix it." Elena poured, examining Samson. She had heard stories of his military feats, and he certainly looked like a warrior with his broad shoulders and warm, bronze skin. But she also saw the makings of a royal within him: the confidence and arrogance in his posture, the sureness in his gaze. He would make a pretty king.

"Let us be frank," she said as he reached for his cup. "Is Ravence your only play for a throne?"

If the question surprised him, Samson made no sign of it. He merely regarded her with his dark blue eyes. *Too much water,* she thought and stopped herself from rubbing the back of her neck. Such eyes were considered bad luck in Ravence. Out here in the desert, water drove men wild with greed.

"No," Samson finally said.

She ventured a smile. At least he knew when to be honest.

"What other queens have considered your hand?" She took a sip from her tea, never averting her gaze.

He held it. "Only two. A queen and a king, in fact. But . . . Farin thought it would be a bad alliance."

"And why would you need Farin's permission?"

"I am but a humble servant of the Jantari, aren't I?" A wisp of a smile played across his lips. "Or at least, that's what people say."

He was toying with her; she could tell by the amusement in his eyes. *All right then,* she thought as she spooned sugar in her tea. *Let's play.*

"Which of the rumors are true?" she asked.

"What, your little intelligence networks can't get the bulletin from the *Jantari Times*?" He grinned. "What have you heard?"

"That you're a Sesharian who sold his brethren just so you could be free," she said.

"Old rumor. Come on, my rani. You must have something better than that."

"You're a charlatan who picks up the scraps from the tables of kings just so that you can feel like one."

"Mm, tough, but I know you can be tougher."

Elena paused. "My apologies. I know what you are."

She leaned forward. "You're lost. A man without a home, serving a king who will never raise his boot from your neck, no matter how many praises he showers upon you."

"Somewhat closer." Samson still didn't flinch.

"No matter where you go, no matter where you run, you will always be lost," she whispered. "Because your home no longer belongs to you."

His breath was warm against her lips. "Wrong."

He was close, so close that if he tilted ever so slightly, he could kiss her. And for a moment, Elena wondered if he would. He was her betrothed, might as well get on with it, for the sake of duty and whatnot.

But then he did something that surprised her.

Samson took her hand, his fingers brushing the backs of hers.

" 'A steady hand and a quick sword,' isn't that what your scriptures say?" He slid his hand down, touching the soft skin of her wrist. "You're the hand, I'm the sword. You command, and I'll burn their names in the sand. How can I be lost then, if I know my purpose? Imagine the Arohassin gone and peace with the Jantari. Your reign—our reign—will bring back the Golden Suns. An age of splendor."

Elena carefully pulled her hand away. "And that's what you are here for?"

"Peace, and freedom." He smiled. "It's not pleasant dancing to Farin's tunes. But I must, at least for a bit. He thinks I've asked for your hand so that I can help Jantar invade, but we both know you'd cut off my hands and tongue before I could open the gates."

At this, Elena smiled. "Glad you're already learning my ways."

"It's my job, isn't it?"

She considered him, this strange man with eyes that trapped the sea. She was good at reading people. Instinct told her that Samson was lying. Not about all of it, but some of it.

"When you asked for my hand, you said you would help me hunt down the Arohassin, and yet you bring one of their assassins into my palace. I ask you for your true intentions, and you dance around the answer." She nodded at the door where her guards stood. "One shout, and they'll take your head off. Or maybe I will. You've seen me in the field."

She leaned back, all pretense and subtleties gone.

"So I'll ask you again, one last time, what are you really here for?"

Samson did not answer right away. But when he spoke, his voice was soft. "I'm not proud of the things I've done, or of the men who died while I stood by, voiceless." He slipped off his ring, a small signet ring with what looked to be a family crest of a serpent. "But I made an oath to the owner of this ring. To be free, and to free the men who have suffered at the hands of oppressors.

"I don't want to live under Farin's boot. And if freedom means marrying you, leading my army with yours to protect this kingdom, I will. But for your sake, and for the sake of the hundreds of Sesharians you've welcomed, I will seek peace first."

He slipped the ring back on, quiet. This time, he did not meet her eyes, and so Elena knew he spoke the truth. Telling a lie took confidence; speaking the truth meant unearthing pain. Before, he had brazenly met her gaze with a look of amusement, even pride, but now he busied himself with spooning sugar in his tea. Whoever had given him that ring had also given him a burden.

Elena knew something of the pain of burdens.

"Well," she said, her voice gentler, "You're brave to risk the anger of Farin. Here I thought only the Ravani did that."

"I told you, I'm a fast learner."

She smiled at the thought of Samson kneeling in a haldi ceremony, bewildered by the song and dance and the gallons of rose-scented milk dumped on his head. "You didn't flinch when you had to put your hand in the flames."

"That's because I know a few things about fire."

"Oh?" Elena spooned more sugar in her tea. "Like what?"

"Fire brings life. Domination. Reverence," Samson said thoughtfully. It caught her by surprise. "But it's an insidious power. It can destroy you from within if you're not careful." And he looked at her with such intensity that for a moment, Elena wondered if he knew her secret.

"I've seen how fire can tear apart its followers," he continued. "The Ravani know all this yet continue to worship the Phoenix. Others call it madness, but I think your people have tapped into an ancient force that no other nation understands." He paused and looked out at the desert that lay beyond Palace Hill. The rain shimmered over the dunes like silver. "Ravence has survived because it knows what it means to burn. It knows loss, yet its people continue to believe."

"'Faith is stronger than any king,'" she whispered, quoting the scriptures.

Samson nodded. "Your father knows this. He puts up with the Fire Order because he needs the image of myth and divinity to ensure his power. He sits in the flames to keep your people in line."

Elena let out a low breath. "I can't hold fire," she said. The words tumbled out before she could stop them. She had never admitted this to anyone; only Ferma and Leo knew. Shame and relief colored her cheeks, but to his credit, Samson only shrugged.

"Does it matter?" he asked. "It's all a show. You just make the people believe you can hold fire, and they'll worship at your feet."

"Maybe," she said. Appearances and deception were the first rules of any statecraft. Honesty, when used strategically, was a finely edged knife. "But if the Prophet were to hear you, you'd be the first to burn."

Samson laughed—a deep, booming sound that leapt to meet the rain. It was a type of laugh that did not often frequent the palace halls. Elena felt herself warming to it.

"I'm sorry about your friend," she said. "I meant to test him, but he cleverly did not take the bait."

"He can handle himself," Samson said. His laughter subsided, and he looked at her with a faint smile. "Give him a chance. Will you?"

Elena glanced out at her garden, at the darkening sky. A breeze whispered through the trees. Beneath the hill and beyond, the dunes sprawled out into the deep desert.

Her desert.

Elena rose, and Samson rose with her. She led him to the door, and when she offered her hand, he kissed it, his lips lingering against her knuckles.

"Think about it," he said and bade her good night.

Long after he had gone, she touched the back of her hand. It wasn't the kiss that had shocked her, but the heat of his lips burning against her skin.

★　　★　　★

The next morning, Elena joined her fiancé and father on the terrace looking down on the capital. Ferma and the royal guards stood behind them
while Yassen waited in the wings. There was a mark beneath his brow
where she had hit him, but otherwise, he looked composed. Oddly, she
felt relief at that, but quickly pushed it away. He did not deserve her pity.

A wide sea of reporters and civilians jostled at the base of the hill. Some
projected holosigns displaying the royal family. Others waved tiny flags.
Most regarded them silently. She could feel the weight of their gaze, the
guarded look in their eyes.

A chant began to echo through the crowd. Elena leaned forward to
listen.

"Son of Fire, Son of Fire!"

She spotted the telltale gold caps, pushing their way to the front like
a wave, their chant growing louder and louder. She spotted Jangir first,
Varun grudgingly following on his heels. Though most of Ravence
believed in the Phoenix, they believed in the Holy Bird with such ferocity
that they would burn themselves to show their piety. Jangir and his followers shamed the nonbelievers, ridiculed the royal family's skeptics, and
threatened the ones who dared to speak of revolution.

Leo raised his hands, and the gold caps roared. Jangir turned, raising his
hands as well, urging the crowd. More and more people began to take up
the chant. Elena saw her father smile.

When the king lowered his hands, the crowd fell quiet. Leo was dressed
in golden robes that shone despite the grey morning. He wore the crown,
the Featherstone pulsing as if alive. Elena stood to his right, Samson to his
left. She glanced at her fiancé and found him looking straight at her.

He winked. She felt a smile slip over her face in response.

"May the sun dawn upon our lands," Leo said.

"And the fire burn within our hearts," the crowd intoned.

Their collective voices lifted from the bottom of the hill with warmth,
seeming to dispel the dark clouds.

"The time has come for a new queen to rise," Leo said, and at this, the
crowd gave another wild roar. Elena tried not to grimace.

"It is tradition that when the heir turns twenty-five, the old sun must
set. He must dim his light for the new dawn," Leo said, his voice amplified

by the sensors surrounding them. "As a king, I cannot be more delighted. This heir is more radiant than our past monarchs." He turned to Elena, and she bowed her head. "But as a father, I must tell you that there is something that your heir needs."

A murmur went through the crowd.

"The sun governs above all. But the flaming sword will make us bow." Leo raised both hands, beckoning for Elena and Samson to step forward. They did so at once. She could hear the crowd inhale sharply, feel their eyes narrow as they began to realize the meaning behind their king's words.

"It is with the blessing of the Phoenix that I announce the engagement of our heir. Ravence, after so long, will once again know the power of both king and queen."

The crowd erupted. Samson held out his arm, and after a moment's pause, Elena took it. He raised their clasped hands, and the people cheered.

And then, suddenly, it was her turn to speak. Her stomach turned, a pit of stinging ants. Elena squeezed Samson's hand. He squeezed hers back.

Gulping down her nerves, she stepped forward.

"My fellow Ravani," she began, and she heard Leo start behind her. Royals traditionally began their speech by calling upon the heavens, not the people. She heard the crowd whisper nervously, confused by her greeting, but she forced herself to keep smiling.

"Yes, countrymen," she said. She willed her voice to become steady. She could feel her father and Samson, her past and her future, watching her. "The people of Ravence create the beating heart of this kingdom. Your blood courses through its veins. I may be blessed with the fire of the Phoenix, but your passion stirs the winds of the desert."

She stood taller, her chest warming.

"They say that it is the sovereign that leads a nation to enlightenment. This is true. As queen, I intend to lead us to great prosperity. But the people, the people of salt and sand, the ones who built Rani alongside Alabore Ravence, bring enlightenment to life. Without her people, Ravence is nothing. Without your faith, she is merely a dream in the desert.

"Every day, we are threatened by those who want to destroy this dream. Those who speak of revolution and a path without Agni," she said, and somewhere within the crowd, a person booed. A gold cap yelled, and others stomped their feet in discontent.

Elena was no fool. She knew there were rebels here who despised her family, despised everything they stood for. Her eyes swept the crowd. One by one, the people quieted under the weight of her gaze. It was a trick she had learned from her father—to stretch out silence and use it to her advantage. When the murmur finally died, replaced now by a tight tension, Elena raised her chin.

"I know there are those of you who disagree with the throne and what it stands for. Those who believe this government has failed you, silenced you. But hear this—I welcome you.

"This kingdom will always serve its people first. As queen, I will protect you. As sovereign, I will lead you. But as a Ravani, as a daughter born of salt and sand, I will work beside you.

"My countrymen, we are the guardians of this kingdom. We are the defenders against the violent metalmen who seek the fire. Will we let them so easily dash our dream?"

"No!"

"Never!"

"Burn them all!"

Elena raised her hand and the crowd quieted. "Then defend this dream. Jantar, the Arohassin, they know little about the power of Ravence or her kindness. Where were the other kingdoms when the island refugees came to their doors? Who let them in? You, my countrymen. To the refugees gathered here today, know that you are always welcome in these deserts. And that we stand with you."

She turned to Samson and let her eyes soften. "A new era dawns upon Ravence. One in which we are not just defending our borders but strengthening them. With the help of my beloved, our future king, we will protect the dream of our forefathers."

She turned back to the crowd. "So lend me your hearts. Let us work together to show the world what Ravence can really do. So we the blessed few."

"So we the blessed few," the crowd cheered. Their voices rumbled up the hill and rolled through Elena with such force that she took a step back. Her bones buzzed with the energy of their chorus. She laughed, stunned.

Samson offered her his arm. In the doorway, they turned and waved—the perfect picture of Ravence's royal couple.

"I thought you said you were going to smooth the rough edges," Samson said once they were inside.

"I made them sharper." She smiled.

"Was the 'countrymen' your idea?" Leo asked, looking at Samson.

He shrugged. "It was merely a suggestion, but everything else was Her Highness."

Her father turned to her, and Elena braced for his usual disapproval. But instead, he placed his hand on her head.

"Preaching unity was a smart move. You will make a mighty queen." Pride colored his voice.

Elena blinked. His hand was heavy, but warmth fluttered in her stomach, making her feel buoyant. When her father left, she let her grin break free. Not even the sight of Yassen Knight could dampen her joy.

"We must take our leave." Samson looked at Yassen. "We've some hunting to do."

"Good hunting." She squeezed his arm. "And thank you."

CHAPTER 13

YASSEN

Belief is stronger than a god, more fragile than a feather.
—from the diaries of Priestess Nomu of the Fire Order

Yassen scanned the crowd in the meat bazaar as Samson's men moved into position. It was a twisting street, wide enough for only three men to walk abreast. There were over thirty shops, brightly lit. Butchers tied up legs of hearty lamb and cuts of delicate hiran in glass-encased freezers as shoppers milled about, watching them work or trying samples of freshly roasted venison. The smell of meat hung heavily in the hot air. It made Yassen feel sick, but his stomach rumbled. He hadn't eaten dinner yesterday.

They were in old Rani, near Radhia's Bazaar, a portion of the capital he had frequented when he was younger. His mother had grown up here, but had moved to the outskirts of the city at his father's wish, to be closer to the wide expanse of the desert.

Yassen could not blame him. His father was as skittish as a hare, constantly searching for exits should the need arise. In old Rani, the buildings crowded each other; neighbors could hear conversations through the walls. Here, there was no escape.

He pulled his scarf tighter around his lower jaw as a man wearing a gold cap walked past. He did not give Yassen a second glance. Yassen shivered to think what would happen if the man had recognized him. Even though he served the Crown now, Yassen knew his presence in Rani was a closely guarded secret. The gold caps, though passionate followers of the king, would not respond kindly to knowing that the man who killed their beloved general now walked freely in their streets. And though most Ravani did not know his face, the gold caps did. Leo had made sure of it.

"He uses civilians," Akaros had said when he first informed Yassen that his photo, captured by a stray holocam in a dark alley of Magar, had been sent to top-level gold caps.

"What?" Yassen looked at the holo. It was dark and grainy, and though his face was slightly blurred, he could make out the telltale flash of his hair, the angle of his jaw. *Shit.*

"He uses civilians as his spy network. Ropes them in by quoting god and country." Akaros had laughed. "At least we have professionals to do our work. He would sacrifice any ordinary man. Fucking hypocrite."

Yassen had said nothing then, but he wished he had had the courage to tell Akaros that he had been a civilian too. An ordinary man who had been given a gun so he could find purpose.

He had realized too late that the purpose would ruin him.

"Brother."

Yassen froze as the gold cap returned, holding out an yron. "Do you have a light?"

"No. I don't." With a sweaty hand, he waved toward the shops. "Maybe someone inside does."

The man narrowed his eyes, and for a moment, Yassen wondered if he had recognized him.

"Ah yes! Good idea." The man bowed his head. "So we the blessed few."

"So we the blessed few," Yassen murmured as the man disappeared into one of the shops.

He leaned against the wall, heart hammering. The Ravani may have mixed feelings toward the royal family, but they all detested the Arohassin. One look, one word, and a mob would be on him.

Elena's speech still rang in his mind. Yassen had never been the religious type. He hated fire, and he always thought the Phoenix was a cruel, vengeful god. But he could not deny the power of her words, for there was truth in them. Ravence was a land of devotion. They worshipped the Phoenix even though it had been a long five hundred suns since they last saw the Prophet. The Arohassin had warned him about the power of faith. But it wasn't until now that Yassen had truly seen it. And he had been terrified by it.

His earpiece crackled.

"Scarlet sighted by Eagle One," a voice said.

Yassen pretended to be preoccupied by the pig's feet hanging from a storefront. He glanced up at the building to his right. Behind a dark window on the top floor, Samson sat before a panel of holos, tracking their movements. *His* movements.

Once they smoked out Giorna, the Arohassin agent, he would cut off her escape. Samson's men would then swoop in, and he could finally, hopefully, earn some trust in this forsaken place.

Yassen licked the sweat from his lips. *This is just another sting operation. Just follow protocol.*

He had worked with Giorna, six suns before. He'd had only a few missions under his belt, and she was his superior in both age and kills. When they snuck through Teranghar to assassinate a Ravani official, she had barely given him a second glance. But he had been a strong climber back then. Scaled canyons in a matter of minutes. She had made him climb to the top of the home where the official met his mistress. When he returned to tell her where exactly in the room they were positioned, she had finally looked at him.

"Can you shoot?"

He had nodded, though his hands had trembled. He was too afraid to tell her of his promise: to never kill a defenseless man. And the official definitely did not have a weapon.

Giorna had watched his face, and then, wordlessly, she led him to a building across from the mistress's home. Assembled a beautiful pulse rifle that she had picked herself, telling him it was a part of her private collection. Then she knelt before the window that faced the mistress's bedroom and shot.

Later, Giorna had told everyone he had made the kill.

Yassen's ear crackled again. "Scarlet heading south down Butcher's Alley. Eagle One and Two are in positions."

"Hawk in position," Yassen muttered.

"Scarlet in the alley. Do you have eyes?" Samson asked.

Yassen glanced around discreetly. He saw red everywhere. The canopies covering the stalls, the castaway feathers of a skinned yuani, the blood dripping down the hanging sacks of meat and pooling in the sand below.

Then he spotted the rust-colored hair.

Giorna was a small woman. Yet Yassen immediately recognized her walk. The straight-set shoulders, the upright chin and chest. The way her eyes, closely set and with an eternal look of disdain under their thin brows, slowly scanned the crowd, her hand always hovering right above her hip where, no doubt, a weapon was concealed.

"I have eyes."

Yassen angled his body so she could not see his face as she drew near. Out of the corner of his gaze, he saw her glance at the window beside him.

Quickly, he made to go inside, calling for the butcher's attention. The merchant turned and yelled at him to wait. Yassen spat back that he was in a hurry, rolling his *r*'s to imitate the rounded southern Rani accent as Giorna passed him.

Her arm brushed against his shoulder. And then Yassen felt the knife point graze across his spine. He whipped around just as she began to push it into his lower back, ramming his hand down. The knife clattered to the ground, but she was already gone.

He darted after her. "Scarlet's on the run," he barked into the comm.

He vaulted over a bin of dried hawk bones that she knocked over as she fled. She veered to the right, threading past shouting merchants. They crowded in, jostling Yassen, but he shoved through them. One vendor pushed a cart piled high with sweet summer apples imported from Cyleon; Yassen tried to swerve but he was moving too fast—he crashed right through it, sending the fruit flying.

"Mother's Gold!" the merchant cried as Yassen hopped over the spilled goods. "My apples!"

Yassen shouted apologies but did not slow. Giorna dashed to the left, and he headed down an adjoining alley to intercept her. His feet pounded against the pavement. The streets began to narrow, twisting north, which meant... *She's heading to the main bazaar.* A small woman like her could easily hide in a big crowd. And if she vanished, Leo would have his head.

Yassen ran faster.

He spotted a man stacking crates of liquor on top of a floating platform. Another stood on the roof of the bar, waiting for the cargo. Yassen swung onto the platform just as it began to rise, wincing as a jolt of pain stabbed up his arm.

"Hey! Hey!"

"Sorry!"

Yassen slid off the platform, dodged the man, and ran across the roof, scanning the streets. For a moment, he thought he had lost Giorna, and his throat closed in panic. But then she reappeared from underneath a fluttering awning.

"Hawk? Hawk, where is she?"

Yassen ignored Samson. Heart pounding, he leapt onto the roof of the next building as Giorna sprinted down the street. He ran alongside her, his shadow flitting over the bricks and awnings of storefronts. Up ahead, Yassen spotted the colorful orange flags of the main bazaar.

It drew closer. Fifty paces, then forty, then thirty.

He jumped.

For a moment he was suspended in the air, weightless, free.

But then gravity took over, and he hurtled down on top of Giorna. She screamed as they hit the ground. The impact stunned Yassen, but Giorna recovered fast, twisting and digging her elbow into his stomach. He grunted in pain, but managed to reach for her arm, rolling and using his weight to pull her under him and pin her down. She thrashed in his grip, but he grabbed her other arm and twisted it above her head.

She spat in his face.

"You fucking traitor," she seethed, her eyes wild. Sand clung to her auburn hair. "Fuck you."

"Quit. Moving," he grunted. Shouts echoed up the street, and Yassen looked up to see Samson's men circling them, distinct in their black-and-blue uniforms.

"They'll have your head for this," she gasped. "Akaros will skin you alive."

"So will they," Yassen said quietly as he looked at the Black Scales, who now pointed their pulse guns at the two of them. Cautiously, one approached. He handed Yassen a pair of handcuffs, and Yassen clipped them on Giorna's thin wrists, tightening them for extra measure.

They hauled her up. Giorna kicked and twisted, landing a blow on one soldier's face before two others grabbed and tied her legs. Yassen turned away. He told himself that this was how it would be now. That freedom came with costs. But Giorna's curses cut through him like a knife, and he wavered.

"You can stand a little taller now, Cass," Samson said in his ear. He gave a soft chuckle. "Squad Dragon and Bear found the two other Arohassin agents. You're cleared."

Cleared.

Yassen sighed. Would he truly be cleared after all of this? Would his comrades ever forgive him?

They would have done the same. They would have sold me out too, if it came to it.

A crowd had begun to surround them. Yassen pulled his scarf tight, winding it around his head.

"Go on, nothing to see here," a Black Scale ordered. "Go on! Back to your jobs!"

A hovercar with the silver feather of the capital police parted the sea of people. The guards pushed Giorna in, but not before she shot Yassen another burning look.

You would have done the same.

He watched the hovercar vanish. With the star of the show gone, the crowd began to disperse. Some gold caps stayed, eyeing Yassen. He knew they noticed his strange, pale eyes, the eyes of a Jantari, but they kept their distance from the Black Scales.

"Good hunting, Hawk," one of the soldiers remarked. "I bet the old king will rest more easily tonight."

"Sure," Yassen replied dryly. "Now let's get out of here."

As he followed the soldiers, one gold cap hawked and spat in his direction.

Yassen stepped back, the familiar sensation of anger and shame burning through him. Suddenly, he was transported to when he was a child, flinching from the unforgiving gazes of strangers who could not understand him. The gold cap gawked at him now, but Yassen forced himself to swallow his pride. No matter how hard he tried, no matter how many Arohassin agents he delivered, Yassen knew he would never be accepted. His was the life between edges. Between Ravence and Jantar, right and wrong, holy and damned.

He ignored the gold caps and got into the car. Just less than a month. He only had to survive until coronation day. Elena would be crowned queen, and his job would be done. He would be free.

The gold caps watched even as he drove away.

CHAPTER 14

LEO

In the end, we must all burn.

—from the diaries of Priestess Nomu of the Fire Order

Leo sighed and pinched the bridge of his nose. He had returned to the library in the night and pulled out more scrolls. They lay in front of him, stoic and indecipherable. He had run his eyes over these runes so many times that they burned in his dreams, in his moments of peace, in the empty shadows of his office.

The door to his chambers rumbled open, and Samson entered. He wore a light blue kurta with the top two buttons undone, revealing his smooth, muscled chest—a strong young man.

Like I used to be, Leo thought. His sudden bitterness shocked him, and he pushed it away. He usually wasn't one for such thoughts.

Leo rolled up the scrolls as Samson bowed.

"I have some good news," he said, and a triumphant smile spread across his face. "We've apprehended three Arohassin agents on Yassen's list. They all check out. *Yassen* checks out. We can trust him."

"No one can be fully trusted," Leo said. He met Samson's eyes. "Surely you know that."

A muscle worked in Samson's jaw, but he held his tongue. *Smart boy.*

"Where are the agents now?" Leo asked.

"Held at a black site in the desert."

"Interrogate them," he said.

He suspected it would not be easy to crack the Arohassin agents. But he felt it was necessary to give Samson a difficult task. Perhaps it would humble the boy.

Samson bowed and turned to go.

"Wait," Leo called out, and Samson stopped. Slowly, he faced the king again and met his eyes.

Too much water.

"My daughter sent word that she spoke with you. That she believes you truly are on our side. But—" Leo leaned back in his seat, his eyes narrowing. "You lied to her, Samson."

"About what, Your Majesty?" Samson asked coolly.

"You said that for the sake of this kingdom and of its Sesharians, you would ask for peace with Jantar. But you and I both know that's not the case."

"And what makes you think so?"

"Because I have heard about your mine."

At this, Samson froze. Leo summoned holos of Muftasa's report. When Samson had first asked for Elena's hand, Leo had made Muftasa run a full investigation of the Sesharian mercenary. Most of the things that she had found were already public knowledge: Samson was the son of a warrior family; he ran away from home and ended up in Ravence; at fourteen, he had joined the Arohassin, only to defect at eighteen and sell the information he knew to the Jantari military. They offered him protection and he rose through the ranks to become, in all aspects, Jantar's poster child of the perfect Sesharian.

Except for one thing.

"Farin asked you to drill for him in the Sona Range. And you are drilling, but only to a point." When Samson made no response, Leo leaned forward. "Muftasa found a man from the nearby mountain town, an unlucky man who went outside for a piss one night and saw hoverpods rising from your mines. He said that they were unmarked, that they headed out to the sea. And curiously enough, when Muftasa's men went to find this man again a few weeks later, they found him dead. Coincidence, no?"

Samson finally met his gaze. There was no fear in his eyes, but a coldness, a frankness that Leo knew lay beneath all that charm.

"What is it that you want?" Samson asked, his voice flat.

"Where are you taking that ore? For what purpose?"

Samson cocked his head toward the crackling fire. When he spoke, it was as if the fire spoke with him.

"For war, what else."

"War against Farin."

"War against Farin." Samson closed his eyes, as if savoring the words. "You don't know what it's like to finally be able to say that."

"You promised Elena you would fight for peace first," Leo said.

"And you and I both know peace will never happen." Samson's eyes were hard, and Leo could not help but see himself in that gaze. The unflinching determination, the dogged zeal. But there was something else in Samson's expression, something he could not decipher.

"I will ask Farin for peace. Follow all the necessary gestures. But in the meantime, my men will slip through the holes in Farin's defenses. And when Elena realizes Farin never had the patience for peace, we will be ready." Samson gripped the back of the chair before him. "I will carve through Jantar once she gives me the word."

And then Leo realized what it was in Samson's gaze: hatred. Pure and dark, full of thorns.

I have invited an animal into my kingdom, Leo thought. For a moment, he felt the cool touch of doubt. What if he and Elena could not tame this animal?

But then he remembered the bombed port in Rasbakan, the Jantari troops along the southern wall. Animal or not, he needed Samson and his men. He needed a king who could see what his daughter could not.

"I have a lie for you," Samson said, voice cold and calculated. "You allowed more Sesharian refugees within Ravence, said it was because you cared for us. But you just wanted soldiers, right? Because you know of all people who would burn Farin's name in the sand, the Sesharians would be the first."

"Yes, and no," Leo said softly. "No man should ever live in fear of the zeemir, Samson."

He stood and walked around the desk. He removed a ring from his finger, a fine green stone with flecks of gold, and handed it to Samson. It was shagun, a present the bride's father gave to the groom as per tradition.

"I've never properly welcomed you into the family," Leo said.

Samson took the ring and slid it onto his right ring finger, the signet flashing on his left. It fit perfectly.

Samson rubbed the gem for good luck. "Thank you . . . Father."

"You'll need to change your name when Elena makes you her king."

"What's wrong with Samson?"

"It's not Ravani." Leo looked at his hand, at his own signet ring that displayed his family's crest. "The people may take some time to get used to a Sesharian king. It's never been done before. But if you take a Ravani name, they'll shower you with blessings. You can take one in the Rani fashion. What about Samu?"

"It's better to be hated for what you are, than to be loved for what you're not," Samson said. He gave a grim smile and bowed his head. "Your Majesty."

He strode out of the room, the flames hissing behind him. Leo shook his head, an uneasy sensation slithering in his stomach.

He's our animal, he reminded himself.

His holopod beeped. Muftasa appeared before him.

"Starlight is in," she said. Her face betrayed no emotion. "We have her down in the tunnels. Should I—"

"No," Leo said. "I will."

If she was the Prophet, Leo doubted that his men would have the courage to kill her. Their belief would hold them back. He, on the other hand, would not balk.

Yet his throat suddenly tightened.

Something flickered in Muftasa's eyes, but she nodded. "We'll be waiting."

Leo closed the holo. Through the glass ceiling, muted light filtered in, painting the room with grey shadows. It was the charged quiet before a storm. He closed his eyes to relish it. To drink in the calm and bottle it up—for he knew that after today, there would be no peace for him.

★   ★   ★

The girl was seated on a bench in a concrete room, far below the palace.

The fluorescent lights made her hair shine, as if it captured the stars themselves. She must have heard the door as Leo entered, for she spun around and looked at the two-way glass that separated the two rooms. Leo knew she could not see him, only her reflection. But her eyes bored through him all the same.

Holy Bird Above, this will be difficult.

She drew her knees in and rested her chin between them. Her eyes held a strange awareness—a clarity Leo had never seen before. She did not seem to be perturbed in any way; she merely sat quietly as he studied her.

Finally, Leo spoke.

"Let me in," he said in a voice too thin. "Let me talk to her."

Without a word, Muftasa turned a dial on the panel before him, and the door separating the two rooms slid open.

Arish gave him a single match. "So we the blessed few," he whispered.

Leo grasped the splinter, but could not bring himself to repeat the phrase. He walked into the other room before he could change his mind. As if sensing his fear, Muftasa shut the door behind him.

The cell felt even smaller now that he was standing in it. On the right wall, a large black hole covered with a metal grating yawned at him. Leo tried not to think of what lay behind it.

The girl looked up. She was frail, with a head too big for her shoulders. She had marks on her hands and arms, light red burn marks that spiraled up like braided rope.

Carefully, Leo dusted the bench and sat on the other end.

"Hello," he said.

The girl blinked.

"My name is Leo," he said and then hesitated. "I'm the king."

The girl said nothing.

Leo felt sweat pool underneath his armpits. On the other side of the glass, Arish and Muftasa watched him, and though he could not see their faces, Leo could feel the weight of their judgment. It wrapped around his shoulders like a slow, coiling snake. But he had to do this. He must. If the girl before him was the Prophet, it was his duty as king to face her.

"I have something for you," he said and revealed the match.

The girl's eyes grew wider, as if he held a prized jewel between his fingers. He saw the curiosity in her gaze, and a deep, creeping madness.

He held the match between them. "Do you know what this can create?"

"Fire," she said, her eyes shining. "Life."

Life. What an odd choice. Out of all the things Leo had seen and known about fire, he had never believed that it created life.

"And what do you do with fire?" he asked.

The girl blinked. Her eyebrows furrowed, and she looked at him as if he had suddenly knocked his head.

"It protects me," she said. Her voice was high and sharp, beautiful even. She reached for the match, but Leo pulled back.

"Can you control the flames?" he asked, but the girl shook her head. She reached for him again, but Leo gently pushed her hand away. "Do the flames hurt you?"

The girl sat back. She looked down at her arms, at the marks that lightened her brown skin. "You're the king," she said. "You should know."

Leo got up. The girl followed him with her eyes. At the door, Leo paused. He looked back at her.

Twelve suns. She had a lifetime before her, a lifetime to grow, travel, fall in love. But if she was the Prophet, it would only be a lifetime of ash. And if she wasn't—well, then whoever the Prophet was, she would burn them all.

Leo knocked on the door, and it slid open. He turned and threw the match to the girl, then stepped out of the cell.

The door closed with a whisper. Through the glass, he watched the girl scramble for the match. With a wave of her arm, she struck the match against the stone bench. It flared to life, the light flickering in her luminous eyes.

"Do it," he said.

Muftasa's face was pinched. With a heavy hand, she pressed the panel.

The metal grate hummed.

The girl turned just as the hum morphed to a screech and a torch of fire flared out. It instantly leapt on her body, ate up the shadows, sucked in the air.

The girl screamed.

Beside him, he heard Arish gasp and Muftasa exhale a prayer. They stepped back.

But Leo did not turn away. He let the sight before him sear into his mind: the girl's flailing limbs, the darkness of her body against the bright, hungry flames.

This was his price to pay. This was his sin to bear.

When it was over, Leo turned to Muftasa.

"Continue the search in the capital," he said, his voice flat and toneless. His stomach churned, and he swallowed down bile. "We have yet to find our Prophet."

CHAPTER 15

ELENA

At 0600 hours, the Hawk Patrol encountered a land mine hidden along the southwestern region of the wall. All six members were killed. This has put the total yearly death toll at sixty-five Ravani soldiers. Even our Sesharian recruits are beginning to balk. Ravence must make a move, and soon.

—a report from Colonel Akbar, stationed at Yoddha Base

Elena fanned herself with the edge of her sari's pallu, which already was beginning to wilt in the sun. They stood on an embankment overlooking a shallow valley along the southern border. At its edge, Samson's army prepared for the demonstration, weapons glinting in the harsh sun.

Tents surrounded them, media prepping their hovercams while dignitaries from Moksh and Teranghar talked softly, throwing glances her way. She had already greeted them upon her arrival. Accepted kisses on her hand. Exchanged polite formalities. Elena disliked small talk, like Leo, but she had more patience for it than him.

A dignitary hurried to her, bowing his head.

"Your Highness, my apologies on my late arrival," he said, sweat glistening on his balding head. "And congratulations on your engagement. And—and thank you for the invitation to see the proceedings! When my office received word, I tell you, I wanted to stand up and salute you then and there. It's time we show the metal bastards what Ravence can really—"

Elena listened politely, her hands fidgeting behind her. She snuck a glance at Samson, who wore a slightly amused expression. He was dressed in the military navy of his Black Scales. He had lined his eyes with kohl, a custom among the Ravani, and one that brought out the strange blue of his eyes.

"Thank you, Akash," she said, finally interrupting the dignitary's rambling. She smiled as he patted his forehead with a handkerchief. "You have served Magar well. Come, take a seat. She will show you your spot."

A servant came forward as Elena beckoned. Akash bowed again and gave a brief salute to Samson before hurrying off.

"Is he usually like that?" Samson asked.

"Always," Elena muttered.

"Skies above." Samson tugged at his collar. "Damn this heat. I'm sweating already."

"Then imagine the state of your poor men," she said.

"They've handled worse."

"Worse than the Ravani Desert?"

Samson smiled slyly, his voice a whisper. "The desert can undo any man."

Elena looked away so he could not see the sudden flush rising on her cheeks.

Across the dunes, a wall of red sandstone jutted against the sky, separating the kingdoms of Ravence and Jantar. It had been erected centuries ago by King Farzand. Though the desert had outwitted the Jantari soldiers and ruined their invasion, Farzand had not wanted to take any chances. He had erected the wall after every single Jantari soldier had been killed or captured, and every Ravani ruler afterward had strengthened it. It was a part of her heritage, as much as the throne.

Elena gazed at the wall. She knew that on the other side, the Jantari watched, waiting, and she wondered if Farin was among them. She hoped he was. The half-metal king would not underestimate Ravence now. Not after this.

Ferma brought over a pitcher of chilled water; Yassen, a platter of dates. Elena smiled to see the deadly assassin of the Arohassin serving refreshments. He had found a new suit, one that fit him properly—*too well*, she thought, observing how it stretched across his broad chest. Oddly enough, he wasn't sweating. She turned away before he could notice her looking.

"Any word from Majnu or Arish?" she asked.

"The king should be done with his meeting soon," the Yumi answered.

Elena glanced behind her at the Yoddha Base. It was a large military compound with gated checkpoints. The base had also been built by King Farzand. Heavy guns sat atop steel towers, while Ravani soldiers worked tirelessly under the desert sun. Her father was in there. When she had tried to join him after greeting the dignitaries, he had quietly told her to stand beside Samson and oversee the preparations.

"Everyone's eyes are now on you," he had said. "So take your place at the forefront and act the part."

A part of her chafed at his tone, the other warmed to think that he was beginning to realize and accept her ascension to the throne. She knew her father did not think she was ready. He had ruled this land for so long, protected it for many suns. But the throne called for the heir to ascend when they reached twenty-five suns, and her father was, above all else, a man of tradition.

What is taking him so long?

Elena scanned the crowd, but she did not spot her father's Astra or Spear. Was he in a meeting? She *had* seen someone in the room behind him, come to think of it. A woman. It had likely been Muftasa, but Elena had not gotten a good look.

Mother's Gold, is he discussing intel without me?

Perhaps Leo's comment had been a diversion, one meant to appease her in the moment. Elena flapped her dupatta harder. She knew he was hiding something. Maybe his meeting was linked to the scrolls, but why would Muftasa—

The sound of a horn ripped through the air. Elena straightened as Leo strode out of the compound, the edge of his red angrakha sherwani flapping in the breeze. A golden silk scarf draped across his right shoulder. He had chosen not to wear his military uniform. It was a slight, but one Elena understood. The king, though the protector of the land, was above all else. He did not need to don his brass and medals to show the world his mettle.

Elena, Samson, and their guards bowed as Leo joined them.

"Shall we begin?" he said.

The soldiers in the valley below were still and erect, waiting for a signal.

Samson withdrew the urumi looped around his waist. It was a Sesharian weapon, long and snakelike, with twin tongues that could bend and cut into a man. With his other hand, he raised a slingsword, the traditional Ravani blade. Both weapons flashed as he raised them to the air.

"The king is the protector of the flame, and I its servant," he intoned. "Together, we shall give our blood to this land. I swear it, or burn my name in the sand."

He brought his swords down, and the first Black Sands Day began.

First came the infantry. Rows and rows of Black Scale soldiers marched through the valley, accompanied by the blare of horns. They moved in unison, their legs and arms weaving in and out like a well-oiled machine. Behind them came the tanks that left no tracks in the sand. Fighter jets shaped like the heads of tridents zipped through the air. They flew low, and as they neared the valley, they rolled off, spreading across the sky like the wings of a bird.

As the infantry approached the embankment where the royals stood, the soldiers swiveled their heads. Commanding officers barked out orders, and five thousand men turned and snapped their heels to attention. They raised their hands in salute.

"All hail King Leo!"

"All hail the heir!"

"All hail her betrothed!"

Elena returned the gesture. Her eyes swept their faces, each as resolute as the last. These were true fighters, men and women of unbendable steel and remarkable courage. She saw it in the jut of their chins, in the furrow of their brows.

"All hail the Kingdom of Ravence!"

The tanks fired up into the sky, one by one. The shots rang through the valley.

The commanding officers gave the order, and five thousand of Samson's soldiers—her soldiers—resumed their march. The valley shook underneath their feet.

"Your Highness, what was the purpose of the Black Sands march?"

"To show the might of Ravence and the Black Scales," she replied to the journalist with the mouselike nose.

"But, Your Highness, some might say it's a provocation against the Jantari," another voiced.

"Are we going to war?" another asked.

"It's a wedding gift," Samson said, placing his arm around her shoulder. She wanted to tell him that she could handle the questions herself, but Samson was already smiling his wide grin, and the journalists zeroed in.

"Five thousand soldiers are a wedding gift?"

"For the queen of Ravence, why not?" He turned to her, eyes bright. "I wanted to show her that I serve her and only her. And now my men do too."

"Does that mean you have cut all ties with Jantar? With King Farin?"

For a moment, Elena saw Samson's eyes darken before he turned to the journalist. "We are looking for peace, not war. Cutting off ties would hardly help with that."

"As a Sesharian, how do you feel about Jantar's conquest of your—"

"Do you want peace?" Elena said suddenly.

The journalist, the one with the mouse nose, blinked. "Pardon?"

"Do you want war against the Jantari or peace?" she repeated, politely.

"Your Highness, with great respect, I am asking the questions and if you could just answer—"

"You're my countryman," Elena said. "What kind of ruler would I be if I didn't hear what *you* want? Your opinion matters to me. Do you want war or peace?"

"Um." The journalist glanced at her colleagues, who seemed just as befuddled by Elena's train of thought. "I want whatever is best for our country."

"And I the same." Elena looked to the other journalists, eyes cold, voice pleasant. "So allow me to do my job and do what's best for our country, yes? If marrying the leader of the Black Scales to get Farin's ear allows me to negotiate for peace, then I would happily do so. As long as he doesn't mind a little foray into the sands." She winked at Samson.

The journalists chuckled at this, though mouse-nose still looked uneasy.

"No more questions, now," Ferma said, stepping in front. "Her Highness and her betrothed are needed elsewhere."

Samson touched her elbow.

"Come, let's meet the men," he whispered.

They turned to go when Elena spotted her father by the gates of the base, looking down at her.

"Wait a moment," she said. Gathering up the folds of her sari, Elena walked up the steps.

"Father, join us," she said.

"You go ahead," Leo said. He stood with his back to the sun, his jade earring glittering. "And, Elena, don't let Samson steal your spotlight. Especially when you're talking about peace. Control the conversation and steer the questions. You know how to do so better than him."

Elena blinked, surprised. "He only meant to help."

"Still." There was a strange look in his eyes. "You're better suited than him."

He kissed his three fingers and pressed them against her head. "Remember, *you* are the heir."

Before she could reply, her father turned on his heel and swept back inside.

Elena watched him go, suddenly uneasy. Slowly, she smoothed her sari, and returned to Samson.

"Lead the way," she said, voice carefully neutral.

She followed her fiancé down the embankment, Ferma and Yassen trailing behind. They reached a tent of the commanding officers. At their approach, the Black Scales came to attention, their hands crossing their chests in salute.

"Hail the sun and her flaming sword!" they cried.

"At ease," Samson said, and they immediately relaxed.

As he introduced each officer to her, Elena could not help but notice how the soldiers leaned toward Samson. How they hung on every word he spoke. His very presence engulfed them. She saw their undying devotion, the forged steel of brotherhood, and she understood a very plain truth. While King Leo had built his reign on fear, Samson had built his power through hard-won victories and shared suffering. He knew his men, and they in turn loved him for it.

She smiled at the last officer and then turned to Samson.

"I just need a moment," she said.

Concern knitted his brows, but Elena squeezed his elbow and offered another smile. She ducked out of the tent, where Ferma and Yassen stood waiting. The day had grown hotter, and the sand baked beneath her feet.

"Are you all right?" Ferma asked.

"Could you bring me some water?" She fanned her face with her hand. "It's too hot."

The Yumi nodded and strode in the direction of the refreshments tent, leaving her alone with Yassen. A sudden, awkward silence loomed between them.

Elena cleared her throat. "Listen, about the game—"

"It's all right. I suppose I deserved it," he said.

"You didn't." She shifted her weight, chewing her lip. "Not really. So. I'm sorry. I should have stepped back when I realized you wouldn't use the Unsung."

"Ah, you noticed."

"Of course. Your feet," she began, gesturing and then realizing how silly it looked to be waving her hand at his feet. She clasped her hands behind her back. "You walk like a warrior. Where did you learn?"

"The Arohassin." It was his turn to shift uncomfortably. "We had a teacher who was trained in the Unsung, and she taught us. Didn't do her much good though, in the end. She was blown up by one of your soldiers."

"Oh. Well, good for us."

Yassen smiled. "She was shit, anyway. Brilliant in the Unsung, but she had very little patience for incompetence."

"Sounds like someone I know," Elena said, thinking of her father. She glanced back inside the tent and hesitated. "Samson," she began and recalled the dark look in Leo's eyes. *Don't let him talk about peace.* "How well do you know him?"

He met her gaze, startled. "Why? Are you getting cold feet?"

She scowled. "I don't—"

"You don't often find men like him," he added and gave a mirthless grin.

"Do you always interrupt people?"

"Not queens, no." For a moment, he looked sheepish. He held out his hands in apology and looked into the tent. "You've had other suitors, but you chose him. Why?"

"The others never offered anything good enough," she responded flatly.

And it was true. She thought of the allergy-afflicted prince from Cyleon and the overbearing bachelor king of Mandur. They and others had come calling for her hand. She had seen the privilege within them, the diffident nonchalance of men who believed everything and everyone served them. They had all demanded that she take the mantle of queen in their kingdom, Ravence a tributary territory. They had all left with bruised egos.

She was Elena Aadya Ravence above all else. And no man would ever take her birthright away from her.

Elena groaned as she sank onto the bench before her great windows. After the Black Sands demonstration, she had gone from meeting to meeting, discussing preparations for the coronation, the ball, and the upcoming festival. Somehow, Ferma had managed to slip in an evening training session. The Spear refused to let her use a slingsword *and* she had blindfolded her. Elena had to use her senses to predict the movement of the sand and her opponent. She had only lasted three minutes.

Sighing, she shook the sand from her hair. Night was falling, and the red sky slowly bled into deeper purple hues. It reminded her of plums, her mother's favorite, the sweet, rare fruit harvested only during the summer. Elena glanced at the bowl in her foyer, but it held only mangoes and unshaved lychees. A pang of nostalgia went through her.

She went to her closet, past the racks of silky saris and spangled lehengas and flowing gowns, to the farthest corner. Bending, she withdrew a brown cloak from the lower shelf. Dust swirled through the air as she shook it out, and she coughed. The cloak was rough to the touch and held no embellishments, no regal bearings. It would do.

Elena donned the cloak. She grabbed a plain scarf, wrapping it around her neck, and the pod with the reports against Jangir. Back in her bedroom, she squatted beside the fireplace. A few flames flickered quietly there, as if dreaming. She took a glass orb and scooped out a single ember. It hissed, reeling. Elena almost dropped the orb, but the flame curled back into itself and held. She let out a low breath.

In the small shrine, the diya lit up the golden statue of the Phoenix. Hesitating, Elena set the orb beside it and knelt before the shrine.

She was not one for prayer. In fact, she did not know all the words, much to Saayna's chagrin, but she knew the songs, the dances. Knew how to imitate the wings of the Phoenix with just a bend of her arms, a flick of her wrist.

"I don't know if you hear me, or if you're listening," she said softly. The Phoenix gazed back at her, stoic and silent. "But I hope you are. I hope you are watching over us all."

Her father did not believe in the Phoenix. Though he hid it well, he regarded the priests and their god with a certain detachment. And Elena understood him, in a way. She could not fathom how her mother, Saayna, or the order could believe in something unseen so completely, so blindly. How they devoted their lives to a god they could not touch, could not hear.

But as Elena poured more mustard oil into the diya to feed the light, she thought she saw a glimpse of what they saw: reassurance. To know that someone, something, was listening to them. And even if that god was false, even if it turned out the heavens were nothing but cold, distant stars, their belief would live on, warmed by their faith.

"Give me strength."

Aahnah had been the one who had taught her how to light the diya, how to sing praises of the Phoenix. As Elena felt the warmth of the flame beneath her cupped hands, she heard her mother's voice. The soft lilt, the measured pauses, the bliss on her face as she had turned to Elena and wafted the smoke over her head.

"You are blessed, my darling," she had said. "My little girl of fire."

Elena pressed her trembling hands against her eyes. She thought of her mother, kneeling before the Phoenix in the palace shrine, the fervor in her voice as she sang, the contentment in her eyes, and Elena willed herself to feel the same. "Holy Bird, protector of our realm. Goddess of this world and the worlds thereafter. Help me learn how to hold fire."

The diya fluttered. The Phoenix gleamed down, silent.

The sky was pitch black as she descended into her garden and approached the fountain. Carefully, Elena turned the stone bird perched on its lip, and the base of the fountain shifted back, revealing marble steps. For a moment, Elena hesitated, hand reaching for her holopod to call Ferma. She planned to meet Varun, then go to the desert to practice the forms

141

drawn in the scroll. But while Ferma may be up for the former, she definitely would not be for the latter.

Fire is dangerous. It's pure chaos, Ferma had said. *You can't learn to wield it with only a scroll.*

But what other option did she have if her father refused to teach her?

Elena descended into the tunnels, yet instead of veering right to the library passage, she turned left. A chill crept beneath the desert, and she pulled her cloak tighter. The scroll rustled within her sleeve.

As she neared the city, the tunnel sloped upward. A metal grate, as tall as a man, covered the exit. Elena peeked out. The alley was dark, empty. Drawing a deep breath, she stepped back and whispered, "As above, so below."

The sensors clicked and the metal grate rumbled and then parted a mere two feet. Elena scooted through, making sure it shut behind her. She walked quickly, careful not to draw attention to herself or her means of arrival as she entered the Thar district, a large, winding network of alleys, bars, and small firestone squares.

Floating orbs and neon signs lit the wide street as drunken couples stumbled out of pubs. On the corner, she spotted a gulmohar tree. Even in the night, its scarlet flowers burned against the dark sky, like little tendrils of flame.

Elena slowed as she approached the beggar who sat beneath the branches. A thin wisp of smoke curled from his blue lips. He looked up at her with dazed, drugged eyes.

"You," he said, and then his lips curled back into a snarl. "What are you doing here?"

Elena stopped. Across the street, city dwellers mingled around a pub, oblivious to her presence.

"What are you talking about?"

"You don't belong here, Sesharian," the beggar cried. He raised a shaky finger. "You and your filthy kind should rot on your island."

She wanted to retort that she wasn't a Sesharian, that she was Ravani, just like him, but something made her hold her tongue.

She looked at the man. "Careful, old man," she said, "Sesharians are welcome here, but I heard there's no place for intolerance under the new queen."

The beggar laughed. "The heir is a whore for that vile islander. I heard his men take turns fucking her."

Her face burned with mortification. Underneath her cloak, the fire in the orb hissed. Elena took a step back. *He's drugged. He has no senses.*

Yet a part of her wanted to punch the man, to drag him through the sands for the vile words. Elena glanced around and saw that some of the pub crowd had noticed them, throwing curious glances her way.

"What's going on here?"

A gold cap was striding toward them. At the sight of him, the beggar paled.

Shit.

"Are you here disturbing the peace?"

The beggar snorted. He met the gold cap's gaze, but Elena saw how his hand shook as he raised his pipe and took a drag. "What's it to you?"

"It means everything to me." The gold cap smiled. "You see, if you're a danger to the king's peace, I'll have to remove you."

"Buzz off," the beggar said, blowing smoke in his face.

The gold cap blinked. Smiled wider. Elena saw more gold caps weaving through the pub gatherers. She stepped back.

"What is it that you're smoking?" the gold cap asked. He sniffed. "Smells like Jantari ganja."

The beggar laughed, wheezing. "Jantari? Not in my lifetime. Their shit tastes like burnt metal."

With his attention on the beggar, the gold cap did not notice Elena back away.

"Oh, so you have smoked Jantari hash?" The gold cap grinned as the beggar realized the trap. "And where did you get it?"

"I don't—"

"Sounds like you have a connection. Maybe you're a spy." He grabbed the beggar, yanked him up. "Why don't we have a chat."

Elena lingered, torn. Even though the beggar had been crude and insulting, the gold cap was worse. But if she helped the beggar now, the gold caps could discover her. They'd find her pod, her scroll. Her father would learn of her ploy with Varun.

She took another step back as the beggar shouted. No one came to his aid; the crowd had hustled into the pub.

"Sister, are you all right?" another gold cap asked.

But Elena was already turning.

Just find Varun. Then it's just you and the desert.

"Sister!"

She walked faster, threw a glance back. The beggar was struggling, and the gold cap who had called to her was now gesturing to his friends.

Elena clenched her fists, but she did not slow. *Damn them.* Her face burned with shame, her chest twisting as she strode farther away. She had no power over the gold caps, not when she was in disguise, not even when she was in her regalia. They ruled the streets without consequence; her father turned a blind eye to their infractions. The flames thrummed underneath her cloak, as if sensing her anger.

Just wait. Wait until I'm queen.

Elena wrapped a scarf around her face as she turned down a street bright with vivid neon lights. Bars lined the entire avenue, and the air was hazy from smoke. A drunk partygoer sang at the top of her lungs. A merchant ignored her and pushed past her with a cart lined with cones of spiced makhana. Elena's stomach rumbled. The late-night food scene in Rani was the best in the nation, and in her opinion, the best on the second continent. The last time she had snuck out alone, she had gorged on aloo chat to the point that she felt bloated and lethargic in the morning.

"Brother," she called out to the merchant and realized with a start that it was Eshaant.

"Dealer," the merchant said warmly. "I know that voice. What brings you here?"

"Business." She smiled and remembered that he could not see it behind her scarf. "I thought you were to leave for Cyleon."

"Soon," Eshaant said. The blue lights deepened the wrinkles on his face, the curve of his grin. "I just need to earn some more coin for the journey."

"Where's the chaas?"

"I'll get to it," Eshaant said. "But I did make the makhanas spicier."

"Well, one cone then."

As he handed her the snack, she leaned closer. "Have you seen a short gold cap with a mole on his left cheek tonight?"

She knew Varun frequented this part of town, mostly to eat and fuck, and had earned a reputation for spending money on boys with pretty green eyes.

Eshaant raised an eyebrow. "You still have business with the gold caps? Dealer, I warned you."

"I'll be fine," she said. "Have you seen him?"

He didn't answer. Sighing, Elena tapped her holopod again, giving him a gracious tip.

"He just left Flower Bud," he said. "Should be off to Karishma now."

"You could have said that just as easily without a bribe."

"Well, how will I get to Cyleon then?" Eshaant grinned, winking. "Good luck, dealer."

Elena smiled as she walked away. She pressed her pod, sending Eshaant another tip, one large enough for the fare between here and Cyleon. Even if he had given up hope on Ravence, she wished the best for him.

Besides, she thought, *he'll make a killing selling chaas to Cyleoni.*

Elena slipped a makhana beneath her scarf as she skirted past the drunk singer, hooking left to the blue doors of Karishma. It was a large, three-storied club. After tracking Varun's movements for the last few months, she knew he was likely on the second floor. She just hoped he would be unoccupied.

Elena crept around the back of the building and stashed her orb behind an abandoned cart. The scroll was too precious—she would keep it with her. She jammed a handful of makhana in her mouth and then threw away the cone. Ducking inside, she pushed past a throng of sweaty bodies dancing under phosphorescent lights that pulsed in time with the music. The beat pounded against the wall like a beast raging against its cage. Whiskey sloshed on her cloak. One drunk, pretty girl grabbed the end of her scarf, pulling her into a kiss. Elena quickly sidestepped her, smiling, and darted up the stairs.

There were more people here, this time dancing to the older tunes of a once-famous cinema star, now dead. As she pushed toward the back, the music faded. A thick red curtain separated the back rooms from the crowd.

"Dealer." The guard nodded. "Here to see Varun?"

"Fai." The Cyleoni was a big man, twice as large as her and twice as slow. "Not going to stop me this time, hmm?"

The last time she had ventured into Karishma, she had caught Fai on a bad day. He tried to demand money from her, for "aiding her in her dealings," but Ferma had been there to step in.

"Your friend isn't here with you." Fai stepped forward, though Elena noticed with a smile that his throat bobbed as he scanned the crowd. "Or is she hanging back?"

"I just need to see Varun quickly," Elena replied. "Is he . . . occupied?"

"Not yet, so be quick." Fai smirked. "But you'll need to empty your pockets before you go in."

"Fai." She sighed. "We've been over this. Do you want me to send you ass over head into the drunks?"

"I'd like to see you try." He stepped forward again, massive under the lights, and for a moment, Elena wavered. Maybe she *should* have brought Ferma. She had the scroll on her, and if Fai ended up ripping it . . .

Fuck.

"You really don't learn, do you?" Elena sank her weight back into her heels, tucking the scroll in her back waistband, but before she could kick him in his solar plexus as she planned, the curtain was thrown back.

Varun, clothing rumpled and buttons askew, stared between her and Fai. "Phoenix's mercy, what is all this noise?" he demanded. "Dealer?"

"I want to speak with you," she said.

"I'm *busy.*"

"It'll only be a moment."

"Dealer, not tonight," Varun said, turning. She glimpsed a rather beautiful young man exiting a room in the back. "Get rid of her, Fai."

"It's about the pod," she said.

Varun froze. Fai raised an eyebrow, but Varun waved him away. He grabbed her elbow and led her to a darkened corner.

"Do we need to talk about this *now*?" he hissed under his breath.

"You haven't leaked the reports," she said. "Why not?"

"I'm timing it." He glanced furtively past her into the crowd. "Jangir suspects I'm up to something, so I'm lying low for now."

"When will you leak it?"

"When I find the perfect moment, I'll let you know. Through the pod, okay. Now, if you'll excuse me—"

Elena grabbed his elbow, pinching the nerves, and he gasped, struck still. "What in the seven hells—"

"My people have chosen you, Varun. But they are impatient. If you don't leak the reports in the next week, they might just choose someone else to be our champion."

She let him go. Varun stumbled forward, rubbing his elbow.

"All right, all right, Phoenix Above." He wiped his forehead. "Just— just give me two days. I'll send you word."

She stepped forward and he automatically stepped back, hands rising in defense. Smoothly, she reached out and buttoned his collar.

"Make sure you do, Varun." She took out the pod from her pocket. "Or else *my* patience will wear thin."

As she turned to go, Varun called out to her. "That...thing you did there. That was the Unsung, wasn't it?"

Elena blinked. "What?"

"It's—it's a trick the boys use in certain places. To, uh, help relax clients. One of them told me it comes from the Unsung." Varun eyed her suspiciously. "How do you know it?"

Elena simply walked away without answering, heart hammering as she pushed through the dancing masses and stumbled into the open air.

Shit, shit!

If Ferma were here, she would curse her down to the bottom of the seven hells. Berate her for potentially blowing her cover.

Everyone knew that only elite soldiers and warriors were trained in the Unsung. Them, and the royal family. Sure, some people knew of pressure points for party tricks, but what she had done was *definitely* not that. If Varun put two and two together, he might puzzle out who she was. And what would people say if the new monarch of Ravence was caught trying to dismantle her father's beloved gold caps?

They'd turn against me, Elena thought bitterly. First the gold caps, then the populace, spurred on by Jangir. Only the rebels and anarchists would be on her side. And they were a group Elena would never want to be a part of.

I need the desert.

There, she could breathe. Think. Maybe salvage her mistake.

She reclaimed her stashed orb and then strode quickly past the bright bars, heading to the western outskirts of the city. She tugged her scarf free as the streets emptied. Eventually, the dunes curved up before her. The twin moons sloped into perfect, mirrored crescents. Nothing stirred or rustled in the night. The stillness felt like a blanket, its silence a cool relief. Elena breathed in the sharp, cold air, her stomach slowly unknotting. To the inexperienced eye, the desert looked endless. Overwhelming.

But Elena knew that the curve of this dune differed from the one before it. She understood how the desert moved in the wind, how it shifted to form new masses. This was her home.

Elena hopped down a rocky face into the bowl of a dune. She came before a stone overhang. Three lines were chiseled into the rock. She had marked this place long ago when she had trained with Mahira's sand raiders. The cave was small but deep.

Perfect to stash a secret.

Elena withdrew the orb as she ducked inside. Its light beat back the shadows to reveal a black tarp, which she flung aside. Beneath was a smooth silver cruiser. With a grin, she rested her hand on its glass control panel, and it flickered to life.

She placed the orb inside the back compartment and mounted. It had been a while since she had been riding, but as she gripped the worn leather handles, it all came back to her. Months in the desert flying over dunes, zipping through valleys, barreling through sand hovels. The wild, precarious nature of it. The thrill of it. The freedom.

Elena pressed the pedal, and the cruiser jolted forward. She shot up the lip of the dune, and then she was off.

Wind whipped back her scarf and the hood of her cloak. Sand sprayed her face. The dunes rose and melted past her as she followed their curves and valleys. The sky opened up for her. The stars spilled out, and Elena felt a contagious sense of euphoria bubble up in her throat.

Here, there were no guards, no generals, no king who could hold her back. Here, it was only her. Her and the wide, unspooling desert.

After some time, when she was sure she had not been followed, Elena slipped into a valley and killed the engine. She estimated she had ventured several miles. The dunes towered above her, blocking out the twin moons, but not the stars. They scattered above her and shone with such brilliance that she almost forgot about fire. Its orange, shifting light paled in comparison to the radiance of the heavens.

Perhaps this was what Alabore Ravence had felt when he first came to the desert. He must have realized that the night held the same power as the day. And so he had sought the help of the twin moons to build his kingdom—his dream of peace.

Elena opened the back compartment and looked down at the orb, at its single flickering flame. She grabbed it, as well as the pulse gun stashed beneath, then moved toward a dune, stepping lightly so that her feet only left shallow depressions in the sand.

As she neared the top of the dune, Elena froze. There, on the other side, silhouetted against the night, was a man. She could make out the light hair, the pale skin of a familiar ghostlike figure. Yassen sat on the crest with his back to her. He looked perfectly relaxed, as if he had been lounging in this desert for countless suns.

"What are you doing here?" she called out. Her heart thundered in her ears as she felt for the pulse gun beneath her cloak. They were alone in the deep desert. She had no guards, no Spear. Here, Yassen could kill her. The palace would not be able to find her body for days.

"Enjoying the quiet night," he said without turning. He ran his fingers through the sand. There was something eerie about him, and a voice in her head whispered to get out, to turn back, but Elena stood her ground.

"I mean, how did you find this place?"

"I didn't," he said.

"No one knows about this spot."

Yassen turned. His eyes almost looked translucent. Again she fought the urge to flee. This was her desert. She would not abandon it.

"But I know my way through the desert," he said. He stood and dusted the sand off his pants. The metal bird on his uniform glinted in the moonlight. A breeze sighed over the dunes.

She gripped the handle of her pulse gun as Yassen approached her. He stopped just a few feet shy. The twin moons peeked over the top of his head like whispering spirits. In their light, he looked younger—his face unlined and his mouth soft. It was as if the desert wind had lifted the weight that bowed his shoulders.

"People only roam the desert when they're running. Or searching for something." His eyes moved from her face to the orb. "What's all this?"

She held it away from him. For some reason, she felt that he would try to extinguish the flame.

"Why I'm here is none of your business," she said.

"And why bring a flame?"

"Also none of your business."

Yassen walked closer, and she took a step back. Her hand went to the gun, but stopped when he held out his hands, his fingers splayed, empty.

"I didn't come to hurt you," he said. "To be honest, I was off duty and visiting the city when I recognized you buying makhana. So I followed you. I thought I lost you in the crowd, but then there you were, leaving a bar and heading to the desert."

"But how did you get all the way out *here* before me?" she pressed. She had made sure no one had been following her.

"I nicked a cruiser and cut through the desert after you. It died just over that hill, so I walked."

"What?"

She leaned over and saw footprints in the distance, coming from the direction in which Yassen pointed.

"How did you know where I was going?" She eyed him but spotted no pulse gun. Not even a slingsword.

Yassen shrugged. "I just followed the noise of your cruiser. You took an awful lot of time getting up here."

The pulse gun felt smooth beneath her fingertips. She could shoot him now, before he tried anything. Yassen still had his hands out before him.

But if she killed him now, Samson and her father would ask questions, and that would eventually lead them to her escapade in the city. To Varun.

"Seems like you needed some space," he said. He lowered his hands and gestured out toward the desert. "All the quiet, with no one to judge your shortcomings. Just you and the stars. A man could disappear out here, and no one would know it." His voice sounded wistful.

Elena regarded him suspiciously. "Don't get any ideas of running away. Mahira's raiders will track you down. *I'll* track you down."

"I know. That pulse gun you're holding could blast a nasty hole." A corner of his lip curled up, and Elena felt a nervous flutter in her chest. *He* had tracked *her* without her knowing. And if he could do that, would Mahira's raiders stand a chance if he ran away? "But you can't kill me now, can you?"

Elena cursed inwardly and drew her firearm. It hummed to life, the chamber glowing an eerie blue as she cocked it in his direction.

"What were you doing in the city?" she demanded.

"I haven't had pav bhaji in ages," he said. "So I went to Thar, which has the best in the city. There's a merchant, small man, on the corner—"

"Before the market," she said with him.

Phoenix Above, his story checks out. She had passed by that corner before turning toward the bars.

When she didn't say anything more, he pointed toward the orb with the flame.

"That's what you came out here for, right? You want to learn Agnee-path."

She inhaled sharply. Agneepath was an ancient word. It meant the path of fire; it was the word the high priestess uttered before her father sat on the dais. It was the word *she* would utter when she became queen—for the path of Ravence was forged by fire. The monarch must learn to hold the flames, to sit in the inferno so he or she could carry out the destiny Ala-bore Ravence had spun for them.

If Yassen knew she had come here to practice, he must know she couldn't hold fire.

"Who told you?" she asked, keeping the weapon aimed at his chest.

"The servants whisper," he said, "and I listen. I heard you almost burned the palace down the last time you tried."

Elena took a step back, her cheeks flushing in shame. Even Yassen Knight knew her shortcomings. Did the whole household know as well? What about the people?

He reached out and touched the barrel of her pulse gun, his eyes never leaving her. "You want me to burn. So be it. But I have a right to Ravence, as you do. This isn't just your home. It's mine too."

"You are a lying bastard," she spat. She shoved his hand away and raised the gun again. Yassen stepped back. "You worked for the people trying to destroy this kingdom. You helped them. You *betrayed* us."

"No," Yassen said, and his voice was thin. It made her hesitate. "That wasn't me. That was *them*," he said, and the weakness in his voice turned to disgust. "The Arohassin tricked us, brainwashed us. We were only kids. I didn't know any better. And now here I am, working with you—working *for* you—to try and amend what I have broken. Even knowing there's no forgiveness for me."

He spoke with a zeal that surprised Elena. She had never seen him so animated, so honest. She blinked; was this truly Yassen Knight standing before her?

He had brought her father the list of Arohassin agents. He served them up like pigs for slaughter. And he had not balked when the redheaded woman had called him a traitor. Samson had told her so.

A breeze swept up the sand as Yassen watched her. Despite the gun, he showed no fear. And a fearless man was a dangerous man. Her father had taught her that.

She could not trust Yassen. Not yet.

The sand drifted lazily across their feet, and Yassen cocked his head, as if listening to it.

"There's going to be a storm," he said.

She could sense the dunes shifting beneath her feet as the desert began to moan. It started as a murmur, an elusive sound, but as the wind picked up, it grew louder. The flame danced in its glass enclosure. Elena cursed and lowered her gun, hugging the orb to her chest to shield it.

"We'd better find cover," she said.

The dunes shuddered as they made their way down. She knew how to move without sinking, how to read the lines of the sands and the stars to guide her back to the sparkling city. To her surprise, Yassen remained only a few steps behind. He too moved lightly, though with half the grace.

They reached her cruiser as the sky clouded over and the heavens disappeared. Elena shoved the orb into the back compartment.

"Get on!" she shouted.

She slammed on the pedal, and they shot forward. Sand slashed their faces and clothes. The wind roared. A large, dark mass surrounded them as Elena revved the engine. She knew they couldn't outrun the storm. The city was too far.

She swerved, and they launched up a dune. The cruiser jumped the lip, skidding before Elena corrected it as they hurtled past rocks shaped like kneeling men. She squinted, spitting sand. She couldn't see any valleys or land markings, but she had grown up in this desert. It claimed her as much as she claimed it.

"Do you know where you're going?" Yassen shouted into the wind.

She didn't respond.

The overhang came out suddenly on their left. She nearly passed it but then yanked the handles, cutting across the rocks and launching into the cave.

A thick layer of sand shifted around the floor, but otherwise, the hovel was still. Elena gulped in air. The engine's hum filled the space; Yassen reached around and turned it off, the sudden silence ringing in her ears. After a moment, she could hear the muffled shriek of the storm raging outside.

She dug out a canteen of water stowed in the cruiser's compartment. Yassen turned, studying the cave as she splashed her face. In its glass enclosure, her flame still lived, though it was smaller now.

"What is this place?"

Elena sighed as she sank to the floor. She cradled the orb, letting the warmth of the small fire seep into her chest. A drop of water curved down her chin, hissing as it fell into the flame.

"I stayed here during my registaan," she said.

Two months into her initiation, she had discovered this spot after chasing a desert hare. The small animal had hidden here, but when she cornered it into the back, it had leapt out and around her, rushing past. She had been too tired to pursue it. Now, as Elena stared around their small shelter, she whispered a silent thanks to the desert.

Yassen sank down across from her. His long legs splayed awkwardly in the small space.

"You knew the way despite the storm," he said, his voice tinged with awe.

"Your desert walk," she said, "it's proficient but sloppy. You've been gone from Ravence for too long."

"Thanks for the compliment, I guess." Yassen looked down at his hands. His voice was quiet. "But I'm here now. Aren't I?"

And he hadn't tried to harm her.

"These storms don't last long," she said.

"Ferma will be outraged."

She shot him a look. "We'll be back before morning."

Sand fell as Yassen ran his hand through his hair. He leaned back and closed his eyes. Elena placed her chin on her knees and listened to the storm. After a while, she heard him snoring softly.

She studied him. It was hard to imagine he was capable of assassinating kings and queens. Before her, she saw only a man too tired to be afraid of her.

As Yassen slept, Elena withdrew the scroll, unraveling it carefully. The fire flickered beside her. She used its light to trace the movements of the dance.

The forms of the woman looked even starker, her expressions fiercer. The text was written in Herra, the same ancient language the priests spoke in, but underneath each phrase, her mother had translated it into Hind.

Elena whispered the words underneath her breath. "Agneepath netrun. Fijjin a noor."

The path of fire is dangerous. Tread it with care.

Care. Did it mean *caution* or *love*—like how Aahnah had taught her to navigate the library and keep it a secret between them?

Elena thumbed the corner where her mother had drawn the jasmine. She remembered watching Aahnah prune delicate stems in her garden, her fingers lifting the leaves, her voice soft as she spoke to the flowers, treating them as if they were listening.

Elena pressed her hand against the warm glass. She needed to hold the flame with care, tenderness—but *how*?

Slowly, she rose. Yassen was as still as before. Elena set the orb before her and began to imitate the dancer.

She had grown up dancing and that skill had transferred to the art of the Unsung. After all, a fight was a dance. There was pull and push, a rhythm set between bodies that could be broken, twisted, or made anew at every turn. And this dance was the same except for one thing.

It wasn't a rhythm between two bodies.

It was between her and the inferno.

Elena folded her hands behind her, as drawn in the second form. The flame flickered. She tried to balance on her right foot, but she teetered. She flung out her arms to steady herself, and her left foot hit the cruiser. She nearly yelped.

Elena hopped on one leg and threw a sour glance at Yassen. His chest rose and fell in a steady rhythm. She let out a breath and resumed the first position.

It resembled the Warrior pose of the sun meditations—one that Ferma had drilled into her. This was a dance that required poise, rigidity, yet also softness. Dance, like many things, was an act of balance. She would need to regulate her breathing, to give and take from the air around her.

To empty her mind and heart and fill them with the brilliance of song. Except there were no drums to accompany her—only the wind's roar.

Elena rose from the Warrior and balanced on her right foot again. This time, she held steady as she folded her hands behind her back like the wings of a bird. She tried to intensify the strength of her pose, the fluidity of her movements. Sweat beaded down her brow, mixing with sand and dirt.

As she unfolded her arms and dipped her head, the fire bowed.

Elena gasped. The flame rose and licked the side of the glass bowl. She watched, transfixed, as it grew taller.

"You keep that up, and you'll set this place on fire."

Elena spun around, and the flame sputtered and died in a pile of ash.

Yassen sat as before, but his eyes were open. He held Elena in his gaze. For a moment, she felt like she couldn't move, that ice had lodged into the space between her bones as she stared into his strange, colorless eyes.

"So that's how the Ravani learn to hold fire," he said.

Elena did not reply as she rolled up the scroll, sliding it into her cloak. Yassen overturned the orb, ash spilling onto the cave floor.

"I've never heard of dancing being involved, though," he continued.

"Only the royal family can do it," she retorted hastily.

"So not us lowly commoners?" He looked up at her. "Don't you think that's a bit unfair?"

"We were the ones who were blessed." She grabbed the orb and stowed it away.

"But the Prophet can be anyone," he said. "They could be a commoner and learn to wield fire."

She scoffed. "As if you believe in the Prophet."

Yassen smiled faintly and looked down at his hands. Elena saw the mark on his wrist. The blackened skin.

"Have you been burned?" she whispered. When he didn't respond, Elena crouched before him and lightly tapped his arm. "How?"

"It's nothing," he said.

"You're lying," she said and grabbed his wrist. He resisted, but when she shot him a look, he allowed her to roll up his sleeve. She gave a tiny gasp.

His arm was covered with burn marks—deep red welts larger than her fingers. In the spaces between the marks, his skin was shriveled and brown.

"What happened?"

He hesitated. When he finally met her gaze, his eyes were cold. "The Arohassin."

"They burned you?"

"No, but—I was foolish. The job, something went wrong. I should have left when the alarms went off, but the Arohassin told me I would be free. One last job, and then it was over." He shook his head. "I was so desperate. So stupid."

She dropped his arm. Yassen looked down, concentrating on unrolling his sleeve. It occurred to her how little she knew about him beyond Muftasa's reports. She had never considered *why* he had defected. He could be playing them all, could still be working for the Arohassin, but one thing she knew for certain: Yassen Knight was too capable to be a blind follower. The Arohassin's ruthlessness may have hardened him, but it could have also nurtured a deep resentment—a resentment he now turned against them.

"No wonder you're afraid of fire," she whispered. Though the wind still roared, she sensed it beginning to tire. The storm would end soon.

"I—I," she began and stopped. Yassen watched her closely, waiting. "I'm afraid of the inferno too. Afraid of the burn. It hurts, when it shouldn't. Not for me, at least. My father can hold it without so much as a blister, but I . . ." She shook her head, suddenly overwhelmed by frustration. Her incompetence. "It's supposed to be my birthright, but I can't even *touch* a single fucking flame without getting singed. I don't understand how he does it. Only that I need to learn his secret before my coronation."

Yassen was quiet for a long moment.

"The path of fire burns everyone in the end," he said finally. "Isn't that what the scriptures say?"

Elena gave him a pained smile because she knew it was true.

They passed the time in wordless silence until the wind fell and the sky cleared. Through the mouth of the cave, they saw the faint colors of dawn splinter along the horizon. Elena started the cruiser as Yassen dusted sand from his clothing.

"We will not speak of this," she said. "Any of it."

He nodded and got on behind her. They zipped through the desert that lay open for them with new, unbaptized curves. It was so peaceful, so still, as if there had never been a storm.

Elena breathed in and felt Yassen inhale with her. His chest pressed against her back, his hands resting lightly on her hips. He was warm and, ever so slightly, she pressed into him as the chill morning air whipped her face. She thought she felt Yassen smile, his lips inches from her neck. When they reached the city outskirts, Elena stashed the cruiser in a run-down hut that had long been abandoned by its owners. She had no fear of anyone stealing it; any thief would need her fingerprints to start the vehicle.

The sun peeked over the dunes and slowly chased away the night's long shadows. She saw Yassen stretch like a cat, the light picking out the gold in his hair. When he noticed her looking, he stopped. A strange emotion shone in his eyes, but she couldn't identify it from this distance.

"I'll go on alone from here," she said.

"You should be careful with fire," he said, apropos of nothing.

She shook her head. It was an unnecessary warning. "Trust me, I know."

She left him standing there as sunlight spilled into the narrow alleyway and the city began to wake.

CHAPTER 16

LEO

Beware the Desert Spider. For she is fearless, and therefore, powerful.
—a Ravani proverb

The hoverpod is ready, Your Majesty."

"Thank you, Arish," Leo said, and his Astra dipped his head, walking away down the tarmac.

Leo turned back to look out at the dunes spreading beyond Palace Hill. Had it been another day, he would have relished the view. Traced the curves of the dunes with his eyes and listened to the wind nipping at his ears. But the urn was heavy in his hands. Its contents even more burdensome.

The girl with hair of starlight had not been the Prophet. He had collected her ashes himself into this urn and tried not to think about her flailing arms, her hair that had lit like a torch.

"Forgive me, damn me." He uncapped the urn and touched the rim. "Do what you must. But I hope you find peace, wherever you are, dear girl. May you find the fire that you believed so beautiful." He hesitated, fingers hovering above the ashes. "And if you are with the Phoenix Herself, I hope She is everything you dreamed Her to be."

Leo raised the urn and slowly spilled out its contents. "So we the blessed few," he murmured.

The grey flakes wavered in the air for a moment before dancing away with the wind. He watched them go and felt a great weight descend on his shoulders, worse than any he had carried in all his suns as king. How many more would he be forced to burn before he found the Prophet? How many more would die when the Prophet came into power?

Surely, the life of a girl will not matter against the lives of thousands. And yet . . . Leo blinked, throat tight. He was finding it harder to believe these days.

With heavy feet, he walked not to the waiting hoverpod but back into the palace. He needed to see Elena. To hold his daughter in his arms and be reminded that she—she was his anchor now. The reason he spilled ash into the singing wind.

He found her dancing. Her guru, a small woman older than he, sang out the rhythm as Elena spun, eyes closed, mouth relaxed. She looked beautiful. Achingly beautiful, like Aahnah. They both seemed so free when they danced.

Leo watched from the doorway, his chest twisting. He was finding it harder to breathe when the guru noticed him standing there. She stopped singing and shot to her feet.

"Your Majesty," she said, bowing. She scanned his face. "Is everything all right?"

Ferma and Yassen, who had been sitting on the benches, rose as well. The musicians stopped playing. Elena turned in confusion, and when she saw him, her face closed like a shuttered window. It hurt. Mother's Gold, that hurt.

"Father." Elena glanced at the guru, the musicians, and her guards. They hurriedly took their leave. When they were alone, his daughter turned to him. "What is it?"

"I," Leo began and stopped. He had come here on a sudden whim, a rush of emotion, really, which was unlike him, but then he remembered the young girl, the urn, and then he was striding across the room.

Elena startled, but he kissed his three fingers and placed them against her head.

"I," he said, voice thin, "I need to bless you. Saayna's orders."

It was a lie, but he could not bear to tell her the truth.

"Oh." And just like that, the hope that had glimmered for a brief moment in her eyes fizzled. "I thought you came to reconsider my request. About learning how to hold fire."

He wanted to tell her that she was better without it. That fire burned, in more ways than one. He may have learned how to withstand its heat, but the inferno devoured him from the inside, plaguing his thoughts.

He wanted to tell her that he only dreamed of ash now, flailing shadows trapped within a light. And that when he woke, he tasted soot on his tongue.

"Elena," he tried, but the words, thick and devious, would not come. "You—you look so free when you dance. So . . . confident. Like Aahnah."

He was evading the issue, he knew, but he could not find the strength now to tell her about the nature of fire and its demand for sacrifice—not when he had just scattered an innocent girl's ashes.

"One of the few things I know how to do well, apparently," Elena said.

She is as stubborn as her mother, Leo thought suddenly, and that truth made him smile.

"Why are you smiling?" his daughter asked cautiously.

"Oh, dear girl," Leo said. He took her hands in his, squeezed. "You are just like her. In the best ways. Stubborn and terrifyingly relentless."

"Terrifyingly relentless." Elena laughed then, low and sweet. Aahnah's laugh. "That is the perfect way to put it."

What did Aahnah always say?

" 'No stubborn woman,' " he said.

" '—has ever gone to bed dissatisfied, Malhari,' " Elena said with him. She grinned. "Mother was right. Because if she ever was upset—"

"Neither I nor she could sleep." He smiled. "And you used that as the perfect excuse to stay awake—"

"—and eat mangoes with her until you came and cleaned up the peels in apology." Elena shook her head, eyes bright with memory. The tightness in his chest eased, just a bit, to see her like this. It would not last for long, he knew. Arish would call him soon to the hoverpod, and he would be thrust back into the world of urns filled with death and a daughter who may grow to despise him for the secrets he kept, but for now—for now, *heavens above, let this moment stay.*

Leo kissed his three fingers again and rested them on Elena's temple. "You are your mother's daughter. Stubborn, yes, but so strong, Elena. So strong. She would be proud of you."

Elena smiled, but slowly her smile faded.

"What would she think of you, Father?" she asked in a soft voice.

Arish rapped on the door then. "Your Majesty, Your Highness." He bowed. "We must go."

Leo turned back to Elena, torn in his answer. Because he knew what Aahnah would think. He had heard her voice in the flames around his study.

Oh selfish, selfish Malhari.

"That I am doing my best to protect you and this kingdom," he said. "That all I do is for you."

Leo rubbed his temples. He had felt the beginning of a migraine crawl up his neck and the back of his head after his meeting with Elena. A cup of tea would help, but he had no time. He had yet another war council with his generals, and the plans for the ball still needed to be addressed, on top of interrogating the captured Arohassin agents—

"Your Majesty," Samson said, interrupting Leo from his thoughts.

Leo closed his eyes. He took a deep breath and then regarded his future son-in-law.

"About the ball—I think it might help if we invite Farin," Samson said.

Leo tried his best to keep the venom out of his voice. "Farin. The king of Jantar? Really?"

They were seated in a hoverpod heading north for Badala, a black site that lay deep within the dunes. It was an unmarked location, invisible on all military maps. It was where they sent high-level prisoners or any enemies of the state. Ravani Intelligence oversaw its daily operations. Muftasa reported occasionally about the site's inner workings, but Leo was careful not to ask too many questions. As far as he was concerned, the base did not exist. Except for today.

Saayna was imprisoned at Badala, but he knew he could not keep the high priestess there for long. Elena was due for an Ashanta ceremony next week, and the coronation would follow. They would need Saayna for both. But until then, Leo intended to make the high priestess sweat.

"I know you think he won't come," Samson said. "But he will. Because *I* am here, and he wants to make sure I'm being a good pet."

"And are you?" Leo asked. "Has Farin contacted you since the Black Sands march?"

Samson nodded. "He found it a bit theatrical, but he thinks I'm playing the part of a chivalrous knight to a queen. You know, lending her my sword even if I mean to take it back. He wants me to pull my troops when he gives the command."

"And when will that be?"

Samson shrugged. "I'm not sure. Could be months from now, perhaps a year. Farin doesn't tell me everything."

"We will have to strike faster, if the peace talks fail." And Leo knew they would.

"I will, but we need to keep up appearances," Samson said. "Invite him. Talk to him. Pretend that you and Elena are earnest in your commitment to peace while I pretend that my fealty is still with him."

"Farin and I cannot sit in one room for long," Leo said. He did not mention how Farin's metal eye unnerved him. "Besides, he's a horrible dancer."

Samson grinned. "Jantari metalmen usually are. You just have to grease their joints a bit. It's nothing Elena and I can't handle."

Leo pursed his lips. He wondered how well his daughter and Samson were getting along. Though they had only known each other for a matter of weeks, Elena could charm anyone. That was her gift. But did she know of the gravity of marriage? His had not been long, but still, a healthy royal couple meant a strong kingdom, a continued royal line ... heavens, he was starting to sound like his own father.

"Fine. Send the invitation," Leo said finally. "Though I hardly believe Farin will come."

"Oh, he will," Samson said. "Especially if Elena and I enclose our personal greetings."

As if that would make any difference to Farin. But Leo kept that thought to himself.

Arish joined them at the upper level of the hoverpod, bearing a cup of tea.

"For your headache, sir," he said, and Leo smiled.

"Heavens bless you, Arish."

After thirty suns, Arish had learned to read all his mannerisms. The Astra had also proved to be the most insightful person in his court; he had an uncanny way of recognizing and predicting the future. He was the first to tell Leo about Yassen Knight's defection, and when Leo had pushed further, Arish had simply answered that he had heard so from a nomad in the market. Leo had no need to doubt him. Arish had strange ways of procuring information, but his information had always proven correct. And he made great tea.

Leo took a sip and almost sighed in contentment. It was delightfully warm and soothing.

He looked out the window. Thick clouds layered the horizon, and without the sun, the desert looked harder, full of sharp edges rather than delicate curves. And there were shadows. Long, black specters that cut across the sand to claw their way toward him.

And then a creeping sensation chilled the blood in his veins. Leo suddenly felt as if his body was not his own, that he was floating. He looked down and saw himself sitting by the hoverpod window, Arish and Samson sitting before him. He could see Arish's lips move, but there was no sound. He tried to cry out. He tapped the window, but neither man turned.

The world turned and shifted into watercolors of grey. The hoverpod dissolved. He was floating over the desert, the dunes stretching on for miles in every direction. The sky began to melt in thick, heavy drops. When it hit the ground, the sand hissed. It blurred beneath him, stretching and mutating until he was floating over a valley.

Leo gasped.

There, burned in the valley, were two runes.

One was a leafless tree. The other was a simple circle with a singular dot in its center. Leo reached for them.

The desert screamed. Shards of sand cut through his body. He fell.

"Stop," he cried. "Stop!"

"Your Majesty?"

Leo opened his eyes to see Arish and Samson staring at him.

"Stop what?" the Astra asked. "We're nearly at the outpost."

Leo stood, his heart hammering. He was in the hoverpod, the dunes rolling beneath him without pause as they flew north. Gone were the harsh shadows.

Leo swiped sweat from his brow. His vision swam, and he stumbled. Arish flung out an arm to steady him.

"I—I—" he stuttered.

Arish gently lowered him back into his seat. Leo felt as if someone were pushing needles into his brain. He looked down at his hands. They were shaking.

"I saw something in the desert," he said. His voice was thin, raspy. "Runes."

"But, Your Majesty, you were here. I'm afraid I may have bored you to sleep—"

Leo straightened. *Had it been a dream?*

Samson offered him water, and Leo drank greedily.

"Are you all right?" he asked, eyes curious.

"Yes, yes." Leo waved him away as the hoverpod began to descend.

The Badala outpost was a series of sand-colored buildings that blended into the landscape. Long ago, this site had once kept and trained the Desert Spiders—a fierce coalition of warriors handpicked by Alabore Ravence himself. But the warriors had fallen out of fashion after Alabore's rule. Now, they were fairy tales meant for Ravani children.

A ring of soldiers stood around the landing pad, their arms crossed over their chests in salute. When the hoverpod docked, Leo shakily rose to his feet. The pain in his head came in waves. In one moment, it grew so gruesome that he felt he would disintegrate on the spot. In another, he could see the world with razor-like clarity.

Leo gritted his teeth and slowly walked out, determined not to appear weak before his men. He motioned for the soldiers to be at ease.

"Muftasa," Leo greeted his intelligence officer as she walked forward.

The small woman was dressed in the garb of a soldier, and she would have easily passed for one if not for her noodle-armed salute.

"Your Majesty," she said. "Arish, Samson. There's something you need to see."

She led them into the dark, quiet halls of Badala to the main room of the largest building, where a wall of holos curved up the domed ceiling. Each holo was a part of a photograph that spanned the length of the room. When Leo saw the image they created, he froze.

The two runes stared back at him.

"I saw this," he whispered, shaken.

Muftasa turned sharply. "That's impossible. Our drones found them not fifteen minutes ago."

But Leo shook his head. These were the runes in his...dream or hallucination or whatever it was. A wave of nausea swept over him, and he swayed.

"Saayna," he said through gritted teeth. *Only she can make sense of this.* "Take me to her."

Muftasa studied him for a long moment. Then she pressed a panel, and a chamber opened to their left. "This way."

Leo and his party followed Muftasa into a white, circular room with skylights. Soft shadows slunk down the bare walls. At its center, Saayna sat cross-legged on a floor cushion. She opened her eyes as they entered.

"So you've seen them," she said, a smile in her voice.

A distant roar commenced in Leo's ears. He staggered forward, but his knees buckled and he sank to the floor.

"What are they?" he asked, spots dancing in his eyes.

"Something the Eternal Fire wished for you to see," she said. Her eyes were wide and bright. "You have sat in the flames, tasted their ash. They can send visions and call to you any time they please."

"But what of the runes? What do they mean?"

The high priestess looked up, and Leo followed her gaze. He thought he would see what she saw, perhaps a shining emblem of the Phoenix or the heavens themselves, but he saw only the dark underbellies of storm clouds.

"They say, 'The Prophet shall be reborn.'" She fixed him with her dark eyes. "And she will begin her warpath at the palace."

Any other king would have balked. Any other man would have pleaded for forgiveness. But his father, before he had fallen into madness, had taught Leo how to root out a lie.

Leo heard it in her voice—the slight tremble, the hitched breath. He had suspected deceit from the beginning, when she had first translated the runes. But as Leo looked at Saayna now, as her eyes shifted away from his, he sensed something else: foul play.

"We will map the runes," he said sharply. "All of them. Join them together and see where they lead."

He heard Saayna inhale, and he smiled. The high priestess had mapped the first two runes and declared that the Prophet was in the capital. But if they led somewhere else? Somewhere the high priestess did not wish him to look.

Samson called for a holopod and, with the help of Muftasa, began to overlay images of the runes on a map of Ravence. Leo kept his eyes on Saayna until they were finished.

When he looked at the holopod, the roar in his ears became distant.

The runes joined together to create a large, smoldering maze that cut through Ravence. And within the center of the labyrinth, there lay no demon, but the Temple of Fire.

"The Prophet is a priest," he whispered.

All this time, she had been in his grasp. All this time, the Prophet had grown in the shadow of his throne and in the care of holy men. He had given her food and shelter, prepared her in the ways of fire. She had watched him perform Ashanta ceremonies knowing one day that the Eternal Fire would claim him and his family.

The high priestess had sent him on a wild shobu chase. *She* had made him kill the girl.

Leo laughed, a dry, bitter laugh. Saayna bristled, shifting away from him.

He looked at the high priestess. She was no Prophet. She had no marks, and she burned just as easily as the others.

Still, he ordered a match. Arish brought it, and Leo struck it against the floor. The match flared to life. Without warning, Leo grabbed Saayna's hand.

"What was it you said to me once—that people go astray without their leaders? That it is the role of the Prophet to lead us to enlightenment?" She struggled as he held her hand to the flame, but Leo only tightened his grip. Slowly, he pressed the match into Saayna's palm. She yelped and flinched as there came a soft hiss and the smell of burnt flesh.

"You are the first to burn," he said, his gaze never breaking. "And all the priests you've taught will burn after you. This is your path of enlightenment, Saayna, the path your Prophet will bring—one of madness. Destruction."

He tossed the match, stamped on it, and stood. Gone was his headache. Adrenaline took its place, along with a surge of hope.

"I will not allow your insanity to endanger this kingdom," he said. "I will burn your priests one by one until I find your Prophet. And then I will bury her in cold stone to end this cycle."

Saayna cradled her hand to her chest, tears pricking the edges of her eyes. Still, when she spoke, her voice was clear. "Watch the winds. They don't dance in your favor."

For a moment, Leo hesitated. He'd already damned himself by burning that innocent girl. What would happen to him when he burned the priests? Killing a child from the street was one thing, killing the priests of the Fire Order quite another. His gold caps, who were frequent visitors of the temple, would sense something amiss. *Elena* would sense something amiss. If the public learned about this, Prophet or no Prophet, *they* would surely call for him to be hung.

Leo glanced at Saayna and then to the city map, his anger cooling. *No, I can't march in and just burn the priests without others noticing. But . . .*

"You made me burn a girl," he told Saayna. "An innocent child. I will not make that mistake again." He turned to Muftasa. "End the search for the girls in the city. Cut off all public visitations to the temple. Say that the holy site is closed in preparation for the coronation and that the priests are secluding themselves within the mountain to fast and commemorate the event. Tell them they won't emerge until after the ceremonial week."

Muftasa accepted the command, but he did not miss her strained expression. Saayna hissed, rising to her feet.

"Word will break," she said.

"Perhaps," Leo said. "But we'll move faster, won't we? Arish, block all signals and communications to the temple, unless they're military or palace. As of today, the Temple of Fire is a black site. Nothing goes in or out without my knowing."

Saayna shook her head. "You cannot stop the Prophet. You cannot kill the order. This is *blasphemy*!" She tried to lunge at him, but Arish held her back. "You're mad, just like your father. So do not blame your crimes on me. *You* did this. *You* will bring chaos on us all."

"I'll do what it takes to secure the welfare of my country," Leo said.

He turned on his heel, leaving Saayna calling after him. He swept out of the Badala outpost, to the darkening desert beyond. Once outside, he stopped and stared at the mountains that lay to the west.

His father had warned him about the power of religion—the way it charmed believers to give up their thinking and follow not with their minds but with their hearts. Their weak, malleable hearts.

The high priestess was wrong. People did not go astray because they had no leader or Prophet. They became lost because they succumbed to weakness, to the soft part that wanted to be safe. They would rather chant hymns and worship a god than realize they had given themselves to a deity who did not care if they lived or died in Her name.

He pressed his fingers into his eyelids. When he opened them, his vision held steady.

The Eternal Fire did not need to burn a man to destroy him. It could eat him from within. Leo had seen it happen to his father. The old king had screamed and pulled out his hair on his deathbed, leaving Leo, a newly crowned king then, to handle the pressures of a kingdom without the former regent's guidance.

But Elena will not be alone. Leo breathed in deeply. Unlike King Ramandra, he still had his wits about him. *I will not go mad. I will not allow it.*

He may not be the Prophet, but Leo knew he was stronger. He was the one who could stand in the harsh glare of the sun and still find his way.

CHAPTER 17

YASSEN

There once were two lovers: a Yumi and a man. They cared for each other deeply, but their kind would not accept their union. One night, in anguish, the pair met under the stars and cried out their love. So moved were the gods that they turned the lovers into the moons, Chand and Chandhini. "They shall live together in eternity," the gods said, "and give light to those who must meet in the secrecy of night."

—from *The Legends and Myths of Sayon*

Hello, Giorna."

Yassen sat down as Giorna settled back in her seat, eyes half-closed. Through the two-way mirror, Samson, Leo, and the king's men watched. They had tried to break the two other agents, but the handlers had been too ignorant. One Arohassin agent had managed to dose himself with a hidden poison pill, while the other had bashed his skull by rushing the door when it was opened, and now lay comatose.

"You finally grew some balls, kid. Too bad you sold them away," she said.

"I'll take the compliment." Yassen regarded her. She was dressed in a plain white kurta. Her eyes were puffy, hair disheveled. He wondered if he was the first to see her, or if Leo's men had tried to interrogate her before him.

She shifted, wincing, and he noticed the uneven outline of her dislocated left shoulder.

They had gotten to her before him.

"I can get you out," he said. Even though the captured agents had been part of his deal with Samson, Yassen felt a twinge of guilt and pity. He had known the Ravani were going to be rough. He had not imagined they would be so cruel as to break her bones and leave her to feel the pain.

"Not interested."

"They'll kill you," he said. "The other two agents are already gone."

"Sounds like you're having a tough time extracting info." Giorna smiled, her lips cracked. "I'm not saying shit."

Yassen sighed. Giorna was playing the game they had all been taught: be evasive. Pick up on withheld information. And, if there's no hope, accept your fate.

"What's your favorite kind of gun?" he asked suddenly. She peered at him with slitted eyes. "I only ask because when I first met you, you carried a pulse rifle, third generation Ravani. Strong guy, but has a nasty blowback."

"It was shit."

"Mm." Yassen patted his waist. "Not shit, just big. Too big for a woman like you. Now me, I like a light guy. Handgun with a silencer, thermaknife if I can't manage the former."

"Thermaknives are for little boys with shitty aim."

Yassen smiled. "I assure you, my aim is just fine."

Giorna sniffed. "If it had been, you would have shot me. Instead, you tackled me into the dirt. That was graceless. Akaros would have made you scrub the cadets' toilets for the lack of elegance."

Yassen did not tell her that he had timed his tackle. That he could not shoot her down because she had been running through public streets. Of course, Giorna would not realize that. She had not promised to avoid civilians like he had.

His ear buzzed. "Yassen, what's your plan?" Samson said. "The others are getting impatient. They're saying I should pull you out."

Speaking of graceless. Yassen snuck a glance at the two-way mirror. He needed time to get anything from Giorna, but the king was watching him closely, waiting to see if he would make a mistake, a sign that he was still sympathetic to the Arohassin. What Leo did not realize was that the typical methods of interrogation—torture, blackmail, starvation—would not work on Arohassin agents. They had been trained to withstand brutality, to sacrifice themselves if all else failed. To break an Arohassin agent, you didn't need cruelty. You needed to be crafty.

"Graceless? Giorna, Giorna." He pulled on a quizzical expression. "A small, fast woman like you wouldn't be lugging around a pulse rifle anymore. Now *that's* graceless," he said, tapping the table. She watched him, alert. *She's listening.* "My guess is that you keep a small pulse gun, no silencer. It'll only slow you down. Thermaknives are for the weak, you've already made that clear. But you used a dagger on me, one that even I didn't notice, which means," he continued, and he noticed how she slightly shifted forward, "it's special issue, possibly Jantari. No, Sesharian! They love their hidden blades. And as for your gun, I'd guess it's Ravani, sixth generation, out of Magar."

Giorna tsked. "You're losing your grip, Knight. It's *seventh*-generation Ravani, out of Rasbakan."

"But." Yassen feigned confusion. "Those guns are off the market. You can't even get them through the sand gutters."

"The sand gutters are idiots. The stepwells know what they're doing," Giorna said. Immediately, she stilled, but Yassen saw how her eyes widened. "Or at least, they think they do," she added carefully.

"Well. Maybe you can get a second one, then. They'd be quite elegant as a pair." Yassen stood. "Take care. And hold on, if you can."

As soon as he was out of the room, Samson grabbed his elbow.

"What the fuck was that?" he demanded.

"I swear he's still one of them," said a general with a hatchet nose. "Your Majesty, why is he still alive?"

Leo sat in his chair, one leg draped over the other, and when he met the king's gaze, Yassen felt a chill run through his body.

"You're wasting our time, assassin."

"Stepwells. Rasbakan." Yassen stepped toward the king. "The Arohassin bombed one of your sand ports in Rasbakan, and Maya was behind the attack. They stole weapons—weapons including seventh-generation Ravani-issue pulse guns. Who do you think Giorna got hers from?"

Understanding slowly dawned in Leo's eyes. "And the stepwells?"

"She's referring to the Raja stepwell in western Rani," Yassen said. "It's a drop point, possibly the one Maya uses. If the Arohassin are planning an attack on coronation day, chances are, she's still there, distributing weapons."

"But we don't know for certain." The general came forward, glowering. "You gave us nothing."

"He gave us a lead, Rohtak," Samson said, stepping in front of Yassen. "We can work out the rest."

Yassen gave Samson a silent thanks. He may not have been able to rescue Yassen from the Arohassin, but he was here now, protecting him. Like he had promised.

Samson turned to Leo. "We have a location now, Your Majesty. We can watch the area, track anyone who goes in and out. Maya is bound to turn up."

Leo said nothing. Instead, his eyes found Yassen once more. And Yassen was struck by how weary they looked, how tired. Perhaps in his fear of Leo, he had forgotten that the king was an old man whose kingdom was full of rebels and traitors.

"Your Majesty," Yassen said, surprising even himself by speaking up. "She's there. I know it."

Finally, the king turned. "Arish, share this information with Jangir. And send in trackers, discreetly. I have a feeling that she is one to spook easily. And, Yassen," he said, his voice cold. Yassen stiffened. "You will bring her in, once she is found."

Yassen knew a dismissal when he heard one. "Of course." He bowed and departed, his heart beating fast.

After a while, he heard footsteps behind him and turned to see Samson trailing behind him.

"Hey," Samson said, grabbing his shoulder. He wore a white silk shirt that opened at the collar, and Yassen caught a glimpse of the scar that ran down Samson's chest to his upper abdomen. "You did great back there. Splendid, really."

"What will happen to her—Giorna?"

At this, Samson's smile wavered. "I—I'm not sure. Does it matter?"

Does it matter? Yassen wanted to retort, but he stopped himself. Giorna meant nothing to them. Giorna meant nothing to *him*. And yet... He could not forget the unnatural angle in her shoulders, her puffy eyes. The king may be tired, and though Yassen felt a twinge of pity for the man, he and his men would not hesitate to kill Giorna. To him, Giorna, Samson, Yassen, the rest, they were chess pieces. Men and women to be manipulated. Tossed aside when their purposes were served.

But I can do nothing for Giorna now. He just hoped that if they found Maya quickly, she would not suffer.

"Make it clean." Yassen looked away, jaw tight. "Clean and quick, if it comes to it."

Samson nodded. He touched Yassen's wrist. "Nothing will happen to *you*. I promise."

Yassen turned to him, and in Samson's eyes, he saw worry and a fierce sincerity, but something else, something deeper, older. Samson's hand still remained on his wrist. Warm, familiar. And at this, Yassen felt his chest constrict in guilt.

"I believe you," he said and pulled away.

As soon as his hoverpod docked, Yassen pulled on his jacket and sprinted to the western wings of the palace.

"Sorry, sorry," he said as he arrived outside the studio, slightly breathless. Ferma leaned against the doorway, watching Elena. Yassen could see her reflections twirling in the mirrors around the room.

"I heard you got us a lead," she said, her eyes on Elena.

"News travels fast."

"Arish sent a message." Finally, she turned to him. She was at least a head taller, and her hair fanned out, unbound. Yassen tried to edge back inconspicuously. "Oh, it's all right, assassin. I don't mean to hurt you." Ferma smiled. "Arish believes you. So does the king, apparently. Maybe I misjudged you."

Yassen blinked. *Is this a trick?* Ferma, like Elena, had kept a watchful eye on him, and often, he felt the weight of both their gazes. The sting of their distrust. But then Ferma laughed and clapped him on the shoulder, no darkness in her eyes, no hint of deceit in her grin.

Oh sands, she means it.

Relief washed over Yassen as Ferma shook him.

"Mother's Gold, you're just as terrible taking a compliment as her." She chuckled. "Lighten up, Knight. You're a king's man now."

Yassen managed a smile, though his stomach twisted at the thought. He belonged to no man. He was here to win his freedom, nothing more, nothing less.

"Come, let's see her dance." Ferma moved aside and followed him into the studio. It was a large room, bigger than his quarters, with gleaming mirrors lining the walls. A large wooden lotus was carved into the ceiling, and incense burned in a corner of the room, beside a small shrine dedicated to the Phoenix. Ferma took off her shoes, and he followed suit.

"Now, sit here and be quiet," Ferma whispered.

Together, they watched Elena. She wore a simple cotton kurta and loose pants, her dupatta tied around her waist, silver anklets around her ankles. As she twirled, her braid loosened. Stray curls framed her face, and he felt a sudden, rash urge to tuck them behind her ears.

Along one wall, musicians played the tabla, pakhawaj, harmonium, and sitar. On the other side, the guru, an old woman with bells tied around her ankles like Elena, sang the rhythm and guided Elena.

"Dha tin tin ta dha din din dha."

Elena beat her feet in time with the rhythm, her anklets tinkling as her bare feet slapped against the wooden floor. *Dha din din dha.* Elena quickened her pace, her arms long and elegant, her poise smooth and precise. Each stamp of her foot echoed through the room. Each flick of her long braid moved sinuously like the tail ribbons of kites he had flown as a child. Her expression began to change. With just an arch of an eyebrow, a turn of her lip, she translated the guru's song into movement, into dance. Playfulness blended into passion, passion into celebration. Yassen shivered as he watched. She moved with such grace, such *freedom.* He tracked her around the room, unable to tear himself away because he feared that if he did, if he so much as blinked, he would miss something essential. He was pulled, like the kites in the desert wind—without protest.

"She's beautiful, isn't she?" Ferma said softly.

"Yes," Yassen said, transfixed. "She is."

When the song stopped, Elena turned to face the guru, her skin flushed, her eyes exuberant. But in doing so, her gaze caught on Yassen. Her smile wavered.

He wished he could tell her how beautiful she looked. How, when she danced, she morphed into something more, something ethereal, timeless. But then he immediately chased the thought away. He could not afford to be thinking of her this way.

Elena bowed to her teacher and turned to go.

"Not so fast, Your Highness," the old woman said. "You need to practice the Phoenix dance."

"What's that?" Yassen whispered to Ferma.

"It's the dance to celebrate the Phoenix, performed by the heir and their partner," Ferma said.

Elena wiped the sweat from her brow. "But Samson is out of the palace. We can rehearse when he's here."

The guru tutted. "He's an accessory to the dance, *you* are the focus. You need to practice more than he needs to." She suddenly turned to Yassen, mouth firm. "You, boy. Can you dance?"

"What?"

"Wait," Elena said, stepping forward.

"You look strong enough. Come, hurry now. Before fire burns to ash."

Yassen hesitated, glancing at Ferma. The Spear considered for a moment before giving him a slow nod. "Just follow the guru's instructions. And leave your weapons here."

He clearly had no choice. His throat felt dry as he slipped off his pulse gun and slingsword, Elena watching, biting her lip as if to hold back a retort. It was obvious she respected the guru, enough to follow her commands. When Yassen stood beside Elena, she did not meet his eyes, only looked to the woman.

"Now, begin," the guru said.

She began to sing an old song, one of desert and fire, one Yassen had not heard in many suns and yet he knew the melody deep in his bones. Elena swooped her arms, imitating the wings of the Phoenix, and he followed suit. Twist and turn. Swing, hands outstretched, face toward the heavens as if basking in the heat of the sun.

Except, Yassen could not concentrate on the guru's song. Nervous jitters ran down his spine as Elena brushed past him, her hair briefly trailing across his forearm. She moved just inches from his grasp, like a leaf flying in the breeze he could not catch. This close, he could smell her sweat mingled with jasmine.

When the guru sang of the two rulers uniting as one like twin flames of the same hearth, Elena finally turned to face him. Her hand was soft, slender. So light in his own. Her gaze met his, and this close, he could see the rich brown in her eyes, like honey and earth mixed. He wondered, distantly, what would happen to a man if he drowned in those eyes.

They spun into the next movement of the dance. Elena gave a small nod, and he grabbed her hips and launched her into the air as she raised her arms, her hair arcing like the crown feathers of a bird. Yassen wobbled, then held still. Pain splintered up his arm, but he ignored it. Only holding her steady mattered to him right now.

He held her as the song's final notes trilled out into silence. Then slowly he lowered Elena to the ground, her dupatta trailing down his face. Her hands grazed his neck, and for a moment, Yassen was frozen to the spot, her fingers on his skin, his arms around her waist. And then the guru clapped, and Elena broke away.

Or, at least she tried.

The end of her dupatta caught on the button of his sleeve, tugging him forward. Yassen held up his hand. Her eyes snagged on him, and his heart hammered as she slowly touched his wrist.

"Where did you learn to dance?" she asked in a low voice as she began to loosen the knot.

"Fighting is like dancing," he said, never breaking from her gaze. "Isn't it?"

She paused, her fingers trailing over his skin. With one last tug, Elena freed her dupatta and turned. Together, they bowed to the guru.

"When you lift her, you must look up," she said to Yassen. "Not at *her*, but at the sky, at the Phoenix Herself."

"Guru Madhu, he won't be here for the next dance," Elena said.

"Well." The guru shrugged, slipping her cymbals in a suede bag. "What a pity."

As Ferma hurried to help the woman, Elena quickly bent toward him, her lips a few inches shy of his ear.

"Have you told Ferma?" she asked.

"No," he said, aware of how warm her breath felt against his skin.

176

They shared a secret now, and it thrilled him in part. To know Elena in a way that Ferma did not. And yet, as Elena turned away, rushing to touch the guru's feet, another part of him worried.

He had seen Elena leaving a club notorious for entertaining gold caps. Arohassin agents avoided it; Akaros had warned him to never step foot in its vicinity.

So who did you meet there? he wanted to ask Elena. A chill ran down his spine. *And did you tell them about me?*

After he was relieved of duty for the evening, Yassen took a hovercar into the capital. He parked the unmarked car beneath a highway junction where two homeless women peered out from their sand hovel. A shobu rummaged in a pile of refuse, growling as Yassen approached. He tossed the women three coins and told them to watch the car. The palace guards knew he was in the city, but if the women stole the car, at least Yassen would have a new story to tell Samson.

Yassen pulled on his hood as it began to rain. He made his way from the overpass to the adjoining street. Distant music echoed down the alley, mingling with the cries of the gold cap who stood on the corner, preaching about the next coming of the Prophet. A crowd gathered around him, faces raised, eyes fervent. Yassen quickly skirted around them.

Vendors wheeled their carts to the end of the street where hungry patrons awaited eagerly. One cart had a line that stretched past the corner, a Ravani merchant who was roasting okra on a makeshift grill and serving it up with a skewer of kabobs. Yassen's stomach grumbled, but he did not have time to wait in line. There was still more of the city to see.

As a drizzle dusted the streets, Yassen breathed in the smell of the desert, the musky scent of wet sand and rock. Sandscrapers rose above copper-and-gold chhatris and tiered squares. He recognized a few of the street names. There was still the covered market on Alabore Street with its mosaic ceiling and banyan tree in the center. Long ago, he had sat underneath the tree while his mother haggled for a bag of figs. When the merchant refused, she had turned on her heel, Yassen following. The next day, he had nicked the figs when the merchant wasn't looking.

Yassen smiled at the memory as he looked at the banyan tree. It shimmered like liquid silver from underneath the skylights.

When he came to the corner of Suraat and Sumput, Yassen found the old bakery he and Samson had robbed together.

They had watched from across the street, behind the bushes that grew along the entrance of the man-made city park. Customers hurried in and out, carrying bundles of honeyed bread and chocolate khajas. When their hunger grew to pain, Samson had hatched a plan. Wait until the baker went to his office and his daughter returned to the kitchen to fry gujiyas.

Yassen had stolen across the street and entered the shop. He had expected the counter to be empty, but the baker had unexpectedly returned from his office, grabbing his hat. When he saw Yassen, he paused.

"Oh, I was just going on my break. But if you're quick, boy, I can give you what you like."

Yassen blinked. Out of the corner of his eye, he saw Samson disappear around the corner. He was on his way to distract the daughter from returning from the kitchen. *Mother's Gold, if Samson came out now* . . .

"Um, ten cardamom and nutmeg infused loaves, please," he had said quickly. The baker began to fill a bag with the bread. Yassen gazed at the glass bins of glazed khajas and freshly cut burfi, mouth watering. "And two bags of khajas and burfi, each," he added.

"Are you having a celebration?" the baker asked as he took out two khajas from the heated rack.

"No, I—yes, I mean, yes," Yassen had said. "Please, can you hurry?"

The baker regarded him, but before he could say anything, a yelp came from the back. The man spun around, calling his daughter's name. As soon as he had disappeared, Yassen scrambled over the counter and began stuffing a bag with loaves, burfi, khajas, anything he could get his hands on. He heard the baker yell. There came a thump, and then the man's bald head loomed over him.

"Hey!"

Yassen jumped over the counter and dashed out into the street, the wind singing past his ears as he ran deeper and deeper into the park. When he could run no farther, he had collapsed, sucking in air. But his hunger was greater than his exhaustion, and he greedily began to devour a khaja.

He had been so hungry that it wasn't until he had finished his third burfi that he became troubled by Samson's absence. He searched the park and eventually found him on a bridge overlooking a sandpit. The khajas were cold by then, and Samson had greeted him with a bloody smile and a split eyebrow.

"Looks like you hit the jackpot," he had said.

"What happened?"

"I was kissing her, and then she bit my lip!" Samson shook his head. "Hand me a khaja, will you?"

Now, Yassen peered into the empty bakery. A holosign advertised that it was available to lease. There were marks on the floor where the glass counter had been. Stealing from the bakery had been the first of many transgressions, but at the time, it hadn't felt like a crime. It felt necessary.

He looked down the street at the unfamiliar neon signs and newly planted trees. Overhead, floating holo billboards advertised companies he had never heard of. A young couple staggered down the street, laughing, their faces red with drink.

Yassen watched them and then looked back at the empty store.

The city had gone on without him, evolving without his supervision. He knew he had no claim on the capital or its ways, but he had been born here, had been raised by these streets, shaken sand out of his hair after winter storms, strained his neck as he and others watched the Fire Birds take on the Metal Warriors in games of windsnatch.

In a way, he felt betrayed by the changed city. Yet a part of him knew such change was inevitable. He had long ago forsaken this place. He could not expect it to bat an eye at his nostalgia.

The neon signs grew dimmer as Yassen entered the park. The sandpit had been hollowed out. Drunks, vagabonds, and storytellers gathered within its crater. As he walked onto the bridge, the sound of quarreling voices made him pause. Yassen peered down and saw a woman with hair the color of polished bronze standing on the foundation of a elevated statue.

A sizable crowd surrounded her. One bearded man with a bull tattooed on his hand argued with a thin teenager still dressed in his school uniform. The woman watched them. She raised her hand, but they paid her no mind.

"Enough," she said as their voices grew louder. "Enough!"

The two stopped, stricken by the steel in her voice.

"My comrades, we need to stop fighting among ourselves," she said.

"Well, he started it," the bearded man said.

"This man's head is not screwed on right," the student retorted. "Fucking refugee."

"We *refugees* sweat and toil as much as you. More than you."

"If you want to complain, then just go back to your own damn land! We can carry on *our* rebellion without you."

"I'll have both of your heads lying in a ditch for the silver feathers if you don't shut up," the woman interrupted. The two men looked at each other, as if weighing their options, then fell silent.

"We will never win if we feud." She pointed north, where the palace glimmered like a distant star. "They will devour us like they have countless times before."

She studied the faces in the crowd. "How many times have King Leo's guards 'taken' our brothers and sisters who spoke out about the state of this kingdom, only for us to never see them again? How many of his mindless *gold caps*," she said, her voice dripping with venom, "have bullied you into silence? They swagger through our streets as if they own this kingdom because Leo has allowed them to." The woman spat in the sand. "The king knows his reign is coming to an end, so he grows crueler. You have heard his gold caps recruit men for war. *War*. Who here thinks we can survive a war against the Jantari?"

There were muffled grunts, but no one raised their hands. No one spoke up.

"We may have the Black Scales on our side, but their leader is a Jantari pet. He will sell us to Farin as soon as he gets the chance. And what does the king do? He organizes a fucking march along the border."

A murmur rippled through the crowd. Yassen recognized it—the whisper of rebellion. He had felt it before.

"Ravence is crumbling, and Leo knows. He sees it and he does nothing. But we won't take it anymore," she said. "Because we know the truth. We know the kingdom is old. It was founded upon death and blood—upon a myth. The Phoenix is gone. There is no Prophet. A new era has come. An era for a government led by the people—not by a bloodline or a false god."

She paused and let her words sink in. Yassen watched as others began to nod, as their murmurs rose to shouts of agreement.

"It is time, my friends, for our revolution. A joint revolution, Ravani and Sesharian alike. This is our chance to stop the bloody cycle of history."

"But they were chosen to rule this land!" someone called out. The crowd pushed an old man to the front. "The Phoenix burned every king's and queen's name in the sand before Alabore. He built us this home."

"If there really was a Phoenix," the woman said, "why did she bless Alabore? And what about her Prophet?"

"The Prophet's time has not come," the old man griped. "But they will come, the both of them. You mark my words; the Phoenix will rise from the ashes and Her Prophet will burn all the unfaithful."

Yassen slipped down the bridge and into the sandpit. Pain slithered down his shoulder to his wrist, but he ignored it. He stood at the edge of the crowd, beside a merchant peddling makhana as the woman gazed at the sky and the palace beyond.

Then, strangely, she began to laugh.

The old man looked at her, confused. Even members in the crowd shifted in unease. When the woman finally stopped, she raised a shaking finger at Palace Hill.

"They—*they* will burn us all." Her voice sharpened. "They will lead us to a war we cannot win, and we will end up like the islands. Dead or colonized."

Yassen walked around the edge of the crowd as she jumped down from the statue and walked up to the old man. She was at least a head taller, with the defiant look of a young martyr.

"Your Prophet is no different than that tyrant on the hill," she said. "Both wage war on this land without regard for its people." She turned away and directed her words to the crowd. "This land is ours to rule and govern as we see fit. And no one, especially not some half-forgotten bird, can tell us otherwise."

Cheers and whistles broke out. The old man shook his head. He grumbled something Yassen could not hear and then pushed his way through the crowd. He began to zip up his jacket, and as he passed, Yassen caught a glimpse of a crumpled hat tucked in his breast pocket.

It was the color of gold.

People surrounded the woman, patting her on the back. Yassen watched for a while.

Leave it, he wanted to tell her. *Do not lose yourself in these fantasies.*

The Arohassin believed in revolution. They decried the Phoenix because She was not real; Alabore Ravence was not a holy figure, but a shrewd general who knew how to manipulate his enemies. They had made Yassen believe that the only way to create change was by destroying the old kingdoms. And for a long time, Yassen had fallen for their stories. He had grown up believing in the Phoenix simply because his mother had. But with the Arohassin, he began to see the vengeful nature of fire. It was only later he had come to learn that hypocrisies existed on all sides. And that fire, no matter who wielded it, was always wild and destructive.

Over the protestors' conversations, Yassen heard a sound. He looked up to see shadows over the bridge. A face came into view, and then another. Angry faces crowned with gold caps. He spotted the old man from before. Beside him stood a thin man with a hooked nose. *Where have I seen him before?* The thin man and the others looked down at the small gathering and sneered. Yassen spotted the glint of a pulse gun.

And then he smelled smoke.

Quick as a fox he darted underneath the bridge as the gold caps opened fire. Screams erupted into the night, and the protestors scattered.

Suddenly, the darkness beneath the bridge erupted with light.

He rounded the column of the bridge as a pulse whizzed past him. Another hit the column, spraying stone. Yassen scrambled up the bank of the sandpit. The rain had hardened the sand, and he found purchase, instinct and training taking over.

The old man hopped onto the edge of the pit with his pulse gun. When he saw Yassen, he raised his weapon. Yassen dove forward, tackling him to the ground. They rolled in the sand, struggling, and then Yassen slipped his arm around the man's shoulder and pinned him down.

"Get off of me, Jantari!" the man cried as Yassen's hood fell, revealing his colorless eyes and light hair.

Yassen froze. With the acceptance he had slowly won in the palace, Yassen had almost forgotten. Almost believed that maybe, maybe he did belong. But as the old man hissed and struggled beneath him, the truth hit him, a bitter and sharp reminder. To this man, he was a stranger. An enemy.

Yassen looked down. He could easily snap the man's neck. Leave his body for his brethren to find. His left hand shook as he cradled the man's head.

But then more pulse fire erupted in the night. Grabbing the man's weapon, Yassen hit the gold cap with the butt of his gun, knocking him unconscious. Then he sprinted toward the park, legs pumping, heart hammering. Bramble snagged at his arms and legs, but he did not slow.

Sirens were screaming in the distance when Yassen finally stopped at the western edge of the park. He hunched over, heaving for air. The roar of gunfire still thundered in his ears.

Despite himself, Yassen felt his throat constrict. Anger, frustration, and a sense of helplessness squeezed his throat. *They are fools, all of them.*

CHAPTER 18

ELENA

There is some comfort in the emptiness of the desert. Here, the past is erased by the wind, and the future is yet to be written.
—from the diaries of Priestess Nomu of the Fire Order

Elena burst into Leo's study.

"You need to stop them," she said. "They're out of control."

Guards scrambled up behind her. Majnu gripped her shoulder, panting. "Your Majesty, I–I'm sorry, she just barged in."

The king looked up. Headlines detailing the civilian attack in Rani floated around him. Images of the aftermath—the pulse-ridden bodies, the red-stained sand—revolved in a carousel of holos.

"So are you," he said mildly to Elena.

The comment stung, more than it should have, and for a moment, Elena wavered. How could he say that? How could he say that after everything *his* gold caps had done? And just like that, the anger was back, thick and vicious. "Your gold caps opened fire in a public place. On innocent protestors."

"They were armed rebels," her father said curtly. "Preliminary investigations say their guns came from the Arohassin."

"You know that's not true. They were civilians! Protestors yes, but civilians." *And one was my friend.* She had seen the reports, the faces of the dead. And she had recognized one: a merchant slumped by his makhana cart.

"That...That's Eshaant, isn't it?" Ferma had said when they saw the holo.

Elena nodded, her hands trembling. In the holo, Eshaant lay on his side, chest ripped open by pulse fire, his head resting on a pitcher of spilled chaas. She had almost cried at that.

But then she had stilled when she saw the pulse gun in his hand. Eshaant was no killer. No Arohassin rebel. At worst, he was a fool, trying to make quick money. But there was a more obvious explanation.

"They did not have weapons on them," Elena said, voice tight with fury. "They were planted. By Jangir and his gold caps, so they had cause for their senseless killing."

"Senseless?" Leo's stone eyes fixed on her. "They were anarchists wishing for the fall of our government, our kingdom. Think, for just a moment. If you were in a room with a gold cap, a rebel, and a gun, who do you think would grab that gun and shoot you?" His voice grew even colder. "The rebels have no love for us, Elena. And we cannot afford them fracturing our kingdom, not now. Jangir said that he visited the rally, but it grew tense, dangerous, and then the rebels opened fire first."

Elena shook her head. "Jangir is lying to you."

"You called him and the gold caps your countrymen."

"This was not what I meant. I called for unity. This—this is destruction."

"You can't call for fire and then blame others when you fail to wield it," he said.

"Are you even listening?" she cried. "We will have a bloodbath on our hands. On all sides."

"And soon it will be over," he said. "Once you're crowned queen, the dust will settle."

Elena let out a slow breath, fists curling in her skirts. With a quiet voice, she dismissed the guards. They looked to Leo, who gave a slow nod. Once they were gone, she met her father's eyes.

"I can't become queen," she said, trying her best to keep the frustration out of her voice, but her hands trembled. "You won't teach me to hold fire. If I can't pass the Agneepath, if I can't hold fire in front of the public, they will *never* accept me as queen."

"They will," Leo said. "I will make sure that they do."

She shook her head. "Stop, stop! This is what you do every time. You crush any utterance of protest, but that doesn't stop our people from distrusting us. You can't make them believe in a lie when they can see it with their own eyes! They will know I can't hold fire. You can't hide that."

"What have I always told you?" Leo said.

"Father—"

"'Control the people, Elena. Tell them how they should think.'" Leo pointed at the holos. "This is what they're going to believe in. Rebels in their city, armed by terrorists, ready to destroy everything we hold dear. Let them focus on that, not you. *You* will be reassurance. You will be their strength."

"I. Can't," Elena said through gritted teeth.

"Trust in me," Leo said. "I have already set the plans in motion. The high priestess *will* declare you queen. The people will believe in you. And you will have the throne."

"Will I?" Her voice was oddly soft. "Will I really control the throne, or will you?"

"What are you implying?"

"Your generals control the military; your gold caps, the city. They owe me loyalty in name, but really, they all answer to you."

"That is not true," Leo said, rising. There was a strange look of worry in his eyes. "Elena, they will follow you. I will make sure of it."

"Of course *you* will." A part of her had tried to deny that her father was not ready to give up the throne, but she saw it so clearly now. He would hold on to any scrap of power he could.

"Everything I do—that they do—is for you. For our throne. Remember that," Leo said. He tried to take her hand, but she stepped back.

"Then call in Jangir and the gold caps who were part of this attack," she said. "For me."

A muscle worked in Leo's jaw. "I will not. The gold caps give us strength, unity. Eyes and ears our military never could."

"They're blind followers, Father," she argued.

"Their blind faith is what makes us strong, Elena. It's what makes this throne powerful."

"I've met them. Talked with them. Father, they are crude opportunists and—"

"And we nearly have a war on our border!" Leo snapped. "Who do you think would make a better soldier: a man who constantly criticizes everything you do, or a man who will follow you, no matter what you ask of him? I don't care if they're blind. They're *mine*. And they will fight and bleed for Ravence, and *that* is what we need."

"That's bullshit," she said.

"That's power," he said, and the look on his face drained her anger, replacing it with fear. "They are loyal men who love this country. And you *will* need them."

Leo's eyes flickered over her, but when she said nothing, he returned to his holos.

"Go," he said in a heavy voice. "If you will not see sense, leave."

Yassen and Ferma waited outside the king's study.

"Ferma," Elena said.

Immediately, Ferma turned to Yassen. "I will take her. You're dismissed."

Elena gave Ferma a tight, grateful smile. Once at her room, she sank into a floating ottoman before her vanity as Ferma waved away the handmaidens.

Everything I do—that they do—is for you. For our throne.

She believed in Ravence, believed that one day the people would shed their fear as a desert yuani sheds her old feathers. Spreads her wings anew and launches into the sky. She believed in the dream so much that it hurt. But her kingdom was crumbling right before her eyes, and it was all her family's fault. Her father did not care. And she could not unite them. She could not wield fire, and without the blessing of the Phoenix, she could not lead Ravence to glory.

Ferma sat down across from her, folding in her long legs. Her tawny gaze fixed upon Elena.

"I don't know if I can do this," Elena whispered.

"You'll learn," Ferma replied. She touched Elena's hand. "No ruler is perfect in the beginning. Your father wasn't, but he knew how to use others to his advantage. He learned by watching them. And your mother." Ferma shook her head. "She taught him the most."

Elena thought of her mother: her mess of curls, her eyes the color of dark banyan roots. She was not here to guide Elena toward queendom, nor advise her on the secrets of marriage. She was a ghost only a few suns from fading. All Elena had left of her was memories of them in a dusty library and a scroll she had written in.

"What did the king say to you?" Ferma said gently.

"He said that even though I can't hold fire, the people will believe in me. But how will they trust in a fraud? *I* don't believe in myself, Ferma. I can't even hold a flame without burning my hand. Me, the ruler *blessed* by the Phoenix." She laughed wildly. "Who is going to believe that? And how long can I hide it?"

"The king will teach you."

"'The king will teach you,'" Elena repeated, voice dripping with derision. "The king wants to stay in control, Ferma. He denies me my birthright so he can remain relevant while I sit on the throne, a dummy ruler he had to prop up because of tradition." Elena paused, the words lying on her tongue before she released them. "Because of my dead mother."

During Aahnah's sickness, Leo had promised her that Elena would take the throne, safe and sound. That she would not burn. Aahnah had laughed in his face.

"She knew," Elena said. "She knew I would not be able to hold fire. That's why she laughed at him."

"Aahnah was unwell and not herself," Ferma said. Her hands were warm and firm around Elena's. "Pull yourself together, Elena. *You* are the heir. You will learn how to hold fire, whether your father wants you to or not. It is in your blood."

And perhaps it was the look on Ferma's face, the sincere belief, the unyielding love, that held back Elena's retort. She grasped on to that look, let it anchor her. Let Ferma wrap her up in her arms and kiss the top of her head like she had done when Elena was a child. Her arms were strong, dependable. Elena closed her eyes and pressed her face into Ferma's chest.

"Oh, look at your hair," Ferma said after a while. "It's a mess. Come, let me fix it," she coaxed, but Elena shook her head.

"I'd rather do yours. Sit here," she said. She needed to take her mind off her father, do something with her hands or else they would stay clenched in fists. Ferma obligingly sat before the vanity as Elena stood and ran her fingers through her long hair—softer than silk, harder than diamond.

Once, after Aahnah had died, Elena had slipped out of the castle and into the squalid slums of the outer city. She could not remember how she had gotten there, only that a man had led her back to his home to show her shobu puppies and then shut the door on her. She had panicked and kicked him between the legs, then bolted into the street—headfirst into Ferma. The Yumi did not say a word to Elena. She simply walked into the hut, her hair writhing behind her. Elena had watched as she had pierced the man's body, blood spilling out. When Ferma came back out, not a single drop stained her strands.

Elena began to weave Ferma's hair into a long, thick braid. Ferma sighed and closed her eyes, relaxing her head back against Elena's knee.

"You know, no one has braided my hair in a long time," she murmured.

"Probably because you scare them."

The Yumi chuckled. "I think *you* do."

Elena smiled as she twisted another strand into the braid. "I'm sure Samson is intimidated by you."

"Ah, the Sesharian." In the reflection of the vanity mirror, Ferma gave a lazy, mischievous grin. "How are things going with our famed hero?"

Elena snorted, though she felt her cheeks warm. "Fine. We're going for a ride later."

"The successful Arohassin hunts are winning him favor with the guards and our soldiers," Ferma said. "Looks like his bet on Yassen Knight paid off."

Elena thought back to Yassen dancing with her in the studio. The way he had held her aloft and lowered her gently. The way his pale eyes had met hers in the desert as he touched the barrel of the pulse gun. *This isn't just your home. It's mine too.*

Despite his past, Yassen believed in Ravence, or he made a good show of it.

Elena turned her attention back to finishing the braid. "When I become queen, I want you to retire," she began. "You deserve the rest—"

"I'd rather you throw me into quicksand," Ferma said, eyes still closed.

"I was going to say you deserve rest before I promote you to be my Astra," she said, giving a teasing tug on the braid.

"Easy." Ferma's eyes fluttered open, and she looked up at Elena. "Astra, eh?"

"I could think of no one else," Elena said.

"But I would better serve you as your Spear," Ferma said. She pulled away from Elena and turned to face her. "You have Samson. As your king, he'll be your closest confidant. That's the way it works."

"It doesn't have to be that way, though," Elena said.

"Shutting out Samson will only weaken your reign. And he's a man. It'll bruise his ego. He'll start to plot against you from the shadows."

Elena scoffed. "Now you're being dramatic."

"I'm being realistic." Ferma drew up. Her thick braid snaked down her shoulder. "You have a strong ally in Samson. *Use him.*"

"But I need *you*," she said and took Ferma's hands into her own. "You're my strongest ally."

"And I cannot be your only one. I'm growing old, Elena." Ferma softened her words with a smile. "I will serve you until my last breath, but it will come sooner than Samson's."

"As my Astra, you won't have to put yourself in the line of fire," Elena insisted. She could not imagine ruling without Ferma by her side. "It'll be a cushy job, and you'll have servants to see to your every need."

"There is no cushy job in Ravence."

"Just think about it, Ferma."

The Yumi sighed. She gave a slow nod, but Elena could see the sorrow in her eyes. "I'll think about it."

Samson and Elena rode north into the desert, the sunset painting the sky in brushstrokes of red and pink.

Her mare fought the lead, eager to run across the dunes. Elena gave her more rein, and they took off. She crouched in her stirrups, sand stinging her skin and the wind singing in her ears. She closed her eyes and breathed in the desert, letting its wildness fill the spaces between her bones.

They climbed up a rock face, and Elena opened her eyes. Pebbles tumbled off the precipice. Beneath them, a deep valley stretched across the desert like an unhealed scar.

She slowed her horse and turned as Samson trotted up beside her.

"You're a fast rider," he panted. "Gave me quite the run."

But Elena had seen how Samson had held his horse back and allowed her to take the lead. She wondered what else he was merely *allowing* her to do.

"Do you know this valley?" she asked.

He peered over the cliffside. "Looks like all the rest."

"You'll need to know everything about this desert if you're to be my king," she said. The smile fell from his face, and Elena hopped off her mare. "Come."

They descended. Unlike Yassen, Samson trudged through the dune. He left a trail, one that an enemy tracker or yeseri could follow. Ferma had insisted she could learn from Samson, but she also had something to teach him.

When they came to the valley floor, Elena stopped. The rock walls towered above them. Spined, prickling plants grew within the crevices, creeping out as if escaping some danger within. Here in the valley, the air was slick and cool.

"This is Alabore's Tear," she said. "This is where he met the Phoenix."

"Don't you think this place is too dark for the Holy Bird?" Samson joked.

"Fire burns brightest in the darkness," she returned.

Samson walked forward, craning his neck. She watched him take it all in: the cold sand, the weathered rock, the tough bramble.

"Have you ever seen anything like this?" she asked.

When he turned back to her, his mouth was a thin line. "Once."

He held out his arm, and she took it. They neared a skorrir bush, and its buds shrank back as they approached. Elena pointed.

"These are helpful markers," she said. "You can tell if something has passed before you."

"We have something like that in Seshar," Samson said wistfully. He studied the skorrir bush, but Elena could tell by the distant look in his eyes that he was gazing upon his homeland.

"Have you gone back to Seshar? Would Farin allow it?"

Beneath her hand, she felt his forearm tense. "I don't want to go back, not yet," he said. "There's so much I want to do here before returning."

"Like what?"

He did not answer. The pensive look grew on his face as they walked.

Long shadows crawled up the red walls, and a heavy silence hung in the air. Elena was about to suggest they return to their mounts when Samson spoke.

"I was born under Jantar's rule," he said, his voice quiet. "By then, they had executed all the noble families on Seshar except mine. They were afraid that my mother would set the evil eye on them. She was a priestess who worshipped the old religion of the Serpent. The metalmen aren't the superstitious type, but..." He shook his head. "My mother could make you believe in anything."

"I suppose you get that from her then."

He gave a wry smile, but his eyes remained dark. "When I was eleven suns, she knew we were running out of time. So she sent me a dream.

"I dreamed of a deep fissure in a desert," he said. "Darkness covered the path, but at the very end, there was a light. An ember. It was so small that a breeze would extinguish it. I ran toward it, but before I could reach it, I woke up."

"You think your mother sent you to Alabore's Tear?" Elena asked.

Samson surveyed the valley. "I think she meant to show me that there is a fire I must seek and protect. It could be Seshar. It could be Ravence, perhaps even Jantar. It could even be you," he said with a wink. "But don't they say that dreams of fire lead to madness?"

Elena said nothing. They stopped before a long crack, one that began from the valley floor and sprouted up across the entire length of the wall. A million tiny fissures splintered from the scar. Gazing upon it, Elena was reminded of a gulmohar tree, dead and bare in the winter.

"Does this have a name too?"

She shook her head. "None that I know." Then, after a moment: "What happened to your family?"

Samson stared at the crevice. He leaned forward, and she thought he was going to reach out and touch the wall when he disentangled his arm from hers and turned around.

"We should head back," he said.

"If you won't tell me about your family, tell me about Yassen," she said. "When did you meet him?"

"In Ravence, stealing the same crate of mangoes." He shot her a glance, but if he sensed something amiss, he made no mention of it. "After my parents died, I ended up in Ravence. I found a merchant with fresh fruit and was about to swipe a crate when Yassen reached for the same one. We fought over it, but Yassen let go. He was smart. Because a second later, the merchant grabbed me.

"Back then, they burned thieves, even children. He dragged me into the street to summon a silver feather when Yassen threw a mug of tea into his face. After that, we ran." Samson stopped and looked up at the sliver of orange sky. "You know, it was on a day a lot like this."

They trekked up the valley, where the guards held their horses. Elena mounted hers, but Samson did not. Instead, he continued standing on the edge of the rock, looking down into the dark valley.

"What is it?" she asked.

"There's so much about Ravence I don't know."

"You'll learn."

He stood there for a moment longer and then turned back to her. "You still don't trust Yassen, do you?"

"Why do you?"

Samson came up to her. He stroked her mare's head, spoke soft words in a language Elena did not know. "Because despite everything, I think back to that kid who saved me. Because I owe my life to him."

When Elena reached the palace, she called the gamemaster and strode into the control room with Ferma.

"Your Highness, y-you're early," the gamemaster stammered and bowed.

Elena slipped on her gamesuit, reveling in the heightened strength of her body: the coiled muscles in her legs, the elasticity in her arms. It was such a shame that gamesuits could not function outside the field. Soldiers in gamesuits would end wars more quickly.

"You can leave," she said to the gamemaster. "Just turn on the field before you go."

"You want to train alone?" Ferma asked.

Elena nodded. As the gamemaster turned dials on the control panel, she grabbed a slingsword from the rack. She balanced it in her hand, checking its weight and trigger mechanism before belting it to her hip.

"I need to clear my mind," she said.

Ferma opened her mouth to retort, but Elena held up her hand. "I need you to do something else for me. About V."

She had given her father the opportunity to correct his wrongs. To rein his gold caps in. But he had made his position clear.

She no longer felt guilt. What kind of legacy was one of blind, violent followers who wreaked terror in their wake? If Varun's reports caused the gold caps to crumble, so be it.

"V had a deadline. Please check that he meets it."

The Yumi nodded slowly, her hair swirling around her shoulders. "I see." She bowed, the gamemaster following suit. "I'll post guards at the door."

"Thank you." Elena watched them go. When the door shut behind them, she exited the glass box and descended the stairs that led to the field. The black sand vibrated underneath her feet.

Elena crouched down as the lights dimmed. A counter sounded through the chamber.

The lights blazed, and the sand rose. It solidified into a large, spiked wall twice her height. Without warning, the spikes shot forward, straight toward her.

She drew her slingsword and slashed down. A spike fell in a spray of sand. Another whistled by her ear. Elena ducked and weaved through the attack, her movements smooth and practiced, her feet light, the sling-sword hilt like an extension of her hand. Sweat trickled down her face, but she did not mind.

She fell into a trance, into the primal physicality of her body.

Lunge.

Duck.

Spin.

Advance.

Her body moved of its own accord, and for one splendid moment, Elena felt attuned to something higher. Forget the gold caps and her father. Here was something she was good at. Here was something she could control.

Elena ran toward the wall, but before she could reach it, the sand collapsed. She coughed as dirt and dust clotted the air. The ground rumbled, the sand shifting as a low hiss crept across the field. Elena held her slingsword in front of her, slowly turning to sense the next direction of attack.

It came from below.

The sand grabbed her feet, sucked her down into a rippling pool of quicksand. Elena grunted, trying to twist out of its grasp, but she only sank deeper.

"The more you struggle, the faster you'll sink."

Her head snapped up. There, standing in the glass box, was Yassen.

"What are you doing here?" she growled.

"Relax your legs and shoot out your blade. You can pull yourself out that way."

She glanced at her sword and then up at the blue lights. The sand gurgled, swallowing her to her waist.

Cursing, Elena raised her sword and pulled the trigger. The blade shot out and embedded into the ceiling. She tugged, but it held. With a grunt, she pulled herself up, climbing the steel rope that connected the projectile blade to the hilt. The sand hissed, squeezing her legs, but Elena put one hand over the other, her muscles screaming as she pulled herself out. As soon as she escaped, the blue lights flashed, and the sand froze.

The round was over.

She sighed and let go. She landed on her feet, but a second later, her knees buckled, and she fell. Elena groaned and rolled onto her back. As she blinked up, a shadow fell over her. Frowning, she craned her neck. Yassen stared down at her, a rare smile playing across his face.

"You've never dealt with quicksand?"

"Oh, shut it."

She pushed herself into a sitting position. When Yassen offered his hand, she noticed the slingsword tucked into his belt.

"Did you have to use that on your hunt?"

"No," he said, hauling her up. "Pulse guns are much faster."

"Only when you don't know how to use a slingsword properly," she said.

"Oh?" Yassen looked down at his hip. He wore no gamesuit, but after a moment's debate, he drew his slingsword, the blade glinting in the blue light. "Show me."

Elena paused. Her legs felt like lead and her arms weak as Cyleon balsa. But she saw the look in Yassen's eyes, the determination and the curiosity, and she thought back to their first duel. How he had held back. How he had taken her blows without protest.

"All right," she said. "But use the Unsung this time."

They crouched at opposite ends of the field. The gamemaster had only programmed one round, so the sand was still, the arena quiet. Elena met Yassen's gaze. He nodded.

They both charged forward. With a snarl, Elena raised her slingsword for an overhead strike. Yassen brought up his weapon, and their blades clashed with a screech. Without missing a beat, Elena stepped back and lifted her slingsword. Yassen cut up for a parry, falling for the feint. Grinning, she sidestepped and wheeled down, the tip of her blade nicking Yassen's shin. He yelped and hopped back.

Elena lunged, using her momentum to knee him in the liver. Yassen stumbled but quickly regained his footing, spinning out of her reach. He swept aside her advance and parried the next.

The clang of their slingswords thundered through the field. The Unsung was a surprisingly simple form, but the idea of it, of using your opponent's momentum against them, attacking quickly and exiting even faster, was hard to execute.

And Elena could feel herself beginning to tire as Yassen continued to fend off her cuts. Her arms shook, and her shoulders cramped. *Mother's Gold, so this is what he's like when he doesn't hold back.* As if sensing her fatigue, Yassen flicked aside her strike and then lunged, his shoulder ramming into her chest.

She gasped, the impact knocking the air out of her. She scrambled back, bringing up her slingsword, but Yassen easily hit her wrist with the flat plane of his blade, knocking her sword from her hand. Her eyes widened. He rushed forward, his blade arcing up, and Elena saw her opening.

She spun down and around, sweeping her leg out as she had seen Ferma do so many times before, clipping Yassen across his ankles. He fell, his slingsword clattering to the ground. Elena snatched it and jumped on top of him, pinning him down as she raised his own blade to his throat.

"Peace," she said, panting.

This close, she saw a bead of sweat run down the side of his forehead and into his hairline. Yassen looked up, his eyes clear and wide.

"Peace," he whispered.

She realized then that he had let her win; that he would always let her win. The opening, though not a rookie mistake, was preventable. Yassen had offered it, knowing that a skilled fighter like her would notice.

Elena suddenly felt aware of how warm his hips felt against her legs. How his lips slightly parted as he looked up at her. She pushed to her feet and offered her hand. He took it, and she helped him stand. A thin line of red marked his throat where the slingsword had kissed his skin. Yassen saw her looking and touched it.

"It'll heal," he said.

Elena hobbled into her room, feeling as if sand was lodged between her bones. She sank into the warm bath Diya, her handmaiden, had drawn for her and soaked in the tub until her toes shriveled like dates. When she closed her eyes, she saw Yassen's pale ones looking up at her.

It'll heal.

He had been fast, so damn fast. And Phoenix Above, the way he had danced away from her attacks like sand in the wind. Absentmindedly, Elena touched her neck. The same spot where she had cut Yassen. The same spot he had touched when he had looked at her.

It'll heal.

Diya brought her a robe, and then Elena dismissed her handmaid with a soft good night. When she was gone, Elena opened the doors to her balcony. A cool wind rustled the curtains. The air felt charged, and she looked up at the burdened sky. Another storm was due.

Elena grabbed a glass orb and took it to the hearth. As tired as she was, she could not rest. Not now. Carefully, she dipped the orb into the fire and scooped up a flame. Then she snatched the scroll from her desk and descended into her garden. By now, the forms and their directions, except the last, were ingrained in her mind, but seeing her mother's handwriting gave her strength.

Lotus blossoms drifted in the stone basin of the fountain. She set the orb on the lip and unfurled the scroll. She imagined herself flowing through the forms like the wind over the dunes. Effortless.

In the distance, lightning flashed through the grey clouds.

She took a deep breath and sank into the first pose. The Warrior.

The path of fire is dangerous. Tread it with care.

Her muscles ached. Elena bit back a groan as she concentrated on her pose. She held out her arms, palms outstretched. Sweeping her right leg, she shifted her weight into the second form.

The Desert Sparrow.

Sweat beaded on her forehead despite the cool night. Elena balanced on her right foot, her left tucked behind her right thigh, her arms folded behind her like a resting sparrow. The fire hissed in its confines.

Empty your mind. See nothing but the fire—for that is all that matters.

Elena stared at the flame until she could see its shape beneath her eyes. She unfolded her arms, raising them above her head like wings. The fire sighed and then lengthened. She unlocked her leg to move into the third pose, but she moved too quickly. She lost her balance and stumbled back. The flame sputtered and died.

Cursing, she took the orb and went back to the hearth. Once more, she dipped the orb in the fire and withdrew a single flame. Back at the fountain, she resumed the pose but lost her balance. The flame left behind a thin trail of smoke. She tried again.

And again.

A sheen of sweat covered her face, her robe slick against her skin as she balanced on one leg for what felt like the hundredth time. With a deep breath, Elena lifted her arms above her head. The flame curled. Slowly, she unwound her limbs, and the fire grew. She sank into the third pose.

The Lotus.

She splayed out her fingers like a flower as she shifted her weight back into her heels. The flame pulsed. Her gaze never wavering, she spun, arms out, chest high—and the flame twisted with her. It expanded, beating against its glass prison.

Think of the brightest light you've ever seen, the scroll said of this form.

Elena thought of the Eternal Fire, the way it spat and crackled as if alive. The way it swayed when the priests chanted. She concentrated not on its form, but on its life. The heat it gave. The power it granted.

Her hands like lotuses, she moved toward the fire. She imagined it rising above the glass and touching her palm, but as she approached, the flame exploded. The orb shattered, glass shards cutting into her outstretched palms.

Elena shrieked.

The fire swelled, licking the air. She lunged toward the fountain, plunging her hands in. She began to splash the fire with water, but it only rose higher. She jumped in the basin and kicked the water onto the flames until, finally, they sputtered and died.

A dark patch of ash lay where the fire had once been. Elena sank into the bowl of the fountain, water spilling over her shoulders. Thick, red drops of her blood swirled within the stone basin. She stared at the ring of ash, and a low sound began at the back of her throat.

It was somewhere between a laugh and a sob.

CHAPTER 19

LEO

Swindlers run with sand in their veins.

—a Ravani proverb

Leo arrived early to watch the burning of the priests. They stood in a grove of banyan trees that grew a hundred paces behind the temple. In the middle of the grove, a singular gulmohar tree held court. Its fiery red leaves danced in the breeze as the priests trudged in, shivering in their thin orange robes.

When all the priests had filtered in, Leo turned to his Spear.

"Make sure none of them leave," he ordered. He then strode out of the grove, his long black kurta fluttering behind him.

Leo entered the temple. As he approached the Seat, the air grew warmer. The Eternal Fire roared in greeting when he entered its sanctuary. It beat against the air, its flames snapping like whips. Saayna knelt below the dais, gathering ash in a brass urn. When Leo came up beside her, she straightened but did not look his way.

"The Phoenix shall judge you harshly for this," the high priestess said.

Her voice was a mere whisper over the crackle of the fire. She wore no shackles this time. Golden robes wrapped around her shoulders and waist, and firelight played across her high cheekbones, giving her an almost regal appearance.

"She is the god of vengeance," he replied flatly. "I would think less of Her if She didn't."

Leo walked up the steps of the dais as Saayna watched. He had brought her because customs were still customs. As high priestess, she would need to oversee his last Ashanta ceremony. And as king, he needed to receive the blessings of the heavens for his last ceremony with Elena.

The Eternal Fire growled, its heat buffeting against his face. Leo did not waver.

He was to commit the highest treason against the heavens. His soul would be eternally whipped and burned in all the seven hells. But all of this was for Elena. For their throne.

The king withdrew a flame in his right palm. He returned to the grove, Saayna trailing after him. The order had not seen their high priestess in weeks, and the assembled priests regarded her warily, as if they knew she was the cause of their suffering.

"Is this everyone?" he asked.

Saayna nodded.

"Check the tunnels," he said to Majnu. "Make sure none are hiding."

The Spear barked orders for a group of his men to search the tunnels beneath the temple. Arish surveyed the priests and priestesses and then bent toward Leo.

"I count forty-eight, but there should be fifty," the Astra whispered. "The high priestess accounts for one, but what of the other?"

Leo studied the nervous faces before him. "The young boy," he said, and he thought back to the priest with the runes burned on his back. "He must be dead. Check just in case."

Saayna watched wordlessly. A light rain began to fall. The trees shielded the order and the royal party, but Leo felt the drops slip beneath his collar. He fought back a shiver.

When his men returned, Majnu faced the king. "The tunnels are empty, Your Majesty."

Leo nodded. A sour taste filled his mouth. He had not slept nor eaten well since his vision in the desert. Nightmares plagued his sleep, and when he awoke in the morning, he saw shadows of twisted trees stretching across his bedroom walls. Yet when he blinked, they vanished.

The heavens were challenging him, waiting to see if he would crumble. Leo stepped forward as the trees rustled and the rain whispered against the leaves. The flame he held hissed.

Well, let the heavens see. Let them laugh after today.

"I have called you all here to search for the truth," he said. His eyes traveled over the orange-robed priests. "The Prophet comes, and I believe she is one of you."

He watched their reactions. Some gasped, others froze, and a few looked down at their hands; he zeroed in on these priests.

"You. The one with the birthmark on your cheek. Come here."

The woman looked at him and then at the others. But when Leo did not avert his gaze, she stepped forward.

"Your Majesty," she said in a frail voice and bowed. This was the girl from before, the one who had tended the burned priest.

"Give me your hand," he said.

The priestess looked at Saayna, but her leader said nothing. She stood, stoic, her mouth set and eyes fixed upon the horizon.

Leo took the priestess's outstretched palm and guided it to the flame.

"Are you the Prophet?" he asked, searching her eyes.

"N-no." Her fingers trembled.

"Prove it," he said and forced her hand into the flame.

The priestess shrieked and tried to pull her arm away, but Leo gripped her wrist and held fast until he saw her skin redden. Only then did he release her.

The priestess stumbled back. She cradled her hand to her belly. Her shoulders shook, but she did not weep. Saayna stepped forward and placed her hands on the girl's shoulders.

"You have done your duty," she said and kissed her three fingers before placing them on the priestess's forehead. "The Phoenix's Light shines upon you."

The priestess's lower lip trembled, yet she bowed and retreated.

He motioned for the next priestess to step forward. And the next, and the next. They came, one after the other, a silent procession of bowed heads and neatly wrapped orange robes. He held their hands over the flame, and to Leo's growing dismay, they all burned.

When the last one shuffled back to the crowd, cradling her hand to her chest, Leo turned sharply to Saayna. His voice cut through the air, dripping with venom.

"You've lied to me," he snarled. "Where is the Prophet? Where are you hiding her?"

When the high priestess made no move to answer, Leo felt his anger grow cold. The flame danced in his hand. Slowly, he turned back to the order, to the waiting priests and burned priestesses. The flame lengthened, eager.

"I intend to burn all of you. Priest and priestess," he announced, his voice cold. "I intend to burn you until I find this Prophet. But, if you are here, Prophet, if you know the true nature of your power, I am giving you the chance to step forward. Announce yourself, and I will spare your brethren. If you don't, I will burn them all alive. And then you will sweep away their ashes."

There was no sound other than the patter of raindrops against the long banyan leaves. Leo scrutinized every face. The flame pulsed. Before him, the smoke from the Eternal Fire twisted into the grey sky.

"So be it."

He nodded, and his guards stepped forward. They formed a ring around the order as they pulled torches from their belts. One by one, the guards struck matches and ignited the torches. Fire blossomed around Leo. The flames hissed against the rain, but they held.

Majnu stalked forward, face grim, and grabbed one priest by the nape of his neck. He cried out, scratching Majnu's arms, but the Spear forced the priest to his knees. The torch crackled. Slowly, Majnu held the priest's face into the flame. He screamed as his eyelashes started to smoke.

The priests panicked then. They pushed and battered against the ring of guards. Some of the guards faltered, looking to Majnu, but his Spear held strong and barked orders.

Some screamed, others begged. A few managed to break the ring and ran. Majnu turned to Leo, who nodded.

"Kill them."

The Spear unsheathed his slingsword and roared out the order. The whistle of thirty slingswords and the smell of burnt flesh filled the grove.

Leo watched a priestess stumble as a blade ripped through her back. Her body crumpled and rolled into the tree line.

Like a rag doll, Leo thought distantly.

He should have wavered. As blood sprayed on the ground, he should have sunk to his knees and begged forgiveness. Given mercy. But as Leo watched his men wield their swords against the sacred priests of the order, he felt nothing.

No fear.

No pain.

All these suns, he had made a show of worshipping the Phoenix. Paying dues to Her Prophet and holding on to the belief that maybe, just maybe, the stories of Her magnificence were true. But now he saw, with brutal clarity. The Phoenix was nothing but a myth, Her Prophet a fanatic. The only true thing that he could believe in with his own two eyes was the Eternal Fire. It was an ancient seat of primal power that, frankly, even his ancestors did not truly understand. But instead of revering it like him, they had created a god and a protector to explain what they could not. A protector who did not even have the courage to face him.

If burning the sacred order before the Eternal Fire was what it took to root out the Prophet and protect his kingdom, then so be it. May today be a reminder of her cowardice. Her silence.

If you are watching, he thought, *know that the servants of your god are suffering, and you can do nothing.*

One priest turned, a wild, desperate look twisting his face. He charged toward Leo, but Majnu stepped in front of his king and struck the attacker down. He yanked the priest up so that his eyes met Leo's.

"Do you know what happens to those who try to hurt their king?" Leo asked softly.

The priest shuddered.

Leo closed his hands, smothering the flame. A pang shot up his arms, and when he opened his palms, a ring of ash marked where the fire had died. He took the bloodied slingsword from Majnu.

"Your Majesty," Arish said, stepping forward, but Leo waved him away.

The king never bloodied his hands. But the high priestess and the heavens were watching. They had sent him on a wild shobu chase, and Leo wanted them to pay.

He placed the edge of the blade against the priest's neck. The man closed his eyes, whispering a prayer, and then Leo slashed down. Blood sprayed across the ground. It splattered across Leo's face and his black coat as the priest's head hit the grass with a dull thud. His eyes stared up at the sky, wide and sightless.

Leo dropped the slingsword. His body suddenly shook, and he gripped his knees. Blood stained his shoes.

Let them see. He pushed back the bile in his throat and straightened. *Let them know that I won't cower.* He unbuttoned his coat and shook out the ceremonial robes he wore underneath, clean and unblemished.

"Do you see, Saayna?" he asked.

The high priestess stared at the horizon, but her eyes were strained as if she held back tears. She clenched her fists so tightly that her knuckles bleached to a bone white.

"Their death is not on my hands," he said. "It is on yours. All the blood that has been spilled today, and all the blood that will spill after, is because of you."

Finally, she turned. Finally, she met his eyes.

"I am merely doing my duty, as you are doing yours," she said.

Through the trees, Leo spotted a black dot on the horizon. A hover-pod. Elena was early.

"Clean this up," he said to Majnu, but he saw his Spear pause. "What is it?"

"The men, Your Majesty, they're beginning to grow squeamish. There are still twenty or so priests left—"

"Then get the Yumi," he snarled. "Make her do what the men cannot."

Majnu bowed his head, his voice small. "As you wish, Your Majesty."

Arish picked up the slingsword and wiped it clean with his handkerchief. "We will still need enough priests for the ceremony. Seven to be precise. Shall I lock up the rest in the tunnels?"

Leo nodded and then held out his hand to Saayna, palm outstretched, the ring of ash grey against his dark skin.

"Come," he said to the high priestess. "Let us do our duty."

CHAPTER 20

YASSEN

A sadness resides deep within these walls. A hollow truth made more crude as the centuries pass. When discovered, it shall chase away one's peace, and their life shall never be the same.
　　　　　　　—from *The Prophecy of the Phoenix*, transcribed into written word by the first priests of the Fire Order

Yassen blinked sleep from his eyes and glanced across the hoverpod.

Up front, by the curved windows, Elena stood with Samson. She was dressed in her gold ceremonial garb, a long lehenga and embroidered blouse. The thin sunrays that managed to peek through the heavy clouds highlighted the pearls woven in the shape of lilies adorning her hair. Samson said something that made her laugh, leaned closer, and whispered something into her ear. His hand found hers. Yassen turned away.

The mountain seemed to rise as they approached, and thick trees older than the kingdom itself reached up to greet them. The hoverpod skimmed over their boughs. Yassen remembered watching the forest as a child when he visited the temple with his mother. How it had amazed him to know that something so lush and beautiful lay across the desert.

The hoverpod descended and docked on the stone ledge beneath the stairs. As they walked out, Yassen breathed in clean mountain air...and something more acrid. He stopped, unease prickling his skin. He could recognize the smell of burnt flesh from anywhere.

Overhead, smoke from the Eternal Fire curled up to meet the grey heavens. His arm ached. The king's guards lined the staircase, and Yassen noted frayed sleeves, rumpled jackets, and smeared drops of blood on their boots, not yet wiped away. A struggle had happened here.

The high priestess and the king came to greet them at the landing. If there had been an attack, they gave no sign of it. Elena went to them with Samson by her side, but when Yassen followed, Ferma grabbed his arm. He tried not to wince as she pulled him aside.

"The king asked me to stay after the ceremony," the Spear said. "You'll have to escort the princess to Rani for the Birdsong festivities, and then back to Palace Hill. I'll send more guards for extra security." Her nails dug into his sleeve. "Watch the sands, Yassen. You'll have to keep a close eye on Elena."

She released his arm. Yassen straightened his sleeve, hiding the mark on his wrist. There was a strangeness in Ferma's voice, a wild look in her eye. And then he understood.

I've never escorted Elena by myself before, he thought. *Of course, she's worried.*

"I'm taloned, Ferma. Don't worry."

They returned to the others. The high priestess held out a branch of red fyerian flowers and dusted both Elena's and the king's shoulders. After a moment's pause, she did the same to Samson.

"Come," she said, "the Holy Bird awaits."

As she pulled her hand back, Yassen spotted something, a dark mark on her wrist, but Saayna folded her hands into her robes and led them into the temple.

Yassen could hear the fire before he saw it. It sounded like a battlefield with the snaps and pops of pulse fire. They turned the corner, and there it was, roaring and lashing at the domed ceiling, its heat hitting Yassen square in the chest.

He backed into the wall, clutching his right arm. The pain returned with a vengeance, as if a dozen needles pierced his skin.

"Are you all right?" Ferma asked.

Yassen nodded. Smoke filtered out of the room through the latticed ceiling, but he still found it hard to breathe. The fire swelled, red forking tongues licking the air. He could barely see the raised dais within its center.

"Mother's Gold," he whispered. "How is Elena supposed to sit in there?"

Leo bowed to the Eternal Fire, and then he took Elena's hand. Together, they walked up the stone steps. The fire swallowed them immediately, but Yassen could see their shadows dancing along the dais.

The high priestess waved her hand, and the priests seated themselves in a semicircle around the pit. Arish and Samson joined them. As Samson leaned toward the fire, Yassen recognized the look in his friend's eyes. It was the expression of a man who saw power and gave himself willingly to it.

Another sharp jolt of pain shot up his arm, and Yassen gripped the stone wall. The Eternal Fire hissed and lengthened. For a moment, the flames parted, and Yassen saw Elena looking straight at him.

"Kneel," Ferma whispered.

Yassen sank to his knees as the priests began to chant. The fire crackled, but as their voices rose, it wavered. Listened. The flames withdrew, caving inward as the high priestess stepped back.

He could no longer see Elena.

The priests chanted and threw white ash into the pit. The air grew thick with smoke and incense. Yassen licked his lips, his mouth dry.

"O Bearer of Hope, we are Your servants," the high priestess sang. Her voice was clear and beautiful, rising over the din. "We will guard Your interests, protect Your lands. We will walk the Agneepath and find succor at its end."

The high priestess threw dried marigold petals into the pit, and the Eternal Fire soared up like the wings of a bird, golden and free. Yassen spotted Elena on the dais, her brow furrowed and her mouth set in a grim line. Leo sat calmly beside her, his face stoic and cool.

"We will feed Your followers, give strength to the weak. And when enemies dare to steal Your power, we will destroy them until they grow meek."

The Eternal Fire flared upward, beating against the ceiling, and then plunged down toward the dais.

Ferma shot to her feet. Even the priests sucked in their breath, their chant faltering. Light pulsed like waves from the fire's core, but neither Elena nor Leo yielded. The fire roared, enraged, its light searing the skin beneath Yassen's eyelids, and still he kept his eyes on Elena. Her flickering form. He felt that if he took his eyes off her, she would vanish.

Suddenly, her shadow rose, and Elena emerged from the flames, coughing. She managed to stumble down the steps and lurch past the priests to the adjoining chamber. The high priestess continued to chant, but Yassen could sense her confusion in the inflection of her voice.

The flames growled, yet Leo remained.

"I should check on Elena." Ferma began to rise, but Yassen held her back. "She wouldn't want you to."

The Yumi slowly knelt again, and they both stared into the fire as it swooned to the rhythm of the chants. Slow and hypnotic. Yassen blinked, his head light. Slowly, the world began to ebb away. The priests' song became a distant drone as shadows pressed along the corners of his eyes.

The fire reared up and swallowed him.

Heat sank into Yassen's bones, but it did not suffocate him. Not this time.

As he stood within the fire, Yassen felt the pain in his arm drain away. The flames found the ache hidden deep in his heart. He saw the faces of his mother and father there, the faces of the boys he had befriended and lost in the Arohassin. He saw the suns of loneliness, of anger, of hate and misfortune. And he felt the fire cleanse the pain away. It washed him as if he were reborn. Soft and new, unknowing in the ways of men.

The flames parted to reveal the bottom of the pit. There, Yassen saw a dark red feather—a feather not of this world, ancient and pure. He felt it give the fire power. And he felt the feather run through him, pull him, call him to the deep darkness that lay beyond this world . . .

"Yassen!" Ferma squeezed his shoulder, and Yassen jolted up.

"Are you okay? You fainted," she said. "And you look pale—I mean, paler than usual."

Dazed, Yassen looked around the chamber. It was empty—only the Eternal Fire remained, sighing. The Ashanta ceremony must have calmed it.

"Where's Elena?" he asked, his voice hoarse.

"With the high priestess," Ferma said with a small frown. "She almost made it."

"And the king?"

"He is with her as well. He sat until the fire had calmed." She hesitated. "Elena's right. The king needs to teach her the way of Agneepath if she is to become queen."

She's learning on her own, he wanted to say but held his tongue. He had seen the dark patches of ash on Elena's wrists in the past weeks; he could not bring himself to stop her. It was not his place. And yet...He wanted to warn her. Warn her of fire's hunger, its white, raging pain.

"Maybe it's a blessing that she can't hold fire," Yassen said before he could stop himself. "It's a volatile power."

Ferma shot him a look that made him instantly regret his words. "Maybe for us. But it is in her blood. The fire *will* choose her." She rose. "We should go meet the royal party."

"I'll join you in a moment," he said. "I want to pray."

Ferma regarded him with skepticism, her tawny eyes glowing in the light.

"I thought those in the Arohassin didn't pray," she said.

"I was Ravani before I joined the Arohassin," he said, "and I'm Ravani still."

Ferma studied him for a moment longer and then nodded. "Hurry. Before you change faith."

He gave a small, rueful smile as the Spear disappeared down the dark corridor.

Slowly, Yassen walked up to the pit. The vision, or whatever it was, had felt so real. Was there truly the Phoenix's feather at the bottom of the pit? Was that the source of the fire? Logic told him no, it was oil or whatever the priests used to feed the flames. It also told him to leave, *now*, but Yassen could not help himself.

He stepped closer.

A single flame rose, like a beast raising its head at the sound of prey. It uncoiled and sniffed the air. Yassen felt time slow and the seconds stretch as the flame slithered closer until it was mere inches from his hand.

The fire snarled and exploded, heat striking his face. Yassen stumbled, but it was too late. He tripped, careening toward the pit when a hand shot out and grabbed him by the collar. He gagged, surprised, and then Elena was pulling him back.

"What are you doing?" she snapped.

With a snarl, the fire smashed down.

Elena screamed as they fell back, the flames rushing toward them. And then Yassen remembered the night on the cliff, the flames eating his hand, and the memory of it, the pain of it, shocked him into action. He hooked his arm under Elena's shoulder and muscled her up. Together, they stumbled out into the corridor.

Elena sank against the wall as Yassen gripped his knees. His body buzzed as if the heat of the fire was inside of him, but he knew it was only the adrenaline. For a while, they said nothing. Only the sound of their heavy pants filled the hall.

"That," Elena said finally, "was utterly stupid."

"I know."

"What were you *thinking*?"

"I wasn't," Yassen said.

"You could have been burned. Phoenix Above, you could have fallen into the pit and died."

"I know," Yassen said, more softly this time.

Elena sighed. Ash dusted her chin and neck. When she spoke again, the anger was gone from her voice. "It was the fire, wasn't it? So beautiful that you couldn't resist."

It was a vision, but he could not say that. "You almost wielded it, right?"

She pulled back her sleeve, revealing patches of burnt skin. "No. But I practice every day."

"Your Highness—"

"Just Elena, Yassen," she said. And when he did not speak, she smiled. "It's no trick."

At this, he laughed. A short, astonished burst, quick and bright, but suddenly, Elena was laughing too.

"Mother's Gold, what kind of mess have we gotten ourselves into?" she sighed after their laughter faded. She spoke quietly, as if to herself.

Yassen hesitated, but seeing her there, hearing her laugh and ask him to call her by her name, he found the courage to speak. "Maybe it's a blessing you can't hold fire," he said carefully. "You've seen what it can do."

And just like that, her face closed, and the softness left her eyes. "Are you implying that I can't control fire?"

"No, I mean—"

"That I can't claim my birthright?"

"Elena, please, I didn't mean that."

She stood. For a moment, he thought she would leave, walk off without a word like before, but instead she stayed, fists curled, face turned toward the inferno as if listening to its hum. When she spoke, he heard a tremble in her voice.

"I need to learn, Yassen. If not for the people, for me." She looked at him, her eyes glistening in the dim light. "To prove to myself that I am not a fraud."

He wanted to tell her that he understood. That when he hung off that cliff, when Samson asked if he was taloned, when pain seized his arm in the dark hours of the night, he felt her same fear. The Arohassin had thought he was useless after his injury; the Ravani thought he was a traitor for his misdeeds and his father, but he was still Yassen Knight. Still capable of winning his freedom from them all.

"I," he began and stopped. Elena waited, but he could only stare, the words lodged in his chest. To tell her the truth would mean damning himself.

Elena scoffed. She pushed past him, her long hair tumbling over her shoulders as she strode through the corridor.

Yassen stood there, waiting for his heart to calm.

When he finally hobbled out and felt the brush of rain on his cheeks, Elena was already heading for the stairs. Ferma hustled after her.

"What did you do to piss her off?"

He turned to see Samson. Smoke writhed from his lips as he drew on a long black pipe.

"I thought you stopped smoking ganja," Yassen said.

"I use it sometimes to calm my nerves," Samson said. "Looks like you need it too." He handed the pipe to Yassen, who raised it to his lips and slowly drew in the sweet, narcotic taste of moonspun ganja. Yassen exhaled; a thin wisp of smoke twisted and dissipated in the air.

"Better?" Samson asked, eyeing him. Yassen nodded. "Good."

They stood in silence, watching the clouds darken and the guards shift their feet. The rain fell steadily now and gave the mountain an eerie glow. Below the lip of the cliff, Yassen caught a flash of Elena's gold skirts.

"Interesting thing, fire," Samson said. "Do you remember the last time we were here together?"

"We met Akaros," Yassen began.

"And then everything changed," Samson finished. He chuckled, smoke puffing out. "Funny, isn't it? That our journey with the Arohassin started in the holiest of places."

"Maybe it's not as holy as we think."

"Maybe." Samson blew out smoke from his nostrils. "I heard from Muftasa just now. They have a lead. A gold cap saw a woman that fit Maya's description near the Raja stepwell. We have a team tailing her but…" He took another draw. "This could be it."

"I'll go." He shook his head as Samson offered him the pipe. "When?"

"Muftasa says after Elena's parade for the Fire Festival. The timing will be better," Samson said. "People will be distracted by the festivities in the city and the stepwell will be quiet. And of course, it'll be coronation week. What better way for Elena to begin her reign than to capture a terrorist." Samson grinned and took one last long pull, then dumped out ash from his pipe. "The world's changing, Cass. If we're not quick to change with it, we'll be stranded."

As Yassen watched Samson descend the staircase after Elena, he felt something nag him, like a painful thorn from a skorrir. Something Samson had said.

The last time we were here together.

He had answered with their first meeting of Akaros, but that hadn't been right. Not really. Because the last time they had been at the temple together, Samson had not known. Yassen had been slipping down the steps holding a freshly pickpocketed pod when he had seen Samson standing at the fountain of the Phoenix.

"Give me strength," Samson had said. "Give me strength to crush their metal hearts."

Yassen had paid it no mind then. But now he wondered what Samson had meant. And what he had bartered. Because though he was no believer, Yassen at least knew that fire did not give without a sacrifice.

An ache lanced up his arm, sharp and precise. Yassen gritted his teeth.

He thought of the inferno, and the deep, ancient pull he felt toward its core. It may have been a hallucination, but the sensation was too visceral to be imagined. A truth lay within the flames, a truth that predated him and the very steps he stood upon.

And it was growing impatient.

Yassen glanced back down the dark corridor. In the sound of the falling rain and the emptiness before him, he thought he heard the fire cackle.

CHAPTER 21

ELENA

*Oh, dear lady, why do you look so pale? You glow like the sun, both
from within and without, selfless, like the honey a mother drips into her
child's dream.*

—from *The Odyssey of Goromount: A Play*

Elena dipped her trembling hands into the basin of the fountain. The
water cooled her skin, but when she withdrew them, they still shook. The
statue of the Phoenix rose above her, and she could see her reflection in its
red eyes.

"Why?" she asked it. "Why am I the only one in our family who cannot hold fire?"

The statue remained silent, like always. Perhaps it did not answer her
because she did not believe in the Phoenix as deeply as her mother. Or
maybe it was because she did not respect fire as greatly as her father. She
was caught in between wanting to believe and being too skeptical to give
in fully; respecting fire and being too afraid to hold it for long.

Maybe it's a blessing you can't hold fire.

She shuddered. Yassen knew the pain of burning—that was why he had tried to dissuade her—but he could not understand. How could it be a blessing to be forsaken? To be denied the gift of her family, the one thing that would grant her the throne?

Without holding fire, she could not be the queen of Ravence.

And without Ravence, she was nothing.

Elena plunged her hands in the water again, her fingers slowly turning numb. She breathed in deeply to still her thundering heart, but it did not calm.

Useless. She was so useless.

Footsteps sounded behind her, and she quickly turned, hiding her hands behind her back.

"Saayna."

The high priestess hurriedly wrapped her scarf around her head, her hands tucked into the wide sleeves of her robe.

"How did you get here?"

"The tunnels. I—I cannot speak for long," Saayna said, glancing up the stairs where they could see a trail of smoke just beyond the cliff. "They are looking for me."

"Who? My father?"

"Elena, you must listen to me," Saayna said, eyes wide, imploring. "Your father has desecrated the order. He believes that he can defy the Phoenix Herself. He is delusional, Elena, blinded by his own ego to see the truth."

"Saayna, what are you saying?" Elena asked.

Suddenly, the high priestess grabbed her hands. Elena flinched, but Saayna squeezed hard, crushing her fingers.

"I would have remained silent. I would have gone through the ceremonies and waited until the Prophet came, but Leo has killed my brethren." Tears brightened her eyes. "You must stop him. Ask him to seek forgiveness on your coronation day and do the right thing."

"Saayna—"

"There you are."

They turned to see Majnu marching up the stairs. He brushed dirt from his shoulders, as if he had come from the tunnels as well. The Spear bowed to Elena, gave a smile to Saayna, who had stiffened beside her.

"The king is waiting for you, High Priestess."

Saayna did not move. Majnu took a step forward, smile still on his face, and as he approached, Elena felt a whisper of danger dance down her spine. She stepped in front of Saayna.

"What does my father want with her?"

"Your Highness, I am not obliged to say. Please, if I may . . ."

"Majnu," Elena said, pulling to her full height, though she was still several inches shorter than the man. "I will escort the high priestess myself."

"That will not be necessary—"

"Elena!"

She turned to see Ferma jogging down the stairs. Ash and sweat streaked the Yumi's face, but she seemed steady.

"Ferma," Elena said, relief flooding her. "What in the seven hells is going on?"

"Majnu," Ferma said with a nod. Her eyes traveled over the three of them. "Is something wrong?"

"The Eternal Fire was not fully satisfied," Majnu said smoothly. "The high priestess is needed to calm it further."

"You will not take her," Elena snapped.

"Your Highness, the king—"

"It's all right," Saayna said as she stared up at the Phoenix. A look of clarity suddenly washed over her face, and she closed her eyes. Whispered a prayer they could not hear. Elena ached to feel what Saayna did; to believe so fully and completely in the heavens and find strength from them. "I will go."

She turned to Elena. Gone was the look of fear and grief. Instead, Saayna's face was composed, calm even. "You will do what is right. I believe in it."

"Saayna, wait."

But the high priestess was already descending the stairs. Majnu bowed and quickly followed.

"Are you okay?" Ferma asked.

"Yes, yes, I'm fine," Elena said, distracted. *What did Saayna mean about the priests?* They had been there during the Ashanta ceremony. Not all of them, but they didn't need the full order for the proceedings. "Ferma, did the priests look frightened?"

Ferma paused. "They did seem...distracted, but I wouldn't say frightened. Why do you ask?"

"It's just," she began, but then Ferma grabbed her hands, studying her reddened fingertips.

"Mother's Gold, you were burned!"

"Oh." Elena looked down at her hands. "It's nothing." Her shoulders sagged. "I couldn't withstand the heat, like always."

"You did better this time. You almost had it."

"Almost isn't good enough."

She needed practice. She needed to be alone in the desert, to lose herself in its dunes, to feel its breath against her skin. She needed time.

The Phoenix stared down at her with hard, unflinching eyes.

Why did you forsake me?

And with that question, mixed with her grief, Elena felt rage spark in her stomach. Rage against herself, against the heavens, against her father. She wanted to drive a blade into those red eyes, to shatter the mirrors that reflected only her and nothing higher. She wanted to weep.

"I thought you were down here."

She looked up to see Samson.

"Leave us, Ferma," he ordered.

Elena paused, taken aback. No one commanded Ferma other than her and her father. Ferma bristled and her hair began to curl at the ends. And perhaps it was the image of Ferma standing beside her, defiant, that broke Elena from her spiraling thoughts and rooted her back to the present.

She faced Samson, shoulders straight. "What do you want?"

It was Samson's turn to be taken aback. He looked between her and Ferma, hesitating.

"Shit. Am I intruding?"

"Yes," Elena said. "But I'll allow Ferma to decide if you can stay."

A small smile touched the edge of Ferma's lips. "Oh, let's spare the man for today, Your Highness. He still has a long way to learn who can grant leave."

At this, understanding rippled across Samson's face. He bowed his head, sheepish. "I apologize, Ferma."

Elena and Ferma shared a secretive grin before Ferma turned back to Samson. "At ease, soldier." As Samson straightened, she whispered in

Elena's ear. "I have to stay behind. Yassen and the guards will be with you." She gripped Elena's shoulder. "And don't fret. You'll find a way. You always do."

Elena squeezed Ferma's hand and watched her vanish up the stone staircase. Then she turned to Samson, who was examining the statue.

"Needs to be cleaned. Doesn't it?" He pointed at marks left from birds and other creatures of the mountain. When she did not answer, his voice softened. "I heard your father say how proud he was to see you sit in the flames for so long."

"Don't lie, Samson. Not to me."

"He believes in you, you know? In his own, twisted way. I see it," he added, when she glanced at him, "when he gets that quiet, dark look. You know it. I'll see him kind of... recede during meetings and I know that he's thinking about you."

"That doesn't mean he believes," she said. "My father refuses to teach me because—" And it was there, on the tip of her tongue. *Because he does not wish to give up the throne. Because he wants control. It's always been about control.*

"Because of some *twisted* reason," she said. "And no Ravani heir can rule without fire."

"Well, I wouldn't say it's too late," Samson replied. "I read that Queen Jumi only managed to sit in the fire on the day of her coronation."

Elena stayed quiet. The numbness in her hands began to ebb away, replaced with tiny prickles of heat traveling up her palms.

"I should leave," she said.

"You know, the Arohassin once instructed me to shoot an innocent woman in the back," Samson said. He stared up at the Phoenix and its sharp, red eyes. "I couldn't do it. So Yassen did it for me and tried to cover it up. But they knew. They meant to punish us both, but I took it. It was my fault anyway. Twenty lashes, ten for me, ten for Yassen.

"The pain was horrible. I lay on my stomach for two weeks wallowing in misery and self-pity. Plagued by fever and nightmares and doubt. I wondered if I should have just shot the girl. But by the time the two weeks were over, and the bandages came off, I knew I had made the right decision."

He looked down, his dark eyes boring through her.

"Sometimes, the moments that define us are the moments in which we spare ourselves. They force us to examine who we truly are and what we stand for." He reached behind her and gently took her hands. Uncurled her fists and traced her skin. "Don't lose hope. Maybe you'll look back and see how this was the moment you decided to give yourself a little mercy."

Elena stared at him. *Mercy.* She had never even considered whether she deserved mercy, much less if it was something she could offer herself. She regarded her fiancé curiously. For all his pride and feats of war, Samson Kytuu was far more poetic than she had imagined. Gentle, even.

"And does that moment define you still?" she said.

"More than you know." He kissed her burnt fingertips. "I'll see you in the city, yes?"

She nodded, and Samson gave a low bow. As she descended the staircase, Elena looked back. Samson stood beneath the Phoenix, gazing into the still fountain.

She wondered what he saw in his reflection—wished she had asked.

CHAPTER 22

LEO

Oh Wanderer! What you seek lies within these veins. Look! You carry the story of the world.

—from *The Odyssey of Goromount: A Play*

I want you to kill the priests," Leo said to Ferma as she bowed before him.

Ferma froze, stunned. "But, Your Majesty." She looked to him in disbelief, as if hoping he would rectify his statement, but Leo only stared back, hard and unflinching.

"They've conspired against the throne, and I have burned their names in the sand," he said. "Now go."

"It is the *order*."

"And I am your king. Do you serve the throne or the order, Ferma?"

Emotions warred across her face, dark and terrible. Her mouth twisted in distaste, the strands of her hair coiling like serpents. For a moment, Leo thought she was going to attack him, but then the Yumi stepped back.

"As the king wishes," she said, and her voice sounded like branches snapping in half. She did not need to hurt him. He could feel her judgment, sharp as knives.

Her hair slashed through the air, through necks and legs, spilling blood down the mountainside. Where his guards had balked, the Yumi was ruthless and efficient. She quickly butchered twelve priests, leaving only eight. Leo watched as a priestess bolted in his direction, but Ferma whipped around, her hair swinging behind her and slicing into the priestess's back. The priestess's eyes widened as they met Leo's.

He saw her hatred, her pain, but mostly, he saw her fear.

Ferma withdrew her hair, and the priestess sagged forward like a puppet, her eyes, lost and empty, staring upward.

Leo bent down beside her. She was a young woman, no more than twenty-five suns. Elena's age. Gently, he closed her eyes.

Bodies lay everywhere—young, old, woman, man. A gale blew through the mountain, stirring the ends of their bloodied robes.

As he stared at the heap of bodies, Leo felt something integral leave him. His fear, maybe, his remorse, perhaps, but as he slowly rose to his feet, he knew it wasn't either of those, but his humanity.

He would never be forgiven. That was all right. The rain would cleanse this mountain and baptize it into something pure. That's what his people did. Like Alabore, they created something holy out of something forsaken. His deed today was but an echo of history. Leo was not the first, and he knew for certain that he would not be the last. Elena may not follow in his footsteps, but her children, his grandchildren, might. And their children. And the ones who came after them. They would repeat the deeds of their ancestors because that's what it took to survive. That's what it took to keep Ravence alive.

Peace is cruel, his father had once told him. *It dances like sand in the wind and blows out of your reach just when you are about to grasp it.*

Leo looked past the flapping robes and to the desert beyond. There, within the dunes, was his home. It had not known peace, not in his father's lifetime or in his. But perhaps Elena might find it. Leo walked past the dead priestess. Elena might enjoy the peace he had killed for.

He found Ferma crouched within the roots of the ancient gulmohar tree, cleaning the blood off her hardened hair with a practiced hand.

"You did well," he said.

The Yumi said nothing as the gulmohar branches whistled in the wind like dry bones rattling in a cage.

"The remaining seven priests and the high priestess will be kept under guard," he said. "That's enough for the coronation. To keep appearances."

But even as he said this, the words tasted false. For what were appearances but a mere shade of truth? The high priestess donned her orange robes, but she was just a puppet for a higher power. The Prophet spoke of bringing ruin upon sinners, but she was a sham, a figurehead who cloaked a harsh reality. The gods were cruel, and the heavens forever out of man's reach.

And him? What was he?

Ferma wiped off the last drop of blood and folded the cloth into a perfect red square. "You need to teach Elena how to hold fire," she said. "If she cannot hold fire before the priests and the people, they will never accept her."

"Won't they?" Leo said softly.

At this, Ferma turned to him, alert. "What do you mean?"

"The priests will not deny her, not anymore. Not after what we've done today. And as for the people." Leo spread his arms like the branches above him. "I've ordered that the coronation ceremony will not be open to the public like the ones before. Danger is too high, with the Arohassin's threat. But one member of the public will attend. Jangir."

Ferma's eyes widened. "And he will repeat anything you tell him."

"He will believe what I want him to." Leo met her eyes. "Don't you see, Ferma? Elena can still become queen without holding fire. She will have the throne."

"But this…this is…" Her hair quivered. "This is unprecedented. People *will* find out sooner or later."

"Not when we have a war on our border," Leo said. "Then they'll be more concerned whether or not Elena can lead armies and protect the kingdom."

"Forget the people then. What of Elena?" The Yumi's eyes bored into him, as sharp as the blades of her hair. "What will you tell her? What will she think?"

She will curse me for denying her birthright, Leo thought. But she will have the throne. *Like she has always wanted, like she has always dreamed.* He hoped it would be enough. Maybe, suns from now, he would earn Elena's forgiveness once she realized fire did not make a ruler—strength, foresight, and discipline did. He would help her protect Ravence, guide her as monarch like his father had not. And if she didn't come around...Leo told himself he could bear her bitterness. As long as Elena and Ravence were safe, he would bear all the hate in the twelve kingdoms.

"If you will not tell her, tell me," Ferma said. "Why won't you teach her, Leo? What wrong has she committed that she cannot receive the blessings of the Phoenix?"

The wind whistled through the branches of the ancient gulmohar tree, and in its song, Leo heard it laugh at him.

Selfish, selfish Malhari.

Leo looked at Ferma, torn. If he told her, she might tell Elena and reveal his true nature to his daughter. And yet Ferma would be the only one to understand. She, like him, had loved and lost Aahnah. She had grieved for her as much as he.

"First you must understand, the Phoenix's blessings are not benedictions," Leo said in a heavy voice. "They are a curse. When Alabore Ravence sought the Phoenix to build his kingdom, She granted his wish with a condition—that if a Ravani heir can hold Her flame, they must sacrifice someone of blood or love to the Eternal Fire.

"When my father told me on the eve of my coronation, I refused. He had sacrificed his own brother, but I could not do the same with my family. I gave the inferno nothing." Leo paused, throat tight. "But Aahnah learned of our curse in the scrolls. And she did what I could not.

"I couldn't control the flames then," he whispered. "No matter how hard I tried, they fought me."

"I remember," Ferma said, her voice hollow. "Aahnah had called to it. Some chant she had discovered in the library. And when the Great Fire rushed to her..."

She had jumped. Without hesitation, without fear, without so much as crying out to him.

The Eternal Fire had never fought him since.

"So you see," Leo said after a while, voice carefully composed. "Elena will need to give a sacrifice if she learns. And who do you think the one of love or blood will be?" When Ferma did not answer, Leo pointed at his chest. "One of blood"—and then to her—"one of love. Would you really want to be burned alive and leave Elena alone to handle the Jantari and the Arohassin?"

"This—this is madness," Ferma said.

"It is the truth."

"But she will make the same mistake as you! You said yourself the Eternal Fire does not forget. It will harm her, one day or another."

"Why do we do the Ashanta ceremonies, Ferma?" he asked quietly.

"To . . . to seek the Phoenix, of course," Ferma said, but her voice lacked conviction. "Or, is that a ruse too?"

Leo glanced up at the temple, at the trail of smoke rising from its center. "We do the Ashanta ceremonies to show the people that the Ravani family is and will always be blessed by the Phoenix. But you and I know the truth now. Elena will no longer have to do the ceremonies or step in this temple again. She will lead negotiations, armies, treaties. The people will forget about the heavens and focus on the Jantari instead."

Ferma pocketed the cloth and wiped her hands against the roots of the tree. Her hair softened, becoming shiny and sleek. As she wound it around her shoulder, her voice was steady, resolute.

"I am *always* willing to die for Elena. It is my job as her Spear. And you—you are her father. Are you not willing to sacrifice yourself for your own child?"

And there it was, the question that haunted him, singing in the desert wind and in the crackle of the flames.

Are you not willing to sacrifice yourself for your own child?

Selfish, selfish Malhari.

Leo turned away, heat lacing around his chest like a vise. He would do anything to protect Elena, but how could he help and guide her if he was dead? Saayna, the order, they did not understand Ravence like him. If the Phoenix asked them to burn for Her, they would build the pyres themselves. But if every man and woman followed the Phoenix to their death, who would be left to pick up the remains? Who would be left to protect their borders, their way of life, against the Jantari?

"I would die for Elena," Leo said finally. "But not meaninglessly. Not by burning. Give me a pulse gun, a slingsword, and I will happily fight alongside my daughter and take a death wound for her."

"She needs us, Ferma. Both of us. The Jantari are at our borders and the Arohassin already in our city. She cannot handle both alone."

He took Ferma's hands in his.

"Would you want Elena to enter her queendom grieving, having lost her father or her most stalwart friend? She will be distracted, vulnerable. And Farin will use that against her." He squeezed, hard. "You can despise me, Ferma, but do not fling yourself into that fire for Elena. She needs you here, by her side."

The Yumi said nothing for a long time. One red leaf fell from above, brushing Leo's cheek. It pricked him on his chin, and a tiny dot of blood swelled. Leo did not break away, but Ferma took her kerchief and handed it to him.

"I will not perform the sacrifice," she said as he dabbed his chin with the same cloth she had used to clean off the blood of the priests. "But you must tell her the truth. Or I will."

When he said nothing, she stood. "She deserves to know."

Finally, slowly, Leo nodded. She did. But he hoped that when he told her, Elena would not judge him too harshly. That she would not think he was as selfish as the fire claimed him to be.

"Your Majesty."

Leo turned to see Arish walking toward them.

"It's Saayna," the Astra said and then hesitated. "And there's something you need to see."

Leo offered Ferma the kerchief, but she shook her head. "Keep it," she said. Her hair curled as the wind rose, the gulmohar tree groaning. "Remember it."

"I heard that you tried to speak with my daughter," Leo said to Saayna. They stood at the entrance of the temple. When the high priestess said nothing, Leo sighed. "What are you hoping to achieve here, Saayna? Sympathy? Salvation?"

Still, she said nothing.

He was suddenly so tired. His conversation with Ferma had drained him, and now, if Elena knew about the priests... *Mother's Gold, it never ends.*

If there was a Phoenix or a god in the heavens, She must be laughing at him.

"You and the order will remain here," Leo said wearily. "And my men will cut down your last seven priests if you do not reveal the Prophet to me. You have until Elena's coronation day. Do you understand, Saayna?"

When she finally turned to him, her eyes were grim. "I pray that when the Prophet arrives, she burns you first. In front of Elena."

Then she was gone, robes whispering across the floor as she slipped back into the temple and its vicious Eternal Fire.

Leo walked down the steps, hands shaking. He knew that if he looked back now, he would crumble. Instead, he carefully stared at the horizon until his eyes burned.

I will find you, Prophet. Wherever you are, I will root you out and burn you before Saayna.

"The Arohassin attacked a patrol near the Yoddha Base," Arish said as they boarded the hoverpod. "We sustained a few injuries, but the Arohassin left this." He motioned and a holo floated to them. It showed something black in the sand, some great, coiling serpent, but as the image came closer, Leo realized it was no monster. It was a rune.

"Who has seen this?" he said through pressed lips.

"Only us," Arish said, and indeed, the hoverpod was empty except for them.

"And the soldiers at the base?"

"The Black Scales and a few of our officers saw, but they think it's some nonsensical mark of the Arohassin."

Leo stared at the rune smoldering on the dune like a fresh brand on an animal. He could not say why, but something was unnatural about the symbol.

"They know," he said. "They know about the Prophet."

And they left the rune to goad me, he wanted to add. And if the Arohassin knew about his search for the Prophet . . .

Mother's Gold, I have a traitor. He gripped his chair, thinking quickly. No one knew about the runes except him, Arish, Muftasa, Samson, and the high priestess. Arish and Muftasa would never betray him. Saayna had been kept under his watch ever since they found the runes on the priest. Was it Samson then? Or Yassen Knight?

"How did they get there?" he asked. "Did we catch any of them?"

"We believe they camped in Teranghar and used cruisers to cross the sands. A Black Scale captured one, Your Majesty," Arish said, and the holo shifted to show the face of a boy with a crooked nose and small eyes. "Goes by the code name Mason. A Jantari, only seventeen suns. He's a new recruit."

"That's why they left him behind," Leo muttered. He shifted the holo back to the rune.

"Do you suppose they know who she is? The Prophet?"

"No," Leo said at once, but a sliver of doubt made the word sound small. *They couldn't.* After all, the Arohassin did not believe in the Phoenix. Why would they then chase a prophet?

Leo peered at the rune. The Arohassin had left black sand in his desert, along the southern border, and the irony did not escape him. They had finally shown their hand, but could it be that they did not understand what they held?

"Maybe they know what the runes mean, maybe not," Leo mused. "But I bet that they burned this because they want me to know they are watching. That they have eyes and ears everywhere."

Before Arish could respond, the door of the hoverpod opened.

With a quick wave of his hand, Arish closed the holos as Majnu and the guards entered.

"What is it?" Arish snapped. "Did I not tell you to wait outside?"

"The high priestess told us to board. She said that the temple..." He hesitated. When he spoke again, his voice was quiet. "It needs to be cleansed. They want to burn their dead."

Leo looked out the windows. In a tangle of thorned rakins, the red buds small and new on the dark branches, he saw an orange robe.

"Leave behind a few guards and the Yumi to help," he said. "It's the least we can do."

Silence crept across the hoverpod. Finally, Majnu turned and barked out orders. A few guards slunk out of the hoverpod, and Leo saw the ashen look on their faces. He had asked them to commit the unforgivable. Perhaps they cursed his name. Perhaps they cursed themselves, but Leo knew they would remain loyal to their king. The desert bred hard men, and their blood ran thick.

The hoverpod hummed as the doors closed and the remaining guards took their places. The pilot engaged the gears, and they rose into the tormented sky. A northern wind played across the desert. Dunes shifted and melted underneath him, but Leo paid no mind. It was only when they reached the southern border and he saw the rune burned along the face of the dune that he noticed the sand hadn't shifted. It remained perfectly still, while the desert around it rolled with the wind.

They docked in a valley, and Leo strode out. Majnu and Arish moved to join him, but he ordered them to stay back.

A Ravani soldier dressed in a sand-colored combat uniform saluted at his approach.

"Your Majesty," the soldier said, his gold stripes indicating that he was a captain. "The Black Scales have the boy in custody, but he hasn't said a word."

"Get out of my way," Leo growled, and swept past the man.

The air prickled. Leo could hear the familiar hiss of fire echoing in his ears. The rune seemed to grow darker as he squatted and ran his hand through the blackened sand that was already beginning to cool. He gathered sand in his palm and watched it spill through his fingers. It fell straight down instead of dancing in the wind.

Leo got up and walked along the edges of the rune. It curved up and over the lip of the dune, and he followed it to the other side.

That was when he saw it. Or rather, did not see it. He had stared at the runes for so long that they were etched into his mind. The mark that had appeared on the back of the young priest looked like the eye of a hurricane, a mass of inward lines. The rune before him was also shaped like a storm, but it did not curve inward. Rather, it jutted out in a harsh line. Like an arrow, like a sword.

The rune was wrong. Did that mean the Arohassin did not know about the prophecy? Were they merely playing games?

"Oi!" he shouted at the captain still standing at the base of the dune. The soldier jumped. "Where's the boy?"

"Well, sir, there's an issue there," the captain said. He paused. "The Black Scales, they took the boy."

"The Black Scales serve Ravence now," Leo said.

"Yes, but—"

"Take me to them," Leo said. He walked right down the middle of the rune, scattering sand.

★ ★ ★

At the makeshift base of Samson's Black Scales, soldiers milled in and out of neatly ordered tents. Leo spotted no refuse, no discarded bottles. He had always heard of the Black Scales' efficiency, their rigid honor code, but he was still amazed by the sight before him.

Samson was prepped for war, just like he had said. Only, Leo realized with bitterness, he had underestimated how ready Samson was to take on the Jantari.

They arrived at a gate flanked by two guards. The men scowled at the Ravani soldier, but when they saw Leo, their scowls dropped away.

"Your Majesty," they said and saluted.

"Let me see the boy," he said.

"Our orders are to keep the gates locked until Commander Chandi has finished her interrogation," one of the men said.

"You serve Ravence now," he said. "You serve *me*."

The Black Scale hesitated, but his partner spoke.

"We apologize, sir, but orders are orders. No one is to see the prisoner."

"Do you know who you're talking to?" the Ravani soldier seethed, but Leo held up his hand.

He looked at the Black Scale, and his voice was chillingly soft, devoid of inflection. "Move aside, soldier. I've already killed many men today. One more makes no difference on my tally."

The Black Scales glanced at each other. An unspoken message flitted between them, and then one stepped back and pressed his hand to the panel.

The gates rolled back. Another Black Scale stepped forward, indicating for them to follow. Several soldiers within stopped and stared at Leo and his gold ceremonial robes.

None bowed.

The soldier led them to an adobe structure.

"Who's in there?" Leo asked.

"The prisoner and Commander Chandi," the Black Scale said. He turned and nodded to the Ravani soldier. "You can stay out here."

They walked down a short, cramped hall that smelled of dust and sweat. When they came to another door, the Black Scale removed a small holopod from his pocket and used it to deactivate the sensor.

They entered a spotless room that had been divided in half by a glass wall. A boy sat on one side. His hands were bound. Three soldiers, one with their back turned, stood before a panel covered in holos and dials.

The two soldiers who faced the door snapped to attention.

"What is it?" said the third soldier.

"The king, Commander."

Slowly, lazily, the soldier turned.

Commander Chandi was a tall woman with dark eyes and blue-stained lips. A tattoo crawled up her neck, a skeletal hand wrapping around her throat like a savage, horrid necklace. When she saw him looking, she smiled.

"Your Grace," she said.

"It's Your Majesty," Leo corrected.

The commander chuckled, the bony fingers rippling over her throat. "My apologies, Your Majesty."

Behind the glass, Leo saw the boy smile.

"Can he hear me?" Leo asked.

"Yes, sir," Chandi replied.

Leo faced the boy. A tiny smattering of hair grew on his upper lip. Blood beaded across his chin and dripped into his shirt. His colorless Jantari eyes peered at the glass from behind deep, hooded lids.

The boy's smile grew wider.

"We knew you would come," he said.

For a moment, Leo wondered if he had walked into a trap, but then Chandi turned a dial and an electric shock ran through the boy, making him shriek and jolt up in his chair. The ends of his hair stood up.

"Why?" Leo said. "Do you have something to tell me?"

When the boy did not answer, Leo's hand found the dial. He turned it, and the boy gasped as pain surged through his body.

Briefly, Leo hesitated. He thought of the young girl with hair of starlight. The fear in her eyes, how her limbs had crumpled.

He stepped away from the panel.

Smoothly, Chandi stepped in and turned up the dial.

The boy gritted his teeth, but a scream escaped his lips. Leo watched his body tremble, and his hands curl into fists, before Chandi relented. The boy slumped forward.

"Why did the Arohassin leave a rune?" Leo asked softly.

"We knew you would come," he said again.

A useless answer, but Leo did not reach for the dial.

"They left you behind," he said, changing tactics. "You're dispensable to them, easily thrown away like a stray shobu. Or an orphan." The boy stiffened.

So he *was* an orphan.

Leo silenced the room and turned to Chandi. "Let me in."

She had been watching him the entire time, a thin, amused smile playing across her lips. "You know, you remind me of him. Our Blue Star." When she saw the quizzical look on his face, her smile widened. "Samson. He's like you. Neither of you would hesitate to pummel a boy."

"I merely want to talk to him," Leo said, his patience wearing thin.

The commander nodded. "Of course."

She pressed a button, and the door to the chamber opened. Mason looked up as Leo swept in. He towered over the boy, making him crane his neck to see his full height. And then Leo rested his hand on the boy's head. Gently, almost tenderly, Leo cupped his cheek.

"You are unwanted," he said, his eyes boring into Mason. "They discarded you just like your parents did. But in Ravence, you are wanted. You're needed." He gripped the boy's chin, gently yet firmly. "Tell me what I need to know, and I'll see that these men won't kill you."

The boy looked at him with his pale, colorless eyes. Eyes just like Yassen's. "I—I don't know," he stammered. "They didn't tell me much."

"Oh, but you do," Leo said. He had seen the shadow of a lie cross the boy's eyes. "You heard something."

Mason gulped. He tried to wrench his face away, but Leo held firm.

"Your time burns, boy," Leo said.

"She's lying to you!" he blurted.

"Who?"

"The one who sees visions in the flames," he said. "That's what they told me! I swear, I don't know her name!"

Leo finally let go. He thought of Saayna standing before the Eternal Fire, the disdainful look in her eyes. Anger rose in him, thick and vicious.

He strode out of the room, the door sliding shut behind him with a click of finality.

"Keep questioning him," he said to Chandi. "Find out what else he knows."

The commander nodded, her blue lips curling into a wry grin. "My men will see you out," she said. "As for the ones at the gate, I apologize for their insolence. They seem to have forgotten who they report to."

Leo accepted her salute and followed the Black Scale, but he was no fool. Double meanings and lies threaded through Chandi's words. Samson may have forfeited his command of the Black Scales to Leo in name, but their hearts still bled for him.

Leo burst out of the building, surprising the Ravani soldier who scrambled into a salute and scampered after him as he stormed out of the base. Arish awaited him on the hoverpod's ramp. When he saw the king's face, he turned to his guards and quickly ordered them in.

"I've been a fool, Arish," Leo said once they were alone. "The runes. They were wrong. The second rune on the priest, the one that Saayna showed me, it looked like a hurricane, bending inward. But the rune the Arohassin have, it points out. It points north. Saayna *altered* the rune."

Arish sat down with a sigh. He appeared to pick his words carefully. "Perhaps there is the possibility that you are wrong, Your Majesty. How can we be so sure that Saayna altered the rune?"

Leo ground his teeth. Raw fury roiled through him, fresh and hot. Suddenly, he understood why the Eternal Fire raged so often. He wanted to burn something too.

"She wants to protect the Prophet," Leo said.

"Yet does she even know *who* the Prophet is?" Arish said. "There is no name in the runes, no clear distinction of who exactly we're looking for. All we know is that the Prophet is a woman who cannot burn. She was not in the city, and now we know she's not a priest."

Leo stared at him. What Arish said could be true, but if so... His anger dissipated at once, leaving ash in its wake. If so, then he had killed all those priests for nothing. Just like the girl.

"No," Leo said, shaking his head violently. "Saayna is hiding something. I know it. She must have warned the Prophet, sent her away before we learned she was at the temple. Search the mountains. Send more guards to root through the tunnels—"

Arish touched his hands, voice soft. "I will always follow you, Your Majesty, but..." He paused. "You are ruining yourself, Leo. Let's stop this awful chase. If Saayna is right, then the coming of the Prophet is inevitable. She will show herself to us. Until then, let us seek forgiveness."

Leo laughed, but the sound was bitter.

"You too, Arish?" He shook his head. "Damn."

His Astra gave a small smile and looked down at his wrinkled hands. "I know you are not as religious as me, but we're growing old, Leo," he said. "After today...Don't you think it's time for us to deserve peace? To rid ourselves of our sins?"

"Do not go soft on me now."

Leo thought of Alabore and what he had seen before building Ravence—a desolate stretch of desert underneath the pale moons. A haven for his people. A chance for peace.

He would not let their dream burn.

"There's no time for redemption," he said.

"Your Majesty—"

"I am not going to throw my hands up!" he snapped. "This is *my* kingdom. *My* desert. My people have fought for it, slaved for it. This Prophet has no claim to this land. She gave it up when she disappeared from this world. And by heavens," he growled, "I will not let her take it."

CHAPTER 23

ELENA

The art of the slingsword is not easy to master. It demands suns of prac-
tice, diligence, and failure. For one can only master the slingsword when
they understand the sting of its blade.
                              —from chapter 14 of *The Great History of Sayon*

Elena craned her neck to see balloons of red and gold rise into the drizzling
air. Dhols beat in the streets, echoing through her chest as people, most
dressed in gold caps, jostled each other along the sidewalks, pushing
against the guards as their hovercar procession wound through the city.

The Birdsong, the prelude of the Fire Festival, was supposed to be a
small affair, but no citizen of Rani knew how to celebrate things quietly.

"Your Highness, I am so *pleased* you will be joining us," Jangir said. He
sat across from her, his gold cap perched on his head like a straight-backed
soldier. "My men have organized everything. Down to the last details.
And we have brought out the loveliest audience. Stalwart supporters of the
king, real men of god and country. Everyone is just so *delighted* to have you
and your betrothed here."

Elena gave a tight, polite smile but it took everything in her willpower not to stop the car and order her guards to imprison Jangir. He and his men were responsible for the murder of innocents, and yet here he sat, with his wheedling smiles.

Oh, Father, you are blind.

She knew it was Leo's doing, having Jangir personally accompany her to the proceedings. At the Ashanta ceremony, her father had not brought up their argument, and afterward, he had disappeared without a word, only to send orders that he would not accompany her to the Birdsong festivities—Jangir would. But she saw the hidden meaning behind his words.

The gold caps are here to stay.

"I'm sure it will be a pleasant afternoon," Elena said.

"Indeed, Your Highness. I don't mean to spoil the surprise, but we have a ribbon-cutting ceremony of a brilliant new statue, which I'm sure you'll be *delighted* to see. Our men have found the best slingsword masters in the country for a demonstration—"

Elena stared out the window, tuning out Jangir. *Varun, you fool, what are you waiting for?* She had told Ferma to pressure Varun, meant to ask for an update after the Ashanta ceremony, but then there had been no time. *I swear, if I see that fucking idiot here—*

Yells erupted in the street, cutting through the dhols. Suddenly, Elena saw guards running toward a knot of bodies.

"What in the seven hells," Jangir growled, turning to the window just as a rock slammed against the door.

Elena gasped, pulling back. The doors were reinforced, and the rock had not even left a dent, but she could only stare in shock, heart thumping wildly, as Jangir let out a lewd string of curses.

"Fucking bastards! Sons of whores! Lash them!"

"What?" she said. And then she saw.

A big fight had broken out in the corner. Men jumping on one another, trying to tear into the center of the knot, shouting. Guards muscled their way to intervene. The hovercar sped up, the guard in the passenger seat shouting orders in his comms, when Elena saw the young man in the center of the storm. He was shouting something she couldn't hear over the din, a holosign projected above his head from the pod stitched into his shirt.

Relief and worry washed over her.

HOW MANY MORE LIVES UNTIL WE SEE JUSTICE? DEATH TO JANGIR!

"Your Highness, are you all right?"

It took Elena a moment to realize that Jangir was asking her a question, perhaps for the fourth time.

"Your Highness, are you—"

"Yes, yes," she said. The guard twisted in his seat.

"Reports say it was an isolated scuffle, Your Highness," he said. "There were two protestors, and they've been apprehended. But if you are feeling unwell, we can return to the palace."

"No, it—it's all right," Elena said as their hovercar entered a large boulevard. She could see a tall, shrouded monument up ahead. *Jangir's statue.*

"These rebels grow too bold. I will see to them, Your Highness," Jangir said, his voice cold. "They'll regret the day they were born. I will *personally* see that they are—"

"Jangir, enough," Elena said. She touched her throat, willing her heartbeat to slow as her thoughts raced. In any other circumstance, she would have ordered that the men be imprisoned for attacking a royal entourage. But the hovercars were not marked to show which one held the heir, so the young man could not have known that he had hit hers. And their sign had named Jangir. But instead of feeling triumph, Elena felt only fear, like a blade within her ribs. If the young man would dare to protest against Jangir among gold caps, then it could only mean two things: that the people were growing fearless enough to openly defy her father's men; and that if she did not do something soon, more clashes would spark through the city.

"If I turn for Palace Hill now, they'll think I don't care for their voices," Elena murmured, more to herself.

"Your Highness, I assure you, I can take care of him," Jangir said. "Enjoy the festivities."

Elena looked at Jangir, sitting before her with hands smoothly folded, gold cap perched starchily, and she thought of Varun and his false promises, of the victims in the park, lying facedown in the sand, clothes cold and damp with their blood, of the young man screaming in defiance.

Damn you for not caring, she wanted to say, to Jangir, to Varun, to her father.

The hovercar came to a stop, and cheers erupted around them as gold caps rose in greeting, but their voices were dimmed by the sound of her blood beating in her ears. By the decision sitting dark and heavy in her pocket.

She still had the pod with the reports, had kept it with her ever since she had given Varun the deadline.

I've waited long enough.

She met Jangir's gaze.

"You're right," she said, "I will enjoy the festivities. But my guards will bring the protestors to me. Unharmed."

A muscle worked in Jangir's jaw, but the door was already opening, the roar of the crowd rushing in to greet them.

He bowed his head. "It will be done, Your Highness."

"*Delightful,*" she said and took the hand of the awaiting guard.

The man gripped her fingers, and Elena turned in surprise to see Yassen, who hurriedly pulled her aside as Jangir opened the opposite door.

"Yassen," she gasped and was stopped short by the look on his face. "What's wrong?"

He wore his palace uniform hat, but he had pulled it so far down that the rim sat right above his eyebrows, covering his hair and shielding his eyes.

"Did you tell them? Did you tell Jangir?" Yassen asked, voice thin.

"Tell them what?"

"Who I am?" Yassen hissed. "Is that why you were at the club, seeing a gold cap? To tell them that an Arohassin agent now served the Crown?"

"Yassen, I don't—" and then she understood. *Of course.* Her father used his gold caps as his eyes and ears in the city. Ferma had said that the king had secretly circulated the photo of an Arohassin agent, a key operative who worked out of a stepwell, to the top-level gold caps like Jangir. Maybe he had done the same with Yassen, long before the assassin had agreed to serve them.

But even she knew her father was not foolish enough to tell the gold caps of Yassen's new allegiance. He had killed Jangir's brother, all those suns ago. The fanatics would storm Palace Hill and drag Yassen out themselves, kicking and screaming.

"Yassen," she said, grasping his hands and forcing him to look her in the eye. "They will not harm you. I promise you. I didn't go there to tell them about you. I went there to turn them against each other."

Yassen blinked, eyebrows crinkling in confusion, when she took out the pod and held it out for only him to see.

"I am setting a timer," she said, thumb pressing against the silver button.

"In about an hour, all the contents of this pod will go out to the media. It will be the end of the gold caps."

"And *what* are those contents?" Yassen asked.

"Your Highness, they are waiting!" Jangir called.

"You, come here," she said, quickly gesturing to a guard as she pocketed the pod. "Give him your visor."

The guard was mid-bow when he paused, glancing between them. "Your Highness?"

"The sun is hurting his eyes. He needs your visor." She held out her hand. "Just for the day."

The guard hesitated, then handed it to Yassen. "Don't break it," he muttered.

As he left, Yassen slipped on the visor. It was too big on his face, resting right on his high cheekbones, but it would do.

"Whatever happens," she said, "don't leave my side."

"Ferma would kill me if I did."

The shrouded monument sat at the base of the city historical museum, a tall building sculpted from sandstone and decorated with stained-glass windows as bright as a monsoon sunset. A crowd gathered beyond the steps, held back by metal gates and armed guards.

Elena met Jangir at the base of the shrouded monument, Yassen on her right, a guard named Mihir on her left. She glanced at the new guard. It felt odd not to have Ferma beside her, to sense her presence like a boulder in the dunes, constant, dependable, solid. But then she caught Yassen's gaze, and he nodded. Offered a tight smile.

Elena returned it, meant it, and her eyes lingered on him a moment longer. Though he was no Spear, Elena realized she had grown to look forward to seeing Yassen on her right like a twin shadow. He cocked his head as she stared, as if asking a question, and she shook her head, turning away before he could see her cheeks warming.

"Your Highness, meet my comrades," Jangir said as two men stepped forward.

The drizzle had stopped, and the sun broke out, blinding the streets with its brilliance. Elena held up her hand, blinking, so it took her a moment to realize that the bowing man on her right was none other than Varun.

"Your Highness," Varun said with an oily smile. "We hope you'll find this monument most breathtaking."

"It is a gift from us all," the man beside Varun said. He was skinny like Jangir, but taller, with a long, hawkish nose.

"My men Varun and Leelat organized it all," Jangir said. He spread his hands as the crowd let out a cheer. "If you will do us the honor."

Elena glanced at Varun, but the man did not seem to recognize her, smile still dripping down his jowls. She wanted to shake him.

Varun gestured to her. "Just pull off the cover."

Dhols beat a new rhythm as she stepped forward and picked up the hem of the red cloth. She could feel their eyes on her back. Heard the soft hush in Jangir's voice as he whispered a prayer of benediction.

"So we the blessed few."

She yanked back the cover, the red cloth rippling to reveal a statue of her. Her *and* her father.

She was sitting on what looked like a throne, but smaller, while Leo stood behind her, arms braced on her shoulders as they both seemed to gaze off into the horizon. A roar broke out through the crowd, but Elena did not hear them. She could only stare, mouth slack with shock.

Because sitting on their heads, in the middle of their crowns, were gold caps. Made of actual gold, glistening in the sun.

Elena Aadya Ravence wore a gold cap, and the crowd cheered for it.

Elena stumbled back. An arm pressed against her, steadying her, and she turned to see Yassen.

"I have you," he said. Though she could not see his eyes, she heard the strain in his voice, felt the stiffness in his arm. "I can get you out of here if you want."

What she wanted was to burn the statue. To melt off the gold caps and hammer the metal until it was flat and formless. Her body trembled.

How dare *they?* Never in her life had she donned the cap. Never in her life would she do so. But her likeness stared back at her with a serene smile, hands folded smoothly like Jangir in the car.

The gold caps are here to stay.

This statue was more than a reminder.

It was an order.

And you will need them.

Elena turned to Jangir, who smiled and clapped. Varun fixed the cap on his head while Leelat raised his hands, egging on the crowd. The dhols began to beat with a frenzy, or perhaps that was her heartbeat as she straightened, fury building in her chest like a fire.

"I'll stay," she said to Yassen. "I want to see their faces when they learn that they've been betrayed."

She strode forward as the sun threw the shadow of the statue up the steps of the museum. Jangir turned from the crowd, hand outstretched. She took it, smiled. As the holocams flashed she gestured for Varun and Leelat to join them. And she wrapped her arm around Varun, slipping the pod in his pocket.

"This way, Your Highness," Jangir said. "We have a *delightful* surprise for you at the tournament."

In the courtyard behind the museum, an arena was set. Spectators sat surrounding a long wooden platform lightly dusted with sand. Sling-swords lined the far wall, their long blades tall and gleaming, etched with messages and names she could not read from this distance.

Jangir guided her to the top viewing box. Candied pecans, roasted pistachios, caramelized jalebis, and other treats sat in pristine bowls on a table. White wine chilled in a pitcher. Varun poured her a glass as Jangir showed her to her seat at the edge of the box.

"We invited the best fighters in the country. In the world." Jangir smiled as the gates below opened and two men strode out. One wore a gold cap; the other, a cloak. "I think you'll find them quite impressive."

Elena nodded, but she did not drink. She glanced at the time projected along the glass. Barely twenty minutes had passed since she had set the timer. She glanced at Varun, who had taken a seat on her right and was already munching on pistachios.

When the timer went off, a seemingly *undisclosed source* would send governmental reports that indicated Jangir's allegiance to Jantar to media outlets and the journalists crowding the seats. At the same time, holos would automatically project from the pod in Varun's pocket. They would show private messages, sent by Varun, to reporters about leaking the reports. The journalists would latch on to the story like a yeseri hunting down a hare. And Jangir would see that Varun was the mastermind. That he was the reason for his downfall.

She watched as Varun reached for another handful of pistachios. Leelat wiped sweat from his forehead while Jangir drank his wine, eyes bright and cold. She needed both of them to believe Varun sent those reports.

Patience, she told herself as the fighters assumed their first stance. *It will happen.*

The men launched forward. The gold cap was short but fast, and he easily darted in and out of the cloaked man's reach. His opponent released his blade, but the gold cap lurched away, his hat not even shifting an inch.

Despite herself, Elena began to follow the duel, tracking every dance of footwork, the arc of blades, the timing of their advances. *The gold cap favors his left leg.* When he parried, his left shoulder would inch forward, indicating the direction of his retaliatory advance. And as for the cloaked man... *He needs to be softer on his feet.* He was tall, yes, and his height gave him an advantage, but the cloak seemed to be slowing him down. Elena wondered why he did not take it off, when the gold cap shot forward, his blade ripping through the air, and the cloaked fighter stumbled back. The crowd gasped, and Elena tensed. Blood spotted the sand. The gold cap raised his sword again, eyes triumphant, when the fighter suddenly flung off his cloak, twisting it around the other's arm and yanking him forward to meet his blade.

Elena shot to her feet, as did Jangir. As did the crowd. The sword rested lightly against the gold cap's throat as Samson smiled and looked to her.

"I believe it's my game, Your Highness."

Oh, Samson, you bastard.

So this was Jangir's surprise. She turned to him as the crowd stamped their feet and whistled their approval. Samson bowed, grinning.

"Your betrothed is a skilled fighter," Jangir said before she could speak. "He organized this tournament and asked me if he could surprise you on Birdsong Day."

"So he did," Elena said. She looked to Yassen, who shook his head. "Though, I think I'm done with surprises for today."

Jangir chuckled, and Elena turned to call to Samson to join them when she saw Varun stand.

"Are you leaving?"

"Unfortunately, Your Highness. Duty calls." He glanced at Jangir, smile faltering for a moment, before recovering. "I hope you enjoy the rest of the tournament."

"Wait!" She peered at the clock. A quarter till the end of the hour. "I believe I am ready for one more surprise."

She turned back to the arena, where Samson clipped his slingsword back on his belt.

"How about one more game, beloved?" she called.

Samson stopped. Murmurs went through the crowd as Jangir began to protest, but she waved him away, eyes on Samson.

"A duel. You and me. Loser will carry the other up the steps of the museum." At this, oohs and aahs rippled through the crowd. Elena pulled a flirtatious smile, one that did not meet her eyes as she held Samson's gaze.

Come on, she willed. *Play along with me.*

Samson considered her, his amusement slowly fading. Finally, he gave a small nod.

"I am at the heir's command," he said out loud, his eyes not breaking from hers.

Elena gave him a quick, true smile before turning back to the box.

"Your Highness, this is absurd," Jangir began.

"Unusual," Varun added.

"Perhaps our fighters did not entertain you?" Leelat said, earning him a glare from Jangir.

"Your Highness." Yassen stepped forward, but she saw him look to the time hovering along the wall. "I'll escort you."

"You've given so much. I think it's time for me to give a gift in return," Elena said to Jangir. She turned to Varun. "Surely you *will* stay for it."

Varun looked to Jangir, then folded his hands, bowing. "Of course, Your Highness."

She left them glowering in the box as Yassen led her to the fighters' chambers.

"What's your plan?" he said.

"Keep them here until the news breaks," she said, walking faster. They had only twelve minutes now.

"Elena, what exactly was in that holopod?"

She paused in front of the chamber doors. When she did not answer, Yassen placed his hand on the door, leaning over her.

"I won't let you through until you tell me."

"Yassen, this isn't the time—"

"*What* is going to happen?" he asked. He had taken off his visor once they were alone, and she could see his pale eyes in the dark, searching her face. Worry dented his brow, a line appearing right above his nose. *Funny*, she thought, how she could read him now. How familiar he had become to her ever since he had vowed to keep her secret in the desert.

She stepped closer. "I gave Varun reports that indict Jangir as a Jantari agent," she whispered. "I thought he would use them to oust Jangir, to lead the gold caps himself, but he hasn't. So I'm doing it for him."

His eyes widened, but before he could respond, the doors flung open.

"There you are." Samson smiled to her, and then he seemed to notice Yassen. How close he stood to her. Something quick flashed across Samson's face, but instead of anger or jealousy, Elena saw only longing in Samson's eyes as he looked at Yassen. But then Samson recovered his smile, and he clapped Yassen on the shoulder.

"Have you come to fight for me, Cass?"

"Samson," Yassen said, hesitating. He pulled away. "I'll be at the box. Both of you just—just be careful."

"We will," Samson said.

"So what is this all about?" Samson said as she returned from the changing room.

The padded pants were a bit too big for her, but Elena pulled the sword belt tighter to keep them up.

"Varun was going to leave. I needed a way to make him stay." She picked up a sword. It was light, well-balanced. She looped it into her belt.

"But why?"

"You remember what you said about mercy," she said, pulling on gloves as Samson watched. "How the moments that define us are when we forgive ourselves?" She met his eyes. "I can never forgive myself if I don't do something about the massacre in the park. My father already made it clear that he'll do nothing for the families. But I will. I'll bring justice to them."

She strode toward the tunnel leading to the arena. Samson hurried after her, falling in step.

"And you think it's wise acting against the very people who support the throne?" he said. "Who will support us when you become queen?"

"Oh, Sam." She closed her eyes to hide her disappointment. "Would you forgive yourself if you did nothing?"

He fell silent as they entered the field. People stamped their feet, a slow roar rumbling through the arena as drummers responded to the crowd, dhols building the beat. The sun hung just above, washing the arena with a soft pink hue.

Elena crouched, and when the rhythm broke, when the crowd erupted, she launched forward.

She swung her slingsword, but Samson blocked her attack and moved to her left. She spun, blade arcing down, nearly swiping his feet. Samson stumbled back. He stared at her for a moment, hesitating.

"Would you, Samson?" she whispered.

He switched the blade to his other hand, sighing. And then he shot forward.

She lunged back, using his momentum to her advantage to dive and release her blade up, catching him by the hilt.

But Samson switched hands at the last second, and her blade caught only air.

She pulled back, spinning, when Samson suddenly made to dart to her left. She slammed her arm down, blade singing. But it had been a feint.

Samson rushed her on her right, and her balance was off. She stumbled as his blade grazed the padding on her leg, tearing the cloth.

And then she felt a breath stir the hair on her neck. She turned and nearly yelped. Samson stood directly behind her; she hadn't even heard him approach.

A smile crept across his face. He was so close that she could see the dark depths of his eyes, deep blue like the uncharted seas.

"You were saying?"

It was as if his words had melted the ice lodged between her joints. Elena tackled him, and though she was not large enough to knock him down, the movement took Samson by surprise. He stumbled back, and it was enough. She spun around him, blade slicing up as he realized the play and brought his own sword to block her attack.

Her blade hovered inches above his throat as he pushed back.

The crowd gasped, some hooting, others crying for her to finish him.

"Three more minutes," she said, breathing hard.

Sweat streaked down Samson's face, but he looked up, flashing her a smile. Above, in the box, she saw Jangir arguing with Varun while Yassen stood apart, watching them, arms crossed.

"I've lasted longer." Samson grinned and pushed away.

She hopped back, but Samson was faster. He rushed forward, slicing down, and her blade met his.

He feinted right, but this time, she anticipated his move, rolling to the left, their blades connecting again in an overhead strike.

"When I say go," he said as he pressed down against her sword, "shoot toward the box and reel yourself toward the ledge."

She grinned thinly, arms shaking as she held her own blade inches from her face. "On your mark, then."

She brought her foot around and twisted from beneath his slingsword. Samson sidestepped, bringing his sword to her leg, but she grabbed his elbow, pinching the nerves. Samson let out a cry, dropping his sword. And then a ripple went through the crowd.

A falter in the cheers and hoots.

As Elena broke away, she saw a woman raise her holopod in the seats, mumbling as she read.

It's begun.

Samson nodded, angling himself toward the box. She pulled the trigger, and her blade zipped through the air, cracking through the wooden support beam. Jangir cried out. Varun fell back as she ran and leapt, pushing off Samson's hand and launching into the air.

The sun flashed in her eyes as she pulled the reel and swung up, crashing through the box. She rolled onto her feet, spinning. Jangir cowered in the corner, eyes wide, hands shaking as he held a pod projecting the reports.

The one she had slipped in Varun's pocket.

"You, you made these false reports!" Jangir shouted, pointing an accusatory finger at Varun. "The outlets are saying they came from an unnamed source, but these messages. These messages to reporters were sent from your pod, *you fucking traitor.*" And with a roar, he launched himself at Varun.

Yassen darted forward, grabbing Jangir's arm as Varun shrieked. Jangir tried to twist away, but Yassen only pulled him back, pressing the mouth of his pulse gun into Jangir's lower back.

"I suggest," Elena said coolly as guards rushed in, "that you come quietly. I don't think your gold caps will take your betrayal lightly."

Leelat looked at Jangir, aghast. Varun stood with his back against the wall, mouth open in disbelief.

"This is a mistake," Jangir said. "A hoax! He is trying to frame me. Please, Your Highness, this isn't true."

Yassen pushed him forward as he bawled, begged, and she followed, sword in hand as they left the arena. The crowd had already spilled out. Some men cried out, begging for an explanation as Jangir twisted in Yassen's grasp, trying to pull free. Others hurled curses. One tried to push past the guards, screaming.

"Traitor! Fucking Jantari traitor!"

The guards shoved him back as silver police cars pulled up to the museum.

"Please, Your Highness, it was not me," Jangir pleaded.

"We shall see," Elena said. She glanced up at the statue glimmering in the distance. The gold cap perched on her head. "I am not kind to ruthless men."

Yassen guided Jangir into the car, slammed the door. He turned to her as she watched the crowd warily. She did not spot Samson in the sea of gold caps. They pressed up against the police barricade, shoving and pushing. Someone threw their shoe, missing the cars by several feet. The air grew thicker, angrier, and she felt the mob's fury rise over her, violent and unstable.

"We need more guards and officers on the streets tonight," she said.

Yassen grabbed her arm. "Yes, but let's get you out of here."

She nodded, and Yassen led her to a car and carefully tucked her in. They pulled away from the museum, leaving the angry crowd of gold caps calling for blood.

CHAPTER 24

LEO

"Peace," the land rumbled.
"Change," the sky whispered.
"Destiny," the fire hissed.

—from *The Legends and Myths of Sayon*

Back in his study, Leo tapped the concrete table before him, the bitter taste of sand still in his mouth. After learning of Saayna's deceit, he had wanted to rush back to the temple. Arish had advised against it, arguing that killing the priests and the high priestess before the coronation would only bring trouble.

"Even if the public won't be there for the Ashanta ceremony, Jangir will. He doesn't know details of the proceedings or know whether Elena must hold or simply *sit* in the flames. He believes in you, Your Majesty, but his belief can only stretch so far. We need the remaining priests. We need Saayna, or else Jangir will question the legitimacy of Elena's reign if she is not properly inducted by the order," the Astra had said.

Grudgingly, Leo had found himself in agreement. The order was a crucial part of the coronation. The high priestess bestowed the blessings of the Eternal Fire onto the next monarch, who then promised to sustain Alabore's vision and lead Ravence into another glorious generation. A divine ruler was nothing without her god.

Everywhere he turned, the Phoenix lay in wait. Her fiery grasp reached every part of his kingdom, his history. He despised Her, yet he could not rule his kingdom without Her.

The coronation was just over a week away, and the Prophet was still free. As he sat at his desk, studying the runes, Leo no longer felt rage. Instead, a cold resolve had hardened in its place, like sand turning to glass.

Arish arrived carrying a tray, and Leo watched him pour tea into gem-encrusted cups. The surrounding fire crackled softly.

"To Ravence and her dream," Arish said, offering a cup to Leo.

"To Ravence," Leo returned.

The tea scalded his tongue, but he swallowed it without complaint. Arish sighed and sank back in his seat. His eyebrows drooped past the corners of his eyes, giving him a sleepy look.

"I suppose there is only one thing left to do," he said, his voice heavy.

Leo nodded. He enlarged the holos of the runes. The burning symbol left by the Arohassin glared at him. Spreading his hands, Leo brought up a topographical map of Ravence with all her dunes and canyons. He looked at Arish over the peaks of the Agnee Range.

"The Arohassin boy said that Saayna lied to us," Leo said. "I think she altered the second rune, and that the one the Arohassin burned in the desert is the correct form." Arish began to argue, but Leo held up his hand to stop him. "If we plot with the new rune, maybe we'll find the true location of the Prophet."

I hope.

He overlaid the first sign, the feather of the Phoenix, onto the map. It stretched across Ravence like a long scar. He then took the second rune—the one left by the Arohassin, the inward storm with an arrow's end—and planted it over the feather. It swept across the valleys and dunes, the eye of the storm settling on the capital.

Leo waved his hand, and the third symbol floated over the others. The leafless banyan tree. He placed it on top of the others, noting how its bare branches brushed the tips of the Agnee mountains while its trunk split the desert in half. Leo called for the last sign, but then he hesitated.

This rune was simple—a circle with a dot in the middle. He had never seen it before in his texts, or if he had, he overlooked it for its mundanity. Yet, it was the final piece to the puzzle.

Leo motioned for the holo. Together, he and Arish watched the fourth rune sink onto the map of Ravence. Its circumference cut perfectly through the southern canyons and western mountains, ringing the trunk of the banyan tree and the stem of the feather.

Apart, the runes looked nonsensical. Together, they created a maze that would hopefully lead to the truth.

Leo let out a deep breath and leaned forward. The maze's path began at the southwestern corner of Ravence, deep within the Agnee Range. He followed it across Magar and the southern canyons, straight through Teranghar and up north. The path skirted around Rani, pierced straight through the deep desert like an arrow, and then curved inward to its destination.

Palace Hill.

Leo blinked. He traced the path again and again, but it always ended in the same place. His palace.

The king sank into his chair in disbelief. He looked at Arish, trying to find words, and saw that his Astra was just as speechless.

All this time, had the Prophet walked within the walls of his home?

"The Prophet," Arish said finally, "is *here*?"

Leo gripped the arms of his chair so hard it left imprints of its carved pattern on his skin. His first thought went to Elena. If this labyrinth was true, she could be the Prophet; yet his daughter could not hold fire. Then there was Ferma. But the Yumi had not controlled fire since the Burning of the Sixth Prophet.

Perhaps it was a servant then, one who prayed at the shrine within the palace. However, Majnu always kept a close watch on the servants and would report if anything was amiss.

"There—there must be some kind of explanation," Arish stuttered. "How can we trust these runes? What if Saayna falsified the first two?"

What if her translations were false? Leo thought wildly. *What if the Prophet isn't even Ravani? Or a woman? Or—*

Leo let out a slow, shaky breath to stop himself from spiraling. He had to keep a steady head if he wanted to find the Prophet.

"I have to become the man I wanted my father to be," he said in a soft whisper.

His eyes met Arish's. "Start a search through the palace. Look for any man or woman with strange marks. Do it quietly though. The coronation is almost upon us, and Elena must not know." He swept his hand across his desk, and the holos dissipated in sparks of blue. "And bring Saayna here."

"Men and women, Your Majesty? I thought the Prophet—"

"The Prophet could be anyone at this point," he snapped. "If Saayna lied about these runes, she could have lied about the gender of the Prophet."

Arish sighed and ran his hand through his hair. "The princess will be back in an hour or so from the Birdsong festivities. I will begin the search before she returns."

"Good. I will await Saayna at the shrine."

He stood and the Astra made to follow, but Leo waved him off.

"I need to be alone."

The fire purred as he swept out of his study. Leo ordered the guards not to accompany him as he walked through his palace. The hallway was quiet. He could hear his footsteps echo and stretch across the stone walls as he made his way past the royal quarters toward the main chambers.

All this time, he had been too busy chasing runes and false words to notice the change around him. The palace was abuzz with excitement for its new queen. He heard it in the whispers of the servants as they hung garlands of golden marigolds and crimson hibiscus, as they lit incense bowls of sandalwood and washed the marble hallways with rose water. Guards wore freshly starched uniforms and lined their eyes with kohl.

Leo passed the kitchens where cooks prepared feasts of roast lamb garnished with spiced pomegranate, buttered bread stuffed with cottage cheese and crushed pistachio nuts, and steamed rice with candied almonds and cashews. Barrels of aged dessert wine and honeyed whiskey were carried and stacked. Leo's stomach rumbled. He had long lost his appetite, but now he wouldn't mind a plate of sweetmeats.

He turned, entering the main courtyard. The sky, for once, was unblemished and lay open for him, wide and pink. He watched servants sweep away sand left behind from last night's storm. It was part of their dance with the desert. It raged, they acquiesced. They built, and the desert watched.

At his approach, the servants bowed and stopped sweeping.

"You," he said to a young woman with an ash mark on her forehead. "Tell me—has the shrine been cleaned?"

"Yes, Your Majesty," she said, not meeting his eyes. "It was cleaned as of this morning."

"Good. Instruct others not to wander there. I want to pray in peace."

"Yes, Your Majesty," she said. "May the Holy Bird answer your prayers."

She shut off her ears for me long ago, he wanted to say, but Leo held his tongue. He motioned for the servants to resume their task.

The sun felt warm against his shoulders as he strolled through the garden. The main courtyard stretched several yards, full of thick banyan and blooming ironwood trees; their pink flowers created a rich, heady scent. In the middle of the plaza, a lone torch hissed. Leo avoided it. He'd had his fill of fire to last a lifetime.

After the library, the main courtyard had been Aahnah's favorite part of their home. She would sometimes take her reading and sit at the stone bench beneath the smallest banyan tree.

Leo went there now and sat, listening to the sound of the feathered brooms sweeping against the stone path, the shrieks of a desert hawk, the distant call of a servant, but their rhythms did not soothe him. Worry crawled in his stomach, knotted and dark. He could not forget the smoldering rune in the sand. How, all this time, the hunt circled back to within his palace. He felt like a fool. A damned, stupid fool.

And Mother's Gold, was he tired.

Leo rubbed his eyes. When he had tried to sleep on the way back to the palace, he saw them. The dead priests. Their limp, torn robes. Their deaths had been fruitless. Like the girl's.

Leo pulled out the kerchief Ferma had given him. The cloth was stiff with dried blood, but he carefully pulled it apart, then folded it into neat squares.

"What a waste," he murmured.

He could ask for forgiveness, like he had with the girl. He could burn the cloth and scatter the ashes from Palace Hill, but Leo knew such words and actions would be meaningless.

He was unforgivable. Saayna had made that clear enough, but strangely, he no longer felt guilt. Or anger. Or pity.

Not anymore.

He held the kerchief for a moment longer before tucking it into his breast pocket, hand above his heart.

He felt free.

The dead could not hurt him, not like the living. Not like the Prophet, waiting for their chance to take his kingdom away from him. And if he was already damned, what could killing the Prophet do to him now?

"Phoenix," he said, eyes closed, "hear me. I will find your Prophet. And I will bring her before you so you can watch her bleed."

When he opened his eyes, he saw the wide expanse of the sky. He had not been struck down for speaking blasphemy. There were no flaming heavens, no hell and brimstone, like Saayna had warned. Just a pink, cloudless sky and warm horizon.

"Your Majesty?"

Leo turned to see Arish hurrying to him. He clutched a holopod.

"What is it?"

"Your Majesty, it's Jangir. These reports were just released, and they claim that he is a Jantari spy. Even Muftasa signed off on it. There's a copy of her report here..."

Leo snatched the pod, quickly scanning the documents. "But that's impossible. I've known Jangir for many suns. He's not a Jantari agent. Why—why would Muftasa sign off on this?"

"I'm not sure, but officers have already apprehended him. The princess was there when they took him in. The gold caps are outraged. Her Highness has called for more security in the city, and I agree," Arish said. "Riots could break out. Varun already has asked to speak with you, and Leelat is saying he believes *he* should take Jangir's place."

Leo listened with growing horror. *Mother's Gold, how did this happen?*

"Father?"

Leo looked up to see Elena approaching with Yassen and her guards trailing behind her. She wore a warrior's clothes with a padded vest, her sweaty hair sticking to her forehead, slingsword at her waist.

"I thought you were at the Birdsong festivities," Leo said, rising.

"There was a slingsword tournament. Samson and I played," she answered.

He noticed the stiffness in her posture, the look she shared with Yassen. An awful certainty rose in Leo as he glanced between her and the holos.

Only a few people could create these reports or access this level of data. Only those with special security clearance, like him, Muftasa, Arish, Majnu, Ferma, and Elena.

And looking into his daughter's eyes, Leo knew.

Skies above, Elena, what did you do?

"Leave us," he said, his voice cracking like a whip. "Now."

The guards, Yassen, and Arish quickly left. A hawk screeched overhead, but then it left too.

Leo sat back down on the bench, and wordlessly, Elena joined him.

For a while, he said nothing, the holos hovering between them. Anger, shame, disappointment, they blurred and passed, morphing until they became shapeless. He wanted to berate her, scold her, shake her, hug her, cry to her, and all that blurred and passed too. Until he could only feel one thing.

"I," he began, voice soft, "I know we don't always agree. And I know that you hate the gold caps, and I see now that going to their rallies was just a ruse. A trick." He paused because it hurt to continue. It hurt that his own daughter would betray him so.

Elena said nothing, but she picked up the pod and closed it.

"Everything that I've built, everything that I do, is for you," he said after a moment. *The killing, the murders, the hunt for the Prophet.* "To protect you, even if you don't realize it yet. I created the gold caps so that when you are queen, they can support you. They can shield you from rebels who wish you and this kingdom harm.

"But what you did today, Elena, was not just foolish. It was destructive. We could have riots in our city, riots when the *one thing* we need until you are crowned queen is peace. You're going to a parade in the city for the Fire Festival, yes? What if there are rebels who take advantage of the falling out of the gold caps and begin protests for kingless governments? What then?"

She did not respond, and her silence knifed through him sharper than her betrayal. She was like her mother in so many ways. Their stubbornness, their anger.

His fingers curled under the lip of the stone bench. He wished Aahnah was here now. He wished it so hard that it hurt.

"I will do my best to clean up your mess. And you will do your best to uphold your duty as queen and denounce these reports as lies. False reports made by rebels to undermine Jangir. And then you will make a speech declaring your support of the gold caps. Maybe then all will not be lost."

It was then that Elena laughed. Harsh, sudden, the sound ripping through her throat.

"Oh, Father, it is lost. It's over." She looked at him, and in her eyes, he saw his defiance, his tenacity. "Have you ever stopped to consider that you are wrong? That maybe, just maybe, the gold caps may not be the beacon of success you've imagined?

"They are greedy, senseless bullies who kill without consequence. And as for the riots, they've already begun. In the park. In the streets. Every time you try to smother a protestor, another will emerge. Every time one of your gold caps tries to scare someone into submission, someone else will grow brave enough to speak up." She held up her hand, and he saw her reddened fingertips. "And every time you avoid teaching me how to hold fire, I only try harder."

He wanted to take her hands then, to kiss the burns from her fingertips as he had kissed her wounds as a child. He wanted to tell her that the Phoenix was a vengeful god, and that fire was its cruel serpent. He wanted to tell her that he had made a mistake. While he had fooled everyone about his devotion to the Eternal Fire, he had misled her in the process. He had driven her further away than he had expected, and he could only blame himself for the distance between them.

He wanted to tell her, but he could not.

Her words cut deep, too deep, and his voice had deserted him.

"You told me that blind followers are useful in a time of war," Elena said. "But how can a blind follower be loyal to you if you're *constantly* lying and manipulating him?"

She let the question hang in the air, floating between them as shadows grew in the courtyard, and the sun dipped below the palace wall.

He thought of Samson and Yassen, how despite their past, they had proven themselves to him; of Arish and Muftasa, who had seen his horrors and still stood beside him.

Elena sighed, a shiver running through her body. Her head dropped back toward her sharp shoulder blades, like a bird dipping its head between its wings. He wanted to hug her, to comfort her, but he fought that urge. What could he say now that would help?

"Have you ever considered what I wanted?" she said finally, and for a moment, her voice wobbled as her eyes searched his. "Have you ever asked?"

Answer, he willed himself.

"What is it that you want?" he said gruffly to mask the tremble in his own voice.

She gave a wry, cold smile. "That you would, for once, ask me on your own."

It felt like swallowing sand. Leo turned away. He could no longer bear her words that had so utterly laid him bare. Whittled him down to his core. He stood, smoothing his kurta and adjusting his scarf.

"I'll send more men into the city," he said, not looking at her.

Elena stood. She slowly slipped off her slingsword and handed it to him, forcing him to meet her eyes.

"What's this?" he asked.

"Courage," she said, "for you to do the right thing."

She left him standing alone in the courtyard.

The shrine room was empty, its golden ceiling reflecting the warm glow of the fire that burned in the center. Floor cushions formed a ring around the pit. Leo sat, setting the slingsword aside, and listened to the crackle of flames and the hiss of sparks. He allowed it to fill his mind, his thoughts, until all he could focus on was the fire and not the pain in his chest.

On the far wall, the Phoenix watched him. Artisans had carved Her likeness out of stone. They threaded Her wings with gold and adorned Her eyes with rubies found deep within the mountains.

Every time you avoid teaching me how to hold fire, I only try harder.

Leo's hand shook as he lit an incense stick. He saw Elena's reddened fingertips as the smell of sandalwood permeated the room. His daughter was burning herself because of him. Because he refused to teach her and tell her the truth, like Ferma had said. Shame, thick and hot, rushed up his throat. Leo swallowed it back and closed his eyes.

Meditation had not initially come easily to him, but after decades of practice, he had discovered a trick. Leo exhaled and sank his weight down so that his feet rooted to the stone, which then rooted to Palace Hill and the desert beyond. He saw his worries flit before him, from Elena's comments to Saayna's lies to his own inadequacies as king. He observed them and then he let them go. With each exhale, he sank deeper. With each inhale, he felt his consciousness slowly untether from his body.

He became adrift. He knew nothing but darkness, a clean, black slate where the world had no beginning nor end. Rather, it was a single, present moment—an entity that existed within him, an entity that would disappear as soon as he opened his eyes.

At once, he was nothing.

At once, he was everything.

He was the desert and the mountains, the valleys and the canyons. He existed in the space between the stars, within a grain of sand, a part of the banyan leaf that struggled and broke in the wind.

He was the sun that beat down from the heavens; he was the twin moons that helped Alabore build his kingdom.

He was Leo, the king of Ravence, the son of Ramandra, grandson of Kishi.

He was a part of history, and he was creating history.

A hand touched his hand, and somewhere far within him, Leo was cognizant of a voice—a woman's voice. He traveled to the sound, treading shadows, and when he opened his eyes, he saw Saayna sitting before him.

"Forgive me for interrupting," she said.

He looked at the fire. Its hiss had been distant; now, it filled his ears, bringing along the voices that haunted him.

"I tried to find some peace," he said. "But I can't seem to remain there long."

Saayna folded her hands in her lap.

"You asked for me," she said.

"You have misled me from the very beginning, Saayna," he said, choosing his words carefully. "But I'm not angry. I understand why." He opened his palm, revealing the ring of ash left by the Eternal Fire. "We both have someone we want to protect."

Saayna dipped her head. He knew she would not divulge the identity of the Prophet if he raged. To win her over, he had to atone. Repent, even if it was useless. After all these suns, he had learned that the best way to cull fanatics was to beat them at their own game—to show reverence.

He lifted his eyes to the Phoenix.

"The Phoenix protects Her fire, like the Prophet protects Her image," he said. "You protect the Prophet, and I protect my kingdom against her." He laughed, a slow and rumbling laugh. "Perhaps then that is the true way to serve. We must sacrifice our lives in order to protect the ones we love. Like Aahnah did for me. But in the act of burning, we become purified by the love we gave them."

He looked down and met her eyes in the light of the dancing flames.

"But what has that love gotten you, Saayna?" he asked. "The blood of your brothers and sisters is on your hands. They burned because you held your secret. Tell me, will you dream of their screams, like I will?"

The high priestess looked away. The dancing shadows made her face a war zone, flickering between regret and piety. Yet when she finally spoke, her voice was unwavering.

"I never expected the runes to point to the temple, but I had suspected the possibility. I put my brethren at risk. I know this. But it is our duty to protect the fire and Her Prophet. We swore an oath. We gave our blood. There is no higher honor."

"You somehow altered the second rune on the young priest's back," he said. "Why?"

The fire sighed out sparks. They danced in the air and then spiraled downward, dusting his hair and hands. A spark caught on Saayna's chin, and she flinched before raising her hand to touch it.

"As above, so below," she murmured. It was an old prayer, one that Aahnah would utter.

The magic of the universe resides in us as much as it resides in the heavens, she said. But if magic was fire, then it was a cruel illusion.

Leo leaned forward. "You said that the first two runes meant 'Daughter of Fire.' First, they led to the city. Then they led to the temple. Now they lead to my own home. So where in the seven hells is she?"

"She," Saayna said, and it was something in her voice: the slight derision, the edge in her mouth that made Leo stop. He blinked.

Mother's Gold, I've been a fool.

All this time, he had thought he knew the nature of Saayna's lie. That she had tampered with the runes only to hide the Prophet's true location. But he realized then that it had not been one lie, but two.

"It's a man, isn't it? The Prophet is a man."

Her eyes locked with his. For a moment, hers almost looked golden, and Leo understood that he had arrived at the truth.

"You wished it was you," he said and laughed. "You wished the Prophet was another woman, another priest, just as the Sixth had been. But it's not. It's a man, and you already know it's not me."

Saayna turned back to the flames, sorrow crossing her face. "The Prophet can never be the same man twice."

"Do you know who he is?"

It was her turn to laugh. It sounded like dry wood snapping when burned. "I do not. But it is my duty to make sure you don't know either."

Leo stood. The flames hissed, retreating.

"Seek forgiveness," she said. "Repent now, and the Holy Bird might give you reprieve in the afterlife."

Overhead, the Phoenix watched. Her red eyes glittered with the harshness of fire, with its cunning shadows and white, hot glare.

"Oh, Saayna," he said. "It's much too late for that."

CHAPTER 25

YASSEN

At some point, we must all grieve for our old selves.
—from the introduction of *The Great History of Sayon*

Yassen stalked through the palace courtyards, unable to sleep. The night air felt sharp, cold. Storm clouds lingered along the horizon, but here on Palace Hill, the heavens were clear. Tiny stars shone in the dark like uncut gems.

The courtyard he entered was one of the smaller ones in the back of the palace. A white path, gleaming with inlaid lights, led to a large banyan tree. The tree stood in the middle of a wide basin carved out of red desert stone. Moonflowers floated in its water, their pale petals curled inward.

Yassen paced underneath the tree. Few people frequented this courtyard, and the servants who did hurried through with a quick nod in his direction. Though they no longer regarded him with distrust, the servants were not rushing to offer him kind words or friendship.

A dark shape broke from the canopy with a squawk, and Yassen looked up. He watched it ascend and circle over the tree, hovering for a moment before soaring off into the night.

Sighing, Yassen sat on the lip of the stone basin. He hugged his arm to his side. He had been practicing his hand exercises every day, but after this morning at the temple, a strange tingling sensation spiraled up his arm at unexpected moments. The burns had not worsened; his arm looked the same as before, but when the pain came, sudden and sharp, it was as if fire crept beneath his skin.

Maybe I need to see a doctor again, he thought.

"There you are." Samson's voice broke through the courtyard quiet. "I was looking for you."

"What for?" Yassen asked as he approached. Samson had changed from his slingsword armor, wearing a black kurta and pants that made him blend into the night.

"You escorted the princess back to the palace," Samson said. "How is she?"

"Quiet," Yassen said. *Unusually so.* "She had an argument with the king and then went to bed for the evening."

"Did you know about the reports? Of Jangir?"

He shook his head. "Only an hour before."

Samson sighed, rubbing his hand over his face. He sat down beside Yassen, their knees brushing.

"She was brave for what she did," Samson said slowly. "But Jangir knew your face, didn't he? Did he recognize you?"

Yassen shook his head.

"He didn't. And now he'll answer for what he did in the park."

"What are you smiling for?" Samson said, nudging him.

"It's like what we Ravani say, 'The desert always knows how to repay its visitors.' Brush up, Sam. You're marrying a Ravani girl soon."

Samson laughed. "She has more taste for swords than old adages. Maybe you can recite the old poems at the wedding."

Yassen nodded, but the thought of the wedding, of watching Elena tie her dupatta with Samson's scarf and take seven rings around the fire made his smile falter. His stomach twisted, and he did not know why.

"You will stay for the wedding, won't you?" Samson said.

"I—I can't," Yassen said. "I'll be gone after coronation day, Sam. Like we planned. You'll be king, I'll be free."

"But we'll still see each other, yes?" Samson gripped his hand, his eyes searching Yassen's face. "After all this time, you can't just leave and never come back. I'll miss you. Hell, I think even Elena would."

Would she? He had grown used to her presence, the smell of her hair, like fresh sandalwood and jasmine. The way her eyes would find him across the room. Their silent game of observation. Yassen looked across the courtyard, half expecting to see her emerging from the shadows with a quip, but the courtyard was empty.

"No, Sam, I will leave. For my sake."

"In that case," Samson said and withdrew an object from his coat.

Yassen recognized it immediately—the map of the tunnels within the Sona Range. The color drained from his face. He looked at Samson carefully as his friend unrolled the map and traced a tunnel branching out from the middle of the range.

"You know it, don't you?" Samson said and smiled. "I figured. Didn't your father have a cabin there when he worked in the mines?"

Blood thundered in Yassen's ears. "Y-yes."

He stared at the map, at the upper mountain range where his father's cabin was tucked away.

He remembered the drone of the machines and the rumble of the rocks.

"Jantar always knows how to disturb a man's peace," his father had said.

Erwin Knight worked in the mines and only came to visit Yassen and his mother in Rani during his short rest periods. Once, when Yassen and his mother had managed to obtain a Jantari visa to stay with him, he had told them about something he had seen in the mountain.

"A metal so fine it could cut through steel," Erwin had whispered. He promised to bring Yassen a piece of this special ore, but when he returned from the mine, he had made no mention of it. Instead, he had hurried Yassen and his mother back to Ravence and told them to stay there until he sent word for them to return.

That was nearly eighteen suns ago. Yassen had not seen him since.

A sudden wave of homesickness swept through him. That, and the familiar feeling of being torn between two places. He had not returned to the cabin since his father's death. Like the remnants of his burnt home in Ravence, it contained too many memories. Memories of the boy he had been—free and decent. A boy who would be ashamed of the man he was now.

He had never seen the metal his father had found, but a part of him knew the Jantari had killed him. Erwin Knight had always been a careful man, private in his affairs. But on the day he had told Yassen, Erwin Knight had shared his discovery with everyone—the miners, his friends, his family—and Yassen had a hunch it had killed him.

"Farin says that there is a special ore deep in the Sona mountains. A metal so fine it could cut through steel." Yassen went utterly still as Samson continued on. "I've tried finding it. I built tunnels beneath Chand Mahal and all the way up to the center of the range. Farin knows about some of the tunnels; the others..." He smiled. "Did your father ever find it?"

"No," Yassen said immediately. He met Samson's gaze, his voice firm. "He never knew anything about it."

"Pity," Samson said. He studied Yassen for a moment longer before shrugging. "Well, anyway, I thought I'd ask." He held out the map. "Maybe when you leave, you can go to the cabin. Rest for a bit. I don't think Farin knows it's there, and it took me a while to find it." He motioned. "Take out your pod."

Slowly, Yassen took out his holopod and scanned the map. It tabled the data, creating a new topographical holo, but Yassen did not study it. He would not need it. The cabin was full of ghosts, those of his family and himself. There was no use in revisiting them.

"Sorry I couldn't be of much help," Yassen said.

"Oh, on the contrary. You've been helpful all along, Cass." Samson stood, squeezed his shoulder. His hand lingered for a beat before he drew away. "Your intel was right. Maya *was* at the stepwell. But our sources say that they've lost her trail. I think she took off after Jangir's arrest."

"Should we track her?"

"Not yet. I think the king is more concerned right now about his gold caps than an Arohassin fugitive," he said, smiling.

Yassen tried his best to return the smile.

"I'm serious, Cass, about before. Stay, or come back soon. Don't leave me in the shadows when we've just seen each other again."

Yassen nodded. "I'll try."

When Samson was gone, he let out a shaky breath. *Mother's Gold, so it was true.* If his father discovered the ore, where had it gone? Why hadn't Samson or the Jantari found it yet?

"No," Yassen whispered fiercely, stopping his thoughts. For weeks, months after his father's death, he had seen his mother obsess over these questions. She would mumble them to herself. Wake up from dreams gasping about shadows and rocks that glowed in the dark. He had seen her slip away from him, bit by bit.

I am not the same.

He closed the map and slipped the pod back into his pocket—just as footsteps rang through the yard. A shadow stretched across the white path.

"Oh, I didn't realize this spot was taken," Ferma said.

"It's all right." He patted the lip of the fountain next to him. "There's plenty of room."

She hesitated but did not depart. Yassen could make out the high curve of her forehead, the elegant bridge of her nose as she stood half-cloaked in shadows.

"Seems like you can't sleep either."

"Most of the palace can't," she said, a bit too quickly. He smiled at the terseness in her voice. "We have a coronation to see through."

"And Arohassin to catch, *and* a festival to celebrate, *and* an angry fire to calm, *and*—"

"What's your point?" she asked, annoyance flashing across her face.

Yassen looked up at the moonless sky. "If you keep worrying about all the things to do, you'll worry yourself to ruin."

She gave a low snort, and Yassen turned to her.

"What?" he said.

"Nothing. You just reminded me of someone I used to know."

She sat down beside him and withdrew a flask. Yassen watched her take a long gulp.

"Rough day?"

She wiped her lips. Her eyes, often bright, looked dull.

She took another swig and then another. She tipped back the flask until nothing was left and then dropped it, watching it bounce and skitter on the stone path.

"Ferma," he began.

"I've done a terrible thing," she whispered.

He looked at her. "We all do terrible things."

The Yumi made a sound caught between a laugh and a sob. "You would know."

He waited for her laughter to die off, and it did. She looked up at the sky, the shadows carving out harsh lines along her eyes and mouth.

"What did you do?"

For a moment, she said nothing. She just looked up at the night. When she finally spoke, her voice sounded as if it came from far away.

"I killed the priests," she said. "The king ordered me to, and so I did."

Yassen felt his stomach drop. "Why?"

"I don't know," she said, and her voice sounded so small. "I never question my king."

Don't ask questions. Wasn't that what he had told himself during assignments? When they sent him the name and location, he never asked *who* he was to murder, nor *why*. He merely did what he was told because he was a good soldier. The Arohassin had trained him like a shobu, and he became their warrior.

Imagine a house, his old mentor Akaros had once said. *Imagine a house with emotions as rooms. One room for sadness. One room for guilt. Another for pain. Let the emotion consume that room, but that room only. And when you're done experiencing that emotion, shut the door. Lock it, and step away.*

It had been hard to do at first. To let nothingness take over and drain away his morality. It felt unnatural. But Yassen had been a quick learner.

He would look into the snake's venom-colored eyes as it wound its way inside him, hissing of his guilt. He saw it, and then he would slowly close the door. Shut it in. Step away.

"Then don't allow yourself to start questioning. Questioning will do you no good."

She blinked. "Is that what you tell yourself?"

"Yes," he said. He felt the familiar rattle in his chest, but he pushed it away. He could not be shaken, not when he was so close to the end.

"If you allow yourself to regret, you'll freeze," he said. "And when that happens, you become useless. The only thing left to do then is die. So either you move on, or you go quietly off into the seven hells."

He stood and picked up her flask, handing it to her. "There's no use in feeling sorry for yourself. We're all going to burn anyway."

He turned to leave, but she gripped his arm. Her eyes bored into him.

"But I *killed* them," she said, her voice breaking. "The Fire Order. The holy ones. He gave the order, and I killed them. I cleaned up their blood. I didn't stop to ask why. I—I should have—"

Gently, he pried off her fingers and folded her hand. Squeezed.

"Don't worry," he said. "If you burn, I'll keep you company."

CHAPTER 26

ELENA

Fire gives both life and abandonment. It reveals your true friends yet lets your enemies lie in its shadows. One should be wary of fire and the things it grows.

—from the diaries of Priestess Nomu of the Fire Order

Elena watched Jangir on the monitor as he paced, wringing his hands. He had only been in the cell for two days, but given the state of his disheveled hair, it seemed longer. His white kurta hung off his shoulders, fluttering behind him as he paced. He stopped suddenly. Cocked his head as if he had heard a voice and then mumbled something the sensors did not catch.

"He's losing it," Yassen said.

"He's in shock," Elena said.

Jangir sank to the ground and rocked back and forth, hands clutching his knees as he whispered. Elena recognized the chant at once.

Holy Bird, may You grant forgiveness in Your fire to us blessed few.

Jangir whispered it again and again, eyes squeezed tight, knuckles white

267

as if the chant was the only thing that could save him, the rock amid the chaos of a sandstorm.

As if his belief could absolve him of his sins, she thought. A part of her refused to pity Jangir. He had orchestrated the massacre in the park, lied that the protestors had been armed. She was sure that when he had returned to his home that night, he did not shake like he did now. *You didn't seek the forgiveness of the Phoenix then, so why would She forgive you now?*

Jangir continued chanting, face fervent—like Saayna. Like the priests and all the Ravani who believed in the Phoenix with all their hearts. *How do you believe so deeply? Even when you're wrong? When you're forsaken?* A pang shot through her, deep and aching. Elena rubbed her burnt fingers. She had applied aloe to heal, but she still remembered the bite of the fire, the sear of its heat.

Yassen touched her hand, slowly uncurling her fists.

"You'll hurt yourself if you keep rubbing the burns," he said softly.

"I can't help it," she said, but as Yassen held her hand, she stopped herself from pulling away. "What is it?"

"You were brave," he said, gazing at her reddened fingertips. "Back at the temple, at the arena. Now." His eyes met hers. "You may not be able to hold fire, but you have more strength than the king to confront this kingdom's wrongs. Like the Phoenix, burning the wicked and bringing justice." He gave a wry smile.

"See, that's where you're wrong," she said. "I'm not like the Phoenix. I can't even commit to believing in Her."

"I saw you," he said. "In the temple, the way you looked up at the statue, the longing in your eyes. You have more faith than them all. You have faith in Ravence."

Elena blinked. All this time, she had thought herself lacking—in faith, in authority. She could not hold fire because she did not believe deeply; and she could not be a strong queen without Her fire. She was not ruthless like her father. *But Ravence is mine, just like it is his.* And she would still lay down her life for it. Elena trembled to be seen so clearly, so completely, but Yassen did not waver. He held her gaze, hand beneath hers, and she found herself sharing his soft smile.

"I see you, Elena," he said quietly.

The door opened, and Ferma entered. Yassen immediately dropped her hand, moving away as Ferma turned to greet them.

"Th-there you are," Elena said quickly and frowned. "Diya said you took sick leave yesterday. Are you feeling all right?"

Ferma's braid, usually so neat, was loose, unkempt, with strands sticking out haphazardly.

"I was feeling a bit...under the weather. But I'm better now," Ferma said, sharing a glance with Yassen. "Sorry that I'm late."

Elena took Ferma's hands in hers, searching the Yumi's face. "Ferma, are you sure you're fine?"

"Yes. Step into the field and I'll show you." Ferma grinned, and Elena nodded, the unease in her chest loosening. Slightly.

"We'll talk more once this is over," she whispered so that only her Spear could hear.

"Look, he's finally done," Yassen said.

Elena turned, saw that Jangir now sat on the edge of his bed. He was no longer shaking, but he glanced around the room, as if waiting for something to leap out of the shadows.

She went to the panel. "Jangir, can you hear me?"

Jangir peered at the two-way mirror. "Y-Your Highness? Oh, thank Phoenix Above! You must release me and ask Varun about the reports."

"Jangir." Elena sighed. Her father had made no press release regarding the man. He had stayed in his rooms, refusing to take visitors. She bit her lip. A part of her had hoped that maybe, just maybe, he had heard her and would act.

She pressed the comms again, voice flat. "Jangir, you are to remain here until I'm queen. Then, you'll be put on trial before your peers to answer to the charges that will be brought forth by my government. They will include murder, treason—"

"You are wrong," Jangir spat. "I am no murderer, no spy. Ask the king! I demand to see him."

"That will not happen," Elena said.

"He is nothing without me!" Jangir cried, standing. "I have brought him believers, crowds to his speeches, information to his soldiers. The gold caps will turn against him without me."

"The gold caps are already turning," Elena said. "Against you."

Jangir began to retort when the comms cut, and a message appeared on the panel.

"Your Highness," a guard intoned. "There is a visitor demanding to see you. Varun."

Elena stiffened. She exchanged a worried glance with Yassen and Ferma. On the screen, Jangir screamed silently.

"Yassen, go to the king," she said. "Say I wish to see him. Say it's an emergency, whatever you can think of. Ferma"—and she turned to her Spear—"bring him to the outer office, where the servants can't see."

Her guards nodded, but a look flitted across Yassen's face, one that made her stomach tighten in apprehension.

"Do you think he knows the truth?" Yassen said.

"Nothing will happen to you," Elena replied firmly. She squeezed his hand. "You're with me, remember?"

Ferma glanced between them, her face a mask. "Let's go find out then."

"This chai is wonderful, Your Highness," Varun said. "I taste, oh what is that, ginger?"

"Adrak wali chai is my favorite," Elena said, but she did not drink. She watched as Varun dipped a biscuit in his tea, crunched loudly. He went to dip again but the biscuit broke and fell into his chai.

"Mother's Gold," he muttered.

"Don't worry, I can have another cup brought," she said, but he shook his head.

"This is fine, thank you, Your Highness," he said.

Elena waited, fingers restlessly tapping the bottom of her saucer. A fire crackled in the hearth, filling the silence. Varun slurped again, gave a sheepish smile. Still, she said nothing. It was always better, she had learned, to let the visitor make the first move. To draw out silences and observe what they hid behind their pleasantries.

And despite Varun's polite conversation, Elena saw the nervous jiggle of his knee, how his eyes darted to the door. Sweat glistened lightly on his upper lip. When he sipped again, his eyes met hers for a moment before he quickly looked away.

He knows something, she thought. *Something that makes him nervous.*

"Your Highness," Varun said finally, lowering his cup, "I . . . find myself in a difficult position."

"How so?" Elena asked.

"Well." He licked his lips. "With Jangir gone, His Majesty's follow-ers are a bit lost. They don't know who to turn to, and with His Majesty remaining silent, they're demanding answers. Accountability."

Elena nodded warily. Though this was what she had hoped to hear, she prevented herself from celebrating. "What kind of answers?"

"For one, will Your Highness and your government pursue legal action against Jangir?"

"Yes, if my father does not already plan to."

"I see. Poor Jangir. Forgive me, I grew quite close with him," Varun said, but Elena noticed how the sorrow in his voice was not reflected in his eyes. How his hands did not tremble around the saucer. "But he is a trai-tor, and I will tell all my comrades to treat him so."

"And your comrades listen to you?" she said.

Varun looked up, and she saw how his eyes sparked at that question. "Oh, yes, they do, Your Highness. But there's a bit of a problem. An-other man is trying to lead them astray. Leelat believes that the reports are fraudulent, that I falsified them. He demands that *he* should be the new leader of our men."

"And what do you believe?"

"The reports do not lie, do they?" Varun said slowly, eyeing her. "Espe-cially not ones like these."

Elena sipped her chai. "They do not."

"I received word a few weeks before from a certain *dealer* that Jangir was a Jantari spy. In fact, she gave me the reports, urged me to release them. But I hesitated because something about her was so very strange."

Elena continued to drink her chai, but her heart began to pound. She met Varun's eyes, voice cool. "And what was so strange about her?"

"She did a trick in a club," Varun said. "A move from the Unsung practice. At first, I thought she was a soldier, one of the elite raiders of His Majesty's army. But then, at the arena yesterday, there was a fighter who moved *just like her.*" His eyes met hers as Elena went still. "Like you, Your Highness."

"I find that quite unlikely," Elena said, but then Varun reached into his pockets and pulled out two holopods. Suddenly, the room became smaller. Varun slowly, so slowly, turned over the pods, revealing the insig-nia of the Phoenix.

But what made Elena stiffen was the emblem of crossed slingswords beneath one of the pods.

An emblem that only royals could wear.

"I believe, Your Highness, that this is yours," Varun said.

Stupid, stupid. You stupid fool. Elena could only stare. She had kept a paired pod to Varun's, in case he called, and like every pod she owned, it had been marked by the symbol of her family: the crossed slingswords.

She had forgotten when she had slipped the pod in Varun's pocket. *I should have thought ahead. Mother's Gold, I should have seen that.*

But she hadn't thought ahead. Not the way Leo did.

Elena set down her chai, smoothing her sari. She forced herself to look away from the pods, to meet Varun's eyes. This time, the gold cap was no longer smiling.

"What is it that you want, Varun?" she asked.

"I want your support. Against Leelat," Varun said. "When you are crowned queen, I want you to invite me to Palace Hill before everyone so that they can see who the queen favors." He patted the pods. "And I want Jangir to get the death penalty."

For a while, Elena said nothing. Varun sank back in his seat, but he no longer fidgeted. He merely sipped his chai. Dipped another biscuit. She listened to him eat, and as she did, the unease, the fear that she had seen in Yassen's eyes and felt coil in her stomach, slowly unspooled.

"I will do no such thing," she said.

Varun stopped mid-bite. "Then I will tell the entire kingdom how the princess conspired against the gold caps. How she engineered false reports to indict an innocent man. My contacts at the RI say that Muftasa's seal was stolen and then mysteriously returned. And I'm sure Muftasa herself will not stay silent and let an innocent man who served your father well be hanged."

"You just asked for Jangir to receive the death penalty yourself."

"Jangir and I have our differences," Varun said. "But still, he is useful. And many gold caps loved him like family."

"Claim all that you want," Elena said. "Muftasa will not speak against me. I will soon be her queen."

"And your father?" Varun leaned forward. "Will he stay silent and not speak against you?"

Elena thought of her father, how he had looked at her with such disappointment when he realized what she'd done. She would have preferred if he had been angry. If he had shouted at her like before. But Leo had remained silent, and now he would not speak to her.

Varun smiled. "You're playing a dangerous game, Your Highness. And I believe that your bets on certain people fell short." He stood, pocketing the pods. "Think on it."

Elena watched him stand, and as she watched, she thought of Eshaant with his chest ripped open, the protestor screaming in the streets. Yassen's eyes as he held her hand and said she believed more than anyone. And then, slowly, she was standing. Varun could not leave with those pods. Not after all that she had done.

Swiftly, Elena crossed the space and grabbed Varun's arm, pinching the nerves as she had before. Varun cried out, crumpled.

At the sound, the doors flung open, and Ferma strode in.

"Elena," she gasped.

But Elena twisted Varun's arm, slamming him against the wall as she withdrew the pods from his pocket with her free hand.

"Ferma," she said calmly as Varun struggled. "Throw Varun in with Jangir. They can keep each other company."

She let go, and Varun sagged against the wall, whimpering. The fire hissed as she approached. Elena tossed the pods and the flames leapt up at once, biting the air, but she did not stumble back. She watched as the pods burned, and Varun's proof with it.

"This—this is injustice!" Varun cried. "This is wrong!"

Injustice. Elena wanted to laugh. *Injustice was what happened in the park.*

"On second thought, Ferma," Elena said, her back to them. "Put Varun by himself. Maybe solitude will do him some good. Announce to the people that we found him in collusion with Jangir and have taken him into custody."

Varun protested, but he was no match for Ferma. There came the scuffing of feet, of struggle, and then his voice faded away.

Elena continued to stare into the flames. A bitter chemical smell rose as her pod started to melt.

"Elena."

She turned. Ferma stood in the doorway. She had redone her braid, and it snaked down her shoulder to her hip.

"Ferma." She expected her Spear to berate her. To caution her and tell her to release Varun. Elena steeled herself for it as Ferma drew near. But to her surprise, her Spear embraced her.

"Next time," Ferma said into her ear, "you just shout. I'll hang the bastard myself."

Elena half laughed, half choked in relief. Ferma squeezed tighter and then released her. There was a knock on the door, and Yassen entered.

"The king," he said, hesitating. "He said that he wishes to be left alone. And to not lie about emergencies."

Elena bit her lip. She had expected silence, and yet, her father's apathy bruised her. Ferma caught her eye, nodded.

"Yassen, will you leave us?" the Yumi asked.

He looked to Elena. "I'll be here, if you need me."

When he left, Elena glanced at Ferma. "What are you thinking? You have that scary kind of look like when you enter the field."

"I am about to do something very stupid," Ferma said.

"Ferma—"

Her Spear smiled. "Come with me."

Faint sunlight illuminated the stone arches as they walked through the central courtyard. Thick ironwood trees with ivory trunks and pale, pink flowers rustled in the breeze.

They turned past the courtyard and entered the rear wings of the palace. Here, the hallways were tall and ornate but with fewer paintings and stone latticework. Above them, on the arched ceiling, the red feather insignia of the palace guards glowed.

Ferma moved swiftly, her hair rippling behind her as they entered a rear tower. They stepped onto a stone platform, and it began to ascend.

"Where are we going?" Elena asked. She had only been to the guards' quarter of the palace a handful of times with Ferma, but the Yumi had never taken her up the tower.

The platform docked, and they entered a narrow, dark hall.

"This way," Ferma said. Strips of light illuminated their path. They passed several doors as they walked, the names of the guards floating before each room.

They came to a plain wooden door at the end of the hall. This one had no name, no design. Ferma pressed her hand against the touchpad, and the locks clicked and spun. They entered a room as big as Elena's foyer.

Training pads lay across every inch of the floor, while a dozen or so mirrors lined the ceiling and walls. A small corridor connected the room to a kitchen fashioned out of black desert stone. Incense burned in the corner before a shrine, but Elena did not see the icon of the Phoenix. She peered closer. A black statue stood inside. A goddess. Her mouth was bright red, open in a battle cry. Her several arms held various weapons, some Elena did not recognize.

"Is that..." she began.

"The Goddess, yes," Ferma said. She clapped her hands, and holostrips shed light across the room. "The Yumi's Goddess."

"I thought you believed in the Phoenix," Elena said. She had seen Ferma kneel before the Eternal Fire. Seen her whisper prayers and dot ash on her forehead.

"I do. And I believe in Her too." Ferma bent before the shrine and cupped her hands around the incense, then draped her hands over her head in blessing. "I find that the Phoenix and the Goddess are similar. Both are fierce protectors, creators of Agni. Yumi legends say the Phoenix and the Goddess were born of the same flame."

"'There are three types of fire,'" Elena recalled, and then her eyes widened. "Is that what my mother was studying? Why haven't you told me this before?"

"Aahnah did not tell me what she was studying or what she found. But I realized something at the temple yesterday." Ferma paused. A darkness crossed her eyes, and Elena took her hand.

"Ferma, what is it? What are you keeping from me?"

When Ferma met her gaze, Elena saw that her eyes were wet, full of pain.

"Oh, my darling."

"What are you—"

"Your father asked me not to do something," Ferma said. "And I pretended to agree. But I won't deny your birthright."

Elena touched Ferma's hand on her cheek. "Ferma," she said slowly, "are you telling me you know how to hold fire?"

For a moment, Ferma's smile faltered, and Elena caught a glimpse of something beneath, something she did not understand, before Ferma nodded, squeezed her hand tight.

"Yes," she said. "That's what I mean. I want you to have everything. Even fire, if you wish it."

"How?" Elena whispered.

"I have an idea." Ferma stood, her reflections glittering in the mirrors. "There are stories of Yumi wielding fire. They were devout warriors of the Goddess, and She gifted them the power of Agni, and to one warrior, Her staff of fire."

Ferma pressed a panel, and there was a hum as the training mats split open to reveal a deep pit with a tiny flame.

"Maybe the dance in the scroll isn't one dedicated to the Phoenix," Ferma said. "Maybe it's of the Goddess. Of the Yumi."

"But—I don't know much about the Goddess," Elena said. "I hardly believe in the Phoenix."

"It takes more than belief to hold fire," Ferma said. "Come. Assume your first pose."

Elena suddenly felt self-conscious and looked down at her burned fingertips. She had only ever practiced the fire dance alone.

"I don't know—"

With a flick of her hair, Ferma knocked her to the ground. "Your center is off-balance."

Elena rubbed her back, groaning. The Yumi's hair prickled, the ends sharpening as she paced. She looked like a cougar slowly stalking its prey.

Elena rose to her feet with a wary look.

"Feet wide," Ferma said and grabbed her by the waist. She tapped Elena's legs, motioning for her to widen her stance. "You need to be strong, like a tree. Rooted to the ground. Immovable like a rock." Ferma sank into her heels, feet wide, shoulders back. "See?"

Elena mirrored the movement, her twelve reflections following suit.

Ferma touched her back. "Straighter."

Elena nodded, though she could already feel her legs beginning to shake.

"Now, flow into the next form."

She balanced on her right foot, raising her arms behind her like the wings of a desert sparrow. The flame slowly tugged left. She moved her hands to the right, and it followed. Elena unwound her legs and transitioned into the next form of the dance—palms outstretched, mind clear.

The Lotus.

Think of the brightest light you've ever seen, the scroll said of this form.

Previously, she had thought of the Eternal Fire, and the flame had exploded. She had been wrong then. The fire was not a bright light. It was a source of rage. Destruction.

Elena blinked fiercely as sweat dripped into her eye. If the Eternal Fire was not the answer, she had to think of something else. Something restorative. Something that brought her peace. She thought of her mother, but the memory of her was already fading. Her father was more of a dark cloud than a source of light. And she knew nothing about the Goddess.

But then her gaze landed on Ferma.

My Ferma.

The Yumi smiled. "Keep your balance now."

Elena blinked. *The brightest light.* That was Ferma's smile, the one she gave now. It was her embrace, warm and strong, and in it, Elena knew she was safe. It was the hope in Ferma's eyes as she watched her, and it washed over Elena, rooted her, as if Ferma's belief alone rid her of her inadequacies. Reminded her that she was strong. That she was enough.

The flame grew.

She called upon her childhood memories—the times when she hid in the garden and Ferma pretended to not already know where Elena was. Elena would watch her from underneath the banyan leaves, holding her breath. And then Ferma would pop up behind her, scaring her into a fit of giggles. She would always find her.

She always knew where to look.

The flame rose in response.

Elena curled a finger. The flame bowed.

Still thinking of Ferma, Elena whirled and transitioned into the next pose. She spread out her feet, held up her arm as if reaching for the stars.

The Spider.

Like the desert spider, the fire sees all, the scroll said.

She envisioned the ancient Desert Spider warriors, and she pictured Ferma in their ranks. Tall and proud, her hair dancing in the wind.

"That's it," Ferma whispered.

Elena bowed her head and swept up her leg, her foot touching the back of her head.

The Tree.

Fire is steadfast and eternal. Root yourself in its heat and the truth it carries.

She thought of the desert on a summer day. How heat shimmered over the dunes in golden waves; how she hopped over hot stones in the courtyard to get to the covered path. Heat could be soft as a mother's kiss, as mean as the sun's glare. It operated in dualities, yet Elena rose to greet it like a flower. She drank it in, opened her heart, and let it blossom.

The flame hissed and grew.

She unwound her leg, opened her arms, and spun as the flame elongated and flickered. She came to a stop and rose on her toes, wrapping her arms around her body and twisting into the Snake.

There are those who fear fire, and there are those who learn to possess it and make it theirs, the scroll said.

Her mother had thrown herself into the Eternal Fire because she loved it. Her father held fire because he needed it. But Elena? What would she do? She balanced on her toes, her eyes trained on the flame as it danced.

Suddenly, the flame began to crawl out of the pit. Its tip flickered, tasting the air.

"Elena," Ferma warned. "Fall back."

In the mirrors, Elena saw the flame rise. She thrust her hands up, one palm out, the other curled into a fist, and beckoned for the flame. It listened. It shot straight into her fist, making Ferma jump back, but Elena cupped the flame in her hands, holding it steady.

"Holy Bird Above," Ferma whispered.

Elena managed a smile even as the small blaze peeled the skin of her palms. Ferma noticed the smoke, her eyes widening.

"Let it go," she said.

But the flame only strengthened, and her hands began to throb. "I can't," Elena whispered.

"Elena," the Yumi began.

Suddenly, the flame hissed and shot toward the mirrors. Her reflections turned, and as the glass shattered, Elena saw herself: ashen and alone, her hands dark and trembling, crumbling.

Ferma sprang and grabbed a mat and leapt on the flame, suffocating it.

The blaze hissed, its pain ripping through Elena. She cried out, falling to her knees.

"Stop it," she gasped.

But Ferma pressed down harder, and the flame gave one last gasp before dying.

They stared at each other in the silence that came after. In the pieces of the shattered glass around them, Elena saw her own doubt reflected in the Yumi's eyes.

"I can't do it," she said.

Ferma stood slowly. Glass snapped as she knelt and took Elena's burnt hands into her own.

"You just need time and practice," she said.

"What time, Ferma? The Fire Festival is tomorrow. Next week is the coronation." She pulled her hands away. "Maybe there's something else. The last form, it's faded from the scroll. Maybe my mother had a copy! Or some other text in her chest that can help us understand this one. Ferma, let's go look."

But the Yumi did not stand. Her shoulders slumped as she stared at the glass, the empty pit.

"Every time someone from your family touched fire, they lost it," she said, almost to herself. She looked up, met Elena's eyes. "It happened to your grandfather, your mother. The king is already losing his grasp, and then it'll be you. I was wrong, Elena. We shouldn't do this. Maybe it's a blessing that you can't control fire."

Elena laughed, and the sound was cruel. "Everyone says that to me. But I never thought you would too."

"Elena—"

"I thought of you, you know," Elena said. "When I was able to control that flame, it was because I thought of how you've always believed in me. How you've fought for me. Mother's Gold, Ferma, it was *you*."

The Yumi stood, her hair twisting behind her.

"Can't you see, Elena?" she said. "Fire is the death trap in your family. Ravence—"

"You said it yourself. It's my birthright," Elena retorted. "I want Ravence, and if I have to walk through fire to get it, I will."

Ferma shook her head sadly. "If you believe that, you truly are a fool."

CHAPTER 27

ELENA

Beware of the Black Hawk of Death. Its golden eyes see the passing of our world into the next.

—from *The Legends and Myths of Sayon*

Elena rummaged through the chest of scrolls. A chill crept through the room, and she shivered despite her shawl. *There has to be an answer here somewhere.* She untied a bundle of bound parchment, pored over the pages. The ink had faded, but as Elena brought the floating lantern closer, she recognized it as a diary entry. At the bottom of the page, her mother had marked her initials, along with the familiar jasmine flower.

Elena set it aside and picked another from the bundle. This one was too faded to read, but it had the same flower on the bottom corner. As did the next, and the one after that. Elena stared at the pages, drumming her fingers.

How does the flower connect these scrolls to the fire dance? Elena studied the diary entry. It was not her mother's handwriting, but it looked oddly familiar. She reached forward but her arm bumped against the lantern, knocking it against a stack of scrolls. The scrolls tumbled to the floor, unrolling and scattering across the room.

"Shit, shit." Elena began to gather the pages when she caught a glimpse of one entry.

Dear Jasmine,

I think I've found it. When you receive this, meet me at your tea shop. After hours. I'll bring it with me.

Yours,
Aahnah

Elena stared, hands trembling. *Jasmine. Meet me at your tea shop.*

The old woman at the tea shop had operated the business for many suns, for as long as her father was king. Elena remembered she had told Jasmine to call her Aahnah, when she had gone there for her meeting with Varun. Jasmine had flinched at that name, as if hearing a ghost.

She knew my mother. Elena ran her hands over Aahnah's note. The handwriting was beautiful with its elegant curves. A familiar ache tightened her throat. She wished her mother was here now. Wished Aahnah could answer her questions. Wished she could teach her how to find peace with her father.

Her pod pinged. Diya, calling her to get dressed.

Elena slowly rose, rolling up the scroll, the ache thrumming through her bones. It was always there, lurking, but here in this library, Elena felt it grab her.

She touched the chest. She had the urge to say something grand, like the hymns the priests sang, like the ones Aahnah had sung to her; or something intimate, like the diary entries she couldn't read, lost to all but the writer and her thoughts. But as Elena looked at the chest, bones weary, throat suddenly threatening to burst, the words fled her.

She leaned forward and kissed the wooden top.

"I miss you" was all she could say.

Elena raised her arms as Diya wrapped an amber sari around her hips and then up over her shoulder, revealing the delicate curve of her waist. The handmaid withdrew a golden brooch set with rubies and pinned the fabric right below Elena's shoulder blade. With a delicate flick of her wrist, she draped the pallu down Elena's arm, the fabric floating and then falling like the wings of a desert eagle.

Elena touched her neck, where a delicate array of gold and diamond insets lay, a gift from Samson. Its singular jade teardrop rested just above her breasts.

Diya smoothed back her hair and clipped on the matching earrings.

"Beautiful," she said.

Elena did not return her smile.

Ferma had come by, but she had not said a word to Elena. She spoke only with the handmaid. At one point, she had glanced over, her eyes tired and strained. Elena had pretended to busy herself with a set of bangles, and when she looked up again, the Yumi was gone. Still, she could feel the Spear's presence outside her door like a cloud's shadow over a dune.

"The Spear wanted me to give this to you," Diya said as she tidied the end of the sari into symmetrical pleats. From her pocket, she withdrew a holopod. "She said it has the list of names of the protestors in the park. For your speech."

Elena took it. "Thank you," she murmured. "Will you bring me some tea, Diya?"

When she was alone, Elena reached inside the drawer of her vanity and withdrew Aahnah's letter and the fire dance scroll. She tucked the letter into her waistband but hesitated over the scroll. The delicate paper rustled against her fingertips. The corners curled up. Slowly, Elena traced the dancer as she progressed through the forms.

Empty your mind. See nothing but the fire, for that is all that matters.

She ran her hands over the words, allowing them to sink in and take root in her mind. She wondered about the scroll's author; if she had a name, a family. Perhaps the author was the dancer. Perhaps this was a map of her life.

"Your Highness," Diya said as she carried in a tray of tea and cloud cookies. Elena quickly rolled up the scroll and slipped it underneath the sash of her sari.

"Thank you, Diya," Elena said.

She took a sip of tea as Diya filled a stone bowl with rosehip oil. The handmaid withdrew a chip of sandalwood from her waistband and set it aflame with a match. The wood began to smoke, and Diya slipped off the clutch that held Elena's hair.

Elena breathed in the smell of sandalwood and jasmine as Diya carefully lifted her hair and let the steam warm her neck. Layers of smoke coiled around her, tickling her ears. She stared at her reflection in the mirror.

She looked beautiful.

She looked monstrous.

A deadly queen who knew how to trap criminals and deliver justice. But as Diya added more sandalwood into the stone bowl, Elena understood that the reflection was only a mirage.

"There," Diya said. She sealed the bowl, suffocating the smoke. Her hands brushed Elena's neck as she began to braid her hair, her fingers swift and deft. She pinned the braids into the shape of a crown and adorned them with jeweled leaves.

"Perfect," she said.

The door opened, and Yassen and Ferma stood waiting.

"The hoverpod is here," Ferma announced.

Like Yassen, she was dressed in crimson, her uniform freshly pressed. Gold ringed her neck and spiraled down her arms. Her hair, threaded with bands of Ravani crystals, rippled down her shoulders. When she moved, they glinted in the light.

"Then let us go," Elena said.

Firecrackers ripped through the air as plumes of colored smoke danced across the sky. The smoke twisted, forming the shapes of animals: the blue dragon of the Ahi Sea; the green vesathri with its scorpion tail and stag head, once said to roam the Agnee mountains; and the Phoenix, Her red plume waving over the buildings. Along the street, performers beat drums and people popped bottles and waved golden flags.

Elena sat underneath a pavilion as her float made its way through Alabore's Passage. Before her, columns of soldiers dressed in red and gold marched down the main road, carrying banners of the kingdom as people whistled and hooted. Unlike the crowds from earlier, they did not all wear gold caps. Elena saw men and women, regular city folk, waving to her joyfully.

After the Birdsong, she had not imagined this many people to show.

"Glory to the queen! Our bringer of justice!" one called.

"Don't let Jangir get away with it!" another yelled.

"Let me kiss your slingsword!"

"All hail the new queen!"

Everywhere, people cheered. The voices of the Ravani rolled through her, swept her up, but instead of feeling a rush of pride, Elena felt sick.

I am a fraud, she thought.

Diya brought her an iced drink garnished with crushed rose petals. Elena thanked her, her eyes traveling to Ferma, who stood at the edge of the float watching the crowd. Curtains roped around the columns of the pavilion. From her vantage point, Elena saw the snipers on the rooftops. She smelled spiced street food and the sweet smoke of cured meats. Farther down the road, she observed a child wave a red ribbon that curled and unfurled like the tongue of a flame.

Elena glanced up at Yassen. "I need you to do something for me." She took a sip, rolling crushed ice in her mouth, and then set down the glass. "After I make my speech at the White Lotus, I need you to sneak me away."

His mouth hardened. "Are you trying to get me killed?"

"Not yet," she said, her eyes on Ferma's back.

He followed her gaze. "Why not Ferma?"

"She would disapprove."

"Rightly so."

"But you, my sweet Knight, like to break the rules," she said and looked at him.

He did not avert his gaze, but she saw color rise on his cheeks. A new roar went through the crowd as the artisans lit up their rockets. They cut through the air with a high whistle and then exploded in an array of colors. The sparks flung out and then sucked back in, forming the wings of their Holy Bird. It soared down the street before exploding once more.

Still, his eyes did not leave hers.

"Where do you want to go?" he asked.

She smiled. "A tea shop in Radhia's Bazaar. There's an old friend I'd like to meet."

"Can't it wait?"

"No," she said and felt the scroll beneath her sari. Her hands itched. "I need to go today."

He turned, and she saw him take in the guards, the police and the soldiers, the crowds.

"It would be impossible," he said finally.

"Yet," she said, knowing he had already found a way.

"Yet it's good you asked me," he replied slowly. The feather on his breast glistened in the sun. He withdrew his holopod, tapped something she could not see, and pursed his lips. When the pod pinged, he stared at it for a long moment, as if considering.

"Well?"

He turned to her, his voice low. "After your speech, we'll bring you back to the float, and the handmaids will close the curtains. There will be a guard change then. I just checked the schedule. We can slip out, get lost in the crowd."

"My dress—people will recognize me."

Yassen looked to where Diya stood by the curtains, dressed in a plain linen cloak. "We can fix that."

Ferma glanced at them just then. Her tawny eyes seemed to glow. Someone began a song, and she heard parts of the crowd catch on until the melody swelled around her.

We are the chosen,
the ones led by Alabore the Great.
We gave our hearts to the desert,
and our mother swept us in.
Her sweet long curves,
the dips of her valleys
the heat of her flames
gave us a home, a home we say,
to tend and call our own.

Elena hummed along with them, but she did not sing.

Alabore's Passage led to the White Lotus, a large sculpture sitting directly in the heart of the city, within a luscious, circular garden. At the center of the flower, a fire burned.

Elena stood, exchanging a look with Yassen as the float came to a rest.

They descended. Ferma led her to a podium at the base of the lotus. Journalists and their crews waited there, shouting and clamoring for her attention as she approached.

She smiled, allowing it to reach the corners of her eyes. When she reached the podium, she held up her hand, and the city lit up with the chorus of thousands.

Slowly, Elena lowered her hand to her heart, and the crowd hushed. Ferma, standing beneath the podium, caught her eye, gave an encouraging nod.

"My fellow Ravani," Elena said, "today we celebrate a Fire Festival like no other. For this sun, you will have a new queen."

Cheers rumbled through the city center, reverberating like heartbeats. In the holos above, Elena saw herself—tall and golden, regal and graceful. At that moment, the sun filtered through the sandscrapers, and the White Lotus was bathed in warm light. Her necklace shone with the brilliance of stars. She understood then why Samson had chosen it.

"You will have a new king trained in the ways of the sword. Already, our southern border is stronger than ever, thanks to the joint operations of our armed forces and the Black Scales," she said and was met by disjointed sounds of approval. Elena remembered the beggar and his scowl as he called her a Sesharian. The way the gold caps had dragged him away. She leaned forward, gripping the podium. "But, my countrymen, we will not have peace. Not when we kill our own in the sanctuaries of our parks.

"We will not have peace if we burn our own names in the sand."

A hush fell over the square. Below her, the reporters whispered and scribbled notes. She waited until she had their attention once more and then withdrew the holopod Diya had given her earlier.

"In the park killings, we have seventeen dead Ravani. Seventeen. Shall I read their names out for you?" She opened the pod. "Ajax Rathore, Jasleen Kumari, Kazenia Bo, Hassan Ruim, Huna Vi, Ramila Neuri, Uday Vyseria, Tia Givan, Anthosh Biswan, Yemani Nour, Eshaant Roy—"

And at his name, her voice wavered. Eshaant with his delicious makhana, his good-humored wink when he wheedled a higher tip from her. With his dream of leaving.

Clearing her throat, she continued. She read every name, heard them echo through the square. When she finished, Elena closed her eyes.

She knew the Phoenix did not hear her, but still, as she whispered the words, it gave her solace.

"May they all find peace in the warmth of Her fire," she whispered.

"So we the blessed few," came the murmur from the crowd.

She closed the holo, and her voice rang through the streets of Ravence. "As queen, I will try Jangir Meena for conspiring against the throne and opening fire on innocent civilians. His second-in-command, Varun Vehta, will also be tried. Today, Ravence will know justice. Today, I will burn *their* names in the sand." She looked up at the clear blue sky. "By the Phoenix's fire, I swear this to you."

She descended from the podium as the journalists closed in, shouting questions. There were disjointed cheers from the crowd, protests from some, silence from others. Elena caught a gold cap spitting on the ground. Someone whistled and another waved a gold flag, praising her name, calling for justice.

"Your Highness, is it true that Jangir conspired against the throne?" a journalist asked.

"Did your father know?"

"Will Jangir and Varun receive the death penalty?"

Elena looked past the guards and recognized the mouse-nosed journalist from Black Sands Day.

"You," she said to the woman. "What was your question?"

"Are you afraid of a divided nation?" the journalist said. "Though people are applauding your efforts for justice, a significant amount of gold caps believe that the allegations against Jangir are a conspiracy."

"It was Varun!" came a cry.

Elena saw a gold cap jostling against the guards. "Varun planted the reports. He did this!"

A guard pushed back the gold cap, who stumbled and fell. A woman laughed, and the gold cap turned, snarling.

"What are you laughing at?"

"Easy, yeseri. Daddy Jangir can't protect you now."

"Why you—"

"Enough!" Elena called out. She motioned to the guards. "Bring him to me."

Ferma stepped forward, her hair glistening. The gold cap fell silent at the sight of the Yumi. They all did.

"Please," Ferma said, her smile sharp as she looked to the gold cap. "Do come with me."

The reporters turned, watching as Ferma brought the gold cap over. He was young and lanky, with oiled hair neatly parted to the side.

"Your name?" Elena said.

"Kiv," he replied nervously.

Elena exchanged a glance with Ferma, and her Spear nodded. They were surrounded by journalists, by the public. She could feel their probing eyes, their confusion, their anger.

We could have riots, her father had warned.

And Elena could see it clearly on Kiv's face, knew that it wouldn't be a stretch for him to raise a torch and raze a park if left unchecked.

She had promised herself that she would not attempt to manipulate people the way Leo had. It was heartless, callous. But as Elena wrapped her arm around Kiv and turned him to the journalists and the people, she realized how easily they could turn against her. How quickly the crowd could become a raging mob.

You learn to control the mob.

"This woman here," Elena said, nodding to mouse-nose, "says that we have a divided nation. A divided kingdom. But we have a war on our borders, Kiv. What do you think will happen if we're still divided when the Jantari come?" Kiv stiffened under her arm. She gave him a gentle, assuring squeeze. "It's not a trick question."

"W-we would crumble," he said.

"And isn't that what Jantari spies like Jangir want?" she said. The lie burned her throat, but Elena held firm. There was no proof to show her involvement now. *Better this way,* she thought. Better to use a lie to catch a criminal. *Like tasting bitter medicine.*

Kiv glanced between her and the journalists. Sweat beaded down his forehead. "Is it true then? Jangir is a spy?"

Elena nodded, looked to mouse-nose. "Our investigations are ongoing, but Jangir will answer for his crimes. He and Varun both." She turned to Kiv. "And we will be a stronger nation for it."

Kiv did not look fully convinced, but before the journalists, before the guards and the people, he fell silent.

Drown out the voice of the dissenter. Control the mob. Her father's voice echoed in her mind as Elena watched Ferma escort Kiv back into the crowd. She hated that he was right, hated that she agreed.

But I am not protecting killers, she argued to herself as she climbed back onto the float, and the handmaids closed the curtains of the pavilion, obscuring the public's view. *I'm protecting Ravence.*

As she passed Yassen, he said quietly: "That was a gutsy thing to do."

She stopped. His eyes flickered over her, and he looked as if he wanted to say something more, something important. But all he said was, "Go, change. We've got little time."

Wordlessly, Elena ducked inside her private chamber.

Diya helped her shed her sari and don a plain linen cloak. Then the maid draped the ceremonial sari over her own body and head, hiding her face. The heat pressed around them, and Elena wiped the sweat off her upper lip.

"Thank you, Diya," she said. Diya nodded, and Elena tried not to notice her hands shaking.

"Ready?" Yassen's voice sounded faint from outside the thick curtains.

Elena squeezed Diya's hands and slipped out. She ducked her head as the trumpets sounded, announcing the end of the parade. Soon, hovercars would arrive to take her back to the palace, where her father was probably seething about her speech. Or not. Perhaps he would regard her with more of the same stony silence. She wondered if he knew how much it hurt her.

Yassen guided her through the curtains. He hopped down and held out his arm to her as the new guards strode up.

"How was the shift, Knight?" one of them asked.

Elena felt him stiffen, but his voice remained easy.

"It's too hot," her guard said. "Her Highness is in the changing room catching her breath. Diya is going to fetch some fresh ice. In the meantime, don't bother her—and keep Ferma away. I think they fought."

The guard chuckled. "Only the princess would dare to get on the bad side of a Yumi."

"You couldn't get on any side of her," another guard said.

They laughed, and one clapped Yassen on the shoulder. Elena saw him wince.

"Did you take a peep, Knight? I'm sure you saw something through the curtains."

Color rose on her face, and she dipped her head as Yassen straightened.

"Just keep the Yumi away," he said gruffly.

He saluted and drew past them. Elena followed, hiding her face. They walked quickly as the guards grumbled something about the Yumi and justice. Yassen led her to the perimeter line, where soldiers stood with their pulse guns. He nodded at one, repeating the same tale about ice for their queen, and they drew back. They did not give her a second glance.

With the parade over, the crowd mingled along the road. Many were drunk. Some whispered about the speech while others laughed and pushed, pointing at the soldiers' banners flapping in the wind. A gold cap warbled off-key.

"Justice in the sweet, harsh dunes," he sang, laughing.

Elena sidestepped him as he wobbled. A friend helped him up, but then the man doubled over and vomited. Elena wrinkled her nose, pushing deeper into the crowd, following Yassen's tall frame. When they reached a corner, he stopped to allow a hovercar to pass.

"A peep, huh?" she teased, and he looked at her, surprised. "Well? Were you looking?"

"What? No!"

"The guards—"

"They joke—"

"But you—"

"I never—"

She glared at him, warmth rising on her face, and not because of the summer heat. To her surprise, Yassen blushed.

"I didn't look, I swear."

He looked lovely when he blushed. The thought startled her, and she turned away before he could see the look in her eyes.

"Come on," he said and tugged her down a side alley.

Colors stained the stones. Ahead, a boy flung crimson powder at a young girl, who squealed and ran, red flying from her hair. They passed an open restaurant where the waiter popped a champagne bottle, and the people at the table laughed and raised their glasses to catch the spray. A hovercar beeped, and Elena slunk along the wall to let it pass.

"This way," Yassen said, ducking into another alley.

Elena pulled the cloak closer as she followed him. She wondered if Ferma had realized their deception by now. She must have. She had probably sent guards to track them down; Elena imagined Ferma stalking through the streets, her hair prickling behind her.

Already, the city had begun to build large fire pits for the coronation. She spotted one in the middle of a square where people piled dried azuri-wood on high, the white branches clawing the air as if to escape their fiery fate. The smell of ash permeated the streets.

Yassen drew close as a group of gawking tourists passed.

"Back there, you confirmed that Jangir was a Jantari spy," he said.

"No." She sighed. "I made those fake reports."

"So you're spinning tales, just like Leo."

Elena turned away, mouth tight. "He spins tales *for* the gold caps. But I am using one, just one, to stop them."

Yassen nodded, his voice quiet. "But how do you feel about it?"

Like I swallowed sand, she wanted to say.

"I'll bear it," Elena said grimly.

"You know, in another life, you would have been a dangerous Arohassin agent."

Elena laughed. "If so, then you'd be a king. Hunting me."

"But I would be there, with you," Yassen said. His eyes met hers and a thrill went through her body. "Even if we're on opposite sides again, I'll still find you."

"I prefer you as a guard," she said, and her voice lowered. "You don't look so bad in the palace uniform. I think serving the Crown suits the infamous Yassen Knight."

He threw her a look, but a smile played across his lips.

They came up to another alley. This one was so narrow that Yassen had to walk sideways to get through, his back and chest touching the two walls. Elena waited for him to pass before she followed.

They turned a corner and another, and then they were at the square. Jasmine's Tea Garden stood quiet, its windows dark. But as Elena followed Yassen, he froze.

Two guards materialized from the shadows under the awning. Yassen held up his hands as they raised their guns.

"Where is the princess?" one growled.

Before he could answer, Elena pushed past him, drawing back her hood so that they saw her face.

"Lower your guns," she said.

After a tense pause, they did.

The square was empty of urchins, merchants, and even stray shobus. As Elena glanced around, she saw the palace guards in the corners. The hilt of their slingswords glinted above their waists.

The door of the tea shop opened. Elena sighed, knowing who waited inside.

Ferma sat at a table with a cup of tea. She looked up as Elena entered, her tawny eyes burning with anger.

"They almost shot Diya for helping you sneak away."

"She did nothing wrong," Elena replied, sitting across from Ferma.

The table was small, yet the distance between them seemed to stretch for miles. Elena folded her hands before her as Jasmine appeared from behind the counter. Her hair, thick and grey, was combed into a long braid that trailed down her back as she bowed.

"Your Highness," she said.

"I need to speak to you, Jasmine," Elena said and looked at Ferma, "in private."

The Yumi regarded her for a moment and then stood. "You know, your stunt today could have cost many lives," she said. "Diya's, Yassen's, mine—imagine the chaos if something had happened to you."

"Ferma, please." Elena stood and took her hands in hers. "I'm sorry. But I'm safe. There are guards and officers everywhere in this city." She squeezed. "Nothing will happen to me."

But Ferma only shook her head, the ends of her hair writhing like angry snakes. Without a word, she brushed past Yassen and walked out. He glanced at Elena, regret crossing his face.

"Don't take too long," he said and followed Ferma.

"Would you like some tea?" Jasmine asked when they were alone.

"No, thank you. Please sit." Elena studied the network of wrinkles that sprouted across the old woman's face. A faint film obscured her brown eyes, making them pale, grey. Had she been younger, Jasmine would have had eyes like her own.

Eyes like her mother's.

Jasmine sat down. Ferma's abandoned tea steamed between them. Elena leaned forward, reaching across the table and wrapping her hands around the old woman's.

"You were my mother's friend. Weren't you?"

"Ah, so you know," Jasmine said with a soft smile. "How did you find out?"

"I discovered a letter and an old scroll of my mother's," she said. Jasmine's hands stiffened, but Elena held them tighter. "She left an odd note for you. About finding something. She said that she would show you."

Jasmine lowered her eyes. "We were dear, old friends," she whispered.

Elena withdrew the scroll and the letter from her cloak and set them down on the table. "Do you recognize them?"

The old woman stared but made no move.

"Yes," she said finally. She looked up, past Elena, to the small window of light pooling in from the door. "She was researching the old diary entries of Priestess Nomu and came across a dance to conjure fire."

"Why did she tell you?"

Jasmine gave a small smile. "Your mother and I grew up in the same neighborhood. We studied together up until after university. We were both mythologists, you know. And Aahnah was so bright. She wandered through the world with a profound sense of curiosity and a yearning for knowledge that humbled everyone. And she was kind. Sweet. When you talked to her, you felt the world slip away. You felt that you mattered simply because she was listening to you."

Elena found herself nodding along, hanging on to every word. Any scrap of memory of her mother.

"Everyone noticed her, including your father," Jasmine continued. "I'm sure you know this, but they met at university. He consumed every part of her—from her mind to her heart and the very time she had. As she grew closer to him, she grew further from me. We had a row. She said I was jealous, and I called her a fool." Jasmine shook her head. "I never received an invitation to the wedding. And once your mother was behind the palace walls, I couldn't reach her. It wasn't until suns later she came here into this shop and sat down in front of me, just like you."

"When was this?" Elena asked.

"You must have been three suns. She had changed then, Aahnah. She seemed worn. But when we began to reminisce about the old days, she became the girl I remembered. Do you know that her favorite sport was windsnatch? She would steal out of the palace, and I'd brew a fresh pot of tea and bake cloud cookies before we watched the game here. She loved the Fire Birds."

Elena blinked. She could not picture her mother, the woman who sang to her flowers, as someone who intently watched players knock opponents from their floating bladers.

There's still so much I don't know about you, she thought with a pang.

"What about the scroll? This letter?" She tapped them. "When did she show this to you?"

Jasmine did not answer right away. Instead, she got up slowly, the scrape of her chair filling the empty café. Without a word, she disappeared into the back of the shop. Elena waited. A minute passed, then two, then five, then seven. Elena drummed her fingers against the scroll, trying to remain patient. Finally, the old woman reemerged carrying a metal tin.

"Here it is," she said. She hobbled over and set it down, then wiped off a layer of dust, making Elena cough.

Inside the tin were two papers carefully folded into small squares. Jasmine delicately picked one up with two fingers. Slowly, she unfolded it and set it before Elena.

Elena peered at it, her heart hammering.

There was a drawing of a woman in a wide stance. She held her arms out before her, one hand curled into a fist with the other flat and open.

The seventh form: the Goddess. Become the fire, the light, for the entirety of the world.

And then, at the bottom: *Give it love. It is as alive as me and you.*

Elena looked up, her eyes wide. "What is this?"

"I think you know."

She looked back down and unrolled her own scroll with trembling fingers. She took the parchment and held it to the place where the paper was torn. The lines bled into each other perfectly.

It was the final form.

"Your mother would send me scrolls—secretly. She kept her findings from Leo. I don't know why, but she thought that, one day, he would stop her. She'd draw a little flower on each, a jasmine, and have them sent to me. And I'd write back to her—on paper—with my thoughts. Where to search next. I couldn't go to the Royal Library, but we'd meet in the city when we could. Until the day she sent me this letter." She tapped the parchment. "Aahnah came here just after I received it. She showed me this same scroll, with the same torn corner. And then she revealed the missing form to me. She wouldn't tell me where she found it. She took back the diary entry and dance scroll, but she left the rest with me. To keep safe. And after that night, I didn't see her again." She gazed at Elena, and there was a dark, hard look in her eyes. "She didn't trust your father with this. I hope you understand the gravity of her decision."

She opened Elena's other hand and set the second paper square in her palm. Elena stared at it. It felt insubstantial. It felt like nothing.

"What is it?" she asked.

"A letter. Something that will keep you safe during the time of reckoning," Jasmine answered.

More riddles. Elena shook her head. Her hand closed around the parchment.

"What else did my mother know?" she asked. "What did she learn after all that time in the library?"

"Oh, child," Jasmine said. This time, she was the one who wrapped her hands around Elena's. "Your mother came across something horrible. But she would not tell me about it. She just said that learning it changed everything. Then there was the Ashanta ceremony and . . ." Jasmine's voice faltered.

"And she died," Elena whispered.

Jasmine's eyes grew blurry with tears. She nodded.

Elena sank back in her seat. A sense of sickening dread filled her, and a question emerged in her mind, one that made the warmth leave her body.

Did she jump into the flames to hide what she knew? Or was she forced to jump to keep her from sharing?

Elena could not find it in herself to move. The only person who could influence Aahnah had been her father. *Did he . . .*

She felt her throat go dry. She did not believe it, of course not, but . . . Elena shuddered. She could not deny her father's ruthlessness. A Ravani never allowed a person to come in the way of his kingdom. It was one of the first lessons Elena had learned as a child. A Ravani held true to the throne. A Ravani was her kingdom, and nothing else.

"Thank you, Jasmine." She paused, meeting the older woman's eyes. "And thank you for keeping this safe for all these suns."

She stood and gathered the papers, hiding them underneath her cloak. "I have to go."

"I'm sorry I could not tell you more," Jasmine said, but Elena was already moving for the door.

She stumbled into the square, blinking furiously in the harsh afternoon sunlight. People, sounds, the city—they all seemed so far away. She wanted to wail. She wanted to drag her father to the Eternal Fire and shake the truth out of him. She was so tired of secrets. Elena swayed on her feet.

Out of the corner of her eye, she saw Yassen. He looked up from where he leaned against the wall, but instead of meeting her eyes, he looked straight past her—and horror swept across his face.

Elena turned just as the sound of pulse fire ripped through the air. She fell on her hands. Screams erupted through the square. A guard toppled over, blood blossoming from his chest.

There were distant shouts, panicked orders. Someone grabbed her arm, and Elena gasped. Ferma loomed over her, screaming, but Elena's ears were ringing, and she could only watch her lips move, dazed.

Ferma yanked her to her feet and shoved her. Suddenly, Elena was running. Her legs moved of their own accord as if her body realized what her mind could not—*run*. She ran down a side street, Ferma sprinting ahead, with Yassen and two guards bringing up the rear. More pulse fire split the air, and Elena saw a woman on a terrace cry out, her body slumping over the railing.

"Move, move!" Ferma barked.

Elena ran. Her heart beat wildly as they rounded a corner and dashed into the open market. A hoverpod was already docked there. Pulses ripped along rooftops as her guards returned fire. But then came a bright flash and a loud smack, and the air exploded. Elena hurtled forward. She fell to her knees, biting down on her tongue. More ringing filled her ears, blood and dirt in her mouth. The blast had torn a gash down the building to her left, and a fine dust coated the air.

She looked up. The hoverpod still stood. Ahead, she saw Ferma rise, her hair sharpening and raking the sky. Elena clawed the ground, found purchase, and lurched to her feet.

Yassen dashed past her, crying out. "Ferma!"

A shot sounded. She felt the pulse graze her cheek, heard its whisper at her ear, and saw it race through the market and rip into Ferma's chest.

She saw the Yumi's eyes widen. Everything was in slow motion, like a dream. The blood sprouting from Ferma's chest. Her hands grasping the air. Her body, her hair, Ferma, falling.

Falling.

A scream tore from Elena's throat, but it sounded as if it came from another being, a wild creature. Yassen held Ferma up, shouting, his eyes wide.

She was so limp in his arms.

And then the world was spinning. A sniper on the roof fell. An urchin lay crushed beneath a fallen wall. Blood spilled down the side of his head, his mouth frozen in a silent cry.

Someone pushed her, but her legs were lead, and she stumbled. But then there was Yassen, yelling, shouting, *Move! Move!* Then he pulled her, nearly ripping her arm out of its socket as they dashed into the hoverpod. The door closed and they were airborne, shooting straight into the sky.

Elena gasped. She clutched Yassen's arm. Everywhere, she trembled. Suddenly, her feet could no longer bear her weight and she sank, taking Yassen with her. He was telling her something, something about the palace, her father, and she turned to him. Somewhere deep in her mind, she registered that his face was bleeding and then realized it was blood from her shoulder. She must have been shot, but she felt no pain.

Everything was distant. Everyone swam. Who took off her cloak? Was that a medic wrapping treated cloth around her shoulder? Someone pushed something into her mouth. It tasted bitter yet sweet. Elena gulped it down, and then the shadows that crept along the edges of her vision grew longer. She was on her side. People were shouting. Her hands lay in front of her and there, in her palm, was the folded letter. Someone had given it to her. It winked at her as her eyes fluttered, and she sank, willingly, into the deep, forgiving darkness.

CHAPTER 28

LEO

When the Phoenix rises, the sky will burn. Dunes shall unravel, mountains shall shake, and valleys shall fill with the bones of generations past. She shall rise from the flames, and She will seek Her Prophet.
—from *The Prophecy of the Phoenix*, transcribed into written word by the first priests of the Fire Order

Anything?" Leo asked.

Majnu shook his head. "No, Your Majesty. They're all clean."

Leo rested his chin in his hands, his head heavy. All morning, the servants had clamored around the palace, preparing Elena for her appearance at the Fire Festival. He had avoided her since their argument, and she had sent messages, night after night. Asking about Jangir, about a statement. But the pain and the sorrow of her betrayal festered in his chest. He did not have the time, nor the heart, to speak with her now.

After Elena had left for the festival, Majnu and his men had searched the servants for strange marks under the ruse of an outbreak. Leo had come up with the idea, had instructed Majnu to round up the palace men because a "sickness" was spreading in the city—one that left black marks on the victim's body.

"The servants will call it an omen," Arish said. "That a so-called sickness descended into the palace before the coronation."

"The Prophet brings plagues," Leo snapped. He turned back to Majnu. "Have you sworn the servants to secrecy?"

"Yes, sir, but I expect some will tell their family members," the Spear said.

"Inform them that the disease is mild, that they shouldn't worry, but that we can't risk infecting Elena," Leo said. "Search your men next, Majnu. The Prophet could be anyone."

"Sir," Majnu said and then hesitated. "I don't believe any of my men are the Prophet. But the new men who've come in . . ." He trailed off. Slowly, he met Leo's gaze. "They might be worth searching."

"Do you accuse your future king of smuggling in the Prophet?" Arish said.

Majnu shook his head. "I mean no harm, sir. But the runes appeared shortly before Samson's arrival. Perhaps the Black Scales are the omen."

"Or it could be coincidence," Arish began, but Leo silenced him with a look.

"There are no coincidences when it concerns the Prophet," he said and thought back to his vision in the desert. He had seen the runes before they had been burned in the sand. The Eternal Fire was warning him, taunting him. "I'll speak with Samson. But search your men, Majnu. No one shall be overlooked."

Majnu bowed.

"Your Majesty," he said at the door, and Leo looked up, meeting his kohl-rimmed eyes. "What if the Prophet does not know that he is the one? What if his power lies dormant? What if . . . he's you?"

Leo did not smile. "I am the furthest thing from a Prophet. Now send for Samson."

The fire around the room purred as Samson arrived. He stood at the door, his eyes traveling over the flames and the mosaic floor before resting on Leo. He bowed.

"Your Majesty," he said. "Arish."

"I had the opportunity to meet a peculiar commander of yours recently," Leo said.

"Ah." Samson shifted his feet, crossing his arms behind his back. "You mean Chandi. She's harmless."

"She's insubordinate," Leo growled. He thought of her dark eyes, her skull tattoo.

"Chandi can be a bit possessive—"

"I cannot have your men defying me," Leo said, his voice slicing through the room like a blade. "They've sworn their allegiance to Ravence. If they cannot even pretend to keep their word, what use are they to me?" His eyes met Samson's. "What use are *you* to me?"

The fire hissed. Samson stared at him, as if shocked, and then nodded slowly.

"I suppose my men do not recognize the true king." He held up his right hand and spread out his fingers. "But I've taken the Desert Oath. And as long as you are king, I'm beholden to it."

Leo rounded his desk. Late sunlight spilled in from the skylights, warming the crest on the marble floor. He stopped at its edge, Samson across from him. Silence wedged between them. Leo expected Samson to fidget, but his future son-in-law stood tall, his face carefully composed.

He knows why he's really here.

"Saayna lied," Leo said, and the crackle of the fire filled the space between his words. "The Prophet is in the palace."

Samson closed his hand. He did not look alarmed. "Do you know her identity?"

"The Prophet is a man," Leo answered. "I've searched the servants and the guards. All who remain are you and your men."

Again, Samson nodded, his face still stoic. "I see."

His composure annoyed Leo. He wanted to see some reaction—a twitch of an eyebrow, a downturn of the lip—but Samson did not yield. He would make a brutal king.

"Come," Leo said.

Samson followed him to the edge of the room. The fire that had listened calmly now grew at their approach. Leo held out his hand, and without hesitation, Samson opened his palm, his signet ring glinting. Leo took his hand and held it over the flames. They grew and brushed the back of Samson's knuckles.

Leo pushed down; the flames bit into Samson's flesh. The warrior sucked air through his teeth, grimacing as the stench of burnt hair filled their nostrils. Leo held both of their hands over the fire until his own arm began to smart. Only then did he withdraw.

Samson cradled his fist to his chest, but he said nothing.

"Aloe will help with the burn," Leo said and then added, "son."

Delicately, Samson pulled off his ring and slipped it onto his other hand. "Do you plan to burn down this whole kingdom to find the Prophet?" he asked, his voice barely a whisper.

"Wouldn't you do the same, if an overly powered lunatic threatened your kingdom?"

Arish drew up beside them and held out a damp towel. Samson took it and wrapped it around his hand, concealing the burn but not the smell of burnt flesh.

"I assure you, none of my men are the Prophet," he said as he tucked in the end of the towel. He met Leo's gaze then, and there was a gravity in his eyes, a depth that belied his charming demeanor. "You run a fool's errand."

"There's the shobu's bite," Leo said with a mirthless smile. "And here I thought you would always roll over to please me."

"You jeopardize our rule," Samson said. "How can Elena and I begin to rebuild the kingdom if you leave us nothing but ash?"

"Don't worry. I'm sure your Jantari king can lend you some metal." Leo waved his hand. "If the Prophet rises, there will be no kingdom for any of us to rule."

"You don't know that," Samson said.

"Oh, but I do. There will be no mercy under the rule of this Prophet, just like there was no mercy under the Sixth. He and his Phoenix will lay waste to Ravence, and they will not stop there. Jantar, Cyleon, Nbru, the islands, they'll all fall."

Leo touched the back of Samson's hand. "This is the small price we must pay to avoid war. A few misdeeds for a greater future." He looked into the younger man's eyes. "So you will search your men with my Spear, and you will report to me if you want this kingdom."

Samson dropped his arm, the towel clenched in his hand.

*   *   *

Leo returned to his desk once Arish guided Samson out. A cloud passed overhead, and sunlight seeped out of the room.

Leo touched the necklace underneath his clothes, the jade bird above his chest. Aahnah's bird.

The day she had jumped into the Eternal Fire, she had told him something odd, something that came to him now as the heavens opened and rain drummed against the skylights.

"I think the desert forgets easily," she had said as she donned her ceremonial robes for the Ashanta ceremony.

"Forgets what?" he had asked, but she hadn't answered.

He had only meant to protect her. The day of his coronation, the Eternal Fire had demanded a sacrifice, but he, selfish and young, had refused. He could not imagine a life without Aahnah. She knew how to root out his faults and iron them into something stronger, better. When they used to lie together at night, she would trace his eyebrows, smoothing out the tension in his brow.

He closed his eyes and imagined her face. Drew it line by line, as if he could conjure her before him. The perfect arch of her brows. The deep brown eyes. The birthmark hidden behind her ear, at the edge of her skull. He rubbed his thumb against her necklace. What was it that she would always say to him?

The dead and the living are full of fear.

Oh, he was afraid. Afraid of what would happen should he fail: the intense fury of the Prophet and the Eternal Fire, the rupture of his kingdom, the death of his daughter. He could feel his fears eating the edges of his mind, racing toward him.

Seek forgiveness.

That's what they all told him—Saayna, Arish, Majnu—but they did not know the cost of forgiveness. Forgiveness required vulnerability, an admission of his faults. It required him to bare his chest to the world and allow others to dig into his flesh.

Leo stared at Elena's slingsword resting on his desk.

Have you ever considered what I wanted?

An ache gnawed in his chest. Leo turned away, guilt flashing through him.

The rain fell harder, yet as Leo looked up, the sky was afire. A bright, living red ringed with pink—Aahnah's favorite type of sunset.

A message popped up on the glass panel of his desk just as Arish returned. The Astra wore a pinched expression, but Leo did not question him as he turned to see his Spear in the holo.

"Your Majesty," Majnu said and then hesitated.

"What is it? Have you found him?" Leo asked, but the look on Majnu's face made his stomach drop.

"There's been an attack in the capital. We believe it was an attempt on Elena's life. We—"

"Is she alive?" he gasped.

"Yes, sir," Majnu replied.

Leo collapsed into his seat. His heart hammered in his chest.

"Her Highness is already on her way to the palace in a hoverpod," Majnu continued. "She should arrive in seven minutes. We suspect the Arohassin are behind the attack."

"Yassen Knight," Leo said, his voice rising. "Where is he?"

"He's with Her Highness," Majnu said. "It appears, according to initial reports, that he was the one who saved her."

Leo's head snapped up. "What?"

"Those are the initial reports, sir," the Spear said. "We've had casualties, both palace and civilian. Some of Her Highness's guards died in an explosion. Ferma was killed by a sniper."

"Ferma?" Leo said, stunned. He felt a pressure in his stomach, as if he was slowly being swallowed by quicksand.

"Holy Bird Above," Arish whispered.

Leo stared at Majnu's floating image. *Ferma dead, Yassen Knight alive. It makes no sense.*

"Seven minutes you said?"

"Yes, sir," Majnu replied, and Leo shot to his feet.

The passage from his office to his chambers rumbled open. He strode through, past the polished halls and bustling kitchens, through the main courtyard and Aahnah's banyan tree, his heart fluttering in his chest like a caged bird. *How in the heavens did the Arohassin get past capital security? Past Samson's men?* He heard a hum and saw a black dot on the horizon—the hoverpod.

He began to jog and then run. Aahnah's necklace jostled against his chest as he sprinted past gaping servants and guards.

And as he did, all that hurt, all that bitterness against Elena evaporated.

He realized now, as he ran to his daughter, that the pain he felt was not because of her betrayal—it was because she saw him. She had revealed the things he had avoided.

Have you ever considered what I wanted?

"I haven't. Please," he begged. He did not believe in the heavens nor the Phoenix—no god would answer his prayers—but as he ran, heart in his throat, Leo called to the one person who he did believe in. "Please, Aahnah. Let her be safe."

He could ward off Jantari armies, root out clusters of Arohassin agents, and burn the Prophet himself, and still, he would have failed his daughter.

Have you ever asked?

That night, she had searched his face for an answer, eyes wet, waiting. But he had never stopped. Never paused and turned to her.

Leo burst through the gates and onto the landing platform that jutted out behind the palace, along the lip of the hill. He saw a team of medics huddled against the rain. Guards lined the platform, and there was Majnu, ordering his men to surround their king.

The hoverpod appeared through the burning sky, and its descent seemed to take an eternity as Leo watched it dock and its ramp slowly unfold before bloodied guards stumbled through.

And then he spotted her. That dark mess of curls.

Leo pushed past the guards, the medics, Arish, Majnu, all of them, and saw Yassen supporting her, helping her down the ramp, pushing her forward. Her eyes fluttered to Leo.

"Elena!" he cried and drew her into his arms. He squeezed her tightly and felt blood on his clothes and his face, but he did not care.

Elena. His daughter. His heir.

She was alive.

Elena made a soft, rasping sound.

"Yes?"

Her eyes locked on him. Her words were faint.

"Ferma," she breathed. "What happened to her?"

But then a team of medics rushed in and unhooked him from her. Leo watched, heart thundering, as they eased her onto a hoverbed, undid the wrapping on her wounds, and sedated her. He watched her go.

"They got Ferma," a dull voice said behind him, and Leo turned to see Yassen. Blood stained his cheek.

"You," Leo said. Yassen flinched and took a step back. "You saved her. Why?"

Yassen looked past him to Elena's fading form.

"Because even though the desert does not claim me as its own, she does," he whispered. "I took an oath."

A medic came up to Yassen, fussing about his cheek, his shoulder, the blood, but Yassen waved him off. He bowed to Leo and followed his daughter. Leo watched him leave, watched the medics guide the hoverbed into the palace, watched Majnu dip his head to say something to Arish. A second hoverpod docked, and more medics rushed to it. Leo could only stare, his hands stiff by his sides.

Standing there, at the edge of the platform, he had never felt so small.

So powerless.

CHAPTER 29

ELENA

The Yumi, above all else, are loyal warriors.
—from chapter 16 of *The Great History of Sayon*

The royal doctor wrapped her shoulder with clean gauze and pulled. Elena winced. The pulse had only grazed her shoulder, drawing blood but ripping no muscle.

He said she was lucky. Elena tried to laugh, but the sound caught in her throat and came out more like a mewl.

The clean white walls of the infirmary overwhelmed her. She was in a small private room, but whenever the door opened, she caught glimpses of a hallway filled with bloodied guards and harried medics.

The doctor, satisfied with his work, clipped the gauze.

"The stitches will heal, but you'll have to come back to remove the scar," he said.

She nodded. She felt weightless, as if she could float away at any moment.

The doctor withdrew glass vials and a syringe from a cabinet by the door.

"For the pain," he said.

The needle pierced her skin, but Elena did not even feel its prick. She felt detached from her body, as if she were watching herself from afar. Distantly, she noted that she still held her mother's letter in a clenched fist.

"You might feel drowsy," he said.

Her tongue felt swollen and clumsy. Her lips would not move. She heard a knock, and Yassen entered.

"Elena," he said as he strode to her bedside.

Her blood caked his cheek and chest. His sleeve was torn at the elbow, and she saw his burn marks. Carefully, Yassen took her hand in his. Squeezed.

"How are you?"

Seeing him, feeling his skin against her, pulled Elena back. Rooted her to the present. This close, she could see worry cloud his eyes. The streak of dried blood above his eyebrow. She had the sudden burning desire to be held, to bury her head in his shoulder and weep.

"She's still too shocked to speak," the doctor answered for her. "But Her Highness has been graced by the Holy Bird Above. She will recover." He pointed at Yassen's arm. "What happened to your arm?"

She felt him stiffen.

"I burned it, months ago," Yassen said.

"Let me see it. It could have gotten infected."

Yassen hesitated, but she squeezed his hand. *Go.*

He sighed and sat down, rolling up his sleeve as the doctor bent closer.

"Hmm, this one is swollen." He touched Yassen's elbow with a gloved hand, and her guard hissed. "Have you been cleaning it?"

"Yes," Yassen said.

"Still, it is infected. It's minor for now, but let's get you cleaned up, before it gets worse. Have you felt any symptoms? Any headaches, nausea?"

His eyes met hers. For a moment, she saw his indecision, his fear. She wished she could reach for him, lend him whatever strength she had left.

"Just some tingling," Yassen said finally.

"Tingling?" The doctor chewed his lip. "Burns can cause nerve damage, but it should fade away, if you address the infection. Is it painful?"

"It passes," Yassen said.

The doctor gathered the empty vials and the syringe. He dropped them in a heated bin and turned on the burner; a warm glow spread along the white walls. He then offered Yassen two bottles of pills and a cream.

"These two are to stop the infection from spreading," he said, holding the cream and a bottle. He then held up the other bottle. "Tell Her Highness's handmaid to give her this every night for the next two nights, but no more. The coronation is nearly upon us, and we can't have her groggy."

Elena blinked. She wanted to tell them that she couldn't take the medicine—that the ball was in a few days, and she needed to practice her dance with Samson, but her mind and lips veered in different directions. She sagged forward, whimpering. Yassen caught her and gently pushed her back into the bed.

"You need rest," he said.

He leaned over, adjusting her pillow, and she smelled death on his shoulder—a sickly, sweet smell that reminded her of overripe grapes left out in the sun. The doctor dimmed the lights. Shadows stretched along the walls, and Yassen paused. He stroked her hair, and then his hand hovered by her cheek.

Stay, she thought.

But he was pulling away. The shadows came down the walls and into her eyes. They washed over her and pulled her down, piled on like layers of sand, like the dunes shifting and growing, burying her alive. Her eyelids fluttered. Yassen grew smaller.

Don't leave, she wanted to say, but he was already gone.

Elena awoke to a cool hand pressing against her forehead. She moaned, and the hand moved away.

"Your Highness."

It was Diya's voice.

She heard a rustle of fabric and felt Diya rise from the bed. Elena opened her eyes slowly, blinking away the heavy mantle of sleep. She was back in her room. A bowl of iced water sat on her bedside table along with the small square of a letter. A breeze stirred the curtains, and she smelled iron.

Diya returned to her side, cradling a bowl of fragrant broth. She stirred, raised the spoon, and held it to Elena's lips.

"Drink," she ordered.

Elena drank. The soup stung her tongue, but its warmth seeped down her throat and fanned out across her chest. Suddenly, hunger pressed against the sides of her stomach. She grabbed the bowl and raised it to her lips. Diya watched as she desperately slurped, catching the drops that dribbled down Elena's chin with a kerchief.

"I can get more," she offered.

Elena shook her head and wiped her lips with the back of her hand. She gazed around her room and was struck by its emptiness.

"Where's Ferma?" she asked.

Diya took the bowl from her hands and set it down. She gently cupped Elena's hands in hers.

"Your Highness, Ferma is dead."

Elena stared at her. "No."

But Diya squeezed her hands, her voice soft and full of sympathy. "She fought bravely."

And then in a rush, it came back to Elena: the burning square, the crushed boy, blood blooming across Ferma's chest like a carnation. Ferma, her Ferma, falling.

Grief stung Elena's throat, her eyes, her nose. The pain felt enormous, intense; it pierced into her chest, cutting down, down, down. Her stomach clenched, and she crumpled inward.

Diya held her as she sobbed, her cries like those of an animal. Her stomach burned. Her shoulder ached. She clung on to Diya because if she let go, she would become unmoored, lost in a deep black ether of grief.

What had Ferma said to her?

You truly are a fool.

And Elena felt like one. She was a fool for going off into the city without her guards, without telling Ferma. Because of her, Ferma was dead.

Slowly, her grief blackened into rage. Against herself. Against the sniper who had shot Ferma. Against the heavens who did not save her.

Elena detached herself from Diya and rose, swaying on her feet. Her hands prickled. Her face felt hot, and she felt a sudden desire to *burn*, to destroy, to create a hole in this world as big as the hole it had drilled in her.

The fire in the hearth flashed. Elena reached for the flames. They reared back, as if afraid, but she ripped one off as if breaking a limb. The flame pulsed in her hand. It resisted, but she held on, squeezed, and it coiled around her fist.

Burn. She wanted everything to burn.

This time, she did not falter. This time, she knew every part of the dance as if it had always been within her.

The Warrior.

She squatted low, feeling heat build in her legs, and then thrust her arms out. The curtains were the first to light. The fire leapt onto the thin blue silk, eating, laughing. She spread out her arms like the desert sparrow, and the flames soared as Diya screamed, rushing out into the foyer. Elena guided the flames onto her bed. The sheets peeled away like the decaying petals of a lotus.

The Spider, the Tree, the Snake, she flowed through the forms, her anger—her grief—building power. The flames cackled. They rushed past her like eager shobus as she descended into her garden. She set them upon the banyans, and the air filled with smoke. Sparrows cried out as they fled from their homes.

The water in the fountain began to boil as the flames swelled. They latched on to an ironwood and tore it apart, split it right down the middle to reveal its white, fragile flesh. Elena heard Diya begging for her to stop, but the flames were louder.

Burn, they crooned. They wanted everything to burn.

Elena closed her eyes, concentrating. A flame grew in her hand, and she willed it to elongate, to strengthen, to strike. She saw the last form of the dance, saw the coiled muscles of the dancer and the heat in her veins. As she crouched back and raised her hand, lifting her fiery spear like a warrior, like a goddess, Elena felt something unlock within her—a spark that flared up her spine.

She felt the power of fire course through her veins, and it tasted delicious.

Elena threw the spear of flame, and the fountain shattered in an explosion of stone and dust. The boiling water splashed out, hissing. Flames burst through, hopping from stone to stone, setting everything ablaze.

And Elena wielded them. She swept her hands, and the flames turned. She beckoned, and they listened. When she pulled her hands in, they surrounded her but did not burn her; their heat licked her face like the kiss of a lover, a mother, a friend.

Like Ferma.

And suddenly the memory of her carved through Elena, through the flames. Ferma as she leaned her head back when Elena had braided her hair; Ferma as she took her hands and told her, *I want you to have everything. Even fire, if you wish it.*

She felt her in the flames. Felt her in the heat that brushed her skin. Elena held out her hand, and a flame curled around her wrist.

Think of the brightest light you've ever seen.

That was Ferma. That *had been* Ferma. But now Ferma was gone, and only the fire remained.

Elena clenched her fist as the ache in her chest reverberated through the inferno. The flames felt her pain. They crowded around her, wept for her.

We remember her, they cried.

"Elena!"

She turned and saw her father at the balcony. Guards tripped down the burning stairs. They made to grab her, but her fire would not have it. The flames plunged toward them.

"Stop! Stop!" Leo cried out.

And then he was running toward her, and the flames were cackling, waiting, but he tore through them as if they were nothing but air. He grabbed her hand, pulled her to him. She gasped. The inferno shrieked and fell inward to attack the intruder, the one who disturbed its wake. And Elena felt its primal hunger to tear into Leo's flesh, to burn his skin down to his bones and then his bones to smoke. She saw what he would become. A pile of char, a heap of soot.

"*No!*" she cried, and she swung Leo behind her and swept her hand. The flames died with a hiss, turning to ash that rained into her eyes.

Behind her, Leo gasped. When she turned to him, he pulled her into a tight embrace, whispering.

She had not heard him over the song of the flames, but now, in its aftermath, she heard him.

"Don't," he choked. "Don't turn into her."

They gave her stronger medicine afterward, and Elena drifted between dreams of burning flesh and dying women. She awoke in fits, slick with sweat, and Diya would place a cold towel on her head and hush her back to sleep.

When her fever finally broke, Elena was alone. She sat up slowly. They had brought her into unused guest chambers. A mirror stood across from the bed.

Her hair was a wild tangle. Dark rings circled her eyes, her lips pale and flaking. Her skin still smelled like the burning banyan leaves.

With a groan, she stood. The floor felt cool, and her toes curled. She heard a soft knock as the door opened.

"You're awake," Leo said, entering the chamber. He hesitated, his voice small in a way she had never heard before. "Should I call for tea?"

Slowly, she nodded.

He turned and whispered to someone outside, but she could not see who. Her father closed the door and gestured toward the seating area.

She sank down, resting her head against the back of her chair.

"How do you feel?"

"Like I've been dragged through the desert," she croaked.

Diya arrived carrying a pot of tea and glazed cups. Leo poured the tea, his hands slightly shaking, and then handed it to her. She held it close to her chest but did not drink.

"Try it," he encouraged. "It's a gift from the Verani king."

"I thought he wasn't coming to the coronation festivities," she said.

"He wants to pay tribute," he said, his eyes meeting hers over his cup, "to the Burning Queen."

Elena stiffened at the name. "Is that what they're calling me?"

"The servants and the guards, yes, but the name will spread," her father said. "Such names tend to."

She could not tell if he was admonishing her, and she was too fatigued to care. Her father avoided her gaze. She waited for him to speak, but he remained quiet. An awkward, heavy silence sat between them. Brutal and familiar, full of all the unsaid things she wished she could tell him.

The ache in her chest grew more acute, and she saw it grow in him too. In the way his shoulders slumped, the way he fidgeted—he never fidgeted—pinching the skin between his thumb and finger. Leo reached for his cup, but he did not speak. She willed him to. Wished for him to ask—just ask. But he avoided her eyes, and for the first time, Elena did not see the man she feared and revered; she saw a broken man full of pain.

Pain that she had inflicted, knowingly.

All I wanted was for you to ask, she thought. But as her father sat before her, unable to even meet her eyes, Elena realized something else.

Grief was a double-edged sword from which they both drew blood. And they had wielded it against each other so callously. She had wounded him by her betrayal; he had punished her by denying her birthright. And at some point, they had gone too far, so that now, in their home that smelled faintly of smoke, they regarded each other like strangers.

And Phoenix Above was she tired of it.

Leo had always taught her to draw out silences. To make the other person uncomfortable, afraid. But silence was also a way to mask vulnerability. It took courage to make the first move.

Elena reached over and placed her hands on top of her father's. And finally, finally, Leo looked up and met her eyes.

"I thought you would leap into the flames too," he said, and at the sound of his voice cracking, at the enormity of his admission, her heart welled.

"Oh, Father," she gasped.

He squeezed her hands tight as he bowed his head, shoulders shaking silently. She rested her forehead against his.

"I would never do that to you," she choked.

A tear fell, then another. Leo Malhari Ravence wept, quietly, and she held him, quietly, so that he could grieve without shame. He raised her wet hands and kissed her burned fingertips. Folded them between his, pressed together like in prayer.

"You were right. I never asked you what you wanted—because I was afraid. And I was selfish." He let out a shaky breath. "I denied teaching you the Agneepath because to hold fire, to wield it like you did, means that you must give a sacrifice."

"Sacrifice?" she said, growing still.

"On the eve of my coronation, my father showed me how to hold fire. And he told me it came with a price: the Eternal Fire would seek a sacrifice. One of blood or one of love. I refused." A mournful smile crossed his face, and her chest tightened. "But your mother learned the truth through the scrolls. She saw how the Eternal Fire grew angrier, and on the day it threatened to kill me, she threw herself into the inferno."

Elena felt as if someone had squeezed her heart, stopping it from beating. It made sense now. Aahnah's obsession with the Royal Library, why she had kept her discoveries between her and Jasmine. *She was afraid that he would try to stop her.*

"Does—does that mean," she began, and when Leo nodded, her hands trembled in his.

"You must give a sacrifice now," Leo said.

"But I didn't learn through you," she said. "I learned through the scroll. The dance. Ferma said it was connected to the Yumi Goddess, not the Phoenix. Not the Eternal Fire. Surely that—"

"Elena," Leo said, and the forced calm in his voice threatened to break her. "It is done. Whenever a Ravani heir holds the inferno, the Eternal Fire will seek a sacrifice."

She shook her head fiercely. "No. I won't give one. I can control the flames. Father, you *saw*. I—I know how to wield them now. When the fire threatened to harm you, I pushed them away." She searched his face, but Leo only looked at her with sorrow. "Please, Father. There must be something we can do. I cannot lose you and Ferma."

For a long time, Leo said nothing. Then he gently released her hands, turning them palm up.

"I killed the priests," he whispered, so softly that at first she didn't hear. "And I made Ferma kill the ones that my men could not."

"Father..." But Elena remembered the haunted look in Ferma's eyes. "Wh-why?"

"I was searching for something," he said, and when he looked at her, she realized that her father was afraid of her. *Afraid of what I will think of him.* "The Prophet is coming, Elena. The Eternal Fire has shown signs of the return. I thought it was one of the priests, but I was a fool." He shook his head. "I—I don't expect forgiveness. But I hope..." He took a deep breath to steady his voice. "I hope you'll understand. This throne drives us to do things that we would have never done before."

His hands quivered, but as he drew away, Elena touched his wrist.

"I do understand," she said. She remembered Kiv, the gold cap in the crowd. How she brought him out under the pressure of the journalists and silenced him. The lies she had spun. How she hated herself for it. But it had been necessary, to break the gold caps and sustain the lies against Jangir. Ravence was better off without them, even if it tasted bitter to do so.

Leo watched her, and his eyes slowly widened in knowing. "What else happened at the parade?"

She told him, all of it. Kiv, Varun, Jangir. The gold caps harassing the poor beggar, how she had watched, powerless; Eshaant with his smile and his makhana, only to end up dead with his chest weeping blood. Her father listened silently, and when she finished, he gently took her hand.

"I won't lie to you. It will get worse. One day, you'll wake up and realize how much you've changed. How much of yourself you've lost. But remember this, Elena," he said. "You will have me. You will have Diya, Samson, Yassen, the guards, the people who knew you as you were before. We can remind you of the woman you once were, so you won't get lost. And if you're not a fool like me," he said with a rueful smile, "you will listen."

She smiled in return, but then Leo's face darkened. "Still, no one will understand what it takes to rule the throne. Not like you. So even if you take our advice, you must think for the kingdom. We might be at war soon, Elena. You must be ruthless. If you must become a villain, become one. Become whatever Ravence demands, because without you, it will die."

And though Elena shivered from the gravity in his eyes, she nodded.

That night, she built Ferma's funeral pyre.

Elena sent for bundles of azuriwood and piled them together herself. When the servants tried to help, she waved them away. Sweat beaded down her forehead as she worked. A cold wind blew in from the north, licking her face, and the Ravani Desert stretched along the horizon, the dunes crested by moonlight.

"You love nights like this," Elena said. Her hands ached as she lugged another piece of wood. "Still and quiet. Well, mostly."

Her voice rang through the courtyard, and Elena saw a servant shift uncomfortably. He whispered to another, glancing her way, and then strode back into the palace.

"They think I'm crazy, Ferma," she said and laughed. "Who cares. You don't."

She grunted as she lifted a log. It was heavy, but Elena shouldered the weight and used her legs to pop the log on top of the pyre.

"Jasmine tea," she muttered as she shifted the wood. "Sprinkled with lavender and a dollop of honey. We will have it in my garden and watch the stars. They're so bright tonight, Ferma. Even with the moons out. Maybe it's a sign for good luck or, I don't know. I suppose I'd have to ask my father or a priest to find out." She chuckled, but the sound died in her throat as Elena remembered her father's hollow gaze, the pain in his voice.

"He told me about the priests," she whispered. "About the Prophet and what you did. It was a horrible thing to do, but, but..." Her fists curled. "You were only following an order, Ferma. It wasn't your fault. It was my father's, and he grieves for it."

She paused, gazing out at the desert. Only the wind answered her. Only the dark, empty desert awaited her. Elena felt an aching gap, and out of habit, she looked over her shoulder, to where Ferma always stood.

Shadows stretched behind her. A servant, catching her gaze, dipped her head.

Elena stared. The absence in her chest widened, and her fingers trembled around the azuri. Ferma was not here. She was not listening or rolling her eyes or laughing at what she had said.

"I am going mad, aren't I?"

"No," came a voice, and Elena turned to see Yassen approaching her with the servant who had disappeared inside the palace.

"What are you doing here?"

He hefted up a log, wincing slightly, before throwing it on the pyre. "I'm here to talk to her too," Yassen said as he bent for another log. She grabbed the other end, and together, they placed it on top. "She's listening and watching, even if it doesn't seem like it. Aren't you, Ferma?" He cupped his ear as the wind blew. "See, she's laughing."

"Nonsense," Elena whispered, but even so, as the night air brushed her cheeks, she found comfort in it. "She's cursing you."

"That's not what I heard." Yassen grinned. "Ferma, you don't have a foul mouth. You do, however, have a wicked sword arm."

"Fast as a rattlesnake."

"Deadlier too." He rubbed his cheek. "You almost got my face in our first duel."

And so they talked to the wind as the night stretched on and dawn began to color the horizon. Elena knew it was madness. Ferma was gone. They spoke to only a ghost, if ghosts existed. But as they spoke, Elena felt the pain in her chest grow duller. She focused on the fresh scent of the wood. The heat in her arms. The memory of Ferma, so bright and alive as they spoke to her, of her.

When dawn arrived, Elena stepped back. The pyre was up to her shoulder, wide and tall. Yassen grunted and rubbed his arm, stepping beside her. Before she could ask him about his injury, her father came.

Leo was dressed in white, like her. Behind him, Samson, Arish, and Majnu followed, then the servants carrying a stretcher with a body. There were no priests.

When they set it down, Elena saw Ferma. Her body had been cleaned, her hair braided in Yumi fashion, and her skin washed with rose water and anointed with ghee.

The servants began to reach for her when Elena stopped them.

"Let me," she said, looking to her father.

Leo nodded.

Carefully, she cupped Ferma's head. Her skin was cold. But her face looked peaceful, and Elena leaned down, kissing her forehead.

"Thank you, for everything," she whispered.

Yassen took her lower body, she the upper, and together, they lifted Ferma onto the pyre. Leo stepped forward with the ceremonial pot of holy water and torch.

"Here," he said. It was usually the monarch's job to burn the body of an Astra or Spear, but Leo handed the torch and pot to her. "She would have liked you to do it."

Elena nodded gratefully and placed the pot on her left shoulder, held the torch behind her back. There was no priest to start the chant, so Elena sang it.

"O beloved of the Phoenix, the skies open for you."

The others sang as she circled the pyre. With each round, Leo hit the pot with the hilt of a slingsword, cracking a hole. On the third and final round, Elena dropped the pot. It crashed to the ground, water hitting her ankles as their voices rose.

"To be forgiven, we must be burned."

She raised the torch and lit the pyre.

The flames spread quickly, efficiently, and as they swelled, Elena felt their heat pulse within her.

"Rise, forgiven, and leave all that was left to you. Rise, forgiven, to find all that is true. Rise, forgiven, for She awaits you."

As the wood snapped and the body caved, Elena felt something break within her. Tears spilled down her cheeks. She sobbed quietly, at the foot of the pyre, watching the flames eat Ferma until she could bear it no longer. She turned away.

The inferno buffeted against her back, but Elena looked to the desert. At the wide, rolling dunes, the ones that Ferma had loved. The wind brushed her face, taking the tears from her eyes before they fell.

A hand touched her wrist, and without turning, Elena felt Yassen beside her.

The scriptures said that when a body was burned, its soul flew heavenward to meet the Phoenix. Elena did not believe in it for certain, but she looked to the stars—to the twin moons, still not yet faded.

Be at peace, my friend, she thought.

The flames sang in the low wind as Yassen stood with her.

Be free.

The guests began to arrive two nights later in a long procession of hovercars that trailed up the drive. Lights illuminated the gorgeous domes and the white marble arches of the palace. The ornate trellises had been newly washed, and they shone in the night as servants escorted dignitaries up the entrance steps. The great doors of the Agnee Palace, carved of wood and metal, inlaid with jewels, depicted the Phoenix, Her wings spread as if She would break through the carving and rise to the sky. They swung inward as the guests came upon the doorstep.

There were diplomats, lords, ministers, generals, and royal heads of state. The ladies wore lavish dresses with long trains or heavy cloaks threaded with gold. Some wore tall feathers woven through their hair while the daring ones wore tailored suits of lightning thread. When they passed, the air gave off a burnt, metallic scent.

Lords wore sharply creased coats with their family crests shining above their breasts. Generals donned their brass and smoothed their hair into neat side parts while the kings and queens glittered among them. They did not need loud ornaments or fancy dresses. They had their crowns.

Elena watched as Leo set the Ravani crown on his head. In the dark halls behind the ballroom, the Featherstone glowed. He wore a rich ivory sherwani with intricate golden embellishments around the collar and cuffs. Over his breast, the Phoenix brooch glistened.

Leo glanced at Elena, and she saw just how much he had aged in the few days since the attack. Deep lines ran across his brow. His cheeks were sunken and his eyes, usually a sharp steel grey, had dulled to worn metal.

He reached across and adjusted the simple gold band around Elena's head. His fingers brushed her ears, hovering over the earrings.

"These are Aahnah's," he said.

She touched them, feeling the groove of the wings. They were jade birds caught in mid-flight, with gold in their eyes and beaks. They matched the necklace Leo always wore, the necklace her mother had gifted him.

"I thought she would like it if I wore them."

"You look beautiful in them." He gently touched her chin, smiled. "She would have loved to see you become queen."

Servants bustled by, carrying large bouquets of flowers. Elena could hear the excited chatter of their guests through the doors. Today, all of Sayon gathered to see her, the young queen-to-be, the heir who would bring fresh life to Ravence.

Elena smoothed out the layers of her heavily embroidered red lehenga, the intricate beadwork glimmering softly in the dim light. The blouse curved off her shoulders as sheer layers of tulle draped down her arms, tumbling down like twin fiery waterfalls. Diya had rubbed her with almond oil until her skin shone like gold. Around her neck, she wore a pearl-and-gold necklace shaped like the Phoenix—an heirloom passed down from Queen Jumi. The bird's head nestled in the dip of her right clavicle; its wings fanned out across her chest and curved toward her ears. From afar, it looked more like a golden tattoo than a piece of jewelry. Jumi had swapped the Phoenix's traditional ruby eyes for emeralds, and Elena preferred it this way. They matched her mother's earrings.

"I assume you reminded your guard to stay out of sight," Leo said, and she nodded.

"Yassen will keep to his rooms."

She had instructed him to stay in his wing. If their guests caught wind that he was here, she would begin her reign with more enemies than friends. Yassen had, after all, targeted or killed members of Sayon's elite, relatives of royal families who now graced their halls. And she had heard of Yassen's mistake with the Verani king. The old man was here now, drinking her wine and flirting with the young princes of Mandur.

Still, she missed him. Elena looked down and felt the ghost of Yassen's arm brushing against hers as they lifted the logs. He had given her more strength than he realized.

"Your king is late," Leo muttered, and as if on cue, Samson appeared at the other end of the hall.

He wore a long black velvet coat that brushed his ankles as he approached them. The coat stretched across his broad chest and shoulders, tracing the pattern of muscles that lay underneath. The necklace she had gifted him, a thick gold band of gems mined from the Agnee mountains, curled around his neck. When he reached her, she could smell the rich musk of mutherwood—a mountain smell.

Samson kissed the back of her hand. He wore kohl, and it brought out the darkness of his eyes against his raven-black hair. "You look beautiful."

"So do you," she said. He laughed, the sound of it lifting the shadows in the hall.

"The Jantari have arrived," Leo said, and he looked at Samson. "Farin believes that you're still his man."

"And I will act like a dutiful servant to Farin, don't worry. He won't suspect a thing." Samson winked. He turned to her and held out his hand. "Shall we?"

Elena looked between the two of them—her father and her fiancé, her past and her future—and she suddenly ached for Ferma with an intensity that took her breath. She wished the Yumi was here now, holding her hand, escorting her into the ballroom with her hair prickling behind them. It felt wrong to enter this next stage of life without her.

The sarangi sounded, indicating their entrance. She took a shaky breath. *I'm sorry, Ferma*, she thought. Then she mustered a smile and took Samson's hand. "The world will be watching us now. Let's give them a show."

Leo led the way as they climbed the stairs, coming to the edge of the landing overlooking the ballroom. Samson squeezed her hand. Through the doors, she heard the muffled voice of the announcer.

"All bow to the Phoenix King, Guardian of Fire, Son of Alabore, the Divine Grace of Desert and Sky, His Majesty, Leo Malhari Ravence."

The doors swung open, revealing the grand hall. Long curtains of roses cascaded down the gold shimmering walls, and their fragrance filled the ballroom with the scent of promise. Delicate chandeliers floated along the ceilings, and tipsy guests danced under their twinkling light, crushing fallen petals as they spun. Servants dressed in crisp white coats with gold lotuses on their lapels served glasses full of honeyed wine and spiced whiskey. Along the far wall of the ballroom, hungry guests milled over tables filled with roast lamb, seared ham garnished with candied pomegranates, and platters full of desert sweets.

A hush fell as the king stepped onto the landing—and then came a thunderous wave of applause, the crowd raising their glasses. Despite the attacks, despite the sorrow they shared, Leo stood tall. Elena admired him for it. He would never show weakness to these people.

Leo raised his hand, and the applause died down.

"Friends," he said, his voice filling the space of the large ballroom. "Thank you for coming. Together, we herald a new age of Ravence, a new dawn brought by a queen of sand and fire. So please, raise your glasses for the blood of Alabore, the Twenty-First Ruler of Fire, my daughter, Elena Aadya Ravence."

Elena stepped forward into the gaze of the hundreds gathered below. She heard them gasp, clap, and shout out toasts as she stood smiling, beaming, hoping they did not see the broken woman beneath.

She raised her hand, beckoning, and Samson drew up beside her.

"My future king," she said simply as Samson looped his arm around her waist.

The lords from Teranghar were the first to approach as she descended the marble staircase. They bowed low and kissed her hand. Next came the ambassador from Cyleon, who presented her with moonspun flowers that blossomed at her touch. The princess of Nbru dipped her head and smiled coquettishly at both of them. Wherever they went, people crowded around them. They laughed, doling out praises and well wishes that did not match the calculation in their eyes.

Their words are sweet now, but how long until they sour? Elena thought. She caught the ambassador of Karven glance her way, saw the tension in

Queen Risha of Tsuana's posture. They all knew about the Jantari threat yet skirted around the issue. She wondered how many secretly supported Farin, how many would turn a blind eye if Jantar invaded?

"Your Highness."

Elena turned, distracted. "Yes?"

"I was just saying," King Bormani drawled, "how I hoped Ravence would open its northern borders for more Verani trade."

Leo shared a glance with her as the king rambled on. Veran was a small kingdom with a disorganized army. If they did increase trade with Veran, how useful would their army be against Jantar?

"In due time, Bormani," her father cut in, finally ending the man's long speech. Leo smiled and gripped his shoulder. "Let the young ones dance now. Eh?"

Elena smiled, mouthing *thank you* to her father, but before she could turn for the ballroom floor, she felt Samson stiffen beside her. She turned, looking up at him, and followed his gaze. There, walking toward them, was King Farin of Jantar.

"Leo," Farin said. His voice was a wispy rattle as air pushed through the metalwork of his neck. He was not a tall man, yet he was square in the shoulders with a large block of a forehead. He was dressed in Jantari blue—a deep, vivid color that mirrored the mountains of Jantar's eastern borders—and wore the silver emblem of a winged ox on his chest. His green metallic eye swiveled across the room, taking in the floating chandeliers, as the pale, colorless one set its gaze on Elena. "Charming place."

Elena noticed how others glanced their way, how the kings and queens pretended to drink their wine but listened as they passed.

"Farin," Leo said, not bothering to hide the distaste in his voice. "You've lost some weight. Hopefully your diet isn't too strict."

"Nonsense. What are pounds if not the result of delight, hmm?" Farin said and looked at Samson. "This chap and I have often challenged each other in drinking games, and I swear he lets me win."

Samson recovered and waved over a servant carrying a tray of drinks. "Not tonight, Farin. I'm going to drink you into the ground."

Farin laughed, a dry, grinding sound. "Only if Her Highness drinks with me."

Farin's ancestor, Queen Rhea, was the first to start the tradition of melding flesh with metal. She sacrificed half of her body to boast of Jantar's superior metalsmiths, had ordered the royal engineers to build a body more capable than flesh. And with each generation the gears became more advanced. The tradition belonged only to the royal family, luckily, or else Elena would have had to deal with a half-metal army along her borders. She supposed she shouldn't be too appalled by Farin. The Ravani sacrificed to fire; the Jantari, to steel. Different gods, but with the same vein of fanaticism.

Elena plastered on a smile as she took a glass and handed it to Farin. Out of the corner of her eye, she saw Queen Risha angle their way.

The other kingdoms are growing wary of Farin's antics, Leo had told her once. *Even Tsuana has asked Farin to not prohibit the passage of refugees.*

"Let us drink to our new friendship," she said. "Oh, Queen Risha. There you are."

Farin paused mid-drink, but he finished his wine with calculated ease.

"Risha, darling, how fares Tsuana?"

Queen Risha was a tall woman with smooth ebony skin and grey braids that cascaded down her back. She wore a shark-tail-shaped headdress, the beaded shells softly jingling as she dipped her head.

"Gentlemen," she said. "Princess. Congratulations on your engagement and your upcoming coronation."

"Thank you," Elena said. "Thank you all for coming."

"Thank your future king," Farin said. He set down an empty glass. "He's a dear old friend."

"I brought us together because I'd like my friends to coexist peacefully with my family," Samson said. He had only taken a sip from his wine. "This is a new era for Ravence, which means a new era for Jantar. Perhaps we can finally bring peace to this holy land."

Farin snorted. "What did this land ever know of peace?"

Ravence would know peace if the Jantari left us alone, Elena thought but held her tongue. She glanced at Queen Risha, who wore a tight smile.

Farin must have noticed it too because he smiled, quickly correcting himself. "Ah, but you are right, my boy. Jantar will keep the peace, so long as all parties are willing."

"Well, my doors are always open if you should need to cement this in a treaty." Queen Risha raised her glass. "You need only ask, Leo, Farin."

Elena turned to her father, who had stayed oddly silent during this exchange. He nodded, raising his glass in response. "My daughter will soon bear the torch of this kingdom. I think your best efforts should be directed at her, Risha."

"Of course, my apologies," Risha said. She turned to Elena, but her smile was cold. "The new generation."

She does not trust me, yet, Elena thought. She did not blame the older queen. She was the latest newcomer in the second continent, and the other rulers awaited to see how she would act on the global stage.

"I will surely call on you, Queen Risha," Elena said. "You have been a great friend to my father, and I hope to continue that friendship."

Risha nodded, her face a mask, as an attendant touched her elbow. "Ah, I must go. Excuse me."

When she had left, Farin turned to Elena.

"I heard that the Arohassin took responsibility for the recent attack in the city." He shook his head. "My condolences to you, Your Highness. To have an attack so close to your coronation. And the death of your Spear on top of that..."

He was trying to unnerve her, but the mention of Ferma twisted a dagger in Elena's stomach. The pain was still too fresh, the grief too sharp. Farin smiled sympathetically, but it was small, thin. Anger rolled through Elena. *You don't deserve to speak of her.* She wanted to take her wine and throw it at his face. But Elena only squeezed the stem of her glass, her smile tight.

"We will find the Arohassin agents responsible for the attack, I assure you," she said.

"Show no mercy, young queen. They all deserve to be shot. Or burned, I suppose." Farin laughed.

Elena thought of Yassen guiding her through the melee, his hand warm and firm in her own. Yassen, who had saved her. She had heard of Farin's cruelty toward insurgents. He forgave no one, not even the smallest of informants. If he caught them, he dragged them to prison, tortured them, and then melted iron onto their heads until their skulls collapsed. Farin's ancestor had done so to Elena's many-times-great-grandfather during the Five Desert Wars. It was a point in history of which Leo had never failed to remind her.

"A heavy hand will only make them hate us more," she said. "But if we turn them against each other, then"—she smiled—"they'll rip each other apart."

"Deception at its finest," Farin said, but his smile did not reach his eyes. "She truly is yours, eh, Leo?"

A muscle worked in her father's jaw. "Did you not do the same, Farin, with the Sesharians? Turned the three islands against each other—only to take them once they were weak?"

Beside her, Samson grew still. Farin glanced at Samson and then threw his arm around his shoulders.

"And they were better for it, weren't they, Samson?"

There was a darkness in her fiancé's eyes, but Samson nodded. "Without the Jantari, Seshar would have regressed into the past. Cut off from the world, from technology."

It hurt her to hear him say it, but she knew it hurt Samson even more to stand there, a smile on his face, spewing lies while the man responsible hung his arm around his neck like a noose.

"See," Farin said, metal eye swiveling, "we raised Seshar to higher standards. Now it has a proper navy, ha!"

Samson's eyes met hers, and she saw the hate in them, so clear and unchecked. She walked forward, touched his hand.

"Come, beloved," she said. "It's time for our dance."

"Ah yes, dance, of course you must." Farin rapped Samson on the back. "Sweep her off her feet, boy."

"Of course," Samson said through tight lips.

Elena shared a look with Leo, and he gave her an encouraging nod, as if to say, *I'll handle him.*

"Enjoy your dance, young ones," Farin said, and he bowed, gears whizzing and whining the brutal song of a body forced into mutation.

Elena took Samson's hand and led him to the ballroom floor. Other couples acknowledged them with bows and curtsies, clearing the space for them. When they reached the center, she turned to Samson.

"Are you all right?" she said.

"Just dance with me," Samson said and took her hand. He placed the other on the small of her back and drew her close. She could smell cologne on his collar, see a flake of stray kohl on the top of his cheek. But his eyes did not meet hers. He looked over her shoulder to where the kings stood.

"You're glowering," she whispered and felt his hand tense.

"If there's war against Jantar, what will you do?" he asked. The question took her by surprise as the musicians plucked the tune of the Phoenix dance, a fusion of Ravani sarangi and sitar with tabla and pakhawaj. The harmonium sounded as her guru, dressed in a fine chiffon sari, sang the tune.

She missed the first beat, stumbling over his feet. Samson quickly turned her so now she could see Farin over his shoulder.

"If peace talks fail," he said, his breath tickling her ear, "how far are you willing to go to win the war?"

Elena glanced at his face, and there was a cold, calculating look in his eyes that she had never seen before. His hand tightened around hers. "How far, Elena?"

"Far enough to protect my kingdom," she said, eyeing him.

They twirled across the floor as onlookers watched. Samson held out his hand, and she dipped underneath his arm. She spun behind him, her hand slinking across the small of his back as he drew her back in.

"Just yours?" he asked.

"I only have one," she said. "What's the meaning of all this, Samson?"

But his dark expression was gone, replaced by an easy smile. "Sorry," he said, shaking his head. "I meant nothing by it. Farin just unnerves me sometimes."

She nodded, though she could not shake off the unease snaking through her. "We will attempt peace first, Samson. We must. If we go to war now without proper cause, the other kingdoms will abandon us."

"Of course."

The guru sang higher, the beat quickening. They fell into the rhythm of the dance, their feet skipping over the floor as roses shed their heady scent. Samson twirled her, and her skirt flared like the petals of a lotus.

"Though first, I have to get him drunk. I can't let him think he can drink *me* under the table." Samson grinned.

"Oh really?"

"It's serious work," he said as she turned back into him.

"Am I to marry a drunk?" she teased.

"No, but as the first decree of our reign, we will order barrels and barrels of wine. Mountains of them." He grinned. They swayed, and his hand dropped back down to her waist. "And we'll ship them out to Farin so he and his metal friends will drown in it."

She bit back a smile. "Attack by wine is your master plan?"

"The most refined type of subterfuge," he said, and this time she actually laughed. It surprised her. After Ferma's death, she had not thought it possible to laugh again. She still didn't.

The music swelled, nearing the end of the dance, as Samson spun her out and held out his arms. When he nodded, she leapt into his embrace, spreading her arms as he lifted her into the air. Slowly, they turned. But his hands were too hard, his nails digging into her skin. Elena flinched in his hold and tried not to wince, tried not to think of how Yassen, when he had held her, had been careful, gentle. But then Samson set her back down as the onlookers clapped.

Elena stumbled back and then corrected herself, managing a smile as Samson caught her eye. They bowed as the music slowed. Surreptitiously, she rubbed her waistline.

"We will make this kingdom great, Elena," he murmured beside her. "That is my promise to you."

The air grew warmer as the dancing couples rushed in.

"I hope so," she whispered, parting from him.

When she found a moment, Elena excused herself and returned to the hall behind the ballroom, the train of her dress rustling behind her.

She slumped against the wall and closed her eyes, drinking in the cool darkness and savoring its still, muted silence.

But as she breathed, a gnawing sensation returned in her chest, and Elena knew it was her grief. In the emptiness of this hall, she felt it— the lack of Ferma's presence—keenly. Her nose prickled. A heavy weight pulled down her shoulders, threatening to sink her like a pebble in quicksand. She clenched her fists, her throat tight. She could not cry. Ferma would not want this. Ferma would want her to put on a fresh face and return to the ballroom with grace.

But her vision blurred and suddenly, the necklace around her throat felt like a noose. Elena grasped her neck. Air, she needed air.

She stumbled away from the ballroom, away from the fake smiles and cloying laughter. The pain in her chest threatened to choke her. She staggered through the courtyard, her feet moving of their own accord. She found herself wandering down the guards' quarters like she had done only a few days ago with Ferma. The hall was silent, empty.

Ferma's door stood at the end, dark and bare. Elena gasped, clutching her chest. She wanted to rap on that door and see it open to reveal Ferma, her Ferma, smiling and inviting her to another spar. She could not bear it. She stumbled down another hall.

She did not know where his room was, but she wanted to see him. To feel his hand in hers and hear his voice. He was the only one who knew Ferma even half as well as herself.

Elena found Yassen's room in the next wing, in the corner, his name floating above the door. She leaned against the doorway, calming her breath. Her hands trembled. Slowly, she rapped against the door. No one answered. She rapped again and again, and still, he did not come.

CHAPTER 30

YASSEN

Forever and forever, farewell, dear friend.
May the moons and the stars bless our parting.
          —from *The Odyssey of Goromount: A Play*

It had been comically easy to steal out of the palace during the ball.
Yassen simply slipped out from the servants' side entrance, dressed in his
guard uniform, and they had been too distracted by the guests to recognize him. Around the front of the palace, he watched hovercars pull up
the long drive. Lords, ambassadors, ministers, and bureaucrats spilled out.
Despite the attack in Rani, they still came with their glittering jewels and
painted smiles. Even the neighboring monarchs weren't thrown off by
security concerns. For them, this was a night to take stock of the Ravani
kingdom—to see how far it had fallen and how brutally it would rise.

    Yassen donned his hood and tried to ignore the ache that traveled up
his right arm. He had taken the pills and treated the infected skin on his
elbow as the doctor had told him; but oddly, the markings on his wrist
had begun to inch up to his fingers. He would need to put the ointment

329

there too. With his left hand, Yassen found the holopod in his pocket. He squeezed it for good measure.

He had received a message earlier in the day.

Honey muffin.

Nothing else. Seconds after he opened the message, the holo dispersed in blue dust, but its meaning had been clear enough.

Yassen began to make his way to his hovercar when he saw a familiar face. The Verani king sweeping forward, his belly straining against the confines of his coat. Yassen froze. The king sniffed the air with distaste as palace servants bowed. Behind him, the Verani queen, a petite woman with eyes the color of amethysts, scowled.

They both wore leather, despite the desert heat. The king said something, and the queen shook her head, fanning herself. Yassen sucked in his breath as they entered, and only exhaled when they were out of sight. Then he slipped out from the shadows and was speeding into the city within seconds.

It began to drizzle as he veered down the overpass, winding through side streets until he came to a narrow alleyway. At its end, two shobus tussled over a scrap of meat. They looked up as Yassen stopped. He leaned down in his seat, ran his fingers along the smooth leather, and found the tracking device—a small black square with a tiny blinking light. Yassen detached it from its holder and got out of the car.

The shobus growled.

"Easy, boys," he said. His hand found the gun tucked underneath his cloak. It was his father's gun, a silver pistol of genuine iron and steel. The police were conducting sweeps, using sensors to locate the heat of pulse guns. His outdated firearm would go undetected.

Yassen wrapped his hand around the holster as he backed away from the shobus.

"Easy."

One shobu barked, taking a few steps forward, but then stopped, its twin tails flicking. Yassen slipped out of the alley, walking quickly. A child in rags stood at the corner, and when he held out his hand, palm outstretched, Yassen dropped the tracking device along with two Ravani coppers.

"Stay off of the streets tonight," he whispered to the boy. "The silver feathers are on their rounds."

The boy blinked, his tiny fingers curling around the coins and the tracker. A small, almost knowing smile touched his ash-streaked face. Yassen turned on his heel and did not look back.

The city was mostly empty. The attack had shaken Rani to its core, and most of the residents—save the orphans and the shobus—hid in their homes after curfew. Yassen sidestepped shards of glass and crumpled petals. In a broken storefront window, a banner from Elena's coronation hung limply.

She had been close to death. Yassen wondered if Elena had realized this as he turned into a narrow alley, walking to an unmarked door at its end. People changed when they saw death's dark face, when they were inches away from its cold grasp. He had. And he had seen it two times already. Each encounter had leached a portion of him, but it had also ignited something—adrenaline and a rush to defy the odds, to defy death itself. Yassen felt that rush now as he rapped on the door, a simple two-beat knock. It swung open, and Yassen stepped in.

The storefront windows were shuttered; shadows filled the old bakery. Yassen could still smell the faint scent of bread and fried gujiyas lingering in the air.

A shadow moved, and a flame flickered. Yassen saw two scarred hands cupping a lighter. Then a man bent into the light, touching the yron in his mouth to the spark; the flame revealed his harsh Ravani cheekbones and dark eyes. He inhaled deeply and blew out smoke. It curled like a writhing dragon, and Yassen smelled the sweet scent of narcotics.

"I trust you weren't followed," Akaros said.

"No," Yassen replied.

His old master nodded. "And the Yumi woman?"

"Dead," Yassen said, keeping his voice flat. "They found her body among the wreckage. She managed to nick a few of our men before she died."

"That's a Yumi woman for you." Akaros chuckled. The end of his yron glowed in the dark like a red eye. "It's a good thing you notified us about the change to the tea shop. Swift feet, Knight. And the princess?"

"She was only grazed by a pulse," he said, surprised at the depth of his relief. When he had pushed Elena into the hoverpod, Yassen had seen a deep, animal fear in her eyes. He recognized the look; he had worn it when he first saw death on his mother's burnt face.

"Good," Akaros said. "Then everything is falling into place."

"Our captured men—"

"Giorna will be freed once we take the city, along with the others. Maya's already slipped out of the city. I'm sure Muftasa will love that."

"We were supposed to be tracking down Maya to bring her in. What should I tell them?"

Akaros shrugged. "Tell them she spooked after Jangir's arrest. Thought there would be too much scrutiny and security." He paused and exhaled smoke from his nostrils. "Speaking of, you spooked too in the square. One of the snipers told me you tried to warn Ferma before he shot her."

Yassen stilled. He remembered the glint of the sniper's rifle, the sound of the pulse as it ripped past him. In that moment, he had forgotten who held the gun. All he had wanted was Ferma to move, to retreat, but he had been too late.

The Arohassin had been careful not to give too much detail. He had only known that there would be a small explosion, a *taste*, as Akaros had put it, of what was to come. *The heir will not be harmed,* he had said. *Just . . . frightened.*

Yassen had known about the snipers, known that he was leading Elena to danger, but he hadn't expected Ferma to die. He still remembered the look of horror and shock on Ferma's face as he held her. Her blood on his hands.

Regret, thick and thorny, wrapped around his throat. Yassen forced himself to meet Akaros's gaze, his voice carefully composed.

"You never told me you were going to kill her," he said. "I was just . . . selling it."

"Hmm," Akaros said. "And did you?"

Too well. Elena had stood beside him before the pyre, and though he had pretended not to notice her tears, he had silently wept with her. He still could feel her hand hovering next to his. *I'm sorry,* he had wanted to tell her.

"Yes," he said simply.

"And you're her head guard now, yes?"

Yassen nodded slowly. "Is that why you called me?"

"Yes," Akaros said. "Now that we've eliminated the Yumi, you're handling her escort to the temple. When she is crowned, we will strike. I want you to remain by her side and help her escape down this path." He withdrew a holopod. The blue light of the holo illuminated the space and threw long shadows across the former bakery's bare walls. A map of the Agnee Range floated before them with a red-marked path snaking down the mountainside. "Lead her to it. Make it seem safe. And then when the time comes, our boys will take care of the rest."

His words filled the empty space. They weighed down the shadows, the air, Yassen himself. He supposed he should feel relief. At least they did not ask him to carry out the assassination. He would not have to dirty his hands with Elena's blood. But her blood had already stained him. Her blood still soaked his ruined uniform, the one he could not bear to wash.

Akaros exhaled, and tendrils of smoke brushed Yassen's face. "Well?"

Yassen looked at him, a bitter taste filling his mouth. When he had made his plea to the Arohassin, bargained for his life after he had been burned, after he had been deemed expendable, they had given him one last task in exchange for his freedom—to destroy Ravence once and for all.

A part of him wished he had run, taken off after his wounds had been treated. He could have escaped to Moksh, the land of volcanoes and debris. He would be miserable there, but he would have been free. Free of Ferma's death, free of Elena, whose eyes haunted him in the dark, in his sleep.

But the Arohassin were no fools. They would have tracked him down before he reached the port. He would have been lying facedown in rubble, body dead and forgotten. And then he would have never met Elena, never faced her torment.

Yassen did not know what would have been better or worse.

Akaros's eyes were boring into him. His mentor waited silently, and in the silence, Yassen heard the unspoken threat. He glanced out the window, saw a shadow move. *Don't falter*, he told himself. *Not now.* But the fear in Elena's eyes, the way she had clutched his arm...He could not shake the feeling nor the guilt.

Shut it out, he thought. *Shut it into a room and never open it again.*

He had told Ferma the same when she had laid out her secrets to him. But what good had his advice gotten her?

"The princess knows how to hold fire," Yassen said. He forced himself to not break Akaros's gaze. "She found a scroll left by her mother, and now she can wield the flames."

Akaros hissed, the end of his yron flaring. The map and its red path glowered between them.

Yassen reached out and touched the holo. It dispersed into blue dust.

"*If* she's crowned..." he began.

"She must be!" Akaros snarled. A hovercar passed by, and its headlights bled through the slats, revealing his burned skin. He dropped his yron and stamped it out. As Yassen watched the ash scatter across the floor, he wondered what the next owner of this bakery would think of the litter. But then, it was no longer a bakery. It was just a building filled with dust and memories.

"We can only kill her if she's crowned. That's what will make this siege legitimate. We need to officially end the Ravani line. The Jantari king wants her head at his feet when he sits on the Fire Throne. Wielder or not, she must die," Akaros said. There was an urgency in his gaze, a conviction and, below it all, a deep, troubling fear.

"Jantari? Her head?" Yassen said, and this time, he could not stop the tremor in his voice. "I thought we were only meant to capture Elena and force her to host an election for the people."

"Plans changed," Akaros said. "Taran is thinking of the long game, and partnering with Farin during the war will help us clear everyone out for a new government."

"Why must she die then?" Yassen said, and he bit his tongue, knowing at once that he spoke too much.

Akaros shot him a look. "Why do you care?"

He shouldn't. Yassen knew he shouldn't and yet, and yet...

My sweet Knight.

Her words felt like a dagger, sharper than the slingsword she had once held to his neck.

"I don't, it's just..." He paused, thinking quickly. "Is it true? If she can wield fire, do you think she's the Prophet?"

Yassen was aware he sounded foolish, but a part of him did want to know. For most of his life, he had abhorred the Phoenix and Her vengeful fire. The Arohassin had taught him that the Ravani kingdom was built on a set of lies, of corpses and mindless mantras. There was no Phoenix. The

Prophet had only been a power-hungry priestess obsessed with infernos. Ravence was only a desert because warfare had stripped it of its once lush forest. Fire only brought madness, death.

But Elena was not like that. He had seen her among the gold caps, in the sandstorm, felt her grief by the fire. She did not kill mindlessly—she fought for her kingdom, for her people.

Akaros snorted. "No, she's not," he said flatly. He did not elaborate further.

"But if she can wield fire, she'll be harder to kill," Yassen said.

"Nothing we can't handle." Though Akaros did not say it, Yassen saw the man's eyes flit to his arm.

Yassen nodded. He took the holopod from Akaros and slipped it into his cloak. The badge of the palace guard glimmered on his chest; he had forgotten to take it off, a silly mistake.

"And, Yassen, give my greetings to Sam," Akaros said.

It wasn't until he had made his way back to the alley, until the door of the hovercar clicked softly beside him, that Yassen realized he did not know Samson's fate. He knew death awaited Leo and Elena. It was the only way for the revolution to begin. But Sam . . .

Yassen looked out the curved windows of the hovercar. The shobus were gone. Rain drummed against the glass. He glanced down and again saw his badge glinting. Elena and Samson dead in one stroke—the thought shattered him. It opened a large, black maw that threatened to suck him in, and Yassen did not dare to even think what lay beyond it.

He gripped the edge of the control panel. *Oh, Sam.* After all these suns, after just reuniting, they would have to part once more. The injustice of it filled Yassen with a sudden, hot rage. Pain jolted up his arm, but he ignored it.

Isn't Ravence enough? Isn't Leo enough? Why do the Arohassin have to claim Samson as well? Samson had given them their due, paid his penance, and fought his way to his freedom. He had been a beacon for Yassen, a hope for better days. His only friend in the whole world; his only family.

Yassen had allowed the Arohassin to take many lives, but he could not let them have Samson's. Samson must live.

And with Samson's name came Elena's, but he pushed the thought away. He couldn't think about her now. If he allowed himself to, he would never make it back up the hill.

The engine thrummed to life, and Yassen pulled out of the alleyway. The streets were still empty as he weaved through the city. The rain grew harsh, lashing at the glass panes; the world blurred into bleeding strokes of color. Only the palace remained clear as it stood atop its hill, watching him.

Yassen could hear the faint music of violins and the tinkle of laughter as he passed underneath the ballroom windows toward the servants' entrance. Two guards flanked the door in the rain. They stepped forward, and he threw back his hood.

"I thought you were inside," the tall guard said, his hand on the hilt of his slingsword. "The king doesn't want anyone seeing you."

"I just wanted some fresh air," Yassen replied.

"More hunting?" The other guard grinned, and the scar along his cheek twitched. "Did you bag any Arohassin?"

"They should've cleared out by now if they know what's good for them," the tall guard said. "No one attacks our queen without facing the sword."

Yassen nodded, his face blank. "If I may, gentlemen."

The tall guard nodded. "Rest well, Knight."

Yassen entered and pulled on his hood again. He skirted the main courtyard where guests strolled underneath the large canopies of the banyan trees. He wondered if Elena was still in the ballroom, dancing among the spinning skirts. He wondered how she hid her grief.

The music and laughter faded as he walked deeper into the palace. A few servants scurried past, heading for the ballroom, and they nodded at him. When he reached the split of the palace wings, he stopped. A figure stood in the garden below. He recognized the tumble of curls immediately.

"I thought you were still dancing," he called out, and Elena turned to look up at him.

Moonlight filtered through the canopy and curved down her bare shoulders, dusting the tops of her cheeks, the bridge of her nose. The golden necklace of the Phoenix shone against her brown skin. But her eyes, her eyes were as dark and tumultuous as a desert sky, and they were fixed on him.

Yassen breathed in sharply.

Fuck.

"I came to look for you, but you weren't in your room," she said.

"I went to get some air." He descended into the courtyard and tugged off his hood. He stopped a few paces away from her, the wide trunk of the banyan between them. "Discreetly, of course."

She did not smile. She stood in the moonlight, and it made her look ethereal, distant.

"I should have never forced you to take me to Jasmine," she whispered.

He heard the tremble in her voice, saw the sorrow in her dark eyes.

He was painfully reminded of the moment he'd seen his mother's charred body after they had cleared the fire. He had thrown up and heaved until there was nothing left within him, until he was as hollowed and empty as the blackened house.

"You can't live with regret," he said for the both of them.

Her earrings tinkled softly as she turned to him.

"How?" she asked, her voice hoarse.

Her eyes pulled him in, drowned him. She stepped closer, rounding the trunk.

"How did you go on when they died?"

He felt his heart hitch as she watched, waiting. He licked his lips, his mouth suddenly dry.

"Why did you come looking for me?" he finally managed. "Aren't you needed at the ball?"

"Ferma liked you," she said, and he flinched, closing his eyes. "You're one of the few who gained her respect."

He wanted to tell her that he had not earned it. That they were all fools for trusting him. His arm felt heavy. The banyan tree rustled in the rain, whispering, and he thought he could hear it tell of his deceit, his treachery.

"You should rest." He stepped back, moving into the shadows of the tree. "Your coronation is in just two days."

"I mean to pardon you as soon as I am queen," she said. She picked her way carefully over the sprawling roots and took his hand, rolling back his sleeve to reveal his blackened wrist, the burns. "And I'll make sure you'll never burn again."

"I'm fine," he interjected and tried to move away, to put the tree between them, but her grip was strong, and her eyes never left his.

"And then you'll be free," she continued as if he had not said a word. She was so close that he could feel her breath on his skin. So close that he could see the tremble of her lips. "But will you stay? Will you help me rebuild what they've destroyed?"

"I can't," he said, and the words dropped like stones. He tried to sound resolute. He had made his allegiance. He could not stop a raging desert wind.

He pulled away, tripping on the banyan roots. Cold drops of rain kissed his cheek.

"Trust me," he said. "You won't want me."

CHAPTER 31

ELENA

Here comes the queen, the young, frightening queen! Make way, make way, I say, for the queen has come! Long live the queen!
—from *The Odyssey of Goromount: A Play*

Elena examined the blackened remains of her room and garden. Dawn had not yet breached the horizon, and the air smelled of ash and promise.

Today, she would be crowned queen, but she could not muster the joy that she knew she should feel. There was only hollowness accompanied by a sense of despair.

She made her way through her courtyard, stepping carefully. The servants had cleared out most of the mess, but she spotted the ghosts of her rampage: a shattered stone from her fountain, the nub of an ironwood tree, shriveled lotus petals. The charred remains of a banyan raked the blooming sky. She reached up and split off a branch. Dry flakes of soot sprinkled from her hands. Elena sat on what had once been a bench, the broken branch in her lap. Nothing stirred. There was no chirp of a morning dove, nor even the faintest whisper of the wind. There was only her, and the skeletons of the things she had destroyed.

In her anger, she had not recognized the depths of her rampage, but now, in this silence, she understood. The aftermath of fire. The emptiness it created.

"Your Highness."

She turned to see Diya approaching, holding a small yellow square in her hand.

"I—I don't mean to interrupt. I'm drawing the bath right now, but I remembered I had this." She placed the parchment on the bench. "I took it when you, when you..." She smiled painfully. "Just come when you're ready. The tub should be full by then."

Elena stared at the perfect square. "Thank you, Diya," she said finally. "And I'm sorry for endangering your life. I did not mean to hurt you."

Gently, Diya touched her shoulder and squeezed. "We all do awful things in grief."

When she was alone, Elena picked up the square. She turned it over, but there were no markings on the other side. Slowly, Elena unfolded it, the paper crinkling as she flattened it against her thigh. At the bottom corner of the letter, she spotted her mother's initials. *A. M.* And beneath that, a faded drawing of a jasmine.

Elena,

If you have received this letter, then you must know how to wield fire. What a horrible, beautiful responsibility. I am sorry I am not there to guide you.

When you were five suns, you asked me why the desert rages—if there was a reason behind the storms. Do you remember what I told you? For the wind to sing, it must destroy the dunes.

When Alabore built this kingdom, he killed his eldest daughter, his first-born. He carved out her chest and buried her heart in the desert. This is how he built Ravence—with blood.

But he did not build Ravence with the help of the Phoenix. The legends say the twin moons helped him, but I have read of a deeper, darker power. I do not know its name, but the writings of Priestess Nomu say it is as old as the Phoenix. This power fed visions to Alabore, led him to the desert, and tormented him into subsequent madness. It imprisoned the Phoenix in a dark, stony hell, and now the Eternal Fire demands sacrifice for Alabore's sin. Your grandfather sacrificed his youngest brother. Your father refused, but I have chosen for him. He will die if I don't, and I would be a terrible ruler by myself. I am sorry for it, my love. We are stuck in an endless cycle, but I hope you will finally be the one to break it.

The Eternal Fire does not rage because it is angry; it rages because it grieves.

Ravence has been built on borrowed time. There will be a day when the Eternal Fire cannot be kept quiet. When the cycle breaks. The Phoenix shall awaken, and She will seek Her Prophet and other brethren. Remember, there are three types of fire.

And you are one of them.

I know it will be difficult to stand aside and let your kingdom be destroyed. Ravence demands loyalty. Blood, above all else. But I pray you will see the light beneath this land—the light that lives in you.

Honor your fire. It is different from the rest. Hone it, love it, and when the time comes, when the Phoenix rises, it will show you the path through the desert.

Forgive me,
Mama

She read the letter again and again, mouthing the words until they ran together like a song in her mind.

Sin.

Sacrifice.

Destruction.

My whole kingdom, a lie.

She crumpled the letter, but then smoothed it out again and folded it back into a neat square. Jasmine had said that Aahnah had found something terrible, and Elena thought it had been the sacrifice. But if this was true, and Ravence was not built by Alabore and the Phoenix like the legends told . . . Elena felt dizzy.

341

Was this why the Phoenix had never listened to her prayers? Was She not Ravence's true god?

Elena stared at the letter. She wanted to believe her mother, but there was a shaky slant to her mother's handwriting, a discordance beneath her words. Aahnah *had* lost touch with reality. Could this letter be no more than delusions?

She turned it over, searching for more clues, but there was nothing else. No further explanation, no peek into the past. Elena chewed her lip. Finally, she slipped the letter in her pocket and stood. She would show it to her father, after the coronation. He was already stressed with the attack and the preparations. Later, when they were alone, she would show him. Surely, he could make some sense of it.

Elena returned to the guest room as faint touches of dawn blushed the sky. Diya was waiting.

She slipped out of her robe, shivering as the cold morning air touched her flesh. She sat in the bathtub as Diya rubbed her with a paste made of haldi and sandalwood. She applied it using long banyan leaves that tickled Elena's skin, but the heir sat still, as stoic as a dune on a winter night. She watched as her handmaid turned her skin into gold, and then washed her with cardamom milk and rose water. Diya squeezed a pea-sized drop of almond oil into her palm and ran it through Elena's hair, buttering her curls until they shone. It was a ritual the reigning queen would perform on the queen-to-be. But Elena had no mother. She had no Ferma. Alone in the bathtub, her skin smelling like the desert, Elena only had herself.

After her bath, she dressed slowly, methodically, Diya helping her. Elena clipped on a large nath around her nose and ear. She donned a thick crimson-and-gold lehenga with a long circular skirt that dragged across the floor. She slipped on necklace after necklace until her neck was weighed down with the wealth of her kingdom. She lined her eyes with kohl like the warriors who defended her borders.

For the final touch, Diya wrapped a white silken belt threaded with pearls and gold around her waist. She stepped back and offered a tremulous smile.

Elena stared at her reflection.

She looked beautiful.

She looked terrifying.

The Burning Queen.

The door of her chambers opened, and Elena turned to see Samson, Yassen, and her other guards. Samson stepped inside.

"It is time, Your Highness," he said. He smiled to her, and though she returned the smile, her gaze crawled to Yassen.

She saw how he stared, eyes widening, mouth slightly slack. When he met her eyes, she smiled wider. He hesitated, returned it.

She cast one last glance at herself in the mirror. This would be the last time she would stand here as Elena. As *only* Elena. The girl who loved to dance and roam the desert, to bicker and argue with her Yumi guard. When she returned, she would be queen of Ravence.

Elena turned, her bangles chiming softly. She palmed the letter and slipped it beneath her silk belt. "I am ready."

Samson held out his hand, and she took it.

Samson, Yassen, and two guards carried an intricate velvet tapestry woven with gems of the desert. They held it up, each at a corner, and Elena stepped underneath it. Yassen remained behind her, and they began to walk.

The palace thrummed with excitement as servants placed the final touches: sprinkling fresh marigold petals in the hall, draping thick strands of jasmine and desert rose along the windows, scenting the air with incense sticks of sandalwood and lavender.

Guards dressed in white and gold lined the corridor; they bowed as she passed. As she entered the courtyard, servants showered petals upon her. They smiled and sang blessings, raising their hands to welcome the new dawn, but she sensed a quiet unease beneath the joviality.

Torches flickered along the path to the landing dock. Hovercams flashed as Elena stepped out, her long train dragging petals behind her. Her image would be all over Ravence, all over the world. She was the Burning Queen. The heir of a land of blood and prophecy. May they all bow to her fury.

Her father waited at the end of the dock. He looked regal in his gold-and-red achkan, with a handspun silk scarf draped sharply down his shoulders. Behind him, his Spear and his Astra were dressed in their ceremonial ivory robes; they bowed as she approached.

The king held out his hand, but all Elena could see was his crown and the red Featherstone glimmering in the morning light.

Today, he would lose his throne to her.

"She would be proud," Leo whispered, and Elena did not know whether he was referring to Ferma or her mother.

The guards and Samson wrapped the velvet tapestry around her shoulders.

"So we the blessed few," they said.

"So we the blessed few," she returned.

Samson bowed and kissed her hand. He was dressed in a gold silk sherwani that shone against his dark skin. Intricate strings of pearls adorned his neck, while a white embroidered scarf hung over his shoulder and looped across to his other arm. He looked like a Ravani, like a king. Beautiful and mighty, and yet . . . Elena found that she could not return the sincerity of his kiss. That her eyes did not search for his across a room. She gave him a small parting smile and squeezed his hand.

"You're an inferno, my darling," he whispered.

"See you soon," she said.

Leo led her into the hoverpod, and she turned back as the ramp slowly lifted. The servants and palace guards stood along the dock, waving. Samson winked at her. He would meet them at the temple, for the heir and ruling monarch must travel alone. Yassen gave a slight, imperceptible nod.

Ferma was not among them.

Elena looked to the desert beyond, felt the wind stir her robes. She blinked, nose burning.

I miss you, she told the desert.

The hoverpod rose into the blossoming sky and Palace Hill fell away. They flew west, and Elena looked over the dunes sprawling in the sun to the mountains ridging the kingdom. Her kingdom. The one she would swear to protect, even from the madness of her family.

Leo came up beside her. They stood silently for a moment, watching as the desert unrolled beneath them.

"The Eternal Fire will ask for a sacrifice," he said finally. His voice was quiet, pained. "And when you won't give one, it will try to harm you. I know this to be true, Elena."

"You're not going to jump, are you?" she asked, trying to keep her voice light. "If so, I'll make Samson and Yassen hold you back."

At this, he smiled. Partially.

"I think they're too distracted by *you* to pay me any mind," he said. She blushed, and her father took her hand, turning her to him.

"Jokes aside, Elena, I need you to understand," he said. "I've asked for extra guards and medics to be present at the temple. If you think—if you even feel the fire swell, I need you to promise me that you'll stop. That you'll run down that dais and leave." He squeezed her hands. "Please, promise me."

Worry lined his face, made him older. His eyes glimmered, and Elena felt a pang as she raised his hand and kissed his ring.

"I promise, Father," she said.

He nodded, his shoulders visibly sagging in relief. She wanted to ask him so much else. About Aahnah, the Prophet, the priests; wanted to tell him about Yassen, what she felt, now that they finally talked to each other openly. But the look on his face stopped her.

Leo smiled on her, looking—for once—lighter. She did not want to weigh him down.

After, she thought.

He brought his hand to his chest and clutched her mother's necklace. The jade glimmered in the light of the waking sun.

"Your mother once told me that the only thing that distinguishes a Ravani from others is our ability to sacrifice," he said softly. "Not to fire, but to our kingdom. This is what it truly means to lead. 'To give yourself to the kingdom that has already claimed you.'"

He slowly pulled off the necklace and held it between them. "I was your mother's keeper. Now, you are hers."

He clasped the necklace around her neck. Elena looked down to see her mother's bird, made of jade found only during a summer eclipse, the same as the earring her father wore, and felt both loss and foreboding. She met her father's eyes. They were the same steel grey, but they were softer now, more vulnerable.

"You were never her keeper," she said gently. "She was yours."

Elena cupped the bird to her chest. It felt warm underneath her touch. She thought of Aahnah and Jasmine, laughing together in the tea shop, sharing secrets. She thought of the women before her mother, the tireless generations of queens. She thought of Ferma, unflinching, a true warrior.

Leo looked down at her. A mixture of pain and pride passed over his face, and he opened his mouth to say something and then seemed to think better of it.

"Take care of it" was all he managed to say.

CHAPTER 32

LEO

And thus the Phoenix rose with eyes afire and a cry of vengeance upon Her lips.

—from *The Prophecy of the Phoenix*, transcribed into
written word by the first priests of the Fire Order

They docked on the stone ledge beneath the temple. A column of smoke writhed above the cliff like a long grey serpent. The smell of ash and incense hung heavily across the mountainside. There were no storm clouds, but the air felt charged.

Leo had already ordered a large swath of guards to sweep through the mountains around the temple, but after the attack in the capital, he made them repeat their sweeps. As he ascended the temple steps, he spotted their white uniforms dotting the mountainside, their pulse guns glinting.

Majnu and Arish greeted them at the top of the staircase with a low bow.

"Your Majesty," Arish said and then smiled at Elena. "Your Highness. May the sun and the moons shine upon you."

"We've swept the surrounding range at least three times," Majnu

347

informed. "We've found nothing. I have revolving patrols searching the mountain. If any Arohassin are hiding, we'll root them out."

"What about the tunnels?" Leo asked.

"Clear," Arish returned and looked at Majnu. "No Arohassin agents are hiding beneath the mountain," he said, and then, after a pause, "or Prophets."

"And the public?"

"No one has been admitted, and we stopped the hoverpods. So far, we haven't met much resistance. I think the attack made people realize the gravity of the threat," Majnu responded.

Leo nodded, glancing at Elena. Disappointment flickered in her eyes. In an ideal world, she would have been anointed before the public. In an ideal world, she wouldn't have had to worry about Arohassin terrorists or vengeful Prophets. He squeezed her hand, and she passed him a smile. Soft, forgiving.

It was enough.

"And Samson's men?" he inquired.

"So far, they're all clean," Majnu said and looked up as the other palace transports descended.

Leo watched the hoverpods dock, Samson and Yassen arriving with more guards. Samson walked ahead, his head high, his shoulders squared, while Yassen trailed behind with his head bowed. There was a heaviness in his step, and Leo noticed how his right arm hung by his side.

"What's wrong with him?" Leo asked, nodding at Yassen.

"He burned his arm." He turned at the sound of Elena's voice and saw that she, too, was observing the men. "The medics treated him after the attack, but it still pains him from time to time."

Leo looked from her to Yassen, noticed the way she gazed upon the assassin; it reminded him of the way Aahnah had once watched him. A dark worry bloomed in his stomach, but he reined it back. He would not admonish her now, not when the peace between them was still so new, so fragile.

"How bad is it?"

"It's treatable," Elena said. "The doctor gave him pills and ointment to apply."

Leo nodded, but as he gazed at Yassen, worry tickled the back of his throat.

He burned his arm. It still pains him from time to time.

With the attack and the coronation, his search for the Prophet had slowed. They had found no leads in the palace. Samson had burned, the servants so far were clean, but Majnu had not found the time to test Yassen, not with the chaos of the attack and the ball.

Leo hesitated. If Elena found out he wished to test Yassen, she might take offense. Their truce, already so delicate, would shatter. She would abhor him, cast him out, and he could not bear her hate. Not anymore.

But the Prophet was still out there. He was watching, waiting, and if it was Yassen, what better opportunity to kill the Ravani family than at the seat of the Phoenix's power?

"I'll take your word for it," he said, but when she turned away, he nodded at Majnu. His Spear nodded back.

When he finally climbed the steps, Samson greeted Elena again, kissing her cheek.

"Your Highness, Your Majesty."

Leo pressed his hand on Samson's head, blessing him. The young man looked like a king from every angle, with his broad shoulders and kohl-lined eyes. The Ravani would fawn over him.

"Come," Leo said, and he took Elena's hand.

He glanced back and saw Majnu block Yassen's path and whisper something in his ear. Yassen faltered. The Spear gripped his arm and led him away.

Samson followed his gaze. "Where are they taking him?" he whispered to Leo.

Leo said nothing as they crossed the landing to the gate, where Saayna stood waiting. She pressed her palms together, bowing deeply.

Leo and Elena returned the gesture. The high priestess held out a fistful of lotus petals, and Leo took them.

"So we the blessed few," she intoned.

"So we the blessed few," Leo and Elena returned together.

They followed the high priestess into the temple, the stone floor growing warmer underneath their feet. Though they walked together, Leo noted Elena was a step ahead. She was eager; never mind her pace, he could see it in her eyes. She saw her kingdom glimmering before her, and Leo recognized her hunger. After all, he had felt the same on his coronation day.

The familiar wall of heat hit Leo as he entered the Seat—but it also felt different this time. There was a new urgency to the blaze. It pushed against the walls, chasing shadows, and Leo was surprised to feel a bead of sweat roll down his forehead.

He glanced worriedly at Elena, and she must have recognized his look, for she paused, taking his hand.

"It's all right, Father," she said. She held up her other hand, curled her fingers inward. In the pit, a flame rose in calling, curling with her. "See. I can still control it."

For a rash moment, Leo wanted to lead her away. Never mind the people, the customs, the coronation, he wanted her to be safe. To be as far away from this cursed fire as possible. But Elena smiled on him, and he saw her hope, her excitement, and he could not find it in himself to deny her.

"Just remember your promise," he said, and she nodded.

The remaining seven priests rose from their seats around the pit.

"Come, blood of Alabore," they sang. "Come and seek blessings from the source of all life, the fire of the one true ruler. Come and share Her benediction with our people."

The priests came forward and, one by one, deposited the lotus petals in their hands. "So we the blessed few."

"So we the blessed few," Leo whispered.

It would be the last time he uttered these words as king.

As the guards took position along the walls, Leo could not help but feel a pang of regret. He had aged so quickly, and Elena had grown so fast. He glanced at his daughter, with her head held high and an intense look in her eyes. She was the spitting image of him, yet Leo was dismayed by it. He had hoped, in some way, for things to change. Perhaps he could have bequeathed her a better kingdom, one that was more forgiving and pliant. Perhaps he could have tried harder to rid their home of its dissenters. Perhaps he could have been kinder.

Leo closed his eyes and let the heat wash over him. He hoped it would cleanse him of his sins, but he knew that was wishful thinking. Leo opened his eyes and cast a shower of petals into the pit. He watched them curl and burn. The Eternal Fire hissed, and tendrils of flames touched his wrist. He stepped back as the priests began to chant, a low, hypnotic drone that reminded him of a rumbling desert wind. Out of the corner of his eye, he saw Majnu take up position by the eastern wall. Leo turned to him, and Majnu shook his head. On the other side of the room, Yassen Knight stood, clutching his right arm, a bruise darkening his lower lip.

Relief flooded him, followed by anxiety.

I will find him. Leo looked up at the golden Phoenix. *Wherever Your Prophet is, I will find him.*

Samson and Arish knelt with the priests as he, Elena, and Saayna walked up the steps to the dais. Leo suddenly remembered how the Eternal Fire had lashed out at him and burned his leg. The white-hot pain. His hand trembled, but Elena squeezed, offering him strength as the high priestess blew into a conch, the single, clear note reverberating through the room.

Together, they knelt as the fire snarled.

"Great One," Saayna sang above its crackles, "we come to serve You. To uphold peace in the holy land." She spread her hands out wide and flung spark powder into the pit below them. The inferno snapped, building in strength. Heat buffeted Leo, but he ground his knees into the stone floor and pressed his hands together. "We ask You to bless the new bearer of Your kingdom. To lead her down the Agneepath."

Leo threw his remaining lotus petals into the fire. It ate his offering with relish. He could hear the flames almost purr in joy. The Phoenix watched from above, wings frozen in forever glory, beak gleaming, eyes raging. Despite himself, Leo shivered.

"From the father, the heirloom of the desert."

Leo bowed as the high priestess lifted the crown from his head. The Featherstone pulsed as if in tune with the dancing flames.

"From the heir, the blood of her youth." And with a silver blade, she pierced Elena's finger. Dark beads of her blood dripped into the Eternal Fire.

"From the keeper of the flames, the bone of truth," the high priestess said and withdrew a tiny black bone from her sleeve, throwing it into the flames. The Eternal Fire growled, the heat growing stronger.

"With these offerings, we bring a new dawn to Your kingdom," the high priestess finished.

She lowered the crown onto Elena's brow. Leo scraped ash from the dais floor and cast it upon Elena. She did not cough nor shirk. She simply stared into the flames, her body steeled, her eyes fierce; she was his daughter, and her reign would be long and true. He was sure of it.

"Now, take what is yours, Daughter of Fire, and rise as Elena Aadya Ravence, the new Phoenix King." The high priestess beckoned, and Elena extended her hand toward the pit. The fire curled around her hand, but she did not tremble. She withdrew a single flame and rose.

"Rise, Queen Elena," the priests said. "Take on the Agneepath."

The priests threw ash upon the dais. Leo still knelt and looked to his daughter. The fire silhouetted her shoulders and the crown on her head. She needed to give the command for him to rise. But as Leo waited, Elena took the conch from the high priestess. In her other hand, she cupped the flame.

"I will walk the Agneepath," Elena said and blew into the horn.

The sound, steady and strong, filled the chamber. It vibrated through Leo, stirring him with the hope—pure, innocent hope—of a kingdom long and true, a kingdom in which every man could find peace. Yet the song also rattled his bones. It made him feel small and insignificant.

The Eternal Fire roared, and Leo looked up. The flames arched over him, and in them, he thought he saw the faces they had taken, the lives they had claimed. He saw Elena, blowing the horn—and then a loud blast ripped the air and threw him onto his stomach.

Leo gasped. Blood was pouring from his nose. Pain splintered up his neck. For a moment, he lay dazed as the walls shook. The rumbling grew louder, and he realized it was not rumbling at all, but the sound of steady explosions and pulse fire. His kingdom. His home.

Leo struggled to his feet, his mouth tasting of blood and ash, as the flames grew longer, larger. Saayna lay crumpled on the steps of the dais, but Elena stood, the horn still in her hand, the flame in the other. She turned to him, her eyes wide. Above them, the Eternal Fire laughed. Leo reached for her as Elena beat back the flames. She spun, and the flames bent away from them, howling.

But then the mountain shook and the ground tilted. She lost her balance.

"Elena!" he cried.

The inferno bucked, laughing.

And then he was falling, falling, the fire rushing to claim him.

CHAPTER 33

ELENA

When the Phoenix rises, the Holy Fire will lay claim to the sinners.
The desert will eat its transgressors. Only the true shall survive. Only
the blessed few shall be forgiven.

—from *The Prophecy of the Phoenix*, transcribed into
written word by the first priests of the Fire Order

No!" Elena screamed.

She felt the flames ripple; felt the sheer *force* of the Eternal Fire as it fought against her. She tried to push it back as she lunged for her father, but then the fire beat her back with such fury that she tumbled down the dais, landing on her back. Her crown skittered into the shadows.

"Father!"

She saw him fall into the pit, heard the flames sing, felt the power pulse through her body as the Eternal Fire swelled. In its cackle, she heard him howl.

"Father!"

She scrambled forward, crying out his name as she swung her arms, trying to peel back the flames, to find him.

No, no, no, she thought. Her arms shook with effort.

Father, no!

He had been there, beside her. Just now. Just mere seconds before. He could not be gone. He just couldn't.

Her rage swelled and Elena grabbed a flame, tearing it from the pit with such vehemence that the Eternal Fire stilled for a moment—as if shocked. But then it recovered with a vengeance, the flame leaping from her hand back into the pit. She watched the inferno rise. She saw their faces: her grandfather's youngest brother, her mother, her father. The sacrifices for Alabore's sin. She saw them open their mouths and wail as the Eternal Fire beat against the ceiling.

Deep rumbles shook the temple, and Elena scrambled to her knees. She could no longer hear Leo's agonized cries. The priests were shouting; one tried to open the entrance of the tunnels, but the fire surged, blocking his path. It lashed out and grabbed the priest by the arm and sucked him into its pit. Saayna swayed to her feet, blood trickling down from a gash in her ear. She clawed at Elena's head and tugged upon her collar, yelling at her to *get up, run, move, girl, move!*

But Elena could not look away from the Eternal Fire. It sang and danced. Curled and sighed. Her father was in there, trapped within the inferno, burned alive.

Burned to death.

Vomit pushed up her throat.

Saayna yanked her to her feet with one violent tug, shoving her forward toward the corridor. Stone and ash rained down on them, the air thick with smoke. The high priestess clutched her wrist, pulling her forward, and they stumbled and ran out into the smoke-filled sky, so dense and grey that Elena began coughing at once. Explosions erupted down the mountainside, and the ground heaved beneath her. Elena teetered.

Pulse fire sparked through the smoke as loud snaps pierced the air.

The trees! They were falling. Down the mountainside, she saw the great forest of her ancestors flatten as if a large hand had crushed it beneath its palm.

"The Eternal Fire, it knows," the high priestess gasped, and Elena looked to the sky. All she could see was ash.

The high priestess grabbed her chin, and Elena winced as Saayna's nails dug into her skin.

"The Prophet, he shall rise, but only in the next life," she said. Her voice was a mix of a wail and a cry of elation. "Together, he and the Phoenix will cleanse the land of our sins."

There came a great groan; flames surged out of the temple and cascaded down the mountain. Elena threw herself off the steps, but Saayna was not so lucky. The fire engulfed her as she screamed. She lurched to the side, flaring like a torch, and ran for the thicket of trees bordering the temple.

"Saayna!" Elena yelled. She whipped around. "Sam! Yassen! Majnu!"

The fire snapped and lunged for Elena, but she jumped, running for the staircase. She took the stairs two at a time as the temple moaned behind her. Her right foot missed a step, and she skidded, slamming right into Yassen. He yelped, and they both landed on their knees. Elena bit back a cry as pain stabbed her leg, and Yassen clutched his arm. In the dancing light of the flames, she thought she saw the marks there elongate and twist, but then she blinked, and the moment was gone.

"Run," she croaked.

Without a word, Yassen took her hand, but then the sound of a great crack whipped down the mountainside. Together, they turned. The temple trembled on the cliff above them, as if resisting the beast within, but then it sighed, finally relenting. One by one, the wings of the temple—Truth, Perseverance, Courage, Faith, Discipline, Duty, Honor, and Rebirth—snapped off the center dome, as if the gods were idly plucking petals from a flower.

They tumbled down the cliff, crashing into the forest below. A wave of rubble and dust rose where the temple once stood.

Without thinking, Elena pressed Yassen to the wall, using her body to protect his as the wave tore over them. She gasped, digging her face into his collar. Dust and plaster stuck to her skin, her hair, her clothes. Yassen gripped her tightly, but when the onslaught of stone and debris subsided, she noticed he was shaking. His right arm hung limply.

"Can you run?" she asked.

He nodded. His skin was pallid, his cheeks sunken. A bruise blooming beneath his lip. Yet when he took her hand again, she sensed strength in his grip.

"We need to head for the forest," he said, coughing. "We're exposed up here."

"The hoverpods—"

"They're gone," he said. "I think the Arohassin snuck through the tunnels and took them out."

"No," she whispered. All around her, she heard the laughter of the fire, and her people's cries for mercy. She heard screams, commands, and the dying wails of injured soldiers. She heard the deep groans of the forest and the rumble of the shaking mountain. She heard her kingdom crumbling.

"I have to stop it. I have to stop the fire," she said and looked down at her hands, but her fingers trembled. "I can wield it, redirect it away from the forest—"

"For once, you have to be a coward," he said and gripped her hand. "*Run.*"

They ran down the staircase that she had ascended countless times. They ran as men died around her. They ran as the fire devoured the last parts of the temple. She could feel its heat nipping at her heels. Elena ducked as a stray piece of a statue flew past her head. Her heavy robes dragged against the stairs, slowing her. She fumbled with the gold clasps, but her hands were shaking. She grunted in frustration and yanked. The clasps popped off, and she tossed the robes away. They plummeted down the cliffside like crippled wings.

Slowly, the landing pad beneath the staircase came into view.

Yassen was right. There were no hoverpods. Only the mangled bodies of men.

Tears sprang to her eyes as she spotted limbs twisted at unnatural angles. From far away, they looked like broken toys, snapped and bent by cruel gods. The fire roared around her, picking up speed, the flames tumbling toward the landing dock like eager children.

Elena sprinted, her heart pounding in her chest. She had to get there before the fire. She had to stop it. Twenty steps, fourteen, ten—

Something shot through the air and then clattered across the landing. Before Elena could discern it, Yassen screamed, "*Grenade!*" but it was too late.

The explosion rent the air, and Elena felt the grenade's heat sear her face as she tried to stop. She fell forward, rolling across the landing. Dirt and rock hit her face and filled her mouth. She flung out her arms, trying to hold on to something, but there was nothing, only air.

Elena tumbled down the mountainside, bramble cutting through her clothes. The heavens and the land merged into one incohesive blur. The mountain was melting. She was melting. She gasped and tried to grab a root of a banyan when she skipped forward and slammed hard onto a ledge.

Momentum nearly carried her over the lip, but she flung her arm out and found a jutting stone. Straining, she pulled herself up and saw the heavens falling.

Torrents of fire washed down the mountainside like great red waterfalls of wrath. Below, clouds from the initial explosions dotted the forest. Pulse shots tore through the trees. *The Arohassin.* Anger and despair filled her as she lay stranded on her meager ledge. She looked up to see the fountain of the Phoenix jutting over the cliff face. And clinging to it, she saw a small figure. Even from this distance, Elena recognized the broad shoulders.

"Sam!" she screamed.

His head whipped at the sound, and as he turned, the flames reached the steps and lunged for him.

"No!" she cried. But she had no time to grieve, for the fire had finally found her. It slithered down the mountain, its hiss filling her ears. It knew her. It knew her fears, her fate, and in its blaze, Elena saw their faces again.

Jump—she had to jump.

Elena flung herself off the ledge. For a moment, she was suspended in the air, the mountain beneath her, smoke above, and then she plunged down, wind rushing past her ears, ash filling her lungs, the forest dark and waiting.

CHAPTER 34

YASSEN

Do not run, wanderer. Arrive.
　　　　　—from *The Odyssey of Goromount: A Play*

The fire was everywhere.

It singed his arm, filled his lungs, blinded him. Yassen wheezed, clawing his way back to his feet. The grenade had knocked him down, and he spat out blood. It sizzled even before it hit the ground.

Behind him, the inferno swelled. It tumbled down the staircase, gaining speed. Yassen scrambled down the remaining stairs, hugging his arm to his body as dots swam in front of his eyes.

Air, he needed air.

"Elena!" he croaked. But the dead around him gave no answer.

He stumbled, panic filling his chest, thick and sharp like barbed wire. Yassen looked down and saw a burst of white smoke from an explosive. Pulse fire lit up the forest. He needed to head west like Akaros had shown him, to the path where the Arohassin assassins lay hidden, but the fire roared toward him, obscuring the way. Yassen ran forward, but there was nothing beyond the landing—nothing but the burning forest. He skidded, nearly falling off the edge when he saw a flash of dark curls.

"Elena!"

But she did not hear him over the din of the inferno.

And then—she leapt off the ledge. Hair flying, skirts flaring around her, she plunged into the trees below.

He did not even hesitate.

Yassen jumped after her.

The wind roared in his ears. The tops of the trees glinted like spears as he hurtled toward them. Yassen braced himself, knees bent, head curled, but the forest met his body too fast. He crashed through the canopy, leaves and branches clawing at his face and skin. Pain lanced up his arm. He tried to stop himself from falling farther, tried to kick out his legs and grab a tree limb with his good arm, but the mountain heaved from another blast and the world swayed as he smacked into the ground.

Yassen gasped. He lay staring at the burning sky in shock. Blood filled his mouth. But adrenaline, training, and the pain that splintered up his arm wrenched him awake and pushed him, swaying, to his feet, retching.

He could not die here on this mountain. Not when he was so close.

He stumbled through the dark forest. Here, the air was cooler, but the smoke lay on top of the canopy like a thick cloud, slowly suffocating everything within. Yassen felt for his old pistol and found it still wedged in the band around his thigh. He pulled it out and clicked back the safety.

"Elena!" he called.

The sound of distant pulse fire answered him. He crept through the underbrush, searching every shadow, every crevice.

"Elena!"

He followed a trail of broken branches and wilted leaves as the pulse fire grew closer. He coughed, his chest burning. A branch snapped to his right, and Yassen whirled, finger on the trigger; then he spotted the soiled edge of a skirt.

Elena lay crumpled within the roots of a massive banyan. It was the only banyan in a thicket of pine, and it was almost as if it was protecting her, the long vines curling around her in an embrace. Blood trickled from her nose, staining the Phoenix necklace wrapped around her throat.

Yassen fell to his knees. He pushed away the necklace as he felt for her pulse and gasped in relief to feel a thrum of life.

"Ferma?" She lifted her head, bleary brown eyes looking up at him.

"I don't have the hair," Yassen said, regret lacing his voice. "Can you stand?"

She licked her cracked lips, her tongue curling at the taste of blood, but she nodded slowly. He helped her to her feet.

"Did you break anything?"

"No, I don't think so," she whispered and looked at him. "You?"

Pain stabbed through his arm, but he shook his head. "There's an escape route Majnu mapped in case of an attack. We need to get there."

She nodded, blinking groggily. Yassen led the way, pistol out. The ground was high and uneven with thick leaves that slapped at them. He tried his best to pick his way through the bramble, but another explosion shook the mountain. He teetered, and then Elena yelped and knocked into him, and they both tumbled down a slope.

This time, the fall was shorter, meaner. Jagged rocks cut across his skin, scraping his knees and elbows. Yassen moaned as blinding pain shot through his arm and shoulder. He nearly fainted.

"Get up," Elena rasped beside him. "We have to get up."

He lifted his head. Her dark brown eyes met his, and he was shocked to see how steady they were, how clear.

She slowly pushed to her knees. He noticed fresh blood staining her shoulder, but she did not seem to be aware of her wound. This time, she helped him stand. She picked up his pistol and handed it to him. When his fingers brushed hers, she touched the black mark on his palm.

"Did you know that the Arohassin would attack today?" she asked, her eyes boring into him.

Yes.

He was to lead her to her death, to deliver her head to the Jantari king. He would bring destruction upon the people who had forsaken him.

But smoke stung his throat, his eyes. In the distance, he could hear screams, the faint patter of gunfire; he could smell the metallic stench of charred flesh, and it gripped him, wrenching his chest. He had caused this. Mother's Gold, he had done this.

Yassen stumbled back under the weight of Elena's gaze. She stepped forward, her voice shaking.

"Did you know?"

A desert yuani shrieked in the canopy, and Yassen looked past her to see a man moving through the brush behind them.

It happened at once.

Yassen saw the pulse gun, the metal snake insignia of the Arohassin on the man's chest. He saw Elena move forward, her lips forming a question, a demand, an answer.

The man raised his gun.

And Yassen saw what would happen: the pulse ripping through Elena's chest, her blood splattering on his body. Her falling, like Ferma before. And the thought of her lying dead, her blood seeping out as she stared at him in horror, stabbed him with an agony worse than any other.

He could not lose Elena.

Yassen jumped forward, tackling her into a neighboring thicket as the pulse ripped through the air. He pushed her against a tree as she gasped. The assassin shot again, and he shielded her as the air exploded with pulse fire.

"Yassen," she began, but then the pulse fire paused.

He's out, he thought, and sprang to his feet just as the assassin cleared the thicket. He reached for his dagger, but Yassen was faster. He shot, once, hitting the man square in the chest.

The man fell back with a cry, his dagger falling into a thicket of bramble. The yuani took to the air in a rush of squawks and golden wings. Slowly, Elena got up and walked to their fallen assailant. She picked up his weapon as Yassen stared at the blood blossoming across the man's chest. At the reddening snake of the Arohassin.

They would recognize the bullets of his gun. They would know of his betrayal. He would never have his freedom.

But he had realized this some time ago. Hadn't he?

"The Arohassin," he said, "they're all over this place. They'll pick us off."

"You knew," she said, and he saw the betrayal in her eyes, the deep, shattering hurt. She stepped back, raising the pulse gun.

He did not move. He did not even lift his pistol in return.

"Do it," he whispered. "Be done with me."

She recharged the chamber and flicked on the pulse gun, its barrel warming to life with a blue light. As he stared her down, Yassen felt a deep weariness. This was it. This felt appropriate. He had betrayed her and deserved to die at her hand.

He closed his eyes, but instead of sweet darkness, he felt the snake in his stomach rattle and hiss. If he died now, Elena would not survive. The Arohassin would find her and kill her. She would never master her fire. She would never bring unity to Ravence. She would never pin him down in the field, so close that he could feel her breath on his skin. He would never be able to let her win again.

Yassen opened his eyes and met her gaze.

"If you kill me now, you won't make it off this mountain," he said softly. "I am your only ally left. And the Arohassin are here. They will hunt you down. I know where they are, and if we move fast, there's a chance we can get out alive."

He watched her calculate the danger, her finger curling around the trigger, her face a war of emotions. The desire to both believe him and to shoot him flashed in her eyes. She tried to mask her indecision, but he knew every inch and curve of her face, every tremble of her lip. Hers was a face he had been forced to study but he had grown to know as if it were his own. He knew of the way her chin jutted when she spoke defiantly; the way her nose scrunched when she drank whiskey; the way her eyes crinkled when she laughed. If there was one thing Yassen could claim, it was this: that even in the darkness of death, he would know her.

The pulse gun whined, and the blue light slowly faded. A look of hollow acceptance settled on her face.

"You traitor," she whispered.

"This way," he said.

He headed east. He knew she would follow.

Ash coated the forest. Panicked squawks filled the canopy as more birds took flight. He heard the crunch of leaves and felt her at his side.

"This way leads to the desert," she said.

"Yes," he said. He inhaled sharply as his arm throbbed.

Elena clenched the handle of the pulse gun, her knuckles white. Without another word, she strode past him. Thick brush blocked their path, but she stomped through it, a grim sureness in her step. She knew the desert; she knew where they were headed. Amid all this chaos, all this madness, the dunes were a beacon.

They trekked on, keeping to the shadows. The pulse fire had given way to eerie silence, and though Yassen knew it was because most of the assassins were on the western path, he still held his pistol at the ready. Distantly, he heard the snaps and pops of burning trees. His chest itched, and he fought down a cough when suddenly there came a rustle in the canopy. He held out his hand to stop Elena, and they both looked up to see a black figure flit between the branches. Before the assassin could shoot, Yassen raised his pistol. His bullet ripped through the leaves and hit the man in the back of the head. His body plummeted to the ground.

Out of the corner of his right eye, Yassen spotted another assassin, but Elena was quicker. Her pulse sliced through the man, and he fell in a spray of blood.

Then the air exploded with pulse fire, and Yassen shoved Elena behind a tree, his ears ringing. Elena scrambled back as a shot hit the tree, leaving a deep wedge in the wood.

"There are too many!" he shouted.

She cocked her gun, but even she seemed to recognize their situation. Slowly, she tucked the pulse gun into her skirts, placed her hands on the ground, and closed her eyes.

"What are you doing?" he asked as the forest groaned.

He heard a low rustle, a low, slithering sound that traveled up his spine. Though he could not see it, Yassen felt it in his bones. Its prickling heat. Its deep hunger. The fire came at once, rushing from behind them in a red wave of destruction. It tore through the forest, snapping leaves and stones, but skirted their tree.

Elena stood. The ground rumbled again, but she did not lose her footing. She darted forward with her arm outstretched, and the flames followed. He yelled at her to stop, but his voice caught in his throat. Heat pressed around him. Elena raised her hands above her head and then slashed down, the inferno ripping through the trees like a stampede. The assassins screamed, their voices piercing the air.

"Come on!" She sliced her hand down again, and the flames bowed to create a path. "Let's go!"

He lurched to his feet as the fire tumbled forward, eager and unchained. Elena ran in front, guiding the blaze. The smell of burning men sickened him, but Yassen forced himself to shut it out as he sprinted after her.

They finally came into a clearing, and Elena doubled over, hands on her knees. Her shoulders shook. The flames coiled, burning along the edges of the clearing to create a protective perimeter.

Yassen panted, his chest tight. He could see the rolling dunes in the distance, free of fire. Elena shuddered. He took off his belt sash and offered it to her.

"Here. Wrap it around your mouth."

Her fingers brushed his soot-covered palm. She swayed, the sash limp in her hand, and he held out his arm to steady her.

"I—I burned them," she said, her voice hollow. But there was a look in her eyes, the same look Leo and Samson had worn at the Ashanta ceremony—reverent, with the unconscious stir of desire. It was a look of the powerful, and it made him shiver to think what else she could do with fire.

"Yassen," she said, "why are you still here?"

"Because I have nowhere else to go," he said.

Her face twisted, and her voice broke. "Neither do I."

They slipped farther into the forest, leaving the past behind. The sky was a deep, boiling red, as if the sun had burst. The inferno crept with them, shielding them from harm and delivering them from the crumbling mountain to the quiet desert. Sand began to line their boots. The dunes awaited, stoic and still as if nothing had changed.

When they reached the desert edge, Yassen raised his eyes to the smoke-filled heavens.

The litany came unprompted to his lips.

"Ash begets ash. Heavens burn to reveal the truth. May the sinners be forgiven, and the pretenders see their doom."

It was a chant recited at the end of the Fire Festival, but here there was no big parade, no city bursting with color. Here, there was only the dry, barren land.

"And thus justice shall bloom," she whispered.

THE DAWN OF THE
KINGDOM OF RAVENCE

–as told in the diaries of Priestess Nomu

*A*labore Ravence was a small man. He barely reached the shoulder of a horse, but he walked as if he knew how to ride one. He had a weather-beaten face and pockmarks down his cheeks, but his eyes were dark and sharp, older than they seemed, as if he knew all along that his meager hut and rusty sword were beneath his destined social station.

He had a conviction about him, so deep and true that it gathered newcomers and travelers like moths to a flame. In that sleepy, unknown village, Alabore Ravence gathered a following of men and women who heard his impassioned sermons of a better life, of a greater future. They all sighed in agreement. Among them were his family: his wife, taller than him, and two daughters.

Alabore Ravence's two daughters, Jodhaa and Sandhana, named under the traditions of their maternal family, bore the effortless, elegant grace of their mother and the hard, ruthless stance of their father. They were quick-witted and sharp of tongue. They could dance circles around a trained swordsman while they followed the beat of dhols. They could shoot arrows with their eyes closed and open them to find a poor lark spasming on the ground. They were their father's fiercest warriors.

One night, Alabore Ravence had a vision that told him his time had come. It showed him an unforgiving land and an ancient flame; the blood of men soaking into the sand while the sky was afire; and him, standing within it all.

He knew then of his destiny.

He took his daughters and they traveled at night from their sleepy, unknown village deep within the Parvata Mountains, though that name has been lost in history now. They rode on the backs of garuds, giant birds with golden beaks and feathers

365

of steel (sadly, the last one was killed in the First Desert War when Jodhaa's great-granddaughter was shot down by an enemy cannon). They rode for fifty nights until they reached the edge of the monstrous desert. It had once been a forest, but fire and belief had burned it to the arid landscape before them. Even in the cold light of the twin moons, they could see that the immovable dunes were giant, stoic mountains.

Alabore Ravence stood before them, his dark eyes taking in all the curves and ridges and valleys of the silent space. After a long moment, he turned back to his daughters, who knew immediately that something about the endless terrain of sand had changed him.

"We will build our kingdom here," he said. "We will work with the moons and slowly gain friendship from the sun."

"But, Father," Sandhana asked, "how can you be sure?"

"Because I will get the Eternal Fire," he said, and they realized that it was not the desert that captivated him but the silence beyond. In the darkness below the horizon, they saw the ghostly shape of the mountains. Jodhaa whispered to her sister that she saw a light—a tiny glimmer, fainter than the stars, but a light nonetheless in that mass of darkness.

"You can't capture the inferno," Jodhaa said, but Alabore Ravence gave a cold, hard smile, unlike any she had seen him wear before.

"I know of a way," he said.

And so it began. Alabore Ravence's ardent followers trekked out to that unforgiving sea of sand, buoyed by his speeches of prophecy and destiny. He preached until his throat was sore and his face red, but his voice never left him. They worked in the cloak of the night, in the steady gaze of the twin moons that Alabore Ravence had already befriended in his dreams. That portion of the year, the nights were long and cool. As kings and queens fought against sandstorms and heatstroke to claim the land as their own, Alabore Ravence and his followers worked deep in the desert, untouched. Even his daughters could not believe their good luck.

Alabore himself knew this was the easy part, that the moons would protect him. The real challenge would come when the city he built could no longer be ignored, and the sun would take notice. The mountains beyond would take notice.

When that day finally came, Alabore Ravence took his two daughters into the heart of the desert. Like before, they traveled at night. And as dawn glimmered on the horizon, they stopped.

"Are we to build sand hovels here?" Sandhana asked. The air was already beginning to warm. A solitary bead of sweat rolled down her father's forehead.

"Close your eyes," he told them.

His daughters obeyed. He watched as the sun drew their shadows on the ground. He knew what he had to do. The vision had shown him how to acquire this desolate land and its flame. But for the first time in his life, Alabore Ravence hesitated. The sun glared. As quietly as he could, Alabore Ravence drew his sword. He closed his eyes and saw his kingdom, and brought his sword down.

Jodhaa shrieked as the limp body of her sister fell to the ground, her blood staining the sand. Jodhaa stared in horror as her father plunged his sword straight through her sister's chest and withdrew her heart. Alabore Ravence knelt and, with his own bare hands, buried his daughter's heart, and the sword that viciously claimed it.

"This is the heart of the desert."

And as he spoke, the light within the dark mountains that Jodhaa had seen grew brighter. Stronger. Higher. A plume of smoke steadily rose from the mountain, and it was then that Alabore Ravence and his daughter knew the deed was done.

The Phoenix came to them in a shower of light that seemed as if the sun had dropped to the earth. Flames rippled across the desert, but it skirted around them, forming a circle. Jodhaa cried, hiding her face, but Alabore Ravence did not balk. He spread out his hands, stained dark with the blood of his daughter.

"This is the heart I give to you."

The Phoenix flapped Her wings, Her voice rising from the dunes, vibrating through his bones until he was full of song.

"So you shall have mine," She sang.

The desert rumbled. The dunes undulated, and the sky burned and filled with smoke. The cries of the warring kings and queens echoed as the Eternal Fire within the mountains roared and burnished the heavens. Amid it all, Alabore Ravence stood tall.

"This will be the Ravani kingdom," he said.

And so it was.

Within months, the kingdom arose. Some fanatics say the desert itself helped, but scholars believe border sandstorms weakened opposition, leaving Alabore Ravence and his followers to build in peace.

Ravence was built three hundred suns ago. Alabore Ravence lived a long, successful life, forging a flourishing kingdom in the middle of a desert. Under his reign, wars ended. The sands finally saw peace.

~~He ordered the image of the Phoenix to be etched onto the Ravani flag, for She had sent him his vision.~~ After his death, he was succeeded by his only daughter, who

wore an eternally haggard expression. But Jodhaa too reigned with a steady, forceful hand. For on that fateful day when her sister died, Alabore Ravence had turned to his daughter and allayed her grief.

"The heavens will forgive us. Every one of us deserves to be forgiven."

Note: The page after this has been torn out, Jasmine. There is hesitancy in Priestess Nomu's prose. Is it because she came to know the truth? That the Kingdom of Ravence was built not on the power of the Phoenix, but through a darker god? I shall resume my studies after searching the libraries at the temple. For now, Elena weeps for mangoes. I must attend to her. —A. M.

CHAPTER 35

ELENA

The night when Alabore Ravence built his kingdom, it is said that men feasted on starlight. For it was Alabore Ravence who brought the heavens closer to Sayon, who brought the power and mystique of the Phoenix into a real, solid hearth. The desert may be unforgiving, but it was spun from stardust, and to stardust it will go.

—from The Legends and Myths of Sayon

They had traveled the desert for two days, and the smoke had not let up. It wrapped around the dunes like a sheet over a corpse.

They trekked north, where there were no cities and no people. The northern Ravani Desert was dry and barren, full of shadowed canyons and brittle plants. Elena watched the dark horizon for the telltale whirl of sand, but no storms came. It was as if the wind held its breath.

Her eyes were heavy. Her palms still smarted, pulsing with heat, but she was too exhausted to summon fire. Her gun had run dry, and she had tossed it into the dunes, along with her heavy jewelry. She kept only her mother's necklace, tucked beneath her blouse. With a pang, she thought of her mother's earrings, lost somewhere in the burning forest behind them.

Flames flickered in the distant mountains. Her kingdom was under attack, yet here she was, stranded.

She had waited for the army. She had waited for Ravani hoverpods or scouts on cruisers to scour the desert for her, but no one came. Not the generals, not the Black Scales, not even the palace guards. It could only mean one of two things: They didn't think she had survived or Ravence had already fallen.

She slipped down a dune, sand spilling before her. *Swish, sip, swish, swoon.* Elena tried to move lightly, fluidly, but she was tired. She turned to see Yassen trailing behind her. He moved slowly, ploddingly, leaning to the right as if his arm was weighing him down.

Swish, sip, swish, swoon.

Blood caked her shoulder where her stitches had ruptured.

Swish, sip, swish, swoon.

The smoke coiled tighter, slowly squeezing her chest.

Swish, sip, swish, swoon.

She wondered what had become of her palace. Had the Arohassin burned the throne? Or did they sit upon it now, laughing like jackals? Did they notice the flowers hovering along the ceiling? Would they tend to them? She had wanted to get rid of the marigolds when she became queen, but her father had always loved them. The memory of him sitting on the throne, the crown on his head, her mother's necklace around his neck, opened a well of grief within Elena. She tried to block it, but that was as useless as trying to stop a summer monsoon.

Leo was dead. Ferma was dead. Samson was probably dead, along with Majnu and Arish and Diya. Her entire world, shattered over the course of a single day.

And what of her god? The one she had sworn to serve, the one who had promised to protect her? Elena looked to the dark sky. *Where are You now?*

She touched her waistband, felt the outlines of her mother's letter in the pocket beneath the lining. Aahnah had said the Phoenix had been fooled. That Alabore derived his power from a darker god. Is that why the Phoenix abandoned her now?

Anger, confusion, and pain threatened to rip her throat. But the dagger of sorrow felt even more acute—so sharp that it cleaved through all other emotions and spilled them into the sand until an aching hollowness filled her chest.

Her family was dead. Her kingdom was burning.

She was the last Ravence.

"Where can we find water?" Yassen croaked behind her.

His voice pulled her from her spiral. She paused on a stone slab overlooking a valley. Yassen slumped against a boulder, wincing.

Elena ran her tongue over her cracked lips. "Maybe we can find a skorrir."

"We don't have a knife to cut off its branches."

"We can use a stone." She fell to her knees, searching the uneven ground. Her knee knocked into something sharp, and she hissed. Gingerly, she drew back and found a stone with a pointed edge, no bigger than her palm. She rose and held it out to Yassen.

Pain flickered across his face as he turned to her. "That's too small."

She chucked it, and they watched the rock skip away. Elena skirted around the sandstone pillars that lined the valley edge, her torn skirts trailing behind her, when a low rumble echoed through the ground. It gradually grew into a buzz that reverberated off the boulders.

Elena hobbled back to Yassen as tiny lights pinpricked the night across the valley.

The scouts!

She began to raise her hand when he grabbed her.

"Wha—"

He shoved her behind a pillar. When she tried to turn back, he pushed her forward.

"Would you quit push—"

But Yassen held his finger to her lips.

"We're exposed here," he whispered.

He motioned for her to follow, and they weaved through the pillars and scrambled up a boulder, watching as the lights in the distance grew bigger. Shapes moved within the valley, but Elena could not make them out. She turned to Yassen and saw the color drain from his face.

"What is it?"

He did not answer. He did not need to, for she heard it then—the whine of a cruiser.

A soldier crested the stone slab where they had stood a few minutes ago. The cruiser's metal hull shone in the night with an uncanny glow, and she spotted a winged ox stamped on its side. The soldier turned, studying the shadows. A long, jagged blade with two metal tongues hung down his side.

Elena breathed in sharply. Only the Jantari carried zeemirs.

Yassen gripped her hand and tugged. They sidled down the boulder as the soldier drew closer. For a split second, Elena thought he would jump off his cruiser and search the pillars, but then he turned and sped off to the south. To Rani.

Her hand tightened around Yassen's.

"The city," she whispered.

They crawled back up the boulder, and Elena finally understood what had been there all along—the Jantari army. After the scout, more cruisers zipped out of the valley, heading toward the capital. The cavalry came next: men dressed in navy, their zeemirs glinting in the darkness. Soldiers on metalboards flanked the formation, their faces as rigid as stone. Tanks brought up the rear. She watched as they crushed the scraggly brush that grew within the valley.

As they passed, the buzz grew louder, closer. Elena stilled as two large metal hovertanks came into view. Thick and blocky, they obstructed her view of the desert beyond. Three soldiers stood in the armored cockpit of each hull. The blue light of holos outlined their gaunt features while thick metal cables latched on either side of their temples. They moved in unison, as if they were one body.

When they were finally gone, Elena let out a shaky breath.

The Jantari were marching through her desert. But they weren't just regular soldiers. Farin had moved past mutilating himself to turning his men into machines. *Mother's Gold, how will we beat them?* Elena slipped down the boulder, all strength leaving her body.

"We should move," Yassen said, but when he walked forward, she did not follow.

"Did you know?" Her voice was a whisper.

He stopped, his back to her.

"You knew about the Arohassin, but did you know about the Jantari? That they were coming like this?"

He turned around, and the regret in his eyes broke something inside of her.

She slapped him hard. His neck whipped to the side, an angry red mark blooming on his cheek. She beat him with her fists, kicking, tearing.

"How. Could. You!" She rained punch after punch, landing in the soft spots that she knew would hurt him: his belly, his cheeks, his chest. She should have killed him on the mountain. She should have shot him that night in the desert. She should have burned him the moment he stepped into the throne room.

He had taken her hand as he followed her through the Phoenix Dance. Held her gaze as she slowly unlooped her dupatta from his wrist. Stood by her side when they had burned Ferma together. Told her that he saw *her*. But when Saayna rested the crown on her head, and the fire took her father, he had watched it all, knowing what would come next.

When her fist slammed into his right arm, Yassen's eyes widened, but he did not cry out. He took it wordlessly. It felt like hitting a dummy in the training arena. And at the look in his eyes, those damned, beautiful eyes—pain, grief—she slowly felt her fury simmer and die. Her shoulders slumped, and her fists fell limp against his chest.

"How could you?" she gasped, sagging against him.

"I'm sorry," he whispered. Blood spilled down from his broken lip. His good hand curled over hers. "I'm sorry. I wish I hadn't."

She shook her head. She felt suddenly tired and alone and useless, all at once.

"I couldn't let you die on that mountain," Yassen said. "I couldn't deliver your head to the Jantari king. I'm sorry. I'm sorry."

And hearing him beg, hearing him plead to her with his hand wrapped around hers, holding her as if without her, he could become adrift, something broke within Elena.

Because she knew that without him, she would be lost too.

She slipped her hand out of his, heat pulsing from her palm.

"You're killing me, Yassen," she said softly, "and at the same time, you're the one keeping me from death." Her eyes met his. "What am I supposed to do?"

"Elena...I..." He paused, looking down at his hands, the blackened and the pale, and then finally met her gaze. "You survive." He took her hand again, almost unthinkingly. "I know a place where you can hide. It's a small cabin, a safe house in the Sona Range. They'll never suspect us hiding in Jantar. You can rest there. Heal."

"How can I save my kingdom from Jantar if I'm hiding in some shack?"

"Don't you see?" he said, and she heard his voice crack. "*You* are what's left of this kingdom. If you die, so does Ravence. It will not win without you. And you can't go on hiding in the desert."

He was right. There was no capital to return to. The Ravani army was scattered. Samson's men were likely in disarray. Teranghar, Magar, and Iktara were too far. Rasbakan, the closest port, was probably sacked.

Even if she tried to reach the Black Scales or the generals, the Jantari or the Arohassin would find her first. They would parade her through the streets, and then they would melt metal onto her head. She would die like her ancestors in the Five Desert Wars.

Elena looked down at her feet, at the sand underneath her toes. Without Leo, she was fatherless. And without her desert, she was motherless.

She was just another orphan wandering through the dunes.

"There's something else." He reached into his jacket, pulled out the holopod from within his inner pocket. It was dented and scuffed, but when he scanned his thumb, it opened. A map of tunnels sprawling under the Sona Range hovered between them. "Samson gave me this map before I left. He has a training base in the middle of the range. There are still some Black Scales left there, I think. We can't get to the base directly, but if we go to the cabin, there's a possibility we can use the tunnels from there to find them."

"I thought Samson pulled all of his troops from Jantar," she said.

"Do you really believe that?" he asked, and she looked away.

"I don't know who to believe anymore."

"You can believe me."

She laughed. "That's rich."

"Now you know everything," he said, spreading his hands. "I have no more secrets left to keep. I took the Desert Oath, and you may think that I've broken it, but I haven't. You're the kingdom now. I'm still willing to give my blood for you. Here." He pressed his pistol into her palm and took a step back. "If you don't trust me, then shoot me. This might be your last chance."

She stared at the pistol. It was heavier than a pulse gun, the trigger more curved. Slowly, Elena wrapped her hands around the grip.

He had betrayed her, and the raw truth burned her throat. *He can betray me again.* A part of her wanted to shoot him, to feel vindicated, relieved, and leave his body to rot for the vultures. But as Elena met his eyes, she was struck by that image: Yassen staring up at the sky, cold and dead. Her, wandering the dunes alone, without a kingdom or a hearth waiting for her.

Her heart twisted at the thought.

Yassen was the only one left standing by her side. He could have left her to perish on the mountain. He could have abandoned her.

The Phoenix spoke of forgiveness as an act of redemption. A way to free oneself of sins.

But now Elena knew forgiveness was not redemption, it was selfishness. Because try as she might, Elena could not tear herself away from his gaze. *Damn him.*

She needed Yassen Knight as much as he needed her.

Elena held up the gun, the barrel facing the earth. "I don't need your gun. I need your word. The desert words. Prove it. Swear it."

Yassen considered this, his eyes cutting through her.

Then he sank to his knees. A low wind finally stirred the dunes as he pressed his palms to her feet, his voice steady and clear as the desert whispered with him.

"The queen is the protector of the flame, and I its servant. Together, we shall give our blood to this land. I swear it, or burn my name in the sand."

"So it is thus sealed," she whispered, and Yassen rose to his feet.

They looked out at the horizon.

There was nothing ahead of them but Jantar. Nothing behind them but sand.

CHAPTER 36

YASSEN

There is no hard line between the servant and the sinner. There is only
a soft blur, a delicate edge in which a man can lose himself.
     —from the diaries of Priestess Nomu of the Fire Order

They slept during the day and walked at night. They applied wet skorrir leaves to their wounds, and ate what berries they could find. Yassen forgot his thirst. He forgot what hunger felt like, for it had become a constant pain, a relentless numbness. When they stopped to rest, he tried to work some feeling into his right arm. He could still move his fingers, still flex his elbow, but his entire hand was darkening to black.

Yassen thought of the pills and ointment resting on his bedside table, forgotten. He wasn't sure if it was the lack of food or his own delusions, but he could feel the infection slowly spreading through his shoulder— like a sickness. Elena often glanced at his arm. They both knew, and they were both too afraid to say it.

He had to treat it, or he would have to cut it off.

A week since passing the Jantari army, they stopped at a shallow canyon in the eastern desert that had once held a river. The rock bed was dry, with skorrir bushes hugging the wash. The landscape had begun to change, the dunes shrinking and giving way to harsh canyons and low valleys. Stars pockmarked the sky, silent and cold. Yassen could no longer see the forest.

He wondered if Samson had burned too, and the memory of his friend, looking so proud and regal before the fire, made his vision blur. *Oh, Sam.* Yassen hugged his knees. *I'm sorry. I'm so, so sorry. I should have told you sooner.*

He thought of Samson squeezing his shoulder with a smile, of Ferma nodding her approval as he took Elena to the Birdsong festivities. The trust in their eyes.

Oh, there are so many things I should have done.

Yassen hugged his knees, staring at the horizon until there were no more tears to give. His vision slowly cleared as the night sky began to lighten to grey. The mountain was behind him. Dead or alive, Samson would have wanted him to aid Elena, to protect her.

"The Jantari base is just north of here," Elena said, awake. Wind tussled with her wild curls, and for a moment she resembled a Yumi, hair writhing, eyes steely, a face so angular and beautiful. "If we head farther into the desert, we can go up and around."

Yassen squinted, studying the shadowed faces of the rocks. He had no idea where they were, but he trusted Elena's judgment. She navigated through the desert without hesitation, following the curves in ways he never thought possible. When they had been on the cruiser, riding out the storm, he had attributed her aptitude to luck. But now he understood that Elena's connection to the desert ran much deeper than he or the Arohassin had ever imagined.

The Arohassin. Yassen wondered if Akaros had already found the wounded assassins, if he recognized Yassen's bullets and his treachery. Or perhaps the Eternal Fire had burned all the evidence.

Fresh pain coiled around his right arm, and Yassen grimaced. Maybe this was his way to redemption—a limb for all the destruction he had caused.

He watched Elena walk a few yards and climb a boulder. She reached the top and paused, her figure silhouetted in the grey smoke. She looked back, shouted. The distance ate up her words.

For the Arohassin, she was the vestige of a crumbling kingdom, an old order of fanatics and martyrs, but for him . . .

For him, she was the way forward.

Gritting his teeth, Yassen hobbled after her. Slowly, using his left arm and his body, he climbed up the rock face. Elena reached out to him and hauled him onto the summit.

"Thanks," he said breathlessly, but she immediately shushed him.

She turned to the north. Without saying a word, she slipped her hand behind her back and pointed to the right and then down. Curled her fist once, twice. He recognized the Ravani guard code.

Danger, two miles to the north.

Yassen scanned the outcroppings beyond the canyon, but he saw nothing. He felt exposed.

She curled her fist again and then opened her hand. *Wait.*

She jumped down, scaling up the other edge of the canyon. Yassen hesitated only for a moment before following. He climbed onto a ledge that opened toward the northeast. Slowly, like a man shaking off the ghosts of a dream, he saw what Elena had seen. The trail of dust and sand rising from the north, toward them.

After a few moments, he saw the cruiser enter the far edge of the basin. It must not have spotted them as it drove through the riverbed, making its way east. Its way home.

Elena slunk down the ledge.

Moving closer, she motioned with her hand.

Yassen slipped out his pistol as she swung underneath the ledge, heading for the riverbed. He steadied the butt of the gun against the rocks and waited. If he timed it right, he could hit the scout right as he passed below.

Yassen considered what they would do if they captured the scout. They could interrogate him to find out the access points into Jantar. Maybe he could even wear the man's uniform and pose as a soldier. But they would have to kill him, of this there was no doubt.

The cruiser grew closer, and Yassen heard its steady hum as it spit pebbles in its wake. Below, Elena crouched behind skorrir bushes, and he emptied his mind. Breathed in. Rested his finger in the curve of the trigger.

One, two, three.

The hum grew louder.

Easy now.

Four, five.

The cruiser neared, but then Elena turned, waving her hands, shouting. The scout whipped around. And Yassen realized it wasn't a scout at all, but a young boy who stared up at him in horror. He tried to right his cruiser, but he lost control; it skidded and spun, slamming into the skorrir bushes.

Yassen cursed as Elena ran to the boy. He did not put his gun away even as he saw her pulling the boy out of the bramble.

"Drop him!" he shouted.

She looked up into the barrel of his gun as she helped the boy. "Stand down, Yassen."

But Yassen did not. The boy looked fourteen or fifteen suns, with a smattering of pimples across his cheeks. Old enough to be an initiate of the Arohassin.

"Step away from him," Yassen said.

The boy shrank back, but Elena held on to his arm. She glared at Yassen.

"He's just a kid," she said.

"Kids can be dangerous too." He looked into the boy's eyes. They were colorless, just like his. "What are you doing out here? Can't you see that there's a war beginning?"

The boy looked between Yassen and Elena. A small visor hung askew from his neck. His clothes were covered in dirt.

Fear and confusion spread across his face as he stammered: "I—I was out here, c-camping, when I saw the army. I tried to run, but a storm hit. I b-barely got out."

Yassen knew he was lying. He could see it in the way the boy tensed his shoulders, the way his eyes darted to the back compartment of the cruiser.

"What's in the cruiser?" he demanded. When the boy did not answer, he edged closer. "What's in there?"

"N-nothing," the boy said, holding up his hands, but Elena was quicker, twisting his arms behind his back, forcing him to the ground as Yassen opened the compartment.

It was full of sawed-off branches of skorrir bushes and red desert berries. A forager's case. A poor boy's livelihood.

A means to survive.

Yassen pulled back his hand as if he had been cut. He knew this kind of desperation. He had done the same: sneaked under the cloak of night into gardens, bakeries, and the desert itself to find morsels of sustenance, something to drown out the deep, inescapable pain of hunger and loneliness.

"Don't you know it's illegal to forage in the desert?" he scolded, but he put away his gun. Gently, he loosened Elena's grip and helped the boy to his feet.

The boy wet his lips. His eyes darted to the cruiser and then back to them.

"I—I only meant to take a little," he said.

"You missed the best ones," Elena said. "There are violet lilliberries that grow underneath the sand of a skorrir bush. Tastes like shobu shit, but three can fill you for a week."

"Wh—" the boy began, but as he looked at Elena, a vague sense of recognition grew in his eyes. "Why are you telling me this?"

Yassen saw the moment understanding finally dawned on him. A look of surprise and horror twisted his face, and he shot forward, but Yassen grabbed him.

"Easy," Yassen said as the boy struggled. "We just need your help. We won't hurt you. I promise."

When the boy finally stilled, Yassen let him sit up.

"If you help us, we won't turn you in for stealing this cruiser and taking berries from Her Majesty's desert," Yassen said.

"It's not the Ravani's desert," the boy spat.

"It's not the Jantari's either," Yassen said. "But if we stay here any longer, the soldiers will find us. So help us, and we'll help you."

"Everyone thinks you're dead," the boy said to Elena. "I saw it in my holos before the storm broke my receptor."

"Let's keep it that way," Yassen said. "Help us get into Jantar, and we won't kill you."

"We invaded Ravence," the boy continued, looking up at Elena. "It's all Jantar now, the capital, the desert, and soon the southern cities. They're fighting back, your people. Even the Landless King's army is defending your southern border, but he's dead too."

"Samson's dead?" Yassen said, his voice hitching.

A part of him had hoped that Samson survived. Just like he had survived after defecting from the Arohassin. Samson was a fighter. He could claw and scrounge his way through anything. But deep down, Yassen had already known that he had burned, too.

Damn this desert. Damn this forsaken land. Damn its fire. Damn it all.

"Get us into Jantar, or he'll kill you now," Elena said bluntly.

The boy turned to Yassen, his brow furrowing as he took in Yassen's pale eyes, his golden hair. "Aren't you Jantari?"

Yassen flinched. "No," he said roughly as he felt Elena staring at him. "I'm Ravani."

"What's your name?"

"Yassen. And yours?"

"Cian."

The boy stood slowly. Elena motioned, and they pulled the cruiser out of the bramble. She swept off the thorns and hopped on, patting the seat in front of her.

"Any trick and I'll know," Elena said. "The desert will know."

Yassen sat behind Elena as Cian slid into the front seat. He revved the engine, and they shot forward, leaving the canyon behind them. Instead of heading east, Cian banked south. They went over a ridge of burnt stone and skirted a sandpit that hissed as they passed.

Yassen kept his eyes trained on the horizon in search of a scout, but none came. Cian led them into a valley and stopped in its bowl. He hopped off, heading toward a boulder the size of a winged ox. Yassen tensed, but Elena rested her hand on his knee.

"Wait," she said.

They watched the boy disappear behind the boulder. Shortly after, the rocks rumbled and the boulder slid a few feet to the left, revealing a passage just big enough for the cruiser.

Cian jogged back to them.

"So the Jantari built tunnels too," Elena mused as he hopped back on. "How many are there?"

"More than I know."

They sped into the darkened tunnel, the boulder groaning as it rolled back into place, sealing them in. The space was long and narrow, and Yassen ducked as they swerved right, barely missing a ledge of rock.

They rode for what seemed like hours, following twisting passages that held no markings before the darkness lightened. Cian slowed the cruiser and stopped underneath an opening; Yassen could make out rusted rungs leading up to a pinpoint of light.

"We have to climb," Cian said.

"Where does it lead?" Elena asked.

"Just inside Jantar, to the shacks," he said.

"The shacks?"

"It's where urchins like him live," Yassen said, and he saw the boy stiffen. "Don't worry. We have orphans in Ravence too."

"Let's get moving then," Elena said, and she prodded Cian forward. "You go first."

Cian glared at them but went to the ladder. He jumped, catching the rung, and pulled himself up. He climbed like a spider, and Yassen thought of how poor boys like him—boys who relied on their wits and their cunning to survive—were easy fodder for the Arohassin.

Yassen followed Cian, with Elena close behind. Slowly, painfully, he hauled himself up the rungs.

"When we get up there, you have to be quiet, all right?" Cian said, pausing near the top to glance down at them. "Everyone will still be asleep."

"You have our word," Elena said.

Yassen only nodded as Cian slid back the grate and scrambled out. A patch of orange, muted sky stared down at them. Cian helped Yassen up, and then they pulled Elena through. The urchin locked the latch back into place and motioned for them to follow.

The shacks were small, lopsided, made of scrap metal, tin, and anything else a scavenger could find. While Ravence's slums were low, brick structures, Jantari slums were built in stacks, with metal fire escapes snaking down the sides. Every window was barred, and a metal sign of the winged ox hung before every door.

Cian was right; everyone was asleep, and the streets were empty. But the shantytown looked outlandish in the reddish haze. It was too quiet, as if the strange sky had descended, wrapped around the homes, and trapped all sounds within. Everywhere Yassen turned, that same orange silence greeted him. Without thinking, he reached for his pistol, but Elena's hand grazed his back. He turned to her and saw the unspoken question in her eyes.

What do we do with the boy?

He glanced at the urchin and then back at her, closing and opening his fist.

Wait.

They followed Cian through narrow alleyways. Lights encased in metal cubes illuminated their path. Everywhere, Yassen spotted the infamous Jantari steel, but it did not gleam. The orange sky blocked the sun, giving their eyes reprieve.

Finally, after they rounded a corner and followed a sloping side street to an intersection, Cian stopped.

"The main road is just off to the right," he said. "Follow it, and you'll find a hovertrain platform. Take it."

"Why are you helping us?" Elena asked, and the urchin smiled wryly.

"Don't have much of a choice, do I?"

"The desert is a fickle place, and it's changing. Be careful," she said.

"Once we expand our cities, there won't be a desert," he said. "This slum will be a part of the metal. We can finally become city folk and conquer the sand."

Yassen saw a muscle work in Elena's jaw as she reached for Cian and squeezed his hand.

"Just be careful," she said again.

He scowled and yanked his hand away, disappearing back the way they came.

Elena watched him go, and then she turned to Yassen. When she saw the look in his eyes, she frowned.

"Yassen," she began.

"Just stay out of sight," he said. "I'll find you."

"But—"

"Think for a moment, Elena," he said. "He's probably going to sell us out to the nearest officer, maybe even collect a reward. We can't let him just walk away."

She chewed her lip, eyes darting between him and the direction in which Cian had disappeared.

"I don't know..."

He cupped her face, met her eyes. "Go to the station. I'll deal with this."

It did not take him long to catch up to Cian. He crept along the side of the alley with the easy, sloping gait of an urchin who knew his streets. Yassen followed, feet quick and light like a cat, like a shadow.

Still, some instinct must have caused the boy to glance back. When he caught sight of Yassen, he took off. They darted through twisting alleys, past quiet houses and small squares full of refuse. Cian feinted right, then jolted left toward a flight of brass stairs. Yassen sprinted after him, taking the stairs two at a time when Cian stumbled.

Yassen pounced.

He clamped his hand over the boy's mouth. Cian beat his hands against his arm, clawed his face, but Yassen squeezed harder. The urchin kicked, his entire body flailing, fighting to survive. Tears slipped down his cheeks.

His eyes met Yassen's.

And Yassen thought of the fleeing prisoner so long ago. He had told Samson then that there had been no choice. Samson had just stared at him, the pain and disappointment clear on his face.

The urchin kicked. Yassen could feel him scream against his palm.

He couldn't.

He released Cian, and the boy fell back, wheezing against the steps.

"We were never here," Yassen muttered. He leaned down and snapped off the visor around Cian's neck. "Don't say a word to anyone."

The urchin nodded, gulping in air. Yassen could already see the hate bubble beneath the boy's film of tears, but he shot up and was gone before Yassen could change his mind.

Shame burned in his chest. Maybe he had made a mistake. Urchins died in shanties like this every day. It was the way of the desert, a land already thick with blood. But Cian was just a kid, a boy who pickpocketed and scavenged the streets for his next meal. How could he take a life that so mirrored his own?

Maybe he had lost his edge. Maybe he wasn't taloned, just like Samson had feared. Or maybe he was just beginning to cut himself some slack. Offer himself a glimmer of forgiveness.

Yassen followed the road to the hovertrain station, an open-air platform on the edge of the slum. It was empty. Holos hovered above him, headlines flashing. A crystal monitor embedded within a pillar of brass announced that the train for the morning labor shift had already passed.

He strode along the edge of the platform, searching for Elena. On his left was a short rectangular track where a hovertrain would dock. The Claws, curved metal fixtures that locked and charged the train, bordered the track. Their buzz filled the morning quiet.

He found Elena huddled beside the ticket booth. Slowly, he sank down beside her.

"They took Chand Mahal," she said, pointing to the holo above the booth.

News streams showed Jantari forces ransacking Samson's garden, overturning the very tables where he and Samson had sat nearly a month prior, reminiscing about their childhood. It felt like a lifetime ago.

"The Ravani royal family has been assassinated by the Arohassin," a reporter said in a clipped voice. "Reports detail that Samson Kytuu aided the terrorists in the coup against the Ravani government."

"That's a damn lie," Yassen growled.

Elena grabbed his hand, her face tight.

"King Farin has officially declared war against the Arohassin and the Black Scales," the reporter continued. "He has invoked his claim over Ravence in the absence of the reigning government. Hail Farin. May our brass prove unyielding against the instigators."

Yassen could only stare as the holos shifted to show footage of Jantari soldiers marching across Ravence's southern borders. Missiles fired. The red wall fell in a blast of stone. Blood drained from his face as he watched the Jantari lay out the bodies of Ravani and Black Scale soldiers in neat, orderly lines.

"That fucking pig," Elena seethed, and sparks flitted from her hands. "He marches into my kingdom, pretending to be the hero? Pretending that *he* has claim over the desert?" Her eyes flashed. "I'll have his head. I'll melt his metal body and throw it into the Eternal Fire."

Yassen clenched his fist to stop it from shaking. Akaros had told him that the Arohassin would deliver Elena's head to Farin, but he had never mentioned this. After all their talks against monarchy, would the Arohassin let another king march in and take Ravence?

And to blame Samson for all of this . . .

Rage bubbled in his chest, thick and hot.

"We need to take a train to the mountains," he said, fighting to keep his voice under control. There was nothing they could do for Samson now. "It'll take us three days. I still have my pod. I can buy us tickets."

Elena turned to him, her eyes reading what he guarded.

"What happened with Cian?"

"Look, the next train is in fifteen minutes," he said, nodding toward the monitor. "It should be less crowded than the morning trains. We'll need a disguise though—something ordinary." He handed her the urchin's visor. "Use this for now."

"Is this his?"

He tried to keep his face as stoic as possible. "We don't have much time."

"Did you kill him?" she asked quietly, and when he said nothing, she squeezed his hand. "Holy Bird Above, you didn't do it."

"I gave him a good scare. He won't talk."

"Oh, he'll talk," she said, but there was a softness in her eyes, a kindness. She touched his cheek. "I'm glad you didn't kill him."

"Let's just get to the cabin—"

"What made you stop?" she said, and her eyes, so dark and large in the waking dawn, stopped him from turning away.

"He reminded me of someone I once knew."

They sat in silence as they stared out at the empty platform. Sand swirled and danced in the wind. Yassen rested his head against the wall and glanced at Elena. Her eyes were distant, but he sensed her sadness, her misery. They were both orphans now.

The air screeched with the approach of the hovertrain.

It was empty, just as he had suspected it would be.

Yassen pressed his holopod on the scanner beside the door and purchased two tickets for the Sona Range. Together, they watched as the Claws unlatched.

With a groan, the hovertrain rose and hurtled east, leaving the orange sky and the desert behind.

CHAPTER 37

ELENA

Distance makes the heart grow fonder, but what of the eyes? Do they show the sorrow of our parting?

—from a Sayonai folklore ballad

Elena watched the desert give way to deep forests and metal buildings. They left the orange silence behind them, the hovertrain zipping past bronze skyscrapers and metal bridges.

The trip to the Sona Range would take three days, and they had already stopped twice. Only two passengers had boarded in that time, both at their last stop. One was a young woman with hair like honey; the other, a younger boy, likely her son. He slumped into her, his face pressed against her stomach, his mouth slightly parted. The mother shifted the boy and rested his head in her lap. She looked up and saw Elena staring. She smiled, but Elena quickly looked away.

Yassen shifted across from her, crossing one leg over the other as he stared out the window. He wore a haunted look and had not said much since their conversation on the platform.

He reminded me of someone I once knew.

She wanted to ask him who, but when Yassen finally met her gaze, Elena faltered.

"What is it?" he asked.

"I," she began. *Who did you remember?* He watched her, waiting, and Elena at once noticed the quiet in the car, felt the gaze of the mother on them. "I'm...hungry."

Yassen nodded as the hovertrain began its third descent. "I can get us something from the station stalls."

They looped past a large sign that read WELCOME TO MONORA, reaching a platform full of people. Elena tensed. Yassen stood, casually studying the crowd as the Claws buzzed and latched on to the train. Steam hissed out of its engines. She turned to Yassen to see him scrubbing the dried blood from his lip with the back of his hand. He had long discarded his palace badge, and the spot above his chest looked dark and empty without it.

"Wait here and save me a seat," he said.

"But there are so many people," she said under her breath, glancing at the mother and sleeping child. "What if someone recognizes us?"

"I know how to shake a tail. Don't worry."

A robotic voice announced that they had arrived in Monora.

"I'll be back," Yassen said, and he strode through the doors.

Passengers rushed in. They carried a rancid smell; for a moment, Elena thought they were day workers bringing the scent of the city, but then she saw the look on their faces, and she realized it was the stench of fear. She twisted in her seat to catch a glimpse of Yassen, but he was already lost in the crowd. Faces of reporters floated along the platform. She could not hear them, but she froze when she saw the headlines.

The Arohassin have claimed Palace Hill.

Someone tapped her shoulder, and Elena glanced up to see a woman with a green visor and pudgy cheeks.

"Is this seat taken?"

Behind her visor, Elena began to sweat. She spread her arm on the seat beside her. "My friend just jumped out, but he's coming back."

The woman scowled. A man dressed in black slacks bumped into her.

"Grab a seat," he said.

"Girl said it's taken," the woman snapped.

"Hey, lady, you can't save seats," the man said. He winced as someone poked him in the side. "It's too crowded for that shit."

"I—I—" Elena stammered. *Where is Yassen?*

The woman in the green visor glowered as the man pushed into her again. "Leave her alone."

"I'm just saying, there's an open spot—"

"She said it's for her friend—"

"—it's too hot for this mess," the worker finished. He jostled forward, teetering as the hovertrain hissed.

"Hey, back up," the woman growled.

"Lady, I've been on my feet all day," the man said. "Can you move on over—"

"I *said* back up—"

"I'm just talking to the girl—"

"Is there a problem?" Yassen's voice cut through the air, silencing the two workers as he pushed to where they stood.

His face was hidden behind a visor, his dirty clothes beneath a new cloak.

"We don't want no trouble. There's already enough coming our way," the woman in the green visor grumbled.

"You can't save seats," the worker said indignantly. He scowled at Elena, but Yassen slid neatly in front of her.

"There isn't any rule against saving seats," Yassen said. He stood a head taller than the worker, and the man seemed to consider this before shaking his head and mumbling something about his legs. Then he moved away in search of an unclaimed seat.

The Claws unlatched, and the hovertrain took to the sky. Elena sighed as Yassen sank down beside her. The sign of Monora winked goodbye as they hurtled past. The sun broke through, and for a moment it was as if the city were on fire, each bronze building lighting up like forks of a flame. She tightened her visor as Yassen handed her a thin folded jacket.

"So you'll look less like a beggar," he said.

She snorted. "It'll take more than that," she said and gestured to her ripped skirts.

"Hey, it's the best I could do. It's not like they have a runway of the latest lightning suits and lehengas," he said, and despite herself, Elena managed a smile.

He reached back into his cloak to withdraw two bundles of pound cake and spiced chicken wrapped in flatbread.

"Here, I found these at the station café."

"And the jacket?"

"I may have nicked it from someone's luggage when they weren't looking." He winked.

"Thanks," she said and paused. "Thanks for handling that too."

He nodded as she bit into the pound cake, savoring its sweet vanilla aftertaste and licking the brown sugar that stuck to her lips. Yassen split the flatbread and offered half to her. She took it as they zoomed past the outskirts of the city for the deeper country beyond.

The hovertrain docked, and the crowd spilled out.

Sunlight poured into their empty compartment. Yassen groaned as he stretched out his legs.

"Skies above." He grimaced as he pulled off his visor, which left an angry red mark across his face. "What?" he said, when he saw her staring.

She had been mulling over the question ever since he had shown her the map, tasting its rough edges. Yassen looked at her, expectant.

"The cabin in the Sona Range, was it your family's?" she asked finally.

He hesitated for a moment. "My father's."

A shadow passed over his face, and Elena could tell that the answer had reopened a wound. One that she knew well—of fathers and their secrets.

"And you're sure it's still there?"

"Yes, although it's been many suns since I've been back," he said, his voice dampened by regret.

He reached into his cloak and withdrew his holopod. He opened the map of the tunnels underneath the mountains.

"My father taught me how to navigate these. One leads right up to the cabin, but we'll need to rent brenni to get there. They're more sure-footed than horses, and they can carry a heavy load of supplies." He moved to pocket the pod, but then hesitated. The holo flickered in his hand. "My father told me once that tunnels underneath mountains are only made to harbor secrets. He wasn't wrong." Sunlight cut across his face, deepening the grooves beneath his eyes. "The Jantari are searching for something in the mountains. We have to be careful."

"Searching for what?"

"A special type of metal, one so fine it can cut steel," Yassen said. "I don't think they've found it, but..." He hesitated, looking away.

"Yassen..."

He sighed. "Samson was trying to find it too. Some deposit of ore deep within the Sona Range. If it's there, Farin might use it to build all kinds of new weapons and fortunes."

"Samson?" she said, confused. *He gave me this map.* Suddenly, a cold realization struck Elena. "Did Samson tell you to go to the cabin? Did he ask you to search for the ore?"

Yassen blinked. "He did. But, to rest. Not to find the ore."

But Elena remembered Samson's urgent whisper in her ear, his strained smile as Farin had looped his arm around his neck. *How far are you willing to go to win the war?* If Samson had been searching for the ore too, did he mean to use it against the Jantari? Had he always planned to forgo peace and attack Farin?

"Do you know where to find it?" she said, heart beating quick. Farin was already mutating his soldiers. If he created weapons from this metal, it would change the war. *Change any war.* "Can you find it?"

For a long time, Yassen said nothing. The hovertrain hummed as it sped across the sky. With each passing minute, she grew farther away from her desert. Her home. With each passing moment, he drew closer to the remnants of his past.

When Yassen finally spoke, his voice was quiet but steady. Full of power like the songs of the priests.

"No, Elena, I won't find it," he said. "The past is binding, and I want to break away. If we carry the burdens of our fathers, we'll never know what it means to be free."

She bit her lip, but he said no more. She wanted to push further, but as he leaned his head back and closed his eyes, she stopped herself. It would be asking too much of him.

For once, Yassen became clear to her: a solid man rather than a ghost.

He was neither assassin nor traitor—simply a man carving his own path in a life bound by fate.

Just as she was.

Elena drew her jacket tighter to fight off the chill. Although the sun had set, people still milled around the platform. News of the war had delayed several hovertrains, their connection included. Now they huddled underneath a steel pillar, and she studied the faces of the people she had been taught to distrust. She spotted a young girl with a lopsided smile; an old man with eyebrows thicker than a sandstorm; a woman who paced across the platform, talking rapidly into a headset.

They were, in short, far more mundane than she had imagined.

All her life, she had abhorred the Jantari. Her father called them zeemir-slinging oppressors, bent on robbing Sayon of her riches and turning her people into machines. But here, she saw only men and women tired after a long day of work, tensing at every new war-ridden headline. Mothers and fathers impatient to get home and wrap their arms around their family to make sure they were safe.

"Here," Yassen said, breaking her thoughts.

Elena turned as he handed her a hot cup of tea from the vendor at the end of the platform. She cradled it between her hands, letting its heat chase away the cold. Yassen leaned against the pillar, sighing.

"The train should be here by now."

She began to tell him that their train had been delayed by another hour when a gasp rippled across the platform. Elena turned as the holos flashed. A brief headline warned viewers of gruesome content, and then it was replaced by a video.

Elena instantly recognized Alabore's Passage, the route of her parade.

The buildings, once adorned by marigolds and streamers, lay in shambles. Walls were missing or blown out. Ripped orange banners and debris littered the streets. But it was not the smoke or the ruined buildings that made Elena's blood still.

It was the body.

A tank rolled across the fallen banners, dragging a blackened form behind it. Though most of the corpse was burned, Elena could tell that it once had been a tall man. It wore long royal-red robes that dragged across the broken ground. Soldiers dressed in black, with the silver snake of the Arohassin on their jackets, marched beside the tank. Their faces were streaked with ash, but their eyes burned with conviction as they shouted: "Long live the king."

The video cut to the White Lotus. The Arohassin soldiers looped a rope around the neck of the corpse. They climbed up the stone sculpture, pulling the body, and then flung the corpse over. It bounced, swaying in the air.

A soldier turned to the camera in mock salute.

"Long live the king."

And then it hit Elena.

She made a sound, something caught between a sob and a scream. People turned. Yassen draped his arm around her shoulder and pulled her close, burying her face in his chest. She tried to pull away, but he only held her tighter.

"My fath—"

"It's not him," he whispered fiercely in her ear. "There's no way they could have fished him out of the Eternal Fire. The Eternal Fire, Elena. He would have burned to ash in a moment."

But the body, the robes. It was her father. They dragged him through the streets like a criminal, like an animal. She struggled against him.

"Elena, think," he pleaded. "If that really is Leo, then where is the crown? They were in the same room. How could they have found his body but not the crown?"

She slumped into him. He was right. She had lost the crown at the same time the Eternal Fire had claimed her father. The body the Arohassin paraded down the streets was merely a decoy.

When she stopped struggling, he let her go. Elena pulled away and drew in a deep, long breath, but her throat hitched. How dare they dishonor the Ravani king? How dare they even *think* to desecrate his body?

"King Farin has issued a statement," a reporter was saying. "All Ravani within Jantar must report to the authorities. If you do not report willingly, you shall be detained. Find your nearest hovertrain station and report to the police. Do not bring your belongings."

A murmur rippled across the platform. The girl with the lopsided smile hid herself within her mother's skirts. The old man snorted, his mouth twisted in disdain. Workers glanced furtively at each other, at her, and for once Elena felt grateful for her awful visor.

Yassen gestured. "Let's move to the other side of the platform."

They turned to leave, but a man stepped in front of them. He was dressed in black, with a winged ox across his chest. A Jantari policeman.

"I need to see some identification," he demanded.

At the other edge of the platform, Elena saw more police officers sauntering through the throng. The crowd split away, revealing those who hid within. There were confused shouts. She spotted a policeman yelling at a young man. When he did not produce a holo, the officer grabbed him by the back of his neck. Elena stiffened, but then Yassen stepped forward and held out his holopod.

"The name's Cassian Newman," he said to the policeman.

Across the platform, the officer clasped cuffs around the young man's wrists.

"You're from Nbru?" the policeman asked as he scrutinized Yassen's holo. His eyebrows furrowed. "Says here that you arrived over a month ago. Why'd you leave?"

"Work," Yassen replied. At once, she recognized the change in his accent. Gone were the heavy, rolling sounds of the desert, replaced by the high, lilting tones of the Nbruian. He gave a bashful smile. "Jantar gives better coin."

"Take off your visor," the officer demanded, and Yassen slowly unclipped his, revealing his colorless eyes. "You're a Jantari?"

"My father was," Yassen replied with a tight-lipped smile.

The office snorted. "And her?" He looked at Elena, and she saw him take in her long curls, her dark brown skin. "Where's her passport?"

"My wife forgot it at home," Yassen said smoothly, and she shot him a look. "We're sorry. We rushed out when we heard the war declaration. My poor mother-in-law, may the Mountain bless her soul, has a frail heart. She lives across the city. We just want to check on her."

You're talking too much, she thought, but she held her tongue.

"Tough luck," the officer growled. He pointed at Elena. "Without holos, I can't let her pass. Come with me, miss."

Elena bristled, but Yassen stepped in front of her. He slipped something into the officer's pocket.

"Sometimes we forget things when we're worried," he whispered.

The officer's lip curled back in a sneer. "Are you trying to bribe me?"

"No," Yassen said, his voice serene. "Just paying my deference to the guards of Jantar."

The officer considered this. Finally, he patted his pocket and nodded.

"Next time, bring your pod. We can't have Ravani mingling with our people," he said. "Hail Farin."

He strode past them, heading for the next man unfortunate enough to catch his attention. Elena let out a shaky breath.

"They're rounding us up." She shook her head. Anger flashed through her—a keen, sudden pain, like needles piercing through her fingertips. She had to protect her people. With her fire, she could burn down every Jantari policeman and Arohassin soldier. With her fire, she would hang them from the rafters.

Yassen must have recognized the look in her eyes because he touched her arm as heat rolled off her. He did not flinch.

"Easy now," he said, glancing around them. "Remember why you're here."

She forced herself to nod. A hissing sound grew in her ears, and she knew at once that it was the fire within her begging to be unleashed.

In time, she told it.

She flexed her hand, and a wisp of a flame, a tiny little thing, danced and died in her palm.

They arrived at the Sona Range at dawn of the third day. On the train, Elena had snagged a scarf left by a passenger and used it to hide her dark, curly hair. Officers, luckily, had not combed the hovertrains once they boarded. They only searched the platforms for traveling Ravani, and Elena shuddered to think what was happening to her countrymen.

The sky bled in drops of rust and carmine as their hovertrain neared the mountains. Like most of Jantar, the peaks glinted unnaturally. Small patches of snow were in stark contrast to the blue and red pines, but what drew Elena's attention were the rigs. Massive metal conglomerations hugged the mountainside like ugly beetles. In the middle, two pressurized glass pipes acted as elevator tubes. One was used to send Sesharians deep into the mountain; the other, to retrieve carts filled with raw ore. Elena was both impressed by the sheer might of the mines and repulsed by the way they gutted the land of its value.

Her father always said that the Jantari did not respect their land. They built and mined without pausing to consider their effects. At least her people knew how to coexist with the desert, to learn its shapes and curves. At least the Ravani knew when to give and when to beg.

Her thoughts turned to Rani, now gutted and burned. How could it be that over a week ago, she had walked through its streets, heard dhols ring through the air as people sang songs about the sands? Elena longed for her home. So much so that her ache felt more intense than hunger, more fervent than prayer.

Yassen groaned, breaking her from her thoughts.

She turned as he rolled onto his back. He was laid out across the seats, asleep. It was her turn to stay on watch, but instead of keeping an eye on their surroundings, Elena found herself studying Yassen. The pale sun outlined the bridge of his curved nose, the high plane of his forehead, softening him. She could see the scar on his neck, small and curved, where she had once held her slingsword to his throat.

Elena hesitated, and then stood slowly. His hair brushed her thigh as she sat down beside him. He stirred, and she froze. For a moment, she thought he would wake, but Yassen remained asleep. His lips were slightly parted, his long lashes dusting the tops of his cheeks. A singular curl of hair fell across his forehead. Age lines crinkled the edges of his eyes, but the sunlight made him young. As if he'd found peace beyond this world.

He looked beautiful, in a way.

Gently, Elena brushed his hair from his forehead as the hovertrain began to descend.

"Yassen," she said softly. She touched his shoulder. "We're here."

With a screech, the hovertrain docked, and Elena glanced up to see another empty platform. When she looked back down, Yassen was awake, his pale eyes staring up at her.

The doors swished open. She felt a cold blast of air, smelled the fresh tang of pine and the acidity of metal, but she did not turn away.

Slowly, Yassen reached up. His fingers brushed her cheek, and she stilled. He ran his thumb along her cheekbone and then gently withdrew, holding up his thumb to reveal a thin eyelash, her eyelash.

"Make a wish," he whispered.

She looked down at him, her breath caught in her chest. A wish? She almost laughed. What would a wish do in a place like this? But he did not break her gaze, and she could not tear herself away.

"I wish for us to survive," she said and blew. The eyelash fluttered and disappeared.

He reached up, and for a moment she thought he meant to touch her cheek again, but he only pointed out of the curved windows.

"There," he said, and she turned to see the vivid shades of the thick, lush forest. No rigs had infiltrated this part of the mountain. At least not yet. "The safe house."

She nodded, and he sat up with a soft groan. He cradled his arm to his chest, and she saw a flash of bruised skin.

"Are you in pain?"

"Always," he said.

"Your hand," she started, but he waved her off.

"Let's go before the train leaves."

They deboarded and walked down the empty platform. An old merchant wrapped in fyrra fur sat behind a rickety stall. His coat made Elena envious as she shivered against the mountain chill.

"Looking to escape the city, eh?" the merchant called out as they neared. His visor bobbed as he spoke.

"Mountain air is good for any man," Yassen said, "but I admit we're poorly packed." He pointed at the musty shelves behind the merchant. "Got any furs back there?"

"Oh, just two," he said. "Though I do have one large overcoat perfect for you lovebirds to cozy up in."

Elena blinked, her cheeks reddening as Yassen hastily pulled out his holopod.

"We'll take the two," he said.

The man scanned the pod and handed them two heavy coats. Elena pulled hers on; it was too big, but she hugged it close to her body to trap whatever warmth she had left.

"Thank you," she murmured.

"Watch out for the autumn snaps, mera," the merchant said. "There's been talk of brushfire. There was one on the other side of the mountain last week that got the soldiers jumping."

"Brush fire? This late in summer?" she said.

The merchant shrugged. "They've been drilling more than usual. Accidents are bound to happen."

"We'll keep an eye out," Yassen said. "Is there a place nearby where we can find a hot meal? Or brenni?"

"Follow the road," the merchant said. "You'll find the handler along it. Oh, and cinch them visors. The mines have been flashing lately, and they blinded a poor girl just last week."

Elena's stomach tightened as she recalled the lumbering tanks in the desert. The soldiers with their zeemirs. Light bounced harshly off the dunes; Jantari's cursed metal would only worsen the effects.

"Have they found more deposits?" she asked nonchalantly as Yassen shot her a look.

"They're still rucking out the old one, but it's a big one. Took them weeks to blast it out. Soldiers will come to collect the ore, so best stay out of their way, or else they'll recruit you." He laughed.

"Do you know when the soldiers will be here?" she asked.

"Hard to say, but shouldn't be too long now," the merchant said.

"And where—"

"I'm sorry, she has a thing for soldiers," Yassen said, squeezing her arm. "Down the road you said?"

"Yes. The handler's the one with the barn."

Yassen thanked the merchant as he nudged Elena forward. His hand pressed into the small of her back, and he did not remove it until they were well out of earshot.

"Did you hear what he said?" she asked quietly.

"I did," he sighed.

She chewed her lip. "I know you said you don't know where the deposit is, and that you have no interest in finding it, but—" She stopped, turning to him. "You know these mines better than me, Yassen. I'm not asking you to look for this ore, but—but what if we can stop these soldiers?"

"What are you getting at?" he asked cautiously.

"They're going to be here soon to pick up the latest draws from the mine. They'll use it to make more weapons, tanks, Mother's Gold, even those tanks with the half-metal soldiers. We can't let them."

"We can't stop an entire army, Elena."

"I know we can't," she said, more to herself. *But there must be a way.* She scrutinized the mountain before her. This was a foreign land, one whose ridges and valleys she did not know as well as her desert. She had no plan, no army. But Elena could not shake off the strange feeling she'd had when Yassen had told her about Samson giving him the map. *Samson knows about the cabin and the ore. He led Yassen here.*

"You said Samson has a small base farther down the mountains," she said. "Is there any way we can contact it?"

"I'm not sure." He stopped when he saw the look on her face. "Elena, what is it?"

"Nothing, it's just..." She trailed off, thinking. "I have a feeling Samson meant for you to come here. To find this special ore for him."

"Maybe," Yassen said slowly, though there was a dark look in his eyes. "But he's dead now. They're all dead. It doesn't matter anymore."

Elena said nothing to that, her throat tight. He did not need to remind her of the people they had left behind. She knew. She knew all too well.

When she remained silent, Yassen sighed. He reached over, stopping her from wringing her hands.

"I'm sorry," he said, voice soft with guilt. "But we can't do anything about the ore right now, Elena. Let's start by getting you somewhere safe."

She did not have the heart to tell him that she was never going to feel safe in Jantar.

By the time they reached the town, the sun was high in the sky. It beat down on the tiny metal shops and glass storefronts that lined the main street. Most were boarded or closed. There were no urchins, no street dancers. Elena spotted a few townspeople, but they hurried by with only a quick nod or smile.

"Where is everyone, you think?" she asked Yassen.

"Too afraid to come out." He kept glancing around them, alert. He walked close to her, his shoulder brushing her own protectively, and she was reminded of his oath. The bitterness of his betrayal had not yet left her, not fully, but Elena smiled as he inserted himself in front of her as they passed a townsman. For better or for worse, Yassen Knight had not gone back on his word.

They finally found the promised barn just past the main street and slipped inside.

A tiny, empty desk sat in a makeshift reception area. Stalls lined the wall, and beyond, the barn opened to a pasture where Elena could see a few free brenni roaming.

She walked to one of the stalls, clicking her tongue. A brenni raised its furry head at her approach. It had large brown eyes and short ears that perked up as it came to the stall door. It was smaller than a horse, its long, thick neck covered in the most luxurious mane Elena had ever seen. Smiling, she touched its soft muzzle.

The brenni brayed, searching her hand for a treat, when a woman mucking the next stall over suddenly jumped up.

"Oh," she said, dropping her rake. "Are you mounting a ride?"

"Just two," Elena said.

The woman hurried out of the stall, rubbing her hands on her pants as Yassen approached. "For how long?"

"A month," Yassen said and lifted his holopod. "And we'll need feed for them, too."

"Month? I can only do two weeks, and you'll need to bring them back right on the mark. This mountain is going to be full of soldiers soon, and they need pack animals. They hit the mother lode."

Mother lode. Elena glanced at Yassen, raising an eyebrow, but he turned away.

"Are there army lodgings near?" he asked lightly.

"On the other side of the mountain, closer to the mines," the woman replied. "But they'll be here in town too. It's got everyone nervous."

"How come?" Elena asked.

"Well, the three mines have been working overtime for weeks. They've extracted enough to get the king excited."

Elena paled. As the woman slipped rope halters on the brenni, she met Yassen's gaze and saw worry in his eyes as well.

"Sorry, I've lived in the city so I don't know much." Elena laughed, keeping her voice mild. "But you said three mines? I thought there were more than that, for some reason."

"There are, but you'll have to go all the way to Janka for the rest. That's about a three-day journey by train. A few hours by hoverpod, but they've shut down all routes to clear out for our boys. But they won't be going to Janka anyway. *Our* mines have done this," the woman said with a touch of pride.

"I'm sure it'll make your town more popular," Yassen said.

The woman beamed. "Say, what city are you from?"

"Monora," Yassen said quickly.

"Monora? You lot have traveled an awful long way."

"We wanted some peace and quiet," Elena interjected with a smile. "The air here is so...refreshing compared to back home."

"The people too." The woman winked.

She saddled the two brenni and swung heavy bags of feed onto their backs. One of the creatures stared at Elena with buttery eyes and flicked its ears. Elena stroked its mane.

"Does this one have a name?" she asked.

"She does," the woman said. "She's Harpa, and he's Henut. They're a pair, actually. Perfect for you two." She winked again.

"Thank you," Yassen said, but Elena noticed the blush rising on his cheeks.

"Bring them back before the two new moons, mero," the woman said to Yassen.

Elena took a brenni's lead. It nuzzled her shoulder, soft and warm.

"Wait here for a moment," Yassen said when they had returned to the road.

He crossed the street and disappeared into a storefront. Elena rocked on her feet. The visor itched the bridge of her nose, and she wished to tear it off. She felt a strange disquiet as she stood alone. It was a whispering feeling, a slippery one. A premonition perhaps, or the knowledge that what lay ahead was uncharted territory—a long, twisting path that she had no hope of controlling.

Yassen jogged back carrying bundles. He stuffed them into the saddlebags and handed her a package of wrapped meat.

"How were you able to buy all of this?" she asked, examining the food.

"Suns of saving and insurance," he said, lifting another pack onto the brenni.

"Insurance?"

"It pays to take out powerful people." He tightened his brenni's girth as it snorted. "Shall we?"

He gave her a leg up, and she swung onto the saddle. The brenni shifted, straining at the bit, but then stilled under her touch. It wasn't quite like a horse, but it felt solid. Sturdy.

Yassen mounted easily and nudged his brenni forward. When they reached the forest road, he twisted in his saddle and looked at her.

"I need you to make me a promise," he said. He took off his visor, his eyes intent on hers. "You have to give me your word that you will do everything I say. If I tell you to hide, you hide. If I tell you to run, you run—even if you have a clear shot. There will be no time to argue. This land may not be as rough as Ravence, but it has its harsh edges, and I know them better than you."

"And what if I have to leave you behind?"

"Then you'll leave me behind," he said, and his words fell like stones.

It saddened her. Yassen was all that she had left of Ravence.

"You took the oath, Yassen Knight. For better or for worse, you're stuck with me." She smiled and spurred her brenni on.

CHAPTER 38

YASSEN

Everything points north, even death.

—a Ravani proverb

Yassen remembered the amethyst pine with the ivory trunk. It hunkered on the edge of the mountainside like a tottering drunk—a sordidly welcoming sight.

"We're almost there," he called out to Elena.

They were already three hours into their journey. Yassen had unbuttoned his coat as they ventured up the mountain, but now, as they wandered deeper into the forest, he wished he had taken it off. A suffocating heat crept through the pines. His brenni shifted nervously, but he patted its neck gently and steered it beyond the tree.

"Why is it so damn hot?" Elena wiped her brow, her face flushed. He tried not to stare as she peeled off her coat. Sweat ringed the neck of her blouse and when she caught his gaze, he quickly looked away.

"There've been warm summers here, but I've never seen one like this," Yassen said as she drew closer.

"You really think there've been wildfires out here?"

"I don't doubt it," he responded.

Yassen hadn't been in the mountain for many suns, yet the path to his father's cabin remained ingrained in his memory. There was the tall sapling with its blue needles; there, the cliffside that resembled the aging face of a king. Yassen nudged his brenni, and it hopped over a fallen log covered with dry leaves and dust from the mines above.

If what the merchant said was true, the Jantari soldiers would be here soon to collect their precious ore. They would most likely go straight to the mines without searching the mountain; after all, they were deep within their own territory. They had little reason to suspect danger. Yassen still made sure to cover their tracks when he could. He guided their brenni over pine roots and weaved them past dry creek beds, where it would be harder to find evidence of their passing.

A spot of blue fluttered above them, and Yassen looked up to see a mountain lark.

"Stay still," he said, and out of the corner of his eye, he saw Elena rein her mount to a stop.

He slid from his saddle and landed on a carpet of pine needles, avoiding the naked black neverwood branches that clawed out from beneath the underbrush. The mountain lark sang. Three soft notes.

"You hear that?" he said to Elena. "Three notes mean no danger."

"What about one note?"

"It means you run."

He stepped in the pockets between roots and came to stand before a long retherin pine. It was an old master of the forest; its velvet blue trunk was wider than three grown men, and its tawny leaves were thick and heavy despite the summer heat.

Slowly, Yassen sank down to study its roots. They spanned the forest floor, a vast network that led to the very base of the mountain. His father had taught him that the roots of a tree were a map that linked the land together—from its valleys to its summits—and that to understand it, he need only to observe.

Yassen traced one that led to the trunk. The bark felt soft, supple even. He followed it diagonally until he found a knot, the pear-shaped bulge that his father had pointed out to him so long ago, and he pressed it.

The wood splintered with a whisper.

The leaves rustled behind him, and the neverwood separated to reveal stone steps that descended beneath the mountain.

"Mother's Gold," Elena whispered. "How did you do that?"

"It pays to get out of Ravence every once in a while," he said and hopped back on his brenni.

The old tunnel's steps veered steeply into the mountain, but their mounts were sure of foot. With a groan, the entrance closed behind them, and they were submerged in darkness. Yassen's hand tightened around the reins. He wished they had some sort of light, but he would have to rely on memory now. Yassen stopped his brenni and called for Elena to do the same, twisting in the saddle to get his bearings as his eyes gradually adjusted to the dark. It came back slowly, piecemeal, like the glowing embers of a campfire: his father leading him across the narrow ridge, through the obsidian rocks that had scared him as a child, and up until he could smell the rotten leaves.

"This way," he said, guiding them toward a ledge. A deep abyss plunged down just beyond it.

The bowels of the mountain glinted despite a lack of light. Unlike the mining tunnels, this one was wide, tall, the walls still rough. When Yassen had asked his father who had created this tunnel, his father had merely shrugged.

"Does it matter?" he had asked.

He made Yassen memorize the tunnels that connected the mines, the cabin, and the foothills of the mountain, often walking alongside him, but he refused to let him explore the ones that led to the middle of the range.

"Stick only to this path," he had said.

As they wound further into the depths, the mountain rumbled. His brenni neighed as dust and dirt rained down.

"They're drilling," Elena said, and though her voice was barely above a whisper, it echoed through the chamber. "I thought you said there were no rigs in this part of the mountain."

"There aren't, but they're close. You can feel the drills everywhere."

Something scuttled between the rocks, and his brenni reared. Yassen squeezed his knees to steady it, speaking softly as his hand dropped to his hip.

They heard a growl. It bounced off the rocks and filled the chamber with a deep, guttural boom. The brenni bucked and tossed its head. Yassen fought for control just as they heard another snarl, closer this time, and he saw a flash of something black—something deeper than the darkness—slither down the rocks. A chill crept down his shoulder and into his burnt arm. Elena's brenni reared; she tugged on the reins, but her mount shot forward, past Yassen. It raced up the tunnel with breathtaking speed, spraying rocks in its wake.

At the sound of its mate's flight, Yassen's brenni also sprang forward. Yassen threw one last look over his shoulder. The black shape sprang into the abyss, and his hand twitched, as if stung.

Yassen cried out at the sudden pain, his grip on the reins loosening, but his brenni was already vaulting forward, screeching. Up ahead, he saw the fork in the path. East and west. Where had his father taken him?

"Left, go left!" he yelled.

Elena struggled, her brenni fighting her every step of the way, but she ripped off her visor and slapped it against its hide. The brenni yelped and swung left, and Yassen's followed.

The path began to ascend. Yassen could smell the forest above. The scent drifted over the rocks as the darkness began to lighten into a muted grey. The path widened, and Yassen urged his brenni on until he was side by side with Elena; he flung out his right hand to grab her brenni's bridle. Perhaps it was the sight of his blackened fingers reaching for its eyes, but Elena's brenni skidded to a stop. She gasped, grabbing its mane to steady herself, and Yassen's brenni suddenly halted as well, almost flinging him over its neck.

Ahead, pockets of sunset peeked through a crumbling stone roof. Roots cracked through the surface, crawling into the chamber. The ceiling sloped downward, so when Yassen dismounted and crept forward, he had to bend his head. Another white-hot flash of pain shot through his arm. He stumbled forward like a drunk, blinded by agony.

"Yassen?" Elena called, her voice laced with worry.

He sagged against the wall. Her voice seemed to come from the bottom of the mountain. He gritted his teeth, forcing himself to breathe.

One, two, three, count damn it.

One, two, three.

One, two, three.

When he opened his eyes, he felt a little less sick, although the taste of the meat they had eaten earlier pushed back up his throat. With his good hand, he felt the rough wall. He followed it until he found the smooth rock—the false rock—and pushed. The stone ceiling hinged open; rotten leaves and dirt fell in, almost burying them in forest litter.

Yassen coughed, pulling himself up. His brenni popped its head out. It snorted in disapproval, but easily climbed onto the steady ground, shaking leaves from its drooping ears. Elena's hand shot up, and Yassen pulled her out.

"Why weren't there steps for this one?" she huffed as she shook pine needles and molorian leaves from her hair.

"Patterns are dangerous," Yassen said as her brenni jumped out of the debris and sauntered about.

He grabbed its reins. The words came unbidden to his lips.

"Bless the ones who carry."

It was an old Ravani saying, one that his mother had taught him, yet the sound of the ancient language calmed the brenni. It snorted and nuzzled his shoulder. He stroked its ears.

"I thought you didn't believe in the Phoenix or the ancient ways of the desert," Elena said softly.

"Maybe I'm just feeling nostalgic," he said. The mountain, the path, this forest, it all brought back the memories of summers spent in Sona Range: hunting with his father, stalking with his mother, searching the sky for falling stars with both at night. As Yassen studied their surroundings, he felt a pain in his chest. It had been there since he had stepped foot in the mountain town, but now it quickened, like a snake constricting its prey.

"Is that it?" Elena said, pointing to a slanting structure within the trees.

Blood beating in his ears, Yassen turned to see his father's cabin.

Fashioned out of molorian wood, it stood on top of a hill between two thick retherin pines. Reflective panels on the roof warded off the sun. The door, black and heavy, with a golden phoenix knocker nailed across its surface, glowered in the distance.

Yassen slowly climbed the stairs to the cabin—every step felt as if he were wading through deep sand. He had been seven suns the last time he had visited. Just a week before his father's death. A week before Yassen and his mother were left alone to pick up the pieces and make peace with the secrets Erwin left behind.

The phoenix glinted as Yassen stepped onto the landing. Its eyes opened, a laser scanning Yassen's face and traveling down the length of his body and then up to pause on his arm. Yassen lifted his left hand. The laser followed.

"Are you supposed to do something?" Elena said.

It was the same question he had asked his father, and Yassen did the same thing his father had done. He reached forward and closed the phoenix's eyes.

Even man needed time away from the gods.

The door swung open, and they stepped across the threshold. It was not a large cabin, yet it seemed to hold thousands of memories. There was the modest wooden furniture covered with colorful blankets that his mother had chosen; the fireplace of grey stone and flecks of Ravani gold that his father had built; the tea set that he had gifted Yassen's mother, resting on the kitchen counter in the back. Sunlight streamed in through the window, brushing the dusty hourglass and cups.

Yassen had never believed in ghosts, yet here they were: the ghost of his mother, father, and the boy he had once been. They crowded the room.

Yassen whimpered, his knees suddenly weak. He dimly felt Elena's arms around him, Elena guiding him into a chair before the fireplace. In the corner of the mantel, he spotted the initials he had carved when his father wasn't looking. Of course, his father had found out. Laughing, he had carved his own next to Yassen's.

Y.K. E.K.

Yassen Knight.

Erwin Knight.

When he would come to the cabin, Yassen had been comforted with the knowledge that he was worth something, that he was loved. Back then, the mountain had been his playground, the cabin his haven. He was free to be whoever he wanted, free to dream, to aspire, *to be something*.

Yet here he was, broken, useless. He had not become the man he had dreamed he would be. He had not even become the assassin he had trained to be.

In the end, he had amounted to nothing.

Yassen's chest constricted. He was too stunned to move, too harrowed to speak. Elena squeezed his shoulder and straightened.

"Let me handle this."

He watched as Elena vanished through the door, tying up the brenni, giving them their feed, returning to fill the pantry with their supplies and set water to boil. He watched her as if he were looking through a foggy window. She must have noticed him staring—she noticed everything—yet she said nothing. She was silent through her work, and when she set the tea on the table, she was soft—not in the fragile sort of way, but in the receiving kind. As if she, too, could sense the ghosts in the room.

"Here."

Yassen stared at the tea but made no move to pick it up. His good hand shook; the other curled inward like a claw. He knew if he picked up the cup, he would spill all of its contents.

Elena sat down beside him and raised his cup. Gently, she touched his chin and brought it to his lips.

"Drink," she said, her eyes holding him, rooting him. He fastened on to her like a wanderer hugs the rock that shields him from the sandstorm's vicious winds. As if those eyes alone could save him.

Holding her gaze, he drank.

When he was done, Elena poured him another cup and offered him another spiced flatbread. He ate, silently, under her watchful gaze.

The sun sank behind the mountain, and darkness crept from the corners of the room. Elena rose and touched the panel beside the door. One by one, the lights in the cabin lit up.

Finally, Yassen found the strength to speak.

"Nothing has changed in here," he said, his voice frail. "Yet everything has."

"The living need to change," Elena said as she sat back down. "Only the dead can remain untouched."

Yassen gave a dry laugh. "I think I've changed too much."

"Maybe." She reached forward and gently took his injured arm, resting his hand in her lap. Slowly, she traced the lines in his palm, the bruises that ringed his wrist. Her touch was warm, light. "But you're still Yassen Knight. That has not changed. And you're alive, despite everything."

"Elena," he whispered.

She met his gaze. "You told me that if I keep living, then Ravence cannot truly die. You're the same. You carry your family with you, their stories. As long as you keep breathing, they live."

She was right, he knew she was. But it felt so strange to be back in this home after spending so many suns away from it. After all he had done.

Yet, Yassen recognized parts of himself in the inscription in the mantel, in the frayed corners of his favorite blue blanket, in the teacup he had chipped on the kitchen counter. They brought back memories, and within each memory, a story.

If a man's life was just a tapestry of the characters he donned, his was the most unusual of all. He had been a boy who was forced to grow up quickly, an assassin who sold out his brethren without batting an eye. He was a traitor who turned on his country, and a servant who saved his queen. These stories were all a part of him.

They *were* him.

Perhaps, then, the man he wanted to be was still here, still within him. Waiting.

Later, when Elena retired to the bedroom and he lay on the sofa, awake, Yassen remembered a story his father had told him.

It was the story of Goromount, the fabled traveler who crossed the Ahi Sea after his home had been destroyed by the gods. Goromount traveled using the stars. He followed them without knowing where they would lead him.

"Why?" Yassen had asked his father. "What if they just led him to another ruined land?"

"Belief, Yassen," his father had said. "He believed that though the gods were savage in their fury, they were also kind in their mercy. And that if they destroyed all the land and all its creatures, then the gods would have no one to worship them. They would truly be forgotten."

At first, Yassen had not understood the story, but now, as he stared up at the ceiling, listening to the creaks in the floorboards and the whistle of the wind, he understood some of it. Goromount had lost almost everything, but he had gathered the pieces that remained and traveled in search of a home to make them whole again.

Yassen wondered if Goromount, when he built a new shelter on a foreign soil, had created it in the image of his homeland. Or had he looked at his surroundings and declared them free of the past? Something entirely new—a fireplace free of inscriptions.

A low, mournful sound drifted through the cabin. Yassen sat up, his hand reaching for the gun on the table. He listened, his muscles tensed. The noise came again.

He stood and followed it to the end of the hall. His bare toes curled against the cold wood. The sound came from behind the closed bedroom door, and he then realized it was Elena. She was sobbing.

Yassen moved to open the door but then hesitated. Maybe he should leave her be. Maybe she wouldn't like it if he saw her cry. But Yassen remembered how he had felt the nights soon after he became an orphan. The rawness in his throat. The crushing loneliness in his heart.

Finally, he knocked on the door. "Elena?"

The noise stopped. He pressed his ear against the dark wood, listening. She did not reply, but she also did not tell him to leave.

He cracked open the door and peeked in. She was lying on her side, her back to him. She did not turn as he sat down on the edge of the bed. He felt her grief; it was as palpable in the dark as a thick, humid night. And he also knew he could not alleviate it. It was a pain that only the bearer could hold, a pain that only the bearer could endure.

The sheets rustled as Elena slid her hand across the bed, her face still turned away.

Without saying a word, he took her hand and squeezed. Her fingers curled in his.

He would stay here all night.

He would stay for as long as she needed.

CHAPTER 39

ELENA

The land is in your blood,
Your blood is in the land.
God above, earth below,
And your life in between.
—from the ancient scrolls of the first priests of the Fire Order

Elena woke and did not recognize the room she was in. Her eyes were raw and her body ached. Panic, quick and sharp, razored down her throat, and she began to rise when she felt an arm warm around her waist.

Yassen lay curled beside her, fast asleep.

At this, she sighed in relief. Smiled. *Never pegged him as a drooler.* Carefully, Elena began to pull away when she hesitated.

He had come in during the night, when she had felt so debilitatingly crushed. He had not said a word, but his presence alone had brought her comfort, like a fire in a cold, dark room. Slowly, Elena lay back.

Just for another minute, she thought. She listened to the sound of his breathing, found herself matching her own breath to his to calm her racing heart.

Just another minute.

This time, it was Yassen who woke her up.

"Mmm," she murmured.

She opened her eyes to see him standing over her, holding a tray of tea.

"Morning," he said. He smiled as she wiped her lips. "You were drooling on your pillow."

"No, you were—" she began and stopped. *I must have fallen asleep again.* Had Yassen then woken up to find her curled up so close to him? *Oh, Mother's Gold.* She felt herself blush, turned away. "J-just leave it here."

"I found these in the cupboard," he said, pointing to the folded clothes on the edge of the bed. "My mother's. I think they might be too short for you but—"

"It'll do," she said, interrupting him. She felt her puffy face, felt the dried spit on the corner of her mouth as Yassen watched, amused. *Holy Bird Above, I must look like a mess.* "I'll change."

"Maybe a bath first," Yassen said. "I've already run it for you."

"Are you saying I stink?"

"You said that, not me." He grinned, and despite herself, Elena returned it.

When he left, Elena rose and discarded her old clothes. The water was a tad cold, but she didn't mind. She rubbed her skin clean with an old bar of soap, trying her best to get rid of the dirt and knots in her hair. Afterward, she picked up the new clothes, and as she shook them out, she caught a scent, strikingly familiar. She sniffed the kurta. It smelled of sandalwood—of the desert. She carefully pulled on the kurta and trousers, and though they were too short, Elena felt a strange comfort.

Before the small vanity mirror, she began to dry her hair, the curls limp and frizzed in her hand. She remembered how Ferma would sometimes oil her hair, braid it herself. And that memory, so sudden, so quick, froze Elena. She felt that wave of grief, black and vicious, threatening to wash and drown her like it had last night.

With trembling hands, Elena pushed back her hair. *Stop it,* she told herself. *She wouldn't want you grieving like this.* The room suddenly felt too large, too empty. Elena got up quickly, heart hammering. Yassen, she needed Yassen.

She found him in the kitchen, studying the map.

"Do you know which tunnel we'll take?" she said, keeping the quiver from her voice.

"Yes," he said and froze when he saw her.

"What?" she said.

"Just," he began and stopped. "Your hair. I've never seen it undone."

"I didn't have the strength to braid it," she said, and it was true.

"You don't need to," Yassen said. After a moment, he added, "It still looks beautiful."

She raised an eyebrow, surprised. And slightly flustered. Yassen seemed to be as well, because he quickly pointed to the map.

"It's, ah, it's this tunnel," he said quickly.

Despite herself, Elena smiled. She drew closer as Yassen highlighted a path.

"We're here. These tunnels skirt the mines and lead to Samson's base." He pointed at the black dot above a crisscross of red lines. "I say we rest for a day, maybe two, and then start heading toward the Black Scales."

"Why are some of the tunnels marked in red?"

"Samson said these were inaccessible, or just haven't been explored recently enough to know. But." Yassen paused, eyebrows crinkling. "I was thinking about what you said. You're right. I have a feeling Samson wanted me to come here." He stopped, abruptly. Grief, quick like a spider, skittered across his face.

Elena lightly placed her hand on his. He turned his palm, curling his fingers around hers.

"He said that there were some tunnels Farin knew about, some he didn't," Yassen continued after a moment, his voice tight. "I have a feeling Samson marked these red to mislead the metal king."

"Do you think they lead to the deposit he is so desperate to find?" she asked, voice soft.

Yassen shook his head. "I don't care to find out."

There was a brittle edge to his voice. Elena pulled her hand away, remembered his darkened expression in the train. *If we carry the burdens of our fathers, we'll never know what it means to be free.*

"Yassen," she began.

"Did Samson really want me to be free?" he asked, as if reading her thoughts. The edge was gone, replaced by a fragile tremor. "Or did he plan to use me to find the new ore?"

Yes, she wanted to say but could not. Samson Kytuu may have been her fiancé, full of charm and sweet words but also ambition. Anger of his own. She remembered their dance when he had looked at her and asked, *Just yours?* The unease she had felt. They did not know his secrets, and perhaps they never would. He had taken them to his grave, and they could not hate him for it.

"He loved you, you know," Elena said. She remembered how Samson had stared at Yassen when he had found them together below the arena. The longing in his eyes. "Sometimes we use the ones we love."

"For better or for worse, right?" he said, his smile grim.

"Yes," she said in a hushed voice.

"But that's love, isn't it?" Yassen said. "To be willing to be used. Again and again, because we can't stop. Because it would be torture to be without them."

He was looking at her, watching her, and Elena felt heat rush through her, as if there was something else he meant beneath his words.

The moment shattered as a sudden drone filled the cabin. She whipped around.

"Easy, easy," Yassen said, touching her arm. "It's just the mines. They're starting work."

Elena glanced out the window. The cabin quivered, ever so slightly, the windows rattling in their frames.

"Phoenix Above," she muttered. "And you would hear this all day?"

"All the fucking time," he muttered.

Elena considered for a moment, looking between Yassen and the map. "Are there tunnels between here and the mines?"

"None," he said.

She drummed her fingers against the counter, thinking. The soldiers would be here soon, which meant their window of time was short. Really short. She eyed Yassen, picking her words carefully.

"You've seen the metal transports before. What are they like? How long does it usually take?"

"Depends," Yassen said. "If this load is as big as the merchants told us, it'll likely take them a few days. They'll need to be extra careful. The raw ore is highly combustible."

"So no pulse guns, then," she said.

Yassen shook his head. "They'll have them, but they won't use them.

I bet if anything, they'll use bullets. But we aren't going anywhere near them, right?" When she did not respond, Yassen touched her elbow. "Right?"

Elena gazed at the holo. What was it that the merchant said?

There's been talk of brushfire. There was one on the other side of the mountain last week that got the soldiers jumping.

She looked down at her hands. She had no army, no slingswords or pulse guns, but she did have her inferno. It thrummed in her veins.

"If the forest is already dry," she began, considering, "then we can start a wildfire. Make it seem like an accident."

Yassen said nothing, merely watched her as she zoomed in to the silver dots indicating the mines on the map.

"This one is the closest. About ten miles east. They've probably cleared the trees around the rig, but if I start the fire half a mile or so away in the forest, it'll catch. I can make it catch and push it toward the mines. Toward the ore." She searched Yassen's face, but still he said nothing.

"Yassen," she began.

"It's too risky," he said. "Sure, you can blow this rig. But there are two more, and we don't have time to get all three. The Arohassin know you're not confirmed dead, which means the Jantari know you're not dead. Cian saw us. Farin's men are probably already on their way to the Sona Range. They could be here any day."

Elena bit her lip. He was right, damn it, he was right. Every day they spent on this mountain was a risk. But she could not forget the screams of the Ravani guards. The echo of pulse fire in the mountains. The thundering feet of the Jantari army as they marched through her desert.

"It can be done, Yassen," she said. "You've seen how fast fire moves. It will spread, and when the smoke finally clears, we'll be long gone."

"And what about the town?" Yassen said. "If the rigs explode, there could be a landslide. It could crush a part of the town."

"Don't you think I considered that?"

She remembered the old man who had sold them their furs, the woman who had rented them their brenni. These people had no role in the war, yet they would suffer.

She ran her hands through her hair, staring at the holo as if it could suddenly produce the right answers. The drone outside grew louder. The windows rattled in their frames, but Elena felt a rattle in her chest, felt the crush of the mountain as if it were already crumbling, already falling onto sleeping homes.

"Hey, hey," Yassen said and stroked her back as she hunched over on the counter. "I didn't mean it to upset you."

She closed her eyes, took a deep breath. But she tasted ash on her tongue, and suddenly she was back in the temple, watching her father fall into the Eternal Fire. She saw the fear on his face. The flail of his hands as he tried to grab her. Heard his scream.

If we carry the burdens of our fathers, we'll never know what it means to be free.

No one understood her burden, not Yassen, not Samson, not even Ferma. The only one who had truly known it had been burned alive, crying out for her.

Elena gripped the counter, her breath hot and ragged in her throat.

No one will understand what it takes to rule the throne. Not like you. So even if you take our advice, you must think for the kingdom.

Her kingdom was burning. And the people who had done it were now coming to this mountain, taking the very ore that would become weapons used against her Ravani.

How could she sit here silent and afraid?

"I—I need air," Elena said.

Yassen began to follow her, but she waved him away.

"I'm all right, I just—" She paused at the door. "I just need to be alone."

He stood awkwardly in the empty room, and she saw his hands twitch as if he meant to reach for her. But Yassen stopped.

"I'll be here," he said. "No matter what. Just... don't wander far."

She smiled sadly. "For better or for worse, you're stuck with me, and I to you, remember?"

He said nothing in response. But as Elena walked down the porch steps and looked back, she saw him through the window, at the counter, studying the map.

In the shade of the retherin pines, Elena rolled back her shoulders and widened her stance. She had carefully brushed away the dry leaves, creating a small clearing. Her visor itched against her forehead, but she did not take it off.

She raised her arms, extending her right hand in front, her left hand behind. The wound on her shoulder still smarted, but after Yassen had applied the skorrir balm, the pain had lessened.

With a deep breath, Elena sank her weight into her heels and breathed out.

A flame unfurled in her outstretched palm like a bird hatching from its shell.

The Warrior.

Elena watched the flame, breathing slowly. She felt the tension in her chest ease as she meditated on the flame, studying its form, feeling its intense heat.

She pivoted and kicked up her left leg, balancing on her right foot as she folded her arms behind her like the Desert Sparrow. The flame sighed and kissed her fingertips. She could feel its pulse, its desire to live. As she flowed into the Lotus, the Spider, and then the Tree, the flame grew and danced with her in her hand.

When she had burned down her room, the fire had burst from her fingertips like a sandstorm on a summer day. Sudden and destructive. Its power had surged through her body like an electric shock. She had used her anger to call it, to punch a hole in the world, and it had responded in kind.

But as Elena unwound from the Snake and once more extended her arms, she could feel the fire's energy coursing through her with a quiet, controlled hum. It followed her without hesitation, bent to her will.

Elena drew the flame close to her chest. It bowed, folding into itself. Slowly, she brought her palms together, and the flame's heat spread down her arms and across her shoulders like wings coming to rest.

She studied the small blaze. How could something so little cause so much destruction? So much pain?

The inferno that had burned the temple and her father had also been full of rage. Vicious and sharp, like a beast tearing through flesh.

And I am to do the same, on this mountain, she thought. But the fire pulsated in her palms, brushing her fingertips. It filled her with a heady heat, warming her limbs.

Elena thought of her father. He had carried the burden of the kingdom for so long. It had driven him to burn the priests, to imprison Saayna. It was unforgivable, cruel and twisted. But as Elena balanced the flame in her hand, heard it whisper, she thought she finally understood him.

You must be ruthless. If you must become a villain, become one. Become whatever Ravence demands, because without you, it will die.

"Everything I do, I do for Ravence. For you," she whispered, echoing him.

The fire sparked in her hand as if in reply.

The realization set heavily in her chest, binding her. When Samson had asked her how far she was willing to go, she had told him far enough to protect her kingdom. But she was wrong.

The burden of the throne, the burden of the Phoenix King, was more than simply protecting her kingdom.

It meant giving up herself. Her conscience, her peace, her very being.

The flame wrapped around her wrist like a bracelet. Like a chain.

Burning the mountain wasn't right. She knew that.

But it was necessary. So she would.

CHAPTER 40

YASSEN

Rest thy weary head, wanderer,
for you have found the honey of life—freedom.
—from The Odyssey of Goromount: A Play

Yassen watched Elena disappear out of view. He had half a mind to go after her, to watch her, but he had seen the look on her face. If she wanted to be alone, he would grant her that.

Sighing, he studied the map. The closest mine was ten miles from them, the farthest about fifteen. Even if they managed to hit the closer one, the other two mines would still be in production. The ore could still be extracted, although at a slower rate.

But Yassen remembered the pride in the handler's voice, the excitement in the merchant's. If the miners had truly extracted enough ore for Farin to celebrate, then Ravence and whatever leftover rebellion would not stand a chance. It was already crumbling. Jantar's new weapons would be the final strike.

He didn't blame Elena for her anguish. Their home was burning, and she could do nothing about it.

If the Arohassin had tasked him to destroy these mines, Yassen would have done a full recon. Scouted the terrain, studied the extraction sequences. But they didn't have time for that. The soldiers would be on this mountain soon.

And the Arohassin, he thought, and that worried him more.

They would have caught on to his betrayal by now. Though Akaros did not know about this cabin, he would put it together eventually.

Samson had been able to shake off the Arohassin because he had joined the Jantari army. He sold secrets and tactical information for higher protection. He and Elena had no army, no protection. Even if they reached the Black Scales in one piece, Samson was not there to lead them.

Yassen sighed and closed the holo.

The mountains lay quiet, and for a brief moment, Yassen saw them for what they really were: giant, intimidating, and gentle. He saw the tall pines rake the pale morning sky. A mountain lark flitted between the canopies, calling.

He had always loved their songs as a boy. When he came to the cabin with his parents, the first thing he would do was run into the trees, armed with a seeing glass, and find a quiet spot. There, he'd watch the treetops for the telltale flutter of blue and listen for the bird's two- or three-note song. Afterward, when he and his mother returned to Ravence and his father to the mines, Yassen would play the birdsong on the piano, relying on memory to find the right notes that captured their voices. No matter how hard he tried, it had never been quite the same.

As the mountain lark called again, he began to hum a song, a ghost of a melody. He could not remember the lyrics—or even the song's name. He only remembered that the tune belonged to an old Sayonai ballad about lovers so morose they became the moons. A melancholy song, yet familiar and warm.

Yassen decided he would tidy up and then go find Elena. He had just gathered her empty teacup when his right arm seized. His muscles locked with such excruciating intensity that he stumbled.

He rested his head against the counter, breathing in deeply. Focusing on the cool touch of stone against his forehead.

One, two, three, four, five . . .

When the pain finally passed enough for him to lift his arm, Yassen pulled back the sleeve.

The sight frightened him. His right hand had entirely blackened, and the skin below his wrist was mottled with angry patches of red and orange.

Yassen rose slowly, swaying. The cabin was eerily quiet, and he stood there for a moment, taking in how sunlight slanted in through the windows and dusted the frayed Ravani rug.

When he felt steady enough to walk, he went to the closet in the hallway and pulled out his father's surgical kit. Injuries were common in the mines.

Yassen pulled off his shirt in the bathroom, breathing in sharply as he took stock of the whole arm. The cuts on his upper arm had become infected and swollen. Dried dirt caked the raised grooves of his skin. Carefully, he drew a bath and began to wash. After drying and wrapping a towel around his waist, Yassen pulled a small towel off the rack and balled it into his mouth. Then, soaking a cloth with the whiskey his father stored beneath the bathroom sink, he began.

Every time he touched his bruised skin, Yassen wanted to scream. Tears pricked his eyes. His toes curled as he slowly washed away the grime. Drops of murky brown blood dripped into the sink. The towel in his mouth became sodden. Yassen spat it out, grabbed a clean one, and shoved it in. When he was done cleaning, he grabbed a needle and surgical thread. He poured whiskey over them and a particularly deep gash in his forearm before inserting the needle.

Yassen nearly fainted. His knees went weak, and he slumped forward.

Come on, he urged himself. *Come on.*

He blinked fiercely and carefully threaded the needle. His fingers trembled as he stitched, but whenever he got too dizzy, Yassen thought of the journey ahead of him, the work that had to be done, and he found the fortitude to continue.

He was trying to snip off the excess thread when the bathroom door opened. Elena stood in the doorway, her eyes wide. Her gaze first fell on the towel wrapped around his waist, then to the kit balanced on the counter.

"*What* are you doing?"

"Mhhm mm," he said through the towel in his mouth.

"What?"

He pulled it out, gasping. "Can't you see?"

"Sit down," she commanded, and when he didn't move, she placed her hand on his left shoulder, forcing him down.

She took the forceps and needle.

"You're a stubborn idiot. You know that?" she said as she cleaned her hands. She examined his arm, but there was no disgust in her eyes, only a resolute sternness, like the steady gaze of a medic.

"How many people have you stitched up?" he asked.

"Few, but enough. Ferma made me volunteer at an army hospital on the southern border," she muttered as she threaded a new needle.

"Really?" He gasped as she pierced his skin, jerking his arm back, but Elena held him firmly, her hands sure and steady.

"Quit squirming," she said, handing him the bottle of whiskey, "and drink."

Yassen hesitated. He never drank. But the pain in his arm made him toss back his head and take a long swig. A mistake. The whiskey burned his throat and his nose. Yassen coughed as Elena knotted the thread.

"Easy there, yeseri," she said.

She was so close to him that he could feel her breath on his skin, see the scratches on her forearms and neck from her fall in the Agnee mountains. He wanted her to sit. For him to clean and dress her wounds. The ones on her skin, and the ones that went deeper.

"Elena," he began.

"Mm?" Her eyebrows were furrowed in concentration, but when she felt his gaze, she looked up. Locked eyes.

He stilled, breath caught somewhere between his chest and throat.

Damn her eyes.

They seemed to hold some power over him, some intoxication that made him want to draw closer, to hold her, to take her arms and kiss the pain that she carried.

"Thank you," she said, her voice low, her breath brushing his lips.

"For what?"

"Last night," she said and looked away. "For staying."

She opened her mouth to speak again, but no sound came out.

"It's all right," he said gently. "Grief is like that."

She looked at him, her eyes bright with tears and a tremulous smile tugging her lips. "There's a song that begins that way," she said. "'Grief is like that, my love, but the stars are here, and they will lend us their eyes.'"

"'So that we may gaze upon each other when we are apart,'" he finished. It was the same song he had been humming earlier.

He began to hum it now as Elena smiled, picking up the needle again.

"Keep going," she said as she threaded.

She worked quickly, her hands gentle yet firm, and despite the pain, Yassen found himself continuing the song.

If only to hum it for her.

"There," she said after a while. She stepped back, surveying her work. "That should patch you up for the next few days."

His forehead was damp with sweat. His arm smelled like whiskey, and he had a sour taste in his mouth, but the stitches were neat, clean. They would prevent further infection.

Hopefully long enough for us to reach the Black Scales.

Elena closed the kit and leaned against the doorframe, crossing her arms. She was silent, and he could feel the weight of her gaze. When she finally spoke, her voice was resolute.

"When I took the crown, I swore an oath. To protect Ravence, no matter the cost." The walls reverberated as the mines began drilling again, and Elena straightened. There was a resolve in her eyes that he had not seen before.

"I don't expect you to agree with that cost. It's mine. I'll bear it. But." She paused, looking out the window. "The war's already begun, Yassen. And if I don't do something now, we'll lose it before we even had a fighting chance."

Yassen stood, blood beating in his ears as he reached for his shirt. It was limp with dirt and sand from the desert.

"The closet," he muttered and slid past Elena in the doorway, trying to ignore the heat of her gaze.

In the hallway closet, he found his father's old shirts folded neatly into two stacks. He shook one out. The fabric was worn and soft and it smelled of iron and pine, just like Erwin.

As he donned it, Elena moved past him, to the kitchen. She was already brewing another pot of tea when he joined her.

"It fits perfectly," she said.

He sank down in a seat at the table. Wisps of steam danced in the air as

Elena drew her knees to her chest. She said nothing, and he knew she was waiting for an answer.

The holopod sat between them, like before. He could open the map. Show the routes, the holes, show how ridiculous and impossible the task was.

But when Yassen met her eyes, he could not bring himself to voice those thoughts. Because she was right.

If they did nothing now, Ravence would be lost. Gutted, ravished, the desert trampled underneath the feet of soldiers who did not understand the dunes in the way he did. The way Elena did.

"It's just impossible," he said finally.

"A few weeks before, I thought it would be impossible to wield fire." She smiled ruefully. "But here we are."

He shook his head. "The Arohassin will track us through the tunnels. They'll find this cabin."

"Yassen," she said, taking his hand. "You know the tunnels better than anyone else. Better than them."

No, he wanted to correct her. He didn't know the tunnels better than anyone else. That had been his father.

Erwin Knight had been a man of few words. He was tall and strong, built like an ox with deep-set, colorless eyes. Yet, when he laughed, it was as if warmth suddenly filled the room, spreading across Yassen's chest.

Yassen would count down the days until he returned to the cabin, but it had been different for his mother. She would lapse into long stretches of muted silence after their visits. In what would be their last trip to the Sona Range, she had stayed in bed with a headache while he and his father set off to hunt. When they had returned, she was still in bed. Wordless. It was as if she had known that his father had told him of his discovery.

A metal so fine it could cut through steel.

"You're filling that boy's head with fantasies, and yours too," his mother had said later that night to Erwin.

"But if I tell the king about the ore, my rani, then we'll be rewarded. Our boy won't grow up poor. He won't be like us."

Yet, Yassen had become like his father. Erwin had taught him how to shoot, how to listen for the warning note in a morning lark's song, how to slow his heartbeat to near stillness as they waited for a stag. Erwin had taught him how to survive.

I'm here, he wanted to say. *Look at me for what I am.*

"It doesn't matter," he said finally. "Even with my knowledge and with your fire, we could get caught. The Arohassin know you can control the flames. What would they think if a fire suddenly burned down a mine, days after the Ravani queen was spotted by the Jantari border?"

She sat back, as if considering this. Two mountain larks took to the sky in a burst of wings. Yassen watched them flutter by the window.

"Why did you join the Arohassin?" she asked suddenly. The directness of her question took him aback.

"You've read my holo."

"I want to hear it from you."

"I—" he began and looked around. He felt a sudden change in the room, a drop in temperature as the ghosts grew nearer.

"I—" he said again. The words felt heavy, yet there they sat, right within his grasp. Memories of the house fire and his mother's burnt body flitted in his mind.

"I was an orphan," he said finally. "My parents were both dead, and I had no one else. The streets of Ravence aren't kind to urchins. The Arohassin seemed kinder. At least they had hot food and a bed."

"So you joined because you were hungry?" she asked, though her voice was curious rather than judgmental.

He shot her a look. "Hungry, lonely, scared, angry. I didn't know who they really were, not at first. They gave us odd jobs like deliver a holopod to someone or keep watch on some corner. It took my mind off things," he said, and he saw the ghosts flicker.

"Samson told me about the training they gave you," she said. "About the prisoners."

When he said nothing, she continued. "He told me you shot your man, and he didn't. He said it changed you."

"They knew what I was," Yassen said bitterly. Unlike the other recruits, Yassen could walk through Jantar without raising an eyebrow. So, they sent him abroad. Ordered him to stake out certain Ravani officials conducting business in the neighboring kingdom. Eventually, the corner watches had evolved into tracking a man in a crowd and reporting his whereabouts. Hot food turned into money if he could find a traitor. A warm bed twisted into long sermons about power and the decaying foundation of divine rule. At first Yassen had regarded those sermons with aloofness, listening only because he was forced to. But when they had placed a gun in his hand . . . He remembered lying beneath neverwood bushes with his father. Stilling his breath. Watching dew form on the tips of grass as they waited for the stag. "Akaros said if we didn't shoot, he would kill us."

With his left arm, he pulled his gun from his waistband and set it on the table. The silver barrel glinted.

"They taught us how to shut off parts of ourselves, to lock emotions in a room and leave them there. I didn't care what I did. I just wanted to forget the pain of losing my family."

"And you felt no remorse?"

"I did. All the time. It made me hate myself," he said. He did not know why he was talking so much. Maybe it was the whiskey, but he could feel a growing pressure in his chest, an urge to let it all tumble out. The house of emotions he had built was crumbling as if sucked in by quicksand. "So I worked harder. I trained, I fought, I meditated. I even let Akaros starve me just so I could block out the world. And they loved me for it. I became the best because I refused to give in to regret. Nothing fazed me. Fear passed through me but could not linger. I was master of myself.

"Akaros told Sam and me that we were different—more alert than the others, cleverer. I don't know if that was true, but it worked. I felt I finally had someone who saw me. Who taught me—I thought—to be strong."

"So why did you leave with me?"

Yassen stopped, staring at her. He felt the air leave his chest.

The memory came back to him, slowly, painfully. The Verani king screaming. The flame leaping onto his arm, tearing through his flesh. It was as if the heat of the sun was trapped within his body, ensnaring him with fiery red whips.

The Arohassin had found him floating far out at sea. For three weeks, he slipped in and out of consciousness, and the memory of his recovery had blurred around the edges. But the fire. Yassen could not forget it.

"When I got burned, it was as if something beat all the fog and numbness out of me until only I remained. No training, no walls, just me. And I couldn't face myself." He looked down at his arm. It had become a constant reminder of that night. "But then I met you. Saw the way you fought against the gold caps. Against your father. Even me, right now, for those fucking mines. And I know you would do it again, if it meant you could help Ravence have a fighting chance."

He paused and met her gaze.

"You showed me what it's like to live for something more. Beyond myself, my desires. That's why I took that oath for you. Because I," he said, his breath catching in his chest as she leaned closer.

Because I would live for you.

"I've never felt like I've fit in," he said, voice soft. He had never said this to anyone, but here before Elena, he felt as if he could tell her his truth. "In Ravence, I was the strange, foreign-eyed orphan. In Jantar, I was the boy with an accent. With the Arohassin, I was constantly moving. Changing identities. But in the desert, you saw me for what I was. And I see you for what you are. You make me feel like, for once, I belong somewhere. Even if it's by your side. Trying to get you somewhere safe."

"It's funny," she said, "because when I'm with *you*, I feel safe."

Elena carefully uncurled his fingers so his palm lay flat. He glanced at her. There were specks of gold in her eyes. A trick of the light maybe, or a quality of a Ravani royal.

"You're free now," she said. "Yet you remain here with me. Surely, you will find some forgiveness for yourself, Yassen."

Free. What an awful word. Yassen had resented it because he had never known it, not truly, yet now the soft light in the cabin and the song of the mountain larks told him otherwise.

Their chorus spread through the morning sky, filling the treetops with joy.

They sang three notes.

No danger—just expanse.

CHAPTER 41

ELENA

Upon seeing the Holy Fire, one cannot help but kneel in reverence. For here in Sayon, we have been blessed with the gift of the gods. Fire is the mainstay of civilization. If it perishes, so shall we.

—from the ancient scrolls of the first
priests of the Fire Order

The tunnel entrance should be here, somewhere," Yassen said.

They walked through the forest, leaves crunching underneath their boots. Elena shivered, despite the heat. The woods were eerily quiet, with a scattering of birdsong, but Yassen did not seem to mind the silence.

His hand was on his hip, above his gun, but Elena noticed a lightness in his step. He was humming again, softly to himself. She glanced around, but she spotted no soldiers, no assassins lying in wait. She did not have the heart to tell him to stop.

Elena caught his gaze, and a small smile played across his lips.

"What?" he said.

"Nothing," she said, but in truth, she could not make sense of what she felt. Of what to make of him, this man who had betrayed her, saved her, and revealed himself to her. Who knew both hardness and mercy. Who made her chest constrict and yet also ease whenever he came near.

"How much farther?" she asked, recovering her voice.

"Not far." He pointed to the right, toward a cropping of thick pines. "There's an entrance just below one of those trees."

"Who built it?"

He shrugged. "They used to be mining tunnels, but now they're barely used. I remember my father saying that they surveyed this part of the mountain for ore, but then they found the deposit farther down the range."

"Was there a rig here?" She looked around, studying the forest. The trees were thick, heavy with leaves. It seemed impossible that an ugly metal contraption had once towered over them, blocking the sun.

"They never got around to it," he said. "Come on."

They stopped before a cropping of pines. One was taller than the rest, skinnier too. Bark flaked off the trunk in patches, and Elena could see the pale, fragile skin underneath.

"It's dying," she said.

"And it'll protect the entrance with its last breath," Yassen muttered as he studied the roots. He knelt slowly, and then pointed to a knot bigger than her fist. "See that? See how it's larger than the rest?"

Elena studied the other roots. They were knobby and thick, but he was right. This knot was different than the rest.

"Why did they hide the entrances like this?" she asked.

"To hide the mines from any raiders and thieves," he said.

As Elena moved to kneel, her foot slipped on the root and she lost her balance. Yassen reached out to grab her, and she fell into him. They landed in a tangle of limbs and leaves.

"Sorry, sorry," she said.

But then Yassen laughed. It was a clear sound, throaty and sweet, and she could feel his chest reverberate with it where her shoulder kissed his skin. She found herself smiling. Laughing with him.

She began to sit up and reached out an arm to help him. He grabbed her hand and pulled her back. Elena stilled. His face was inches from hers, and his eyes watched her, held her, and she could not break away.

He touched her cheek.

"If the Arohassin or the Jantari find us on this mountain, I want you to come here," he said. His voice was soft yet urgent. "Press this knot, and the tunnel will open."

She nodded, slowly. "And you'll come with me. Right?"

"I'll be right behind you," he said.

As they made their way back up the hill to the cabin, a sudden drone filled the mountain. Elena froze. Yassen drew his gun, and they watched, hearts leaping in their throats, as the silver hull of a hoverpod grazed over the trees in the distance. It was heading toward the mines.

"Mother's Gold," she whispered.

Yassen turned. There was a stricken look in his eyes.

"They've already come for the ore," she said.

"They still don't know we're here," he said.

But she did not hear him. She could already see it, the metal lifted from the mountain. Heading to Jantar's factories, where it would be melted lightning quick into zeemirs, long-range guns, *Phoenix Above, into those damn metal tanks.* Fear spidered down her throat, thick and hairy.

Have we already lost? she thought. *Will Ravence ever be saved?*

And then she heard Yassen, heard him repeat, *They still don't know we're here.*

"You're right," she said, and she felt the heat of her inferno, the weight of its burden sink into her chest. "They don't know. So we still have a chance."

"Elena."

She hurried into the cabin. The holopod wasn't on the kitchen counter. She rushed into the bathroom, the bedroom, found it on the bedside table.

"Summon the map," she said as Yassen entered the room.

Yassen hesitated, standing in the doorway. "Press your thumb against it."

She looked at him in confusion, but when she pressed her thumb to the pod, it opened. "How?"

"I programmed it for you," Yassen said, and there was a tired acceptance in his voice. He looked at her. "I know you won't sit still."

She went to him. "I know it's dangerous. But we *must* do something, Yassen."

He did not say anything, but she saw the war on his face. The lines between his brows that appeared when he was thinking hard. The tightness of his lips. She saw him as well as he saw her.

He pushed past her, walking to the window. Beside it, two wooden shelves lined the wall. They were bare except for one holo, frozen in a crystal like a traditional photograph.

She had not noticed it last night, lost as she was in her grief. But now she approached the shelf and studied the image. There was a tall, burly man with straight, pale hair combed neatly to the side. Next to him stood a small woman with desert-black hair and kind brown eyes. She had a gentle smile, and that alone seemed to balance the man's stern expression. Between them stood a small boy, perhaps six suns. He had the same pale hair and eyes as the father, but his smile was that of his mother: soft and easy, uninhibited by the demands of the world. The boy seemed to lean away from the man, as if to shirk his influence, but Elena recognized the similarities in their posture, the clarity in their eyes.

She lifted the crystal and brought it closer. Though the boy stood nearer to the woman, he was more of the father than the mother.

"I'd forgotten about that picture."

Elena turned to see the boy in the crystal, watching her. Except he was older now, stronger, and more haggard.

"When was this taken?" she asked.

"The summer before my father died," Yassen said.

"You have your mother's smile."

"Some would say so," he said. "I wish she and Father were here now. A queen in their cabin! Me, bickering with her." He gave her a small smile. "They would've been beside themselves."

She glanced at him. "I think they would've been more excited to see you come home."

She noticed a slight tremor in his hand as he took the crystal and set it back down. She touched his elbow.

"The mines," she began.

"Elena," he sighed. "It's dangerous."

"I know," she said quietly. She felt the thrum of fire in her veins, heard its whisper. "And if we do it, we'd explode the mines. Start wildfires. Endanger the town. But," she said, forcing her voice to stay steady and sound strong even though her stomach twisted into a knot, "if we don't, if we simply pass beneath those tunnels and run, then hundreds, thousands of Ravani will die. Maybe not today, but in a week's time. A month. A sun. Ravence will become the new Seshar, Yassen, and then where will we run?"

He said nothing, and she stepped closer.

"You don't have to go. You don't have to follow me," she said, even though the idea of leaving him broke something in her. He'd sworn himself to her, taken the Desert Oath, but she could release him from it. Ravence had failed him, and she owed him his freedom. He *deserved* his freedom.

But Yassen stepped closer.

"I go where you go," he whispered.

He drew her into his arms, and she pressed her face into his neck, breathing in his smell of ash and fresh mountain air. Felt the thrum of his heart beneath her cheek. They held each other for a long time, drinking in each other's warmth. And somewhere in that black ether of anguish, Elena felt a sliver of solace. Of all people, he understood her grief. How could she ever let him go?

When they parted, Yassen stepped back.

"Shall we—" he began.

She stood on her toes and kissed him.

His lips were warm, sweet. He tasted of spice and honey, of the desert and the mountain. He tasted of home.

"I see you," she whispered and met his eyes.

At this, he smiled. It was small, but genuine, kind, and it made her bloom to think that she could make him smile. That this smile, the one he gave her now, was hers and hers alone.

He touched his forehead against hers. Sunlight spilled onto them, and Yassen cupped their hands as if to catch the light and keep it between them.

"And I see you," he whispered.

She gently took the sunlight in her hand and cupped his face. With his eyes still on hers, Yassen kissed her wrist.

"I see you," he said.

Kissed the inside of her arm. "I see you."

Down her elbow, up her shoulder, until she felt his breath brush her neck and his hot lips against her collarbone. "I see you."

He drew her to the bed, and she gasped, digging her fingers in his hair as he moved down her chest, her breasts, rolling up her shirt as he kissed the soft skin of her stomach. Up he traveled again until it was he who pressed sunlight to her face, his lips a breath away from hers.

"And I give myself, utterly and completely, to you," he said.

He kissed her, a kiss that seemed to send an electric shock through her body as he slowly peeled off their clothes, bit the insides of her thighs.

"Yassen," she moaned, breathless. He drew her into his lap, and she locked her legs around him, running her hands across his shoulders, down the arm she had tended. When she moved her hips against his, he shuddered into her neck.

"Fuck, Elena," he groaned.

Elena bucked, flipping them so he was on his back and she was straddling him. Yassen looked up, surprised. A slow grin spread on his face as she traced the wide span of his chest, the ridges of his stomach. She rocked her hips against his, and Yassen moaned. That sound itself threatened to undo her as Elena drove him into the bed, moving faster, deeper, their breaths hitching together, his hands clasping her waist, hers tangling in his hair. And when she gasped, verging on the brink, he held her closer. Kissed her scars as she touched his. Whispered sweet love into her ears as she trembled in his arms.

He took it—all the broken parts of her—and she forgot, for once, her burden, as if nothing in the world mattered, not Ravence or Jantar, but her, but them.

Elena curled into Yassen, her arm draped across his chest. She could feel his breath dance against her hair. His chest rose and fell in slow, steady beats, and she heard the song of his heart in her ear. She could just stay, wrapped in this bliss.

But as she saw the light gradually seep out of the room, Elena knew that was an impossible dream. People like her did not deserve bliss like this.

She tried to disentangle herself without waking Yassen, but he stirred against her.

"What are you doing?" he murmured sleepily.

"I have to go," she whispered.

"Why?"

She touched his cheek, tracing the arch of his eyebrows. He smelled of sandstone and musk.

"Dream well," she said softly.

He had told her that he would go where she went. But as Elena watched Yassen's eyes flutter, his face peaceful, she did not wake him. She wanted to spare him this. The first fall of the sword, the first counterattack of Ravence, would be hers and hers alone. If the mountain burned, it would be because she lit the match. She would bear the guilt—not him.

Elena waited until he fell back into deep sleep, and then she rose.

On the shelf, the crystal glimmered in the growing darkness. Though the Phoenix did not hear her prayers, Elena whispered one.

"Protect him," she told the ghosts.

She took his gun and tucked it into her waistband. As the cabin door shut with a soft click, a pang of regret cut through her chest. The twin moons hung heavily in the sky, as if swollen with the weight of what was to come. Her brenni snorted nervously as Elena tightened its girth. She mounted in one fluid motion, and then they set out into the forest.

Shadows stalked through the trees like the shards of a nightmare, cruel and unshapely. Despite herself, Elena shivered. The thick canopy blocked out the moons and any hope of light. A chill crept through the forest, dampening the foliage. Elena cursed as she passed the amethyst pine for the third time.

From her calculations, the rig was ten miles to the east. She had followed the path marked in Yassen's holopod, but the terrain was strange, unshapely. All her life, Elena had trained to survive in the desert, to withstand its harsh demands. But she did not know the ridges and curves of this forest, could not discern a shadow from a threat. Without the moons or the stars, she could not tell which direction she was heading.

I need to find higher ground.

Something stirred in the tree above her. Elena twisted in her saddle, yanking out the gun. A shadow darted through the branches, and she recognized the blue wings of a mountain lark. It sang three notes.

Elena relaxed but did not holster the weapon.

She nudged her steed to start up a slope, hoping to find higher ground. Her brenni panted, and Elena tried to lean forward in the saddle to ease its strain when she saw a glimmer of light.

She squinted but could not make out the source. Her brenni shuffled its feet anxiously.

"Easy," she whispered.

The light flickered. Elena realized then it was not merely a light but a reflected moonbeam. Given the angle, moonlight was bouncing off a smooth surface, which could only mean one thing. She was getting closer to the mine.

She went in the direction of the light, hoping that once she reached it, she could see where the rig stood. They trotted past glades of neverwood until they reached a clearing. Up ahead, the ground rose to form a steep hill. Elena jumped down and tied her brenni to a tree before creeping up the grade.

The rig sat in a clearing to the east like a giant parasite. It loomed over the treetops, stretching several hundred feet with a guard tower standing watch at each of its four legs. Unlike the rig she had seen earlier, this mine had not two, but several glass-armored chutes dissecting its length and descending into the depths of the mountain. Three hoverpods floated on the landing beside the mine. Elena spotted soldiers walking across the platform, their bodies lit by floating lanterns as carts were guided to the transport entrance of the mine.

They were already loading the hoverpods.

Elena bit her lip. Heat buzzed through her hands—but she would have no cover if she crept closer to the mine.

She set off once more, but instead of going straight to the edge of the forest, Elena steered her brenni south, toward the southernmost point of the rig. Neverwood branches clawed at her hair and clothes, but Elena paid them no mind. She stopped before a thick huddle of molorians with dry, wilted leaves.

Perfect.

She tied her brenni a safe distance away and stalked forward. Here, the forest crept closer to the mine. It towered above her, blocking the twin moons. Even from this distance, Elena could see the giant water tanks and the gleam of the glass chutes.

A guard post peeked through the treetops several yards to the right, and Elena saw a soldier patrolling it, his pulse gun glinting in the distance.

She slunk farther into the neverwoods. As the sound of the hoverpods echoed across the clearing, Elena began her dance.

Heat jolted up her arms. The intensity frightened her, and Elena stumbled back.

She tried to breathe, to calm her mind, but doubt wormed its way into her chest. The image of the sleepy town, hunkered within the mountain foothills, flitted before her. If she did this, she was no better than the Jantari. *Seven hells*, she was no better than even the Arohassin. They killed innocent people for their own gain. She was supposed to be the Golden Queen of Peace. But here she was, sparks flitting in her hands, fire on her tongue like the goddesses of lore, like the Burning Queen.

Be ruthless. Become whatever Ravence needs you to be.

Elena closed her eyes. She saw her father as he fell into the flames. The twisted, burned bodies of the palace guards on the temple steps. Blood on Ferma's chest. She saw it, and she let her fire bloom.

Sparks sizzled in her hands, and then a flame burst forth. Elena spun, flowing through the forms of the dance. She willed the flame to grow stronger, unwavering like the fire of the desert, like the fire of a Ravani.

The flame swayed, listening. It flared and hissed at the air. With a sharp jab, she hurled it onto the molorians.

The blaze sang and licked the base of the trees. The dry roots began to crackle, but they did not catch. Sweat beaded down her forehead. She could not doubt herself, not now; doubt would kill the flame. She could do this.

She had to.

Straining, Elena focused on the blaze growing taller. She stretched her hands, and the flame yawned. *Again.*

She thought of Ravence, of Leo, of the energy that had buzzed through her body when she had first wielded an inferno.

The flame lengthened.

She thought of Yassen and the way he had held her, the warmth of his embrace. The touch of his breath as he had whispered into her ear that he would follow her, no matter what.

The flame howled.

Elena stepped back and closed her eyes. She felt the hum of power, the song of fire, coursing through her body. She imagined it strengthening, solidifying as a spear flashed in her hand. Her eyes flickered. The flame danced, waiting.

With a cry, Elena released it.

It struck the canopy, the leaves immediately catching. The blaze at the base doubled and then tripled before leaping up the grove. Wood snapped, and Elena gasped.

Sweat drenched her face as she pulled the blaze higher, willing it to grow brighter, and soon the treetops were filled with flames. Smoke buffeted out, dispersed by a sudden wind. Elena spun, and her inferno roared at the heavens.

Alarms began to blare, alerting the soldiers. They were too late. Elena gritted her teeth, her arms shaking as she pushed the fire toward the rig. The flames tumbled and spat, growing louder, stronger. They reached the base of the mine, and then Elena fully let go.

The inferno raged on.

In the distance, soldiers stumbled out onto the guard post. She whirled around and sprinted back south where she had left her steed. Her brenni neighed in fright at the smoke writhing through the trees.

"It's okay. We're going," she said.

She swung onto its back and kicked hard. Her brenni shot into a gallop, and Elena clenched her thighs to hold on. The inferno grew behind them with an insatiable haste. The high-pitched wail of the alarms and the roar of the fire filled the air, but as they hurtled deeper into the forest, the sound grew fainter until Elena thought, rashly, that she had made it.

She began to slow her brenni to a canter when a mighty roar ripped through the heavens. The mine exploded with a blinding flash. The mountain heaved. Her brenni shrieked, losing its footing, and they tumbled to the ground. Elena fell out of her saddle. Pain, hot and fierce, ripped through her knee as she rolled to a stop beneath a molorian. She gasped, trembling. Her brenni nickered.

"It's all right," she called out. It stilled, listening to her voice. Slowly, Elena lurched back to her feet. Her ears rang. Blood trickled down from a cut on her forehead. But the ground did not rumble again. There was no landslide.

Smoke filtered through the trees, and Elena remembered, suddenly, the temple. The fire raging down the mountainside, the dying cry of soldiers.

She stumbled. Her hands shook, and her fingertips glowed like embers.

Burning Queen, the inferno sang.

And then she saw what the flames observed. She spotted flashes of metal shards, the spray of blood, a man sprinting away from the mine, his clothes afire.

Burning Queen.

The hoverpod's alarm wailed into the light as it tilted, flames tearing through its hull. It crashed into the mountain.

Burning Queen.

But then she saw another face in the flames, heard another voice.

Become whatever Ravence demands. Leo's face was frozen in shock, in pain.

She saw Ferma, her Ferma, falling.

She saw Samson, his blue eyes suddenly bright and glowing. He grabbed her hands, his voice filled with the song of fire.

How far are you willing to go?

Elena clenched her fists until they no longer trembled. She stood.

With a steady hand, she grabbed her brenni's bridle. It nickered but held still as she patted its mane. And as the smoke grew thicker, as the inferno's song grew louder, doubt and inhibitions fled from her mind until all she felt was the sweet, intoxicating, dangerous power rippling through her veins.

"I'll go far enough," she told the fire.

CHAPTER 42

YASSEN

To be forgiven, one must be burned.

—a Ravani proverb

Yassen awoke at dawn to the smell of smoke. It permeated the cabin, lining the floorboards, and when he saw the bed empty beside him, fear leapt up his throat. Had there been another attack? Had the Arohassin already taken Elena? He threw on his clothes, dashed out of bed, and stumbled down the porch stairs.

Elena's brenni was gone. With a groan, Yassen lifted his saddle with his left arm and threw it on his steed. It neighed, nostrils flaring. Yassen fumbled with the clasps of the girth. His fingers felt swollen, clumsy. He cursed. He tried to use his shoulder and lean against his brenni while he yanked up the girth, but the animal threw back its head in protest.

"Easy, easy," he said, but it backed away from him.

Just then, he heard hoofbeats.

Yassen turned as Elena tore up the hill. Soot coated her face, and her expression was grim, resolute. The pressure in his chest burst. As soon as she jumped down, he grabbed her and pulled her close.

"It's all right. I'm fine," she gasped.

She was alive. She was here. The Arohassin still hadn't found them.

"You idiot," he whispered into her ear. "You stupid, beautiful idiot."

She pressed her face into his neck, squeezing him hard for a moment, and then drew back.

"The mine exploded," she said.

"Did they see you?"

"Only smoke," she said.

But Yassen knew it would not be long. The Jantari might be tricked into believing it a forest fire, but the Arohassin wouldn't take it at face value. How could a forest fire spread so quickly, so close to a mine? If the Arohassin were here, they would come for them.

"Elena..." He shook his head. "Why did you go alone? Why didn't you wake me?"

Her smile was sad, pained. Early-morning light stole through the canopy, highlighting the dirt and ash in her hair. She touched his cheek.

"I got soot all over you," she said.

He leaned into her hand. "I'm just glad you're safe. But we must go. *Now.*"

"I need to finish what I've started, Yassen," she said, and there was a heaviness in her voice, an ache he had never heard before. Her eyes met his. "You saw the army. You saw what they're doing at the hovertrain stations. I have to spread the fire, just a little more. And then I can go."

"But the tunnels," he said, his voice dry. "If we blow up the other mines, they might collapse. How will we get to the Black Scales?"

"The new mining tunnels might collapse, but not the old ones," she said. Her eyes glimmered as she stepped closer. "You said it yourself—the red ones skirt around the mines. It's a chance I'm willing to take."

Yassen chewed his lip. A part of him screamed for him to turn and run. To leave.

But hadn't he been running all his life? From Ravence, Veran, Jantar, the Arohassin—himself?

"I—" he began. He looked to the sky, to the smoke that was eating the horizon.

She touched his hand, and he met her gaze. Her eyes looked even darker with ash coating her lashes.

"You don't have to stay," she said. "I free you from your oath, Yassen Knight. If you decide to leave, I'll honor that decision. If you stay—it'll be your choice."

Yassen looked down at her hand on his. Not long ago, she had vowed to kill him. But when he had revealed his betrayal, she had spared him.

He knew he was never destined for a quiet life. He had cursed himself ever since he had shot the poor prisoner. Time and time again, fate had given him crossroads; time and time again, he had allowed it to push him down a path of its choosing. All his life, Yassen had believed that his life was caught between edges because fate had demanded it be so. He believed that he had no freedom, no home. That one more job, one more kill, would finally bring him closer to those things.

But as Yassen looked at Elena and saw the burning conviction in her eyes, he realized that *he* had kept himself from peace by switching loyalties, countries, people. That if he left now, if he ran, he would never find it. His home was not a place. It was her.

And she was worth fighting for.

"Leave me, or"—Elena kissed her three fingers and placed them on his forehead—"fight with me."

He closed his eyes and leaned into her hand.

"So we the blessed few," he said. The words fell like stones that sealed his decision.

"So we the blessed few," she whispered back.

They pored over the map, memorizing the network of tunnels that snaked beneath the mountain. The two remaining mines lay fifteen miles north, high up on the ridgeline, separated by only two miles of forest.

"Why would they be so close?" Elena asked as she peered at the holo. She had washed the soot from her face with an old bar of jasmine soap but there was still a smudge beneath her ear. Yassen reached to wipe it off, and she turned, surprised.

"You missed a spot," he said.

She smiled and leaned into his hand.

It was the fragile calm before the storm, but Yassen wanted to stretch it like the twin moons had stretched the long night for Alabore. To remember the way she looked at him now, her eyes dark and liquid, and lock it forever in his heart.

"What is it, Knight?" she whispered, holding him in her gaze. "Are you getting cold feet?"

No, he wanted to say. *I just want this.*

Yassen withdrew his hand, turning back to the holo. "The deposit must be heavy up there, and that's why they need two mines." He pointed at the silver dots indicating the locations of the rigs, and the red tunnel farther down the ridgeline, about five miles south. "This is what we'll need to take. Once we blow up the first mine, the fire should spread to the second. We can escape before then."

Elena traced the tunnel, the shadows curving around her face, her lips. "And it won't collapse."

"It won't collapse," he repeated, hoping that saying so would make it true.

They departed as night fell. The trees and the smoke began to thin as they pushed farther north. Moonlight filtered through the forest, coating the pines in an eerie hush. Yassen slowed his brenni to a stop at a dry ravine filled with dead leaves. The old magazine bullets dug into his waist. He had found them in the hallway closet, underneath his father's hunting clothes.

"We're close," Yassen said as Elena drew up beside him. He could see the ridgeline peeking between the trees. It skirted around the mines and would lead them to their western border.

"If the soldiers start shooting, we run," he said, turning to her. Her face was hidden behind her scarf, but her eyes met his. "Understood?"

"Yes," she said.

Yassen took the lead as Elena followed. He held his gun against his thigh, his finger curling around the trigger. So far, they had encountered no soldiers nor assassins lying in wait. The forest was quiet save for the occasional scuttle of a rodent or the whispering of the wind.

His brenni grunted as it hopped over a fallen tree. Yassen stood up in his saddle and peered down through the heavy foliage. The cliff now rose above the trees, but he still couldn't spot the telltale glimmer of metal. Suddenly, Elena whistled. He turned to see that she had stopped and was pointing to a crop of pines.

There, partly hidden by the trees, lay a stone path. It snaked down the bluff, weaving between the pines for the forest beyond. As he joined her, he saw it.

A thin trail of smoke, glimmering from the north.

Elena stilled, her eyes alert, fingertips glowing.

"I can feel it," she said slowly, "a small inferno."

"But how?" The fire that Elena had started was in the east, but the smoke was coming from the north, the direction of the second mine.

"An accident?" he thought aloud. Jantari ore was highly combustible.

Elena twisted the reins in her hand. "Only one way to find out."

Yassen hesitated. "How strong is the inferno?"

"Not very. It feels . . ." Elena closed her eyes. "Weak. Like it just started."

"Then maybe something did go wrong out there." He urged his brenni forward, trying to ignore his unease.

Based on their location, he felt fairly certain the smoke was coming from the second mine. If they could grow the inferno, if Elena could strengthen it, then perhaps this job would be over sooner than expected.

"Hurry," he said.

They broke into a gallop, cutting through the trees. As they rode closer, the smell of ash grew stronger, mixed with something he couldn't tell for certain. Metal glimmered from between the treetops. With a screech, his brenni threw back its head.

And then it hit Yassen.

The acrid stench of burning metal.

The second rig rose out of the pines, glinting from the light of the flames beneath it. Fire was flickering under the western leg of the mine. A cart had fallen, and ore spilled onto the ground, burning rapidly.

Men danced around it as they tried, vainly, to put it out.

But it was too late.

Above, soldiers streamed out of a hoverpod docked on the northern platform. *Strange*, Yassen thought. *There's only one hoverpod.* Some soldiers stood on the upper stairs of the rig, directing water tanks toward the blaze.

Elena had tied her steed beneath a molorian and was already dropping into the first form of the fire dance. She looked up at him with a tight smile.

"I can hear the fire calling," she said.

He tightened his grip around his gun. His brenni nickered nervously.

"Make it quick." A siren began to wail, and Yassen watched as more soldiers hurried toward the blaze.

Elena raised her arms, sparks raining down from her fingertips. She twirled, and the sparks flared into a flame that leapt onto the canopy. The branches wilted and blackened like his arm, the leaves curling into ash. Elena coiled her wrists. The fire snaked up the spine of a retherin. The pine groaned, resisting, but then its trunk snapped with a loud crack that resounded through the forest. Everything fell to the inferno. Even the stones darkened as flames devoured the underbrush, the leaves, the trees.

Yassen shrank back, heat buffeting his face. In the distance, the rig fire swelled as if sensing the new blaze. Soldiers cried out. He saw them turn, point in their direction.

"Let's go," he called over the crackle.

When Elena turned around, he saw a bewitched look in her eyes as the flames spat behind her. It crackled, and for a moment, Elena swayed, as if listening. Tiny flames curled around her toes.

"Elena," he called in warning.

His voice seemed to break her trance. She quickly untied her brenni and swung into the saddle, looking over her shoulder with a mirthless smile. "Ride, Yassen," she said.

Yassen nudged his brenni, but it needed no encouragement. It shot forward into a gallop. He could barely make out Elena in the thickening smoke. He wanted to call out to her, to stop her, but he could only cough. His eyes stung. Worry nagged at him in the darkness. *How did that cart catch on fire?*

Yassen did not see the neverwood; its branches raked him across the cheek, and he cried out. He felt something warm drip down his jaw as his brenni brayed and vaulted to the right, nearly bucking him from the saddle.

With a grunt, Yassen slowed his brenni and hauled himself straight.

"Are you all right?" Elena called out.

Suddenly, the drone of a hoverpod filled the mountain. It appeared above them, a dark, smooth shape against the rolling grey sky. Yassen turned to Elena, reaching for her when light flooded the grove. His brenni brayed, blinded.

Then the mountain shrieked as the rig exploded.

A force wave rippled through the forest. Yassen hit the ground hard, the air rushing straight out of him. He gasped. His mind spun: the mine, the explosion, *get up, run, run!* But his body was slow to respond. Ash rained down and blotted out the pale moons, the sky. It reminded Yassen of the temple, of Samson, of Elena. He scrambled to his knees, felt around for his gun. His fingers grazed metal, and Yassen grabbed it. Blinking, he brought it in front of his face and realized it was not his gun, but a stray scrap of the rig.

"El-Elena!" He vaulted to his feet. The heavens swam, and Yassen reached out to steady himself. Instead of bark, he found flesh. Elena pulled at him, her hair covered in bramble, her eyes wide, her mouth moving, telling him something. He shook his head. Sound came roaring back.

"The brenni!" she shouted.

He looked around but did not see the animals. He hoped they were okay. He began to reach for his weapon but only felt his empty hip. *Where is my gun?*

Elena grabbed him, and they ran into the trees. Many of the pines had snapped in half from the blast, and the ones that were still standing leaned precariously.

"This way," he croaked. He tugged her to the left, and they tore through the underbrush. Elena kicked something, and Yassen saw a flash of silver.

The gun! He shot forward as it fell in a patch of splintered neverwood. Yassen winced as he pulled out the pistol, thorns digging into his skin. Elena slid to a stop beside him, doubling over.

"Can it still shoot?" she panted. When he did not respond, she shook him.

"Yassen. Yassen!" she yelled, but he had finally answered his question.

The blackened path. The sudden fire.

Dread spread down his throat and chest.

"The Arohassin."

It was the only explanation. The Jantari soldiers must have created a fake blaze to lure Elena and him to the mines. They had deliberately burned ore at the second mine—that's why it had been so small. Why the fire had not spread to the forest.

They had wanted the queen to show her face.

"He knows," Yassen croaked. Only Akaros could have designed a trick like this—a trick that came with sacrifice and reward. "The second mine was bait," he said. "They know we're here."

Elena shook her head. "But why would they destroy their own ore? It makes no sense."

"The hoverpods." Yassen's eyes widened. "You said at the first mine, there were three. Here, there was only one. They must have already taken the ore away."

"And we never saw the other hoverpod burn down," Elena said. "Which means, it got out. They got all their fucking ore out."

A staccato drone cut through the roar of the flames, and Yassen looked up to see two tankers flying up the mountain. *The reinforcements.*

"Elena." He took her hand. "Run."

But she stood still, and he could see the wheels turning in her mind, could see her weigh the options. The tunnel was their only chance at survival, and when Elena's mouth hardened into a grudging scowl, he knew she saw it too.

"We won't be able to get far," she said, and he was surprised by how measured and calm her voice was. "Not without the brenni. We need to slow them down."

"How?"

Her gaze met his, and he saw a smoldering look in her eyes as she raised her hands.

"We burn the way to us."

Elena whirled before he could stop her. She widened her stance and raised her hands. A hiss slithered up the trees. He saw a wink of red in her palm, and then it grew into a flame. With a jab, Elena threw the flame onto the molorian that sheltered them. It lit up like a torch. Elena turned, and the fire moved with her, leaping down the mountain.

He could not deny her power. He could feel it ripple off her like heat waves over a dune. The Arohassin preached that fire was cruel and so were its masters. But Elena was not the hell and brimstone he had been taught to fear. She could be harsh, but she was a queen. A protector rather than a destroyer. She had a responsibility toward her people, and no one, not even he, Yassen realized with a chill, could stand in her way.

"Elena," he called.

For a moment, she stared at the burning branches and the smoke, her shoulders outlined by the light of the inferno. *The Burning Queen*, the servants had called her. But then she turned to him. This time, the bewitched look was not in her eyes. There lay only somberness.

She touched his hand. Her skin was hot.

"The fire will find its way," she said.

He was not sure what she meant, but he felt himself answering, "Fire always finds a way."

Slowly, she nodded. "Then let's go."

They headed southeast, toward the tunnel entrance. They stumbled along the edge of a dry ravine as the fire followed, surrounding them like a shield. Tankers flew over the mountain, their searchlights vainly sweeping over the broken, burning trees.

The heat dried his eyes and lips. Yassen began to cough, and as he doubled over, spitting out blood, a pulse sliced into a branch above him— exactly where his head had just been. He hit the ground, calling for Elena.

Pulse fire shredded the air. The fire roared in return. Ahead, he saw Elena raise her hands, the flames curling, but then a pulse cut through the pines, and she yelped, tumbling into the ravine.

"Elena!"

The fire swept past Yassen to surround her. Pain shot up his right arm. It felt as if his bones were ripping apart. He stifled a cry as he inched forward on his stomach and rolled into the ravine after her.

The flames circled them. Yassen dragged himself forward to where Elena knelt, clutching her arm.

"Are you okay?" he panted.

She looked at him with glazed eyes. Blood streamed down her forearm. Her wrist hung at an unnatural angle, and the sight made Yassen's stomach roil.

"It's all right," he said to assure them both.

She had been hit right beneath the elbow and had sprained her wrist during the fall. Yassen quickly took the scarf around her neck and tightened it around the wound. He then ripped off a part of his cloak to make a sling.

"Mother's Gold," she rasped as he pulled tighter, her face grey with pain. "I'm going to kill them."

Pulses zipped overhead. From their direction, Yassen estimated that the shooters were to the southwest. The cabin's tunnel entrance lay farther to the east, past the flames and fallen trees.

In the ravine, they were easy prey for slaughter. The fire would buy them time, but they only had one gun. Yassen stared at the flames as the pulse fire screeched overhead, as the forest crackled and burned, as Elena hugged her bloody hand, and the decision came to him with a quiet, unwavering gravity.

He thrust his holopod into Elena's hand, his words rushed. "Follow the ravine. Stick to the trees for cover and use your fire to get to the cabin. Look for that thin pine. Take the tunnel and head south until you find the dragon. The Black Scales will know you've arrived even before you do."

He watched the realization dawn on her.

"No," she said. "No."

"Remember before we went up the mountain? I said you had to listen. If I told you to run, you run. If I told you to leave me, you leave me." He tied the knot of the sling. "Now for once, listen to me."

"We're supposed to leave here together," she insisted.

"Plans change," he said as he fumbled with the bullets strapped along his waist. "I'm expendable, and you're not."

"Not to me," she whispered.

"I burned my name in the sand. Remember?" His smile was tight. He checked the chamber of his gun and slid back the safety, but when he met her gaze, his smile cracked. He did not want to let her go. Of all things, he wished he could turn back time to that moment in the cabin, the moment when he had held her in his arms, and she had pressed her face into his neck. "Ravence needs you. Your people need you. Now go. Please, Elena."

Slowly, Elena rose to her feet. The flames drew back. He tried to smile again, but his chest was too heavy.

"I'll find you," he said, and he wondered if she heard the tremor in his voice.

Her eyes glimmered. She squeezed his hand.

"You'd better."

Then she took a step back. Still, her eyes did not leave his. A pulse smacked into the edge of the ravine, dislodging soil and rock. Still, his eyes did not leave hers.

Another pulse hit the tree above, and the molorian groaned then fell, crashing between them.

And then Elena turned. She ran. Farther and farther away, around the bend.

As he watched her go, Yassen felt a quiet settle in his chest, a calmness that came with finality.

He climbed the ravine bed. Crouched just along its edge and trained his gun. Through the flickering flames, Yassen could make out movement. They had spread out around him, just as he had predicted. Yassen breathed in smoke. Let it curl in his chest. And when he breathed out, he pulled the trigger.

A shadow fell. Yassen turned and found another. He fired twice to bring it down. The flames crawled up the fallen molorian and licked at his feet. He breathed in more smoke. Shot down another shadow and its partner.

A pulse zipped past his ear, cutting through a pine on his left. A soldier ran between the trees and Yassen fired, but he missed. The man ducked behind a trunk. Yassen waited, the flames crawling up to his ankles, and when the soldier reappeared, he fired again. This time, the man fell.

Yassen inched forward on his stomach as more soldiers gathered, lighting up the forest with their pulses. He huddled behind a smoldering neverwood bush, coughing. Heat and exhaustion tightened his throat, but they did not unseat his sense of clarity.

Peering through the smoke, Yassen spotted movement in the thicket of trees to his left. He fired, and his assailants responded. Pulses slashed through the trees, cutting deep wedges in the bark. They all came from Yassen's left, and he fired twice in that direction. A man cried out. Yassen pulled the trigger again, but the chamber only clicked, empty.

Cursing, Yassen unlatched the empty magazine. It clattered to the ground. He tried to grasp a new magazine with his right hand, but his fingers were frozen. *Damn this arm!* He gripped the pistol between his knees and pulled out a new magazine with his good hand. A pulse slammed into the pine. A branch fell just to Yassen's right. He gritted his teeth. *Focus.* He finally managed to line up the magazine, and it slid into his pistol with a satisfying click.

He turned, searching the smoke, when a shot rang out. It ripped through the forest. Tore through branches. A bullet sliced through his right arm and out.

Yassen tumbled into the ravine. There was a warm, liquid sensation in his chest. He rolled onto his back, struggling for breath as he looked up and saw the burning heavens and the sky full of smoke. The stars glinting like uncut gems. The fire surrounded the ravine, but this time, its heat did not suffocate him. It kissed him.

And in that swath of darkness that came after, Yassen Knight saw a light.

He did not fear it.

Finally in his cursed life, he would find untroubled sleep.

CHAPTER 43

ELENA

Though I have the memory of you, I see you from before, in a land where roads are rivers and the sun is aglow, and we will wade to that wilderness that claimed us forever ago.

—from a Sayonai folklore ballad

Elena raced through the forest of fire and smoke. She did not know where she was going, but she followed the ravine as Yassen had told her. The mountain larks screeched singular notes. A pine groaned and snapped, sparks raining down. Elena yelped, falling. Pain pounded through her elbow, her wrist. She rolled in the dirt, the world spinning, the flames hissing at her feet. The inferno came to her as if urging her to get up and move. With a grunt, she pushed herself up onto her knees.

Pulse fire sliced through the forest. It was like the temple all over again, except this time, she wouldn't get out.

She stared up at the burning sky, blood wetting the bandage Yassen had tied around her arm. She tried to rise only to fall again; it was as if her body had given up. All she wanted to do was sleep and wake up back in

Ravence. For Ferma to tell her it was a bad dream.

But if she died here, no one would weep for her. She would be known as the shortest reigning monarch of Ravence, a footnote in history and nothing more. Would they sing of how she died? Would they say that she had put up a good fight, and that when all was said and done, she had died buying Ravence a little more time?

The sky had burnished into shades of orange like a glowing ember.

Like the desert sky after a storm had nearly passed. She could still see grains of sand in the air, still taste salt on her lips. Her desert, her home, connected by a sky just like this.

She had to reach it.

Slowly, Elena clambered to her feet. Placed one foot in front of the other. Her chest clamored for air. *Don't look back.*

With every step, her heart cracked. With every step, she abandoned Yassen. *Don't look back.*

If this was strength, if this was weakness, she did not know. She could only fight against the pressure in her lungs and the tears clouding her eyes. She could only put one foot in front of the other, until she was jogging, running again, because it was all she could do. *Don't look back.*

The ravine curved off to the east and Elena climbed the bank. She hauled herself over the edge, gasping. The flames crawled up the trees, shaking the dead leaves with a sadistic hunger. Far off in the distance, she saw the third mine. It jutted out, cold and silent, and for a moment, all Elena wanted to do was to hurl fire onto its metal face. She didn't just want to see the mine implode; she wanted it to melt before her, to ripple down the mountainside, dragging away Jantar's precious ore.

The flames pulsed, sensing her desire. Elena reached out and they curled around her hand, ready to leap, but instead of sending the inferno toward the mine, Elena made a fist. The flames flattened, hissing in displeasure. She did not care. She opened her palm, and the flames peeled back as she began to run again.

The cabin.

She headed south, the fire following. Her legs burned and every breath felt like a sharp stab in her chest. The cabin's tunnel still lay several miles away. *Skies above, it's so far.* Elena skirted around a pine when her foot got stuck in a root. She yelped, falling onto her knees.

Suddenly, something brayed.

Elena gasped, looking up.

There in the distance were three brenni. Three brenni with soldiers on them.

She scrambled to her feet, trying to hide behind the tree, but it was too late.

The soldiers had seen her.

One shouted, and a pulse smacked into the pine. And then they were all shooting, shredding the trunk, filling the air with the horrid screech of their pulsefire.

Elena winced, covering her ears. She couldn't outrun them, not when they were on brenni. Maybe, when they were out...

There came a click, and the pulsefire stopped as the soldiers went to recharge the chambers. With a cry, Elena hurled the inferno onto them. The fire rushed down the slope, picking up speed, hunger. She spun, forming a spear of fire in her hand. She flung it on a soldier, who screamed and fell from his brenni. The other steeds bucked, violently. One soldier fell off while the other remained in his seat. He charged up the slope with a snarl, shooting. Elena looped the fire around, and his brenni, ever the wiser, screeched and bucked him off.

"Come back here!" the soldier cried, but his voice was lost in the roar of the inferno.

Elena grabbed the reins of the brenni as it rolled its head. "Easy, easy, the fire won't hurt you," she said.

The brenni brayed but held still as she jumped on. She urged it forward, and the flames swept back, clearing a path for them.

Elena ran for it.

The blaze had reached the cabin before her. It crackled along the edges, the phoenix knocker gleaming in the glow of the flames. Seeing it, her heart cracked, but Elena did not have the luxury to weep. Not now. She cantered to the cropping of pines that Yassen had shown her and jumped down. Her brenni took off without so much as a goodbye.

Look for that thin pine. Elena whirled around.

Where is it? Where is it?

She stumbled and fell on the tangles of roots. Got to her knees and crawled forward, searching as the inferno hissed. Suddenly, she saw it.

The thin, tall pine with a flaking trunk. She scrambled to it, searching for the knot bigger than her fist. She recalled how Yassen had followed the roots of the tree; how he had pressed his pale hand into the knots; how the mountain had listened and opened for him.

Her throat tightened, but Elena forced herself to concentrate on the task at hand. Her fingers brushed over the rough bark until she found the large knot.

She pressed it.

The ground rumbled, and Elena scrambled back just as the floor beneath the pine slid away, revealing darkness.

Elena hesitated. The forest groaned as the fire ate up the pines, the molo-rians, the neverwoods, everything. She thought of the cabin and the crystal and the family frozen within. She thought of the boy who now lay somewhere on this mountainside, dead or alive, to buy her time. And she thought of Ravence. The ever-shifting, singing dunes. Her father sitting on the bench in the garden, watching the birds. Ferma challenging her in a duel, her smile easy and wide. The expectant faces of the crowd when Elena had stepped to the podium and hushed them with her raised hand. Ravence lay at the other side of this. Ravence was waiting for her.

Elena jumped into the pit.

She plunged deep into the mountain, wind rushing past her ears, stone scraping her elbows, before she hit the ground. The impact shocked her. Elena moaned, rolling onto her back. Above, she saw fire dancing over the opening of the tunnel, so far away.

Slowly, she sat up.

The darkness was so vivid, so textured that Elena almost thought it was alive. As her eyes adjusted, she could make out jagged stones and a path snaking from the ledge she stood on. She did not know if it led south, but it was the only path she had.

She took it.

It was as if she had stepped into a different world. The shadows weren't shadows. They were pools of black liquid that rippled as she walked. A spider as large as her hand scuttled over a rock. It stopped and watched her with a hundred inky eyes as she scooted past it. Large, sharp obsidian jutted out from the bowels of the mountain like frozen innards. Perhaps it was the darkness playing tricks on her, but the rocks seemed to glow.

Elena peered at them and realized with a start that, actually, they were glowing.

Everything was.

As the tunnel veered deeper into the mountain, a blue, internal light emanated from the obsidian. Some stones shone brightly, others so faintly that they seemed to disappear. It was the ore; it existed in every part of the mountain, from the tiniest pebble to the largest boulder. Manufactured Jantari metal could blind a man if he wasn't careful; the ore alone merely trapped tiny flecks of light. For this, Elena was grateful.

With her other hand, she felt for the holopod. Its side was badly dented, but when Elena pressed her finger against the sensor, it flickered open.

With shaking fingers, Elena traced the red tunnel. It bore south to a single dot. There lay the Black Scales, or so she hoped.

Suddenly, the mountain quaked, dust and dirt raining down into her eyes. *The third mine.* The inferno must have spread farther north. Elena grasped the wall, fear bounding through her body as the tunnel quivered. A deep groan echoed through the chamber. The shaking intensified, and the mountain seemed to groan, guttural and deep, as if it had lost some part of itself. And then Elena realized why. *Landslides.* The third explosion had finally triggered what she had feared.

Stones fell from the ceiling, but the tunnel held. After several minutes, the shaking finally stopped. Elena cautiously pushed herself to her feet.

Impossible.

Except for loose dirt and crumbled rocks, the tunnel was intact. She pressed her hand against the stone, and the wall quivered. She gasped, shrinking back. The blue light from the ore pulsed, but when Elena touched the wall again, it lay still. Nothing crept through the darkness. The tunnel lay as quiet as it had before the rumbling.

Her mind was playing tricks on her.

With one last look at the wall, Elena darted down the path. It snaked deeper and deeper into the bowels of Sayon, and she walked until she could walk no farther, her legs buckling from exhaustion.

She slept where she fell, fitfully, dreaming of people choking beneath the earth. The old merchant. The brenni handler. Yassen. Their eyes were red and leering.

Burning Queen, they sneered. *Burning Queen.*

She woke to the sound of her own screaming. Her voice echoed through the mountain, but no one answered.

Elena stumbled on in a delirious state. The blood on her elbow crusted over. Her sprained wrist grew stiff. Hunger gnawed her stomach until it became familiar. She walked until she fainted, slept until she woke from nightmares. She had no sense of time but felt like she had been walking for days, weeks. She felt a strange presence throughout the mountain, as if someone were holding a deep breath.

Her throat was so dry it hurt, and her eyes were raw and swollen from tears. She did not know when she had started crying, only that it felt as if she had never stopped.

She had long known the stinging stab of grief. She had first learned it when her mother died; felt it, so excruciatingly deep, when Ferma fell; almost drowned in it when her father burned.

But this, this was something more. This was a creeping wail that threatened to spill out of her throat. A wail that hummed in the deep marrow of her bones. A wail that defied even the strongest of desert winds, the deepest of tunnels.

And finally, she let it out.

It reverberated through the bowels of the mountain and beyond. So keen was her cry, so sharp her anguish that the mountain trembled. It seemed to sense her loss. But the tunnel still stretched on, the same as before. No matter what she endured, no matter how many lives she sacrificed, Elena could not change the path ahead of her.

But she dared not stop.

Faintly, she registered the tunnel was beginning to rise. The path snaked past stalagmites shaped like fingers, reaching upward. Elena raised her hand to push back a lock of hair and saw a jagged line of dried blood from her index finger to her elbow. She touched the wound, and fresh dots of blood oozed out. One grew heavy; she watched as it fell to the floor.

Somewhere deep in the mountain, there came a growl. Elena froze. *Am I still dreaming?* The sound seemed to have come from far below, from beneath the ground itself. The darkness before her rustled like a fabric being pulled tight. Again, Elena had the odd feeling that something was holding its breath, but now, as the growl came again, louder this time, she realized it wasn't waiting anymore.

It was coming toward her.

Elena began to run. The tunnel narrowed as it rose higher and higher. The walls closed in on her, and she was forced to crawl on her knees. Her heart pounded in her ears. A sharp chill cut through the air. It knifed down her throat as she dragged her way forward. Suddenly, she felt something touch her ankle, and she almost shrieked. She remembered how she had heard a similar growl when she first entered the tunnels with Yassen. When she had seen a mass of black so dark that even the shadows seemed to fear it. She began to scramble faster, her shoulders scraped raw by the walls. Finally, the tunnel widened. Elena lurched back to her feet and dashed forward, following the curving path.

It led her to a tall chamber full of light. Ore trapped within the rocks glinted, illuminating a staircase chiseled out of the wall that rose to a gate twice as tall as a man.

She sprinted up the stairs as she heard something scraping in the tunnel behind her. It growled again, and the mountain shuddered in response. Elena took the steps two at a time, her breath tearing her chest. Runes were carved along the staircase, and she recognized the symbols of the inward storm and the fire.

Finally, she reached the landing. The mountain moaned. It was a frightening sound, cold and jarring like a metal nail dragging across a tin roof. She slammed her hand against the gate. She could tell at once it was old, fashioned out of pure silver rather than Jantari steel. Several gears and bolts lay across the doors in an intricate pattern. She saw no doorknob, no handle. There was no inscription above the gate, no other runes to give her clues.

The growl came again. Stalactites snapped and shattered on the floor. Elena grasped the gears, running her fingers frantically over them. There had to be a key, there was always a key on this damned mountain.

She dragged her hand down the gears, feeling the sharp grooves. *Odd.* The gate seemed as old as the mountain, yet the gears had not dulled with time. They snaked and twisted, slowly creating a figure, and then she saw it—the dragon.

Head south until you find the dragon, Yassen had said. *The Black Scales will know you've arrived even before you do.*

Samson.

Elena banged on the doors again as the ground shifted beneath her feet. The shadows around the room shrank back from what came from beneath the mountain. She could feel its presence, or rather the absence of air behind her, but Elena dared not look back.

"Hello?" she yelled. "My name is Elena Aadya Ravence! I'm here!"

The gate remained shut. The air around her grew thinner. Elena looked at the coiled dragon hidden in the gears and tried again.

"My name is Elena Ravence, daughter of Leo Ravence and Aahnah Madhani, queen of the desert kingdom."

The door did not move.

The world grew colder. Her eyelids felt heavy, her body weak.

"My name is Elena," she whispered.

The gears turned and the bolts receded. Slowly, the doors swung open. A gush of fresh air and light hit her, and she stumbled forward.

At first, she was blinded by the sun and how it bounced off a silver mass spilling between the mountains. Little by little, the world took shape around her. She saw that she was standing on a bluff and that the silver body was actually a large blue lake, bluer than the sea or the sky. A concrete compound sat on its bank, flanked by tankers and hoverpods.

The Black Scales.

The gate slammed shut behind her, trapping whatever lay within. The mountain groaned. Elena shook, with adrenaline, with shock, with fear of what would have happened had the doors not opened.

She sank to her knees. She had no idea what day it was, whether the Black Scales were in this compound, whether the Ravani kingdom still existed—but she was alive.

Elena raised her face to the sun. She drank in its warmth and savored its light. A wild, desperate laugh shook her, and she realized she was crying too, but she did not care. The sky was a deep blue, an endless expanse.

She wondered if Yassen saw it too.

"Hold," a voice came from behind her.

Slowly, she wiped her tears and turned. There, on the ridge above the door, stood a soldier, and then another, and another. They were dressed in combat black and had their pulse guns trained at her head.

"What did you say your name was?" one asked, and she saw the blue insignia of a dragon on his chest.

She gasped in relief.

"Elena Aadya Ravence." She pushed to her feet and looked at them with clear eyes. "Queen of the Kingdom of Ravence."

"Well, queen," the soldier said. "We've been waiting for you."

EPILOGUE

CORONATION DAY

It was a pleasure not to burn.

Samson sighed as the inferno raged around him. Underneath the Phoenix statue, he watched the sky redden. The Eternal Fire ripped down the temple, filling the mountainside with agony and smoke.

Flames wrapped around his arms, healing the burn on his hand.

"I know," he said as they crooned, "I shouldn't have let him burn me."

He closed his eyes. Felt the quiet, steady hum of energy coursing through his veins. The rush of power. It was calculating. It knew when and how to burn.

When Samson opened his eyes, blue embers danced in his palm. He let them fall from between his fingers.

Slowly, he climbed onto the back of the Phoenix's statue. A woman called his name, but when he turned, the inferno washed over him. The heat buffeted his face, warm and sweet like a lover, the crackle of the fire like a song. It whispered to him about how many men it had caught, how many trees it had taken. It told him about the assassins crawling up the mountainside.

He had expected the Arohassin to keep their word about attacking

Ravence today; what he hadn't expected was Yassen's role in it. *Poor Cass.* Even when he had dangled freedom before Yassen, his friend had chosen the Arohassin.

"But I can't hate him," Samson told the flames brushing his feet. "It is my fault for leaving him there for too long." Akaros must have brainwashed Yassen, coerced him. Given him a deal he thought he could not refuse. If Yassen managed to live, he'd finally give his friend the peace he had earned.

The flames hissed, and Samson turned to listen. Suddenly, he felt an inferno flare down the mountainside, a blaze of heat that ripped through his body, and he knew at once it was Elena.

Despite himself, Samson smiled. He had sensed the Agni within her. Her energy was like a low buzz, humming every time she came near. She was Fireblood, the same as him. When he closed his eyes and felt for her Agni, he saw a deep red soil and white sandstone. There was something ancient to her spark, something raw and untamed. It tasted of salt and earth. He reached out to touch it, but then the flare flickered and grew faint.

Samson dipped his hand and lifted a flame. He whispered to it. The flame purred and then leapt back into the inferno, his message spreading down the mountainside.

Bring her to me, it hissed.

Samson turned back to the desert. The dunes were still. The heavens burned a deep incarnadine as smoke coiled through the air like a snake ready to strike. Somewhere across the sand, across forest and stone, deep within the mountains, the old power rumbled. Samson felt it call to him.

He swung down and looped his arm around the Phoenix's neck. The inferno danced in its mirrored eyes.

"Am I all you ever asked for?" he asked, and then, with a snarl, he shattered the red eyes of the bird. The glass popped as it fell into the fire.

He began to climb the stone steps. The flames bowed and touched their heads to the floor as he passed. When he found the high priestess curled beneath the debris-laden boughs of a banyan tree, he nudged her with his foot. She stirred, moaning. Half of her face was burnt, the flesh red and weeping.

Samson slowly cupped her bloodied cheek. She was half-dead and opened one bleary eye. Blue embers sparked in his hand, undoing the damage of the burns, knitting back the skin and soothing her scalded flesh.

As he stood, Saayna wheezed. Her hands flew to her face. She had lost one eye, but the new skin stretched tightly over her cheek, marked by the sign of his Agni.

The black serpent.

It slithered down her cheek and throat. Her mouth curled in shock. She looked up at him and, at once, threw herself down at his feet, her body quivering like the flames.

"Prophet," she cried.

Prophet. What a strange word.

The people wanted their Prophet, and so he had come. He, the Landless King. The orphan whom they had spurned. The Sesharian they had tried to enslave. Yet, when he stepped out of the fire reborn, they would flock to him as waves bowing to the shore.

Samson walked past the high priestess without bidding her to rise. He came before the fallen temple. The walls caved, the dome crumpled inward, but the gate still stood. Only thin hairline cracks slithered down the pink marble.

Samson slashed his arm down, and the inferno tore the gate apart. It collapsed with a boom.

Saayna gasped.

"Why?" she croaked.

Samson turned to her. As he spoke, the flames cackled, their song lending to his voice.

"Because we will no longer pray to false gods."

Read on for a special bonus chapter from

The Phoenix King by Aparna Verma

BONUS CHAPTER

FERMA

Aahnah, they're ready for you."

"There's a secret, a secret I can't keep," Aahnah murmured.

"Aahnah—" Ferma strode into the room to find the queen whispering to herself as she slipped on her chudiya, the bangles tinkling softly.

"There's a secret, a secret."

"Aahnah." Ferma touched her shoulder, and the queen jolted. "Darling, it's time to leave for the temple."

Aahnah looked up at her, her gaze cold and distant, as if she didn't recognize her own Spear, but then Ferma saw her eyes widen.

"Aahnah," Ferma said, more firmly this time.

The queen gave a slow, sweet smile. "Ferma, darling, what are you doing here?"

"Fetching you," the Yumi said. "The king is waiting."

At this, Aahnah's smile faltered. It was a momentary slip, but Ferma had seen it happen more than once when she mentioned Leo. Worry, thick and familiar, wormed its way through her chest.

"Aahnah, the hoverpod is—"

"Mama."

They turned to see Elena standing in the doorway with Diya. She was dressed in a dusky rose kurta with a white chunni draped down her shoulder in the same style as her father's.

"Elena, why aren't you dressed properly?" Ferma said. "Diya, where's her lehenga?"

"She refused to wear it. Again," Diya sighed as Elena skipped forward.

"Elena," Ferma scolded, but she smiled as the girl jumped up, trying to touch the end of her braid.

"Open your hair, Ferma," Elena said. "Please, please."

"Only if you can reach it."

Elena jumped again, swiped, missed. She tried again as Ferma watched, arms crossed.

"You're too tall! Like a tree!"

Diya and Aahnah laughed as Ferma grinned, finally relenting. She undid her braid and leaned down. Elena slowly, cautiously, touched Ferma's hair. She gasped as Ferma hardened an end, yanking her hand back. A tiny dot of blood bloomed on her pinky.

"Do it again!" Elena cried.

Ferma laughed, shaking her head. Elena laughed too, and climbed into her mother's lap.

The queen pulled Elena closer and kissed her ear. "My little raja," she said. "As stubborn as Leo. Why must you be more like your father than me?"

"The skirts are so heavy and itchy," Elena whined. "I hate them."

"Just wait until you grow up," Aahnah said. "Then you'll love them, same as me."

"Never," Elena said.

"We'll see, my darling," Aahnah said, and though she still smiled, Ferma noticed how her eyes slipped away again, how they seemed to go to that faraway place that Ferma so desperately wished she could pull Aahnah back from.

Elena noticed, too, as the queen fell silent. She touched her mother's arm, but Aahnah said nothing, simply put Elena back down and turned to her mirror.

It was like this even on the good days. Wordlessly, Diya took Elena's hand and led her away, and the princess did not protest. She knew better, too. Ferma wished she could shake Aahnah. Wished she could say something to wake her up, to bring her back as she was before when she was *present*. But Ferma merely squeezed Elena's shoulder as she passed.

It's not your fault, she wanted to say.

When they were gone, Ferma found the queen staring at her in the mirror with eyes like flint.

"I want you to promise me," she said, her voice strange and hollow. "Promise me that when Elena knows the truth, you will be there to guide her."

"What truth, Aahnah? Why won't you speak plainly?" Ferma said, exasperated. "You haven't confided in me these past few moons."

"Promise me," Aahnah said.

Ferma closed her eyes. She did not want to make a promise. Promises were meant to hold someone accountable, to forge an unbreakable bond between two people who were honest with one another. How could Aahnah speak of truth when she evaded all questions?

"What secret were you whispering about?" Ferma said, eyes still closed.

"Promise me," Aahnah repeated.

At last, Ferma opened her eyes. The queen met her gaze without faltering. *You are the stubborn one*, she thought.

"Fine." It was pointless arguing with Aahnah, especially when she acted like this. "But you must promise me something too."

She knelt and took her queen's hands in her own. They were soft, the skin unblemished, while Ferma's were hard and etched with many scars.

"Swear that you will come with me to Moksh. There is a Yumi guru there, one of the Yamuna priestesses. Maybe she can help you."

Aahnah stilled. "Help me with what?"

Ferma considered the words carefully. "Your trances," she said.

"I have no trances," Aahnah snapped and began to pull her hands away, but Ferma held firm.

"Please, Aahnah, for the Great Mothers' sake," she pleaded. "All I'm saying is that the Yamuna may understand you. Whatever this thing is, whatever secret that's been eating you, she will know how to handle it."

"How will we even get into Moksh? They allow no visitors."

"My grandmother will let us in," Ferma said. "She will have to."

Finally, Aahnah bowed her head. Her forehead touched Ferma's. "I'm terrible at promises," she whispered.

"You must try with this one," Ferma whispered back.

At the temple, Ferma listened to the Eternal Fire seethe as she sat against the wall with the other guards. The great flames cackled, heat buffeting her face with such force that she was forced to take shallow breaths.

Sparks rose in the air, dancing as they fluttered before the feet of the Phoenix. Leo sat on the raised dais. Aahnah and Elena knelt by the steps with the high priestess.

"O Bearer of Hope," the priests sang. They swung multitiered diyas as Saayna scattered marigold petals into the fire. The heat intensified. Ferma coughed, sweat dripping down her nose. Usually she could chant along with the priests through the ceremony, but today her throat thickened, and she was finding it harder and harder to breathe.

Saayna continued to fling more petals into the pit. But Ferma heard the growl of the inferno, heard its fury beneath the melody of the prayers. She looked to the fire, trying not to shut her eyes against the brightness of its blaze. The flames swelled at the base of the pit, and above, the Phoenix glittered as She watched.

Though she could not pinpoint it, there was something about the Eternal Fire that made Ferma uneasy. She scanned the room, but nothing had changed. The priests sang. Leo was as still as the statue of the Phoenix. Saayna began to sway, eyes closed, voice vibrating with reverence. And then there was Aahnah.

The queen leaned toward the fire, chanting. For once, she was *present*. She sprinkled holy water into the flames, and when Elena trembled beside her, she squeezed her daughter's shoulders and whispered something in her ear that made the princess giggle.

Suddenly, the fire snapped, shooting sparks that whipped through the air. Elena gave a small shriek, and Ferma rose, but Aahnah simply brushed the stray sparks away from Elena's cheek. She tapped Elena's chin, and the princess smiled sheepishly.

"You are brave." Ferma read Aahnah's lips.

And it was this picture of them, of mother and daughter kneeling before the Eternal Fire, that Ferma would remember forever. Aahnah, face aglow, touching Elena's chin. Elena, looking up, blushing in embarrassment and relief. The recognition between them, the comfort in knowing that the other cared just as deeply as she.

Great Goddess and Phoenix Above, Ferma prayed as she saw Elena lean into her mother. *May you grant them both peace.*

She sat back against the wall. The Eternal Fire rumbled again, but no one paid it any mind. Ferma fought back her misgivings, her gaze staying on the queen. When this was over, she would take Aahnah to Moksh. She would ask her grandmother to allow them to see the Yamuna. Beg, if she had to. Because Elena deserved a mother who was present, and Aahnah deserved to find peace. And because—selfishly, Ferma knew—she wished for the old Aahnah. The one whose mind did not wander away midsentence but who would regale her with stories for hours as they ate their way through a plate of mangoes, eyes alight, hands sticky with juice as she spoke about the findings of Priestess Nomu. The one who sat before Ferma now, arms folded around her child in an embrace.

Ferma's eyes stung. She dashed away a tear, her nose itching from the smoke. Phoenix and Goddess above, when had her eyes started watering? She fought back a sneeze as the Eternal Fire roared again. This time, the flames leapt over the confines of the pit. One stray spark snapped just inches from Aahnah's face, but the queen did not move. Ferma noticed how the priests tensed. They took a step back even as Saayna chanted faster.

Leo and Aahnah remained still.

"To the wings of glory, to the keeper of peace," Saayna sang, rising. The priests all rose with her. "May you bless the ones who carry your dream."

On the dais, Leo stood slowly. But then he seemed to sway, as if drunk. He stumbled down the steps, wheezing, and Ferma started when the Eternal Fire shot after him. It folded into itself, the flames bearing down upon the dais.

Leo screamed.

Elena shrieked and darted back.

Saayna stumbled, tripping over her robes.

Aahnah walked forward.

It happened slowly, achingly, each second seared into Ferma's memory. Each movement, each glance.

A flame latched around Leo's ankle as he tried to escape. The Eternal Fire snarled and dragged him back towards the pit. He twisted, crying out in pain. Aahnah strode forward, calling to the fire. Ferma did not hear what she said, but for a moment, the fire stilled. As if listening.

And then Aahnah was at the edge of the pit. Her shoulders were straight, her head high. She turned to Leo, but for a moment, her gaze caught Ferma's.

Ferma remembered shouting her queen's name. Reaching, as if suddenly she was standing beside her. As if she could pull her back. But Aahnah only smiled. And then she turned to Leo, but her words seemed to be for them both.

"I'm sorry," she said. Then she jumped into the Eternal Fire.

There had been no ashes to collect. Nothing to discern what had been Aahnah from the ashes of a lotus or marigold. Nothing physical that Ferma could touch. Nowhere to place her grief.

So it hung around her, like the flower wreaths they would have put on Aahnah's corpse. "She is gone now," Saayna had said. "Welcomed into the heavens by the Phoenix. She has found peace, and she would wish for you to do the same."

The flags were lowered. The cities went into mourning. Even the sounds of the desert seemed to be muffled. A sandstorm raged past Palace Hill a week after Aahnah's death. Ferma saw shadows of sand flicker past her window, but she did not hear the gale. For hours, she watched the storm pass. She tried to cry. Tried to vent this grief that would not leave, would not let *her* leave and find peace. But her eyes remained dry.

Finally, she got up. She did not know where she was going—her feet moved of their own accord—and she found herself before Aahnah's room.

With a trembling hand, Ferma opened the door and stepped into the past.

The curtains were drawn. Aahnah's glittering array of chudiya sat on the vanity. Strands of her hair were caught in her comb. Ferma ran her hand along the chair before the mirror. Aahnah had sat here before. Aahnah had pulled Elena onto her lap and kissed her nose and met Ferma's eyes in this mirror and told her to keep a promise—

Ferma sank into the chair, shaking. Tremors racked her body, and she inhaled harshly, but still the tears did not come.

Promise me, Aahnah had said. Ferma gripped the edges of the chair. *Promise me that when Elena knows the truth, you will be there to guide her.*

"You knew," Ferma said to the empty room. "You knew you wouldn't be here. That *I* would be the one to guide Elena, not you."

Ferma looked to the mirror, but only her reflection stared back.

"You cheated," Ferma said, her voice cracking. "You held me to my promise, but I can never hold you to yours. You cheated. You cheated. You—"

There was a soft sound, from the closet. Ferma stilled. *Aahnah?* she thought wildly.

She whipped around, smoothing the ends of her hair that had sharpened in reflex. Slowly, she crept toward the darkened wardrobe, but inside, she didn't find Aahnah.

She found her promise.

Elena was curled up in her mother's saris, sniffling. She had wrapped one around her entire body, propped her head on a bundle of dupattas. When Ferma entered, she gasped.

"Mama?"

"No, darling," Ferma said as she knelt. Gently, she touched Elena's hair. It was knotted, still tangled in the same braid she had worn the day of the ceremony. "Come, let's go back to your room."

"Mama said she would be back," Elena said in a small voice. "When we were in the temple, she told me she would come back someday to tell me a truth."

Ferma's chest tightened. She did not have the heart to tell her that Aahnah was not returning. That the queen was a liar, a cheater. A woman who kept secrets, even from her own family and friends. But as Elena peered up at her, eyes dark and luminous like the queen's, Ferma touched her head. Drew her into her lap.

"I will not lie to you, ever. You deserve that," Ferma whispered. "Your mother is not coming back. But she made me promise something. Do you want to know what?"

Wordlessly, Elena nodded.

"She told me to help you, in any way that I can."

In the darkness, Elena seemed to consider this. "How?"

"Well, for starters, by fixing this hair," Ferma said, tickling Elena's neck.

"It's a mess." Elena giggled, cautiously, as if she did not know whether it was appropriate to laugh. But Ferma saw how she leaned toward her, hopeful, trusting, and she made another promise then. Not to Aahnah, not to Elena, but to herself. Between her and her gods.

Great Mothers above, I swear this, she prayed as Elena asked, softly, if she could have her hair braided like a Yumi. *I will make her strong. Stronger than her king and her queen. Stronger than myself. Stronger than the fire.* Her fingers moved gently but deftly as she smoothed and twisted Elena's hair. *And she will not feel the same grief of losing a mother again. I will not allow it.* She knotted the end of the braid. Elena smiled, held it up. Ferma returned the smile and held up her own braid.

Because when I die, she will have a body to mourn.

The story continues in...

Book TWO of the Ravence Trilogy

GLOSSARY

Agneepath: The path of fire.

Agnee Palace: The royal governmental home of the ruler of Ravence.

Agnee Range: Mountains that create the western border of Ravence. The Agnee Range is lush and covered with diverse plant species and trees. It stands in sharp contrast to the Ravani Desert.

Agni: The very spark and essence of fire. It is the primordial power.

Ahi Sea: A large body of water that splits Sayon in half.

Alabore's Passage: A long lane that runs east to west in Rani.

Alabore Street: A long lane that runs north to south in Rani.

Alabore's Tear: A long, dark valley north of Palace Hill. Legends say that it was created by Alabore Ravence himself when he met the Phoenix.

Arohassin: An underground network of criminals and terrorists who are known to assassinate leaders and take down governments. The leader of the Arohassin goes by the name of Taran, but no one truly knows his name.

Ashanta ceremony: A fire blessing ceremony used to bestow the ruler(s) of Ravence with the power of the Phoenix.

Astra: The closest advisor and right-hand man of the ruler of Ravence.

Ayona: A large island nation in the northern Ahi Sea. The Ayoni do not welcome outsiders.

Azuri: A delicate tree whose white branches are often used to build pyres.

Banyan: A tree that can grow to be several feet wide, while its roots can be several miles long. It was introduced to the desert after intense years of environmental development under the rule of Queen Tamana.

Beuron: A southern city of Cyleon.

Birdsong: A small festival celebrated before the official opening day of the Fire Festival. It is meant for the Ravani to open their hearts and fill their spirits with song.

Black Scale: A soldier of Samson Kytuu's army. Known for their strength and skill, Black Scales have never lost a war.

Brenni: Furry, llama-like animals. They are often used to transport heavy loads in the Sona Range.

Chand Mahal: The moon palace, otherwise known as the abode of Samson Kytuu.

Chhatri: An elevated, dome-shaped pavilion often found within the architectural style of Ravence.

Claws, the: Curved metal fixtures that are stationed around the track of a hovertrain station. When a hovertrain docks, the Claws latch on to the sides of the train and recharge its engines.

Coin Square: A popular square in the Thar district of Rani.

Cruiser: A floating vehicle used to traverse the desert.

Cyleon: A kingdom that lies north of Ravence. Cyleon has been an ally of Ravence for nearly two hundred suns.

Desert Spiders: The band of female warriors chosen by Alabore Ravence to protect the Ravani kingdom.

Desertstone: A fine, purple crystal found within Ravence.

Dhol: A large drum used in Ravani music.

Diya: An oil lantern fixed at the end of every petal in the Temple of Fire.

Dupatta: A long scarf.

Enuu: An entity considered to be the evil eye by the Jantari.

Eternal Fire: A large inferno that burns within the Temple of Fire. It is said to have been created by the Sixth Prophet to remind men of the wrath of the Phoenix. It needs no fuel but demands sacrifice from all those who wish to claim its power.

GLOSSARY

Featherstone: A large gem that contains the only Phoenix feather given to men. It rests in the center of the Ravani crown.

Floating bladers: Metal and/or wooden boards that hover slightly above the ground. They are powered by batteries and can go up to thirty miles per hour with a full charge.

Fire Festival: A weeklong festival that celebrates the founding of Ravence by Alabore and his followers.

Fire Order: A religious order of priests who serve the Phoenix and protect Her temple.

Five Desert Wars: Five bitter years of war between Ravence and Jantar during the reign of King Fani of Ravence and Queen Runtha of Jantar. Both kingdoms lost thousands of men, but Ravence emerged victorious in the end.

Fyerian: A bush that grows within the Agnee Range and produces vivid red flowers.

Fyrra: A large white wolf known to live in the Sona Range.

Gamemaster: A trained official who can code gamesuits and create obstacles within the training field.

Gamesuit: Thin yet sturdy armor that is specifically programmed to fit its wearer. Gamesuits can reknit broken bones during training sessions. They can only be used within the constraints of a training field, due to the magnetic fixtures that help power the suit.

Ganja: Marijuana.

Gold cap: An ardent supporter of King Leo. Gold caps fiercely believe that King Leo is blessed by the Phoenix and has the divine right to rule Her desert kingdom. They are often vocal (and sometimes violent) in showing their support.

Gujiyas: Sweet pastries that are stuffed with sugar and crushed nuts, like pistachio, almonds, and cashews, and then fried for the perfect treat.

Gulmohar: A tree with fiery red leaves found within Ravence.

Herra: An ancient language that used to be spoken in Ravence. It is the language that the first priests of the Fire Order used when creating scrollwork within the temple.

479

Hind: The common day language spoken in Ravence.

Hiran: Deer found within Ravence.

Holopod: A small, circular handheld device that is activated by scanning one's fingerprint. One can store personal data, money, images, videos, and more in this device.

Holosign: A floating, holographic poster and/or advertisement.

Homeland dock: The main dock within the port of Rysanti. It is full of shops, restaurants, and entertainment. It is often a newcomer's first glimpse of Jantar.

Hoverboat: A boat that hovers slightly over the sea.

Hovercam: A camera that can float in the air and is controlled via remote.

Hoverpod: A powered flying vehicle shaped like a large black ovoid. These vehicles vary in size, depending on their escort type: civilian, governmental, and/or military.

Hovertrain: A train that flies through the air. They can travel a great distance if properly charged (see **Claws**).

Iktara: A southeastern city of Ravence known for its fine artisans and scholars.

Immortal: Ancient beings of Sayon who never die, such as the Phoenix.

Jantar: A kingdom that shares the southern and eastern borders of Ravence. Jantar is known for its metal and brass cities. Jantar was founded before Ravence and believes the desert should be a part of its kingdom. Throughout the centuries, Jantar has waged countless wars against Ravence, but it has never won.

Jantari: The people of Jantar. They are known for their pale skin and white, colorless eyes.

Karven: A kingdom that borders Cyleon and Jantar. It has been a steadfast ally of Jantar.

Karvenese: The people of Karven.

Kavach: A gamesuit designed by the Arohassin.

Khajas: Flaky, layered pastry that's dipped in chocolate and garnished with crushed pistachio.

Kurta: A long, loose collarless shirt commonly worn in Ravence.

Kymathra: An ancient fighting style of the Ravani.

Lehenga: A large, embellished skirt commonly worn in Ravence, often paired with a choli (blouse) and dupatta (scarf).

Lilliberries: Berries that grow off the deep roots of a skorrir bush.

Loyarian sparks: Floating specks of light that appear in shadowed areas during the summer in Ravence.

Magar: A southwestern city of Ravence known for its red canyons and bountiful gems.

Makhana: Foxnuts.

Mandur: A kingdom across the Ahi Sea that borders Nbru and Pagua. It is well known for its outstanding army. It has been in constant conflict with Pagua.

Mero/a/i: A term of endearment spoken in Jantar. Its masculine form means boy; its feminine form means girl; and its third form means a genderless person.

Metalman: A colloquial name given to the Jantari.

Mohanti: A horned, winged ox, the national symbol of Jantar.

Moksh: A kingdom across the Ahi Sea that borders the volcanic region of Pagua.

Molorian: A tree with purple leaves and dark bark found in the Sona Range.

Monora: A northwestern city of Jantar.

Monte Gumi: A mountain within the northern parts of Veran.

Moonspun flowers: Lavender buds that bloom when touched.

Moonspun ganja: A mild psychoactive drug often smoked with a pipe. It is harvested from the ganja plant, found within the Sona Range.

Mutherwood: A pine that grows within the mountains of Seshar.

Nbru: A kingdom across the Ahi Sea that borders Mandur and Pagua. It is often the peacemaker between Mandur and Pagua, and never participates in wars.

Neverwood: A thorny plant that grows beneath the underbrush in the Sona Range.

GLOSSARY

Pagua: A kingdom across the Ahi Sea that borders Nbru, Mandur, and Moksh. It is well known for its stealthy air force. It has been in constant conflict with Mandur.

Pakhawaj: A two-headed, barrel-shaped drum often used in Ravani dance

Palace Hill: The large rise north of Rani upon which the Agnee Palace sits.

Palehearts: White flowers shaped like tiny hearts that grow within the Sona Range.

Phoenix, the: The fiery god known for Her vengeful fire and penchant for justice. The Phoenix is said to choose a Prophet when the world is full of strife. She is worshipped by the Ravani.

Prophet: A man or woman chosen to enact justice as ordered by the Phoenix. The Prophet can wield fire and cannot burn.

Pulse gun: A weapon that shoots out "pulses," or bursts of lasers. Depending on the size and weight of the gun, some pulse guns can cleanly cut off limbs.

Radhia's Bazaar: A large, teeming network of shops, restaurants, and alleyways located south of Rani's city center.

Rakins: Thorny bushes that grow around the Temple of Fire.

Rani: The capital of Ravence.

Rasbakan: A port city that lies on the eastern border of Ravence.

Ravanahatha: A wooden stringed instrument popular in Ravence and used in traditional dances.

Ravani Desert: A large swath of dunes and canyons. The southern desert is lusher and better suited for crops; the northern desert is harsher. Desert storms are known to appear and disappear suddenly within the northern regions.

Ravence: A desert kingdom founded by Alabore Ravence three hundred suns ago. The kingdom is considered to be part of the holy land created by the Sixth Prophet. Alabore Ravence named the kingdom after himself, bestowing upon his bloodline the burden of maintaining his dream of peace.

Receiving dock: An immigration and customs dock within the port of Rysanti used to check non-Sesharian visitors.

Red Rebellion: An uprising within Ravence led by rebels who wished for a democratic government. It was crushed by Queen Akira.

Registaan: A six-month-long desert test in which the Ravani heir is given no food, water, shelter, or protection. It is a rite of passage in which the heir must learn the sands of her home and why it runs through her veins.

Retherin: A pine with a velvet blue trunk and tawny orange leaves located within the Sona Range.

Royal Library: A tall chamber built underneath the Agnee Palace that houses ancient scrolls and texts.

Rysanti: The Brass City of Jantar; it is a port city and popular immigration access point. All of its buildings are made out of brass, glass, and shining steel.

Sand raider: A Ravani soldier who is skilled in operating a cruiser and fighting underneath the surface of the Ravani Desert. Sand raiders were formally a unit within the army; however, Queen Jumi created a separate branch for the sand raiders after expanding the kingdom's underground tunnels.

Sandscrapers: Tall buildings made of sandstone and steel within the Ravani kingdom.

Sandtrapper: A large, scaly tree found within the Ravani Desert.

Sarangi: Instrument that resembles the violin; its sound is said to most closely resemble the human voice.

Sari: A garment of unstitched fabric that is wrapped around the waist and draped over the shoulder, exposing the midriff; it is commonly worn in Ravence.

Sayon: The name of the world.

Seat, the: The center dome within the Temple of Fire.

Seshar: A nation of three islands that lie within the middle of the Ahi Sea. Jantar invaded the country, turning the three islands against each other. Jantar emerged victorious and has maintained a seventy-sun colonial rule over Seshar, forcing its citizens to work within the mines of the Sona Range.

Sesharian: The people of Seshar. They are known for their raven-black hair and insurmountable strength.

Shagun: Presents given by the bride's father to the groom and his family.

Sherwani: A long coat-like garment often worn by royals in Ravence.

Shobu: A small dog with two tails and the mane of a lion, often found within Ravence.

Silver feathers: A colloquial name for the capital police of Rani.

Sixth Prophet: A priestess of the Fire Order believed to exist five hundred suns ago. She burned down the forest beyond the Agnee Range, creating what is now known as the Ravani Desert. The Sixth Prophet killed many kings, queens, generals, and Yumi as punishment for constantly waging war. After many suns of burning, the Sixth Prophet disappeared.

Skorrir: A thorny bush found within the Ravani Desert. Its buds recede when a predator walks by.

Slab grenades: Explosive devices that shoot out spikes; they are detonated by pulling out a pin.

Slingsword: A weapon with a long, sharp blade and a trigger in the hilt. When pulled, the trigger releases the blade. The blade is connected to the trigger via a steel rope. A user can recall the blade back to the hilt by pulling the trigger again.

Sona Range: A mountain range located within the southeast regions of Jantar. The mountains have a rich deposit of metal ore. Before the Invasion of Seshar, Jantari miners worked the rigs. Now, Sesharians work the mines while Jantari soldiers keep watch.

Spear: The head guard of a Ravani royal.

Sun's breath: Dawn.

Tabla: Twin drums often used in Ravani music.

Tanker: Military aircraft vehicle.

Temple of Fire: The place of worship of the Phoenix. Shaped like a large white lotus with a dome in the center, the temple was built by the first priests of the Fire Order.

Teranghar: A southern city of Ravence known for its rolling hills and training bases for Ravani and Sesharian soldiers.

Thar: A southern district of Rani.

Tsuana: A kingdom that borders Veran. Like Nbru, the country has sworn off war. Peace treaties between other countries are often signed with Tsuana.

Unsung: An ancient fighting style of the Ravani.

Veran: A kingdom that lies east of Jantar.

Vermi: A type of tea grown within the Agnee Range.

Vesathri: An ancient, mythical creature with the body of a scorpion and the head of a stag.

Visor: Made of plastic and/or fiber sheath, visors are used to shield the eyes from blinding Jantari metal.

White Lotus: A large, lotus-shaped sculpture that sits directly in a garden in the heart of Rani. A gas-powered flame burns in the center of the sculpture.

Windsnatch: A game in which two opposing teams ride floating bladers. The goal is to get the ball into the opposing team's net.

Yeseri: A desert lion.

Yoddha Base: A Ravani military compound that sits along the Ravani southern border.

Yron: A type of cigarette only found on the black market. Its nicotine is harvested from the Beldur plant, which can be found within the volcanic regions of Pagua.

Yuani: A sand-colored desert bird.

Yumi: A race of skilled fighters. The Yumi women are known for their long, silky hair that can suddenly harden into sharp shards; their hair can cut through diamonds. The Yumi men are known for their healing abilities. Once plentiful, the Yumi were nearly wiped out by the fires of the Sixth Prophet. Now, many serve as soldiers, guards, or mercenaries.

Zeemir: A long weapon with a sharp blade and the butt of a gun. They are often used by the Jantari army.

ACKNOWLEDGMENTS

I've always skipped the acknowledgments of a book, but only when I began to write one myself did I realize the importance of the people behind the story. So, dear reader, stay a while. See the magic these people have spun.

First and foremost, I want to thank my agent and my editor, Lucienne Diver and Priyanka Krishnan. Thank you, Lucienne, for diving into this story with so much enthusiasm and passion and for being a guide in the quagmire of publishing. Thank you, Priyanka, for loving these characters and seeing the potential to make them even greater. Readers have you to thank for making me include even more tender Elena and Yassen scenes.

To my past editors, Kristin Gustafson and Clayton Bohle, who saw the beginning of this journey when the book was still *The Boy with Fire*, thank you for believing in this story and in me.

To my team at Orbit, thank you for your badassery and talent. I would like to especially thank Jenni Hill, Tiana Coven, Tim Holman, Alex Lencicki, Ellen Wright, Angela Man, Paola Crespo, Natassja Haught, Nazia Khatun, Rachel Goldstein, Stephanie A. Hess, and Lauren Panepinto.

A huge thank you to my cover designer, Lisa Marie Pompilio, for making a jaw-dropping cover. I still can't stop staring at it.

Writing can be a lonely journey. I have been blessed to have friends and family to mitigate that loneliness. To David Snyder, thank you for your love, your patience, and your belief in me. I'm grateful for you, desert boy. To my friends Sarah Schisla, Anthony Flores, and Carlos Ciudad, thank you for the laughs and the debauchery. To my cousins Nikki and Neha, thank you for fangirling over the characters with me. To my brother,

ACKNOWLEDGMENTS

Romi, thank you for pushing me to explore new narratives. You inspire me, though I won't tell you this in person—because you're never going to read this book. To my parents, thank you for never forcing me to pursue an engineering or medical degree like most Indian parents. You both recognized my love for storytelling, and instead of crushing it, you nurtured it. Papa, your tenacity inspires me. Mama, your gentleness protects me. Thank you for driving me to the library when I was younger. Thank you for constantly rereading the *Ramayana* to me even when I complained. You helped me build the foundation of my stories. Maybe that's why I'm so obsessed with myths.

To Ngoc, Manish, and Gehan, thank you for bringing my characters to life with your amazing art. You made Yassen, Elena, and Leo far cooler than I imagined.

Thank you to everyone who picked up the book when it was self-published as *The Boy with Fire* and who has followed me on this wild, amazing journey. I would be nowhere without your support.

I kept writing all these suns because a part of me always believed someone out there in the world would read my story. In moments of self-doubt, I always thought of you, dear reader. So last but not least, I want to thank you—whoever is holding this book right now. Thank you for giving this story a chance.

extras

orbit

meet the author

Aparna Verma

APARNA VERMA was born in India and immigrated to the United States when she was two. She graduated from Stanford University with honors in the arts and a BA in English. *The Phoenix King* is her first novel. When she is not writing, Aparna likes to ride horses, dance to Bollywood music, and find old cafés in which to read myths about forgotten worlds.

Find out more about Aparna Verma and other Orbit authors by registering for the free monthly newsletter at orbitbooks.net.

if you enjoyed
THE PHOENIX KING

look out for

THE JASAD HEIR
The Scorched Throne: Book One

by

Sara Hashem

In this Egyptian-inspired debut fantasy, a fugitive queen strikes a deadly bargain with her greatest enemy and finds herself embroiled in a complex game that could resurrect her scorched kingdom or leave it in ashes forever.

At ten years old, the Heir of Jasad fled a massacre that took her entire family. At fifteen, she buried her first body. At twenty, the clock is ticking on Sylvia's third attempt at home. Nizahl's armies have laid waste to Jasad and banned magic across the four remaining kingdoms. Fortunately, Sylvia's magic is as good at playing dead as she is.

When the Nizahl Heir tracks a group of Jasadis to Sylvia's village, the quiet life she's crafted unravels. Calculating

*and cold, Arin's tactical brilliance is surpassed only by his
hatred for magic. When a mistake exposes Sylvia's magic,
Arin offers her an escape: Compete as Nizahl's Champion in
the Alcalah tournament and win immunity from persecution.*

*To win the deadly Alcalah, Sylvia must work with Arin
to free her trapped magic, all while staying a step ahead
of his efforts to uncover her identity. But as the two grow
closer, Sylvia realizes winning her freedom means destroying
any chance of reuniting Jasad under her banner. The
scorched kingdom is rising again, and Sylvia will have to choose
between the life she's earned and the one she left behind.*

CHAPTER ONE

Two things stood between me and a good night's sleep, and I was
allowed to kill only one of them.

I tromped through Hirun River's mossy banks, squinting for
movement. The grime, the late hours—I had expected those. Every
apprentice in the village dealt with them. I just hadn't expected the
frogs.

"Say your farewells, you pointless pests," I called. The frogs had
developed a defensive strategy they put into action any time I came
close. First, the watch guard belched an alarm. The others would
fling themselves into the river. Finally, the brave watch guard
hopped for his life. An effort as admirable as it was futile.

Dirt was caked deep beneath my fingernails. Moonlight filtered
through a canopy of skeletal trees, and for a moment, my hand
looked like a different one. A hand much more manicured, a little
weaker. Niphran's hands. Hands that could wield an axe alongside
the burliest woodcutter, weave a storm of curls into delicate braids,

drive spears into the maws of monsters. For the first few years of my life, before grief over my father's assassination spread through Niphran like rot, before her sanity collapsed on itself, there wasn't anything my mother's hands could not do.

Oh, if she could see me now. Covered in filth and outwitted by croaking river roaches.

Hirun exhaled its opaque mist, breathing life into the winter bones of Essam Woods. I cleaned my hands in the river and firmly cast aside thoughts of the dead.

A frenzied croak sounded behind a tree root. I darted forward, scooping up the kicking watch guard. Ah, but it was never the brave who escaped. I brought him close to my face. "Your friends are chasing crickets, and you're here. Were they worth it?"

I dropped the limp frog into the bucket and sighed. Ten more to go, which meant another round of running in circles and hoping mud wouldn't spill through the hole in my right boot. The fact that Rory was a renowned chemist didn't impress me, nor did this coveted apprenticeship. What kept me from tossing the bucket and going to Raya's keep, where a warm meal and a comfortable bed awaited me, was a debt of convenience.

Rory didn't ask questions. When I appeared on his doorstep five years ago, drenched in blood and shaking, Rory had tended to my wounds and taken me to Raya's. He rescued a fifteen-year-old orphan with no history or background from a life of vagrancy.

The sudden snap of a branch drew my muscles tight. I reached into my pocket and wrapped my fingers around the hilt of my dagger. Given the Nizahl soldiers' predilection for randomly searching us, I usually carried my blade strapped in my boot, but I'd used it to cut my foot out of a family of tangled ferns and left it in my pocket.

A quick scan of the shivering branches revealed nothing. I tried not to let my eyes linger in the empty pockets of black between the trees. I had seen too much horror manifest out of the dark to ever trust its stillness.

My gaze moved to the place it dreaded most—the row of trees behind me, each scored with identical, chillingly precise black marks. The symbol of a raven spreading its wings had been carved into the trees circling Mahair's border. In the muck of the woods, these ravens remained pristine. Crossing the raven-marked trees without permission was an offense punishable by imprisonment or worse. In the lower villages, where the kingdom's leaders were already primed to turn a blind eye to the liberties taken by Nizahl soldiers, worse was usually just the beginning.

I tucked my dagger into my pocket and walked right to the edge of the perimeter. I traced one raven's outstretched wing with my thumbnail. I would have traded all the frogs in my bucket to be brave enough to scrape my nails over the symbol, to gouge it off. Maybe that same burst of bravery would see my dagger cutting a line in the bark, disfiguring the symbols of Nizahl's power. It wasn't walls or swords keeping us penned in like animals, but a simple carving. Another kingdom's power billowing over us like poisoned air, controlling everything it touched.

I glanced at the watch guard in my bucket and lowered my hand. Bravery wasn't worth the cost. Or the splinters.

A thick layer of frost coated the road leading back to Mahair. I pulled my hood nearly to my nose as soon as I crossed the wall separating Mahair from Essam Woods. I veered into an alley, winding my way to Rory's shop instead of risking the exposed—and regularly patrolled—main road. Darkness cloaked me as soon as I stepped into the alley. I placed a stabilizing hand on the wall and let the pungent odor of manure guide my feet forward. A cat hissed from beneath a stack of crates, hunching protectively over the half-eaten carcass of a rat.

"I already had supper, but thank you for the offer," I whispered, leaping out of reach of her claws.

Twenty minutes later, I clunked the full bucket at Rory's feet. "I demand a renegotiation of my wages."

Rory didn't look up from his list. "Demand away. I'll be over there."

He disappeared into the back room. I scowled, contemplating following him past the curtain and maiming him with frog corpses. The smell of mud and mildew had permanently seeped into my skin. The least he could do was pay extra for the soap I needed to mask it.

I arranged the poultices, sealing each jar carefully before placing it inside the basket. One of the rare times I'd found myself on the wrong side of Rory's temper was after I had forgotten to seal the ointments before sending them off with Yuli's boy. I learned as much about the spread of disease that day as I did about Rory's staunch ethics.

Rory returned. "Off with you already. Get some sleep. I do not want the sight of your face to scare off my patrons tomorrow." He prodded in the bucket, turning over a few of the frogs. Age weathered Rory's narrow brown face. His long fingers were constantly stained in the color of his latest tonic, and a permanent groove sat between his bushy brows. I called it his "rage stage," because I could always gauge his level of fury by the number of furrows forming above his nose. Despite an old injury to his hip, his slenderness was not a sign of fragility. On the rare occasions when Rory smiled, it was clear he had been handsome in his youth. "If I find that you've layered the bottom with dirt again, I'm poisoning your tea."

He pushed a haphazardly wrapped bundle into my arms. "Here."

Bewildered, I turned the package over. "For me?"

He waved his cane around the empty shop. "Are you touched in the head, child?"

I carefully peeled the fabric back, half expecting it to explode in my face, and exposed a pair of beautiful golden gloves. Softer than a dove's wing, they probably cost more than anything I could buy for myself. I lifted one reverently. "Rory, this is too much."

I only barely stopped myself from putting them on. I laid them gingerly on the counter and hurried to scrub off my stained hands. There were no clean cloths left, so I wiped my hands on Rory's tunic and earned a swat to the ear.

The fit of the gloves was perfect. Soft and supple, yielding with the flex of my fingers.

I lifted my hands to the lantern for closer inspection. These would certainly fetch a pretty price at market. Not that I'd sell them right away, of course. Rory liked pretending he had the emotional depth of a spoon, but he would be hurt if I bartered his gift a mere day later. Markets weren't hard to find in Omal. The lower villages were always in need of food and supplies. Trading among themselves was easier than begging for scraps from the palace.

The old man smiled briefly. "Happy birthday, Sylvia."

Sylvia. My first and favorite lie. I pressed my hands together. "A consolation gift for the spinster?" Not once in five years had Rory failed to remember my fabricated birth date.

"I should hardly think spinsterhood's threshold as low as twenty years."

In truth, I was halfway to twenty-one. Another lie.

"You are as old as time itself. The ages below one hundred must all look the same to you."

He jabbed me with his cane. "It is past the hour for spinsters to be about."

I left the shop in higher spirits. I pulled my cloak tight around my shoulders, knotting the hood beneath my chin. I had one more task to complete before I could finally reunite with my bed, and it meant delving deeper into the silent village. These were the hours when the mind ran free, when hollow masonry became the whispers of hungry shaiateen and the scratch of scuttling vermin the sounds of the restless dead.

I knew how sinuously fear cobbled shadows into gruesome shapes. I hadn't slept a full night's length in long years, and there were days when I trusted nothing beyond the breath in my chest and the earth beneath my feet. The difference between the villagers and me was that I knew the names of my monsters. I knew what they would look like if they found me, and I didn't have to imagine what kind of fate I would meet.

Mahair was a tiny village, but its history was long. Its children would know the tales shared from their mothers and fathers and grandparents. Superstition kept Mahair alive, long after time had turned a new page on its inhabitants.

It also kept me in business.

Instead of turning right toward Raya's keep, I ducked into the vagrant road. Bits of honey-soaked dough and grease marked the spot where the halawany's daughters snacked between errands, sitting on the concrete stoop of their parents' dessert shop. Dodging the dogs nosing at the grease, I checked for anyone who might report my movements back to Rory.

We had made a tradition of forgiving each other, Rory and me. Should he find out I was treating Omalians under his name, peddling pointless concoctions to those superstitious enough to buy them—well, I doubted Rory could forgive such a transgression. The "cures" I mucked together for my patrons were harmless. Crushed herbs and altered liquors. Most of the time, the ailments they were intended to ward off were more ridiculous than anything I could fit in a bottle.

The home I sought was ten minutes' walk past Raya's keep. Too close for comfort. Water dripped from the edge of the sagging roof, where a bare clothesline stretched from hook to hook. A pair of undergarments had fluttered to the ground. I kicked them out of sight. Raya taught me years ago how to hide undergarments on the clothesline by clipping them behind a larger piece of clothing. I hadn't understood the need for so much stealth. I still didn't. But time was a limited resource tonight, and I wouldn't waste it soothing an Omalian's embarrassment that I now had definitive proof they wore undergarments.

The door flew open. "Sylvia, thank goodness," Zeinab said. "She's worse today."

I tapped my mud-encrusted boots against the lip of the door and stepped inside.

"Where is she?"

I followed Zeinab to the last room in the short hall. A wave of incense wafted over us when she opened the door. I fanned the white haze hanging in the air. A wizened old woman rocked back and forth on the floor, and bloody tracks lined her arms where nails had gouged deep. Zeinab closed the door, maintaining a safe distance. Tears swam in her large hazel eyes. "I tried to give her a bath, and she did *this*." Zeinab pushed up the sleeve of her abaya, exposing a myriad of red scratch marks.

"Right." I laid my bag down on the table. "I will call you when I've finished."

Subduing the old woman with a tonic took little effort. I moved behind her and hooked an arm around her neck. She tore at my sleeve, mouth falling open to gasp. I dumped the tonic down her throat and loosened my stranglehold enough for her to swallow. Once certain she wouldn't spit it out, I let her go and adjusted my sleeve. She spat at my heels and bared teeth bloody from where she'd torn her lip.

It took minutes. My talents, dubious as they were, lay in efficient and fleeting deception. At the door, I let Zeinab slip a few coins into my cloak's pocket and pretended to be surprised. I would never understand Omalians and their feigned modesty. "Remember—"

Zeinab bobbed her head impatiently. "Yes, yes, I won't speak a word of this. It has been years, Sylvia. If the chemist ever finds out, it will not be from me."

She was quite self-assured for a woman who never bothered to ask what was in the tonic I regularly poured down her mother's throat. I returned Zeinab's wave distractedly and moved my dagger into the same pocket as the coins. Puddles of foul-smelling rain rippled in the pocked dirt road. Most of the homes on the street could more accurately be described as hovels, their thatched roofs shivering above walls joined together with mud and uneven patches of brick. I dodged a line of green mule manure, its waterlogged, grassy smell stinging my nose.

Did Omal's upper towns have excrement in their streets?

Zeinab's neighbor had scattered chicken feathers outside her door to showcase their good fortune to their neighbors. Their daughter had married a merchant from Dawar, and her dowry had earned them enough to eat chicken all month. From now on, the finest clothes would furnish her body. The choicest meats and hardest-grown vegetables for her plate. She'd never need to dodge mule droppings in Mahair again.

I turned the corner, absently counting the coins in my pocket, and rammed into a body.

I stumbled, catching myself against a pile of cracked clay bricks. The Nizahl soldier didn't budge beyond a tightening of his frown.

"Identify yourself."

Heavy wings of panic unfurled in my throat. Though our movements around town weren't constrained by an official curfew, not many risked a late-night stroll. The Nizahl soldiers usually patrolled in pairs, which meant this man's partner was probably harassing someone else on the other side of the village.

I smothered the panic, snapping its fluttering limbs. Panic was a plague. Its sole purpose was to spread until it tore through every thought, every instinct.

I immediately lowered my eyes. Holding a Nizahl soldier's gaze invited nothing but trouble. "My name is Sylvia. I live in Raya's keep and apprentice for the chemist Rory. I apologize for startling you. An elderly woman urgently needed care, and my employer is indisposed."

From the lines on his face, the soldier was somewhere in his late forties. If he had been an Omalian patrolman, his age would have signified little. But Nizahl soldiers tended to die young and bloody. For this man to survive long enough to see the lines of his forehead wrinkle, he was either a deadly adversary or a coward.

"What is your father's name?"

"I am a ward in Raya's keep," I repeated. He must be new to Mahair. Everyone knew Raya's house of orphans on the hill. "I have no mother or father."

He didn't belabor the issue. "Have you witnessed activity that might lead to the capture of a Jasadi?" Even though it was a standard question from the soldiers, intended to encourage vigilance toward any signs of magic, I inwardly flinched. The most recent arrest of a Jasadi had happened in our neighboring village a mere month ago. From the whispers, I'd surmised a girl reported seeing her friend fix a crack in her floorboard with a wave of her hand. I had overheard all manner of praise showered on the girl for her bravery in turning in the fifteen-year-old. Praise and jealousy—they couldn't wait for their own opportunities to be heroes.

"I have not." I hadn't seen another Jasadi in five years.

He pursed his lips. "The name of the elderly woman?"

"Aya, but her daughter Zeinab is her caretaker. I could direct you to them if you'd like." Zeinab was crafty. She would have a lie prepared for a moment like this.

"No need." He waved a hand over his shoulder. "On your way. Stay off the vagrant road."

One benefit of the older Nizahl soldiers—they had less inclination for the bluster and interrogation tactics of their younger counterparts. I tipped my head in gratitude and sped past him.

orbit

Follow us:

/orbitbooksUS

/orbitbooks

/orbitbooks

Join our mailing list
to receive alerts on our
latest releases and deals.

orbitbooks.net

Enter our monthly
giveaway for the chance
to win some epic prizes.

orbitloot.com